Tan[illegible]ght
[illegible]

TANGO MIDNIGHT

BY MICHAEL CASSUTT
FROM TOM DOHERTY ASSOCIATES

Missing Man
Red Moon
Tango Midnight

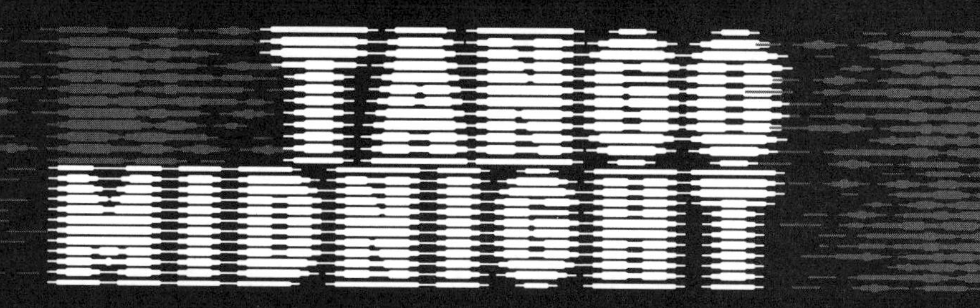

MICHAEL CASSUTT

A TOM DOHERTY ASSOCIATES BOOK
NEW YORK

This is a work of fiction. All the characters and events portrayed in this novel are either fictitious or are used fictitiously.

TANGO MIDNIGHT

This book is printed on acid-free paper.

A Forge Book
Published by Tom Doherty Associates, LLC
175 Fifth Avenue
New York, NY 10010

www.tor.com

Forge® is a registered trademark of Tom Doherty Associates, LLC.

Library of Congress Cataloging-in-Publication Data

Cassutt, Michael.
Tango midnight / Michael Cassutt.—1st ed.
p. cm.
"A Forge book"—T.p. verso.
ISBN 0-765-30645-X
1. Space stations—Fiction. 2. Biotechnology—Fiction. 3. Millionaires—Fiction. 4. Actresses—Fiction. I. Title.

PS3553.A812T36 2003
813'.54—dc21

2003049143

First Edition: November 2003

Printed in the United States of America

0 9 8 7 6 5 4 3 2 1

For Ryan and Alexandra

NASA STATION STATUS
Lyndon B. Johnson Space Center
Houston, Texas 77058
281/483-5111

International Space Station Status Report #13-13
10 A.M. CDT, Monday, April 17, 2006
Expedition 13 Crew/Taxi Crew 10

Space Station Alpha's Canadarm2 is scheduled for a workout today, as Expedition 13 flight engineer Nate Bristol takes a turn operating the manipulator in order to maintain proficiency.

Station commander Viktor Kondratko and science officer Jasper Weeks are to continue maintenance on the Vozdukh air-regeneration system, which has been off-line since Sunday evening. There is also an anomaly in the station's command and control alarm system that requires troubleshooting.

The Eridan glovebox materials processing unit aboard the Harmony module is scheduled for operations today by spaceflight participant Tad Mikleszewski.

Filming on the MosFilm/DreamWorks production *Recoil* with spaceflight participant Rachel Dunne continues. Cosmonaut Igor Gritsov will be serving as director and camera operator. Expedition 13 crew members Kondratko and Weeks will offer assistance as time allows.

PROLOGUE: X-DAY ZERO

It was one little slip. One tiny puncture. Nothing more than a gash several microns long in a sheet of Mylarized rubber.

But it was enough to allow ten thousand molecules to fly free, the flow eased by the difference in air pressure between the interior of the glovebox and the module outside.

On paper, the accident was an impossibility. There was no direct path from the substance to the atmosphere of the module. Three different barriers intervened.

All three were breached.

Tad Mikleszewski had waited impatiently all morning to return to his experiment, as five other crew members of International Space Station Alpha floated in and out of the Harmony module at various times, preempting his scientific program. Finally, at one P.M., when he should have been breaking for lunch, he heard the magic words from Nate Bristol, one of two NASA astronauts in the current Alpha resident crew: "Tango, you've got the comm."

The comm. After six days on the station, Tad was still amused by Bristol's nautical jargon. Of course, Bristol had spent ten years as a flight officer in the navy prior to being selected as an astronaut. And the first Alpha crews had adopted several naval traditions—ringing an honest-to-God brass bell to signal arrivals and departures, for example.

And using the military alphabet for difficult combinations of letters, such as "Tadeusz Mikleszewski," known most of his life as "TM," and now designated "Tango Midnight."

"I'll do that," he said. With Bristol's help, he closed and dogged the round hatch between Harmony and the Unity module. Then he donned his headset and pushed through the narrow throat of Harmony into the wider lab section. Following protocol, he closed a hatch here, too.

Within minutes he was finally at his station and linked via a NASA Tracking and Data Relay Satellite to his own small support team in a back room at the Russian mission control in the Moscow suburb of Korolev. "How's everybody today?" he asked.

"Fine and dandy." That was Lanny Consoldane, the young engineer he had hired to modify a Russian germ warfare glovebox for use on Harmony. Today Lanny was serving as payload communicator. "We slept in and had a late brunch." Everyone on TM's team was used to the Russian style of working that had been adopted aboard Alpha. It meant that you could reasonably expect to accomplish your daily task *sometime* during a given day, possibly within an hour or two of the schedule uploaded the night before, but just as often at the end of the day. In the early months of Alpha ops this had been frustrating to NASA astronauts used to the minute-by-minute scheduling of ten-day Shuttle missions. They had learned, however, that the more flexible method clearly worked better on the long haul of a five-month Alpha increment. TM, who was not a NASA astronaut, whose scientific chops were at least twenty years out of date, found the Russian method perfectly congenial, especially when the Vozdukh air scrubber acted up—again—or the caution and warning system needed testing, or breakfast just required a few extra minutes of cleanup.

This morning, however, TM had been kept out of Harmony because three crew members were making a *movie.*

And it wasn't the latest IMAX tour of Alpha, either. This was a Hollywood thriller about an astronaut trapped aboard a dying space station. Since it was Hollywood, of course, the trapped astronaut was a female under thirty whose natural beauty placed her in the ninety-ninth percentile of the human race. Rachel Dunne's surgical enhancements put her at the very top of that bracket. TM and Rachel had shared a Soyuz launch and two-day drift to Alpha, along with Igor Gritsov, their cosmonaut-pilot and fledgling movie director.

"Now that you're all rested," TM told Lanny, "let's go to work."

"Copy that, Tango." Lanny had obviously picked up the jargon. "Heaters are on. You want to spin up the motor, or should we?"

"I'll do it." It was a simple matter of clicking a cursor on a screen. But the mundane action made TM feel like a real experimenter.

The motor controlled two sound guns that generated an invisible bottle in a small chamber inside the Eridan glovebox. In Harmony's microgravity environment, chemicals that would normally separate due to gravity would bond freely, creating unique compounds. This was why TM had spent thirty million dollars of his own money to fly in space.

While he waited for the sonic bottle to stabilize, a process that usually took several minutes, TM looked over his to-do list for the day, his ninth on board Alpha, his sixth working in Harmony. He couldn't help glancing out the window.

The daytime earth below was deceptively peaceful. From 240 miles up, you couldn't see the fear and desperation on people's faces, as they worried about where X-Pox would strike next—

A beeper sounded, reminding TM of the microwave he had installed in his crappy little apartment at Star City, the cosmonaut training center. Russian appliances had improved mightily since the fall of the Soviet Union, but were still fifteen years out of date. The glovebox apparatus was a perfect example. The state-of-the-art Raytheon system in TM's company's lab in Irvine compared to this Russian Harmony hardware the way . . . well, the way Rachel Dunne compared to the average woman in a grocery store.

With the same bonus: you were unlikely to encounter Rachel Dunne in real life, but you could approach the woman in the grocery store. The Eridan, left over from biowar research on some island in the middle of the Aral Sea, had not had to run the gauntlet of U.S. technology export laws that kept the Raytheon gear in Irvine. The Russian equipment had been installed on Harmony in record time.

The fact that it was here, and usable, didn't mean it made TM especially happy. The displays had been hastily modified, with English terms and Roman letters replacing Russian and Cyrillic. The buttons were chunky plastic things. TM's zippy new ThinkPad kept crashing the old software. The thick plastic walls of the chamber already showed fogging and scratching. Even the gloves themselves were stiff and left his hands smelling like burnt tires.

"Tango, it's Bristol." Nate Bristol was calling him from another part of Alpha. "Am I interrupting?"

"Sure," he said. "Will it stop you?" It wouldn't stop him.

"Jasper thinks he left his tape in there."

Jasper Weeks was one of the three long-duration Alpha residents, a tall, thin, African-American astronaut who treated TM like sand in his bed. Weeks was the self-appointed tape monkey in the crew, forever grabbing loose items and securing them to walls and cabinets, complete with bar codes he would then scan and feed to the equipment control teams below. "Can't he ask me himself?"

TM heard Bristol sigh. "He asked me to ask you. He's afraid to bother you."

"That makes one of you."

A moment later, Bristol opened the first hatch, floated into the work area, eyes scanning walls, floor, and ceiling. "I don't see it." Bristol almost shouted. The drone of fans in Harmony, especially with the glovebox up and running, made TM feel as though he were standing by the side of the 405 Freeway at rush hour.

"How can you tell?" The Harmony module was a relatively new addition to Alpha, but it was already cluttered like a college dorm room at the end of a school term. Cameras, microphones, lights, and movie props were stashed behind mesh netting on the few bits of surface area not taken up by the scientific and life support gear. The module was also used as a pantry; Jasper Weeks's food supplies lived here, too.

Bristol ignored TM's question. Instead he clicked his waist-mounted intercom. "Jasper, you better take a look yourself." Now he made a face at TM. "This is going to cost you time. I'm sorry."

"Well, as they kept telling me in Houston, I'm just a guest here."

Bristol grunted. "I know that drill." As astronauts went, Bristol was one of the less territorial. He had been actively helpful to TM during their sole joint training session in Houston, unlike the other NASA astronauts, whose reactions ranged from indifference to open hostility.

It wasn't Jasper Weeks who opened the hatch, but Rachel Dunne, in a faint, invisible cloud of Lancôme perfume. The actress was followed closely by Igor Gritsov. No surprise there: the Russian commander had taken his filmmaker role to heart, and was now, it seemed, hopelessly in love with his leading lady. He couldn't bear to have her out of reach. "I saw it right on the nadir in the lab portion," Rachel was saying, proud of her fluency with the up-down terms used on Alpha.

Now there were four people in the module, three of them talking. And TM felt crowded. "Why don't we just invite *everyone* in here, and I'll work somewhere else—"

Lanny chose that moment to call up from Korolev. "Hey, TM, you might want to look at your temp—"

"Give me a second!" TM snapped. "I can't hear a goddamn thing!" He actually pushed himself out of the lab section into the other half of Harmony, where he bumped into Viktor Kondratko, the Alpha commander. Neither saw the other one coming, so there was sufficient impact to send both rebounding toward the walls. "Shit!" TM said.

Viktor looked amused.

Just then, Jasper sang out from the lab. "Here it is!" Swimming back into the now extremely crowded lab section, TM saw Jasper pulling a fat roll of gray duct tape from mesh at the top of the section.

"We call that the 'zenith' or 'top' or 'plus Z,' as opposed to the 'nadir,' " Bristol said to Rachel, who responded with a contemptuous sneer only a teenage girl—or Hollywood actress—could deliver successfully.

It took several more minutes to clear everyone out of the module. "If you need us, we'll all be right here!" Bristol joked, as he closed the hatch.

TM finally turned to his work. And saw an immediate problem: the temperature gauge was at the top of the scale. "How'd that happen?" he asked Lanny.

"It just started to surge a few moments after you turned on the guns."

"What do you recommend?" The temperature was still in the safe zone, but only barely.

"We're watching it. The consensus here is that it's okay, for now."

"Copy." TM turned his back on the glovebox to reposition his ThinkPad, which had been moved in the chaos of the duct tape search. He called up the menu for the day's runs, four different mixes at different temperatures and proportions. TM had his own theories about which would turn out to do the trick.

He would not admit the possibility that none of the mixtures might result in a cure for X-Pox—

Was that a hiss?

He was twisting toward the source of the sound, which was the glovebox itself, when a bell started ringing.

"Lanny . . ." TM said.

He had time to see that the temperature gauge was right at the redline, and that fully half of the plastic readouts on the glovebox were flashing, like a VCR after a power surge.

"We're already shutting down," Lanny said.

Sure enough, the whirring clatter of the power units driving the sound guns began to die. But the alarms still jangled.

Bristol was on the comm next. "Everything all right in there, Tango?"

"Yeah," he said, finding himself out of breath. "Started running a little hot."

He safed the whole mechanism, shutting it down piece by piece.

The alarm stopped.

But he could still hear hissing!

"Lanny," TM said, "do you show any leakage—?" He didn't finish the sentence, because he could smell something unusual, a hot, damp odor that overwhelmed Rachel Dunne's perfume as well as the tang of sweat that lingered after any gathering on the station.

TM's eye went to one set of stubborn red lights at the top left of the display, so far out of the way that the labels had not been translated. "*Prolom*," TM said aloud. "Lanny, what's *prolom*?"

Lanny, whose Russian was better than TM's, hesitated. "Uh, that means 'breach.' " TM had just realized that. Breach? The glovebox had leaked! How could that happen? And what had leaked? Some sort of benign mixture?

Or the deadly X-Pox itself?

"Uh, Tango," Lanny was calling. "Still there?"

"Yeah."

"We've got some . . . weird readings here."

TM barely heard him. He fought to regain mobility, checking to see that the hatch to Alpha was dogged. Then he closed the hatch between the two sections. Not that it would do much good, but the sections could be isolated.

Lanny undoubtedly noticed the closure of the intervening hatch. "Tango . . . what's going on?"

"Don't get alarmed," he said, "but I may just have killed myself."

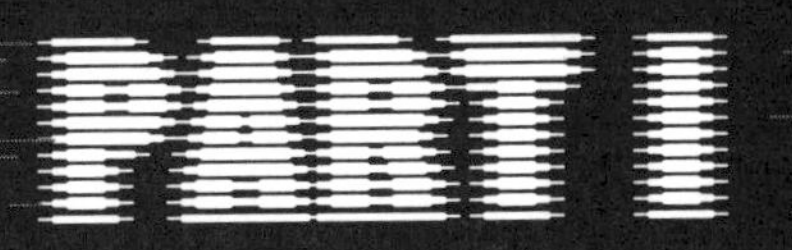

X-Minus Six Months
(October 2005)

NASA NEWS

Monica Kaveny
October 4, 2005
Headquarters, Washington, DC
(Phone 202/358-1400)

(EMBARGOED UNTIL 12 NOON EDT)

NASA ADMINISTRATOR APPOINTS JOHNSON SPACE CENTER DEPUTY DIRECTOR TO SPECIAL ADVISOR POSITION

NASA Administrator Michael McEwen today appointed Lester Fehrenkamp, Deputy Director of the Johnson Space Center, as special advisor for program management. This appointment comes after Fehrenkamp's highly decorated thirty-year career at NASA which began with the Apollo-Soyuz Test Project.

"Les Fehrenkamp has done an outstanding job as director for flight crew operations and as JSC deputy director, effectively preparing crews and hardware for the continued safe operation of the Space Shuttle and International Space Station. America owes Les a debt of gratitude.

"In his new position, Les will assist me in the coordination of new programs, such as the Orbital Space Plane and Project Prometheus, where his insight and experience will be greatly valued."

JSC Center Director Robert Hutchings says that a new deputy will be announced shortly.

DAY OF THE DEAD

Tuesday was the day of the dead.

Not the upcoming Mexican holiday celebrated at Halloween with special relish here in southern New Mexico. To Mark Koskinen, that would have been fine, an occasion for bad costumes and excessive candy consumption.

No, this Tuesday in October had real death looming over it. First there had been the report on KTEP that the number of X-Pox fatalities in the United States had reached 100,000. A city four times the size of Las Cruces—gone! God only knew how many others were sick, and would die.

And that was just the U.S. The figure for the Middle East, where X-Pox had first been launched, was much higher.

Reports like that always made Mark nervous. He actually put on rubber gloves to take out the trash, one of a series of ultimately pointless but nevertheless reassuring actions he was taking lately.

Then, as a further waste of time, he sat down at his computer to update his X-Pox map: the New England states (with the exception of Maine) colored red, for their advanced level of contamination. The West Coast, including California, was the same, and rates of infection in the Phoenix and Tucson areas were now pink. (The contagion had entered the United States with returning naval personnel and was now spreading inland.)

He had long since given up on charting the disease in Asia, Africa, and Europe: too depressing. Not that it mattered. Before he could close the file, the phone rang: his mother in Iowa. They barely exchanged greetings when he said, "How bad is he?" Meaning his father.

"Oh, they found something else," she said, meaning the doctor had found another tumor, though she had never uttered that word in Mark's hearing.

Mark felt his heart rate rise, his breathing quicken, his voice thicken. "Jesus," he said, even though the misuse of the Lord's name would upset his mother even more. "What are they saying?"

"Oh, you know," she said, sighing so she wouldn't break down. "They just didn't get it all during the last operation. They want another round of chemo . . ." She trailed off.

Mark could picture her, at the telephone in the kitchen. "Where's Dad?" He hadn't seen his father in four months, partly because of continuing disasters at work, partly because he could just not face a trip like the last one, when Dad was midway through the first round of chemo. With the loss of forty pounds he couldn't spare, along with the rest of his hair, he had looked like a victim of famine.

"He's resting," she said. There was no obvious hesitation between the two words, but Mark was attuned enough to his mother's peculiar syntax to hear it, and make the translation: *he doesn't want to talk.* "You must be on your way to work," she said, offering him a chance to end the conversation.

"The place won't fall apart if I'm five minutes late."

Here came his mother's well-known dismissive sigh. "I need to call Johanna," she said, naming Mark's younger sister.

"Say hi for me, then," Mark said. "I'll call Dad tonight."

Dazed at the growing certainty that his father would not be alive a year from now, Mark grabbed his backpack. One last look around the increasingly lonely condo and its rental furniture reminded him how much he disliked his life.

The offices of Harriman Industries/Pyrite Group's X-39 Spacelifter project occupied two floors of a beige brick building at White Sands Missile Range. Until Harriman, reeling from the dot bomb sell-off, had been forced to allow Pyrite to buy in, the project had occupied two additional buildings as well as a test stand on the range itself. Pyrite's mysterious management had cut the staff by two-thirds and returned two buildings and the test stand to White Sands.

The move had struck Mark as foolish, since it forced the program to lease the test stand at premium rates, and to fight for time on the range schedule. The whole rationale behind the X-39 was to demonstrate a radical new hybrid rocket that would serve as a prototype for a successor to NASA's troubled Space Shuttle. No hybrid, no project.

But there was no arguing with Pyrite. This morning, for example, the hybrid motor was scheduled for a sixty-second run at 80 percent power—the most demanding test so far, and one that could easily have taken place a week or ten days earlier. But the test stand had been preempted by some spooky DARPA activity, and as of last night there was some doubt the instruments would be recalibrated in time for use by Spacelifter.

Which was another reason Mark felt no guilt about arriving twenty minutes later than usual, pulling his battered Explorer into the lot at ten to eight. His presence wasn't strictly required for the test, anyway. His title—director of flight operations—and background—NASA astronaut on leave from the agency—meant that he was responsible for the development of mission control, tracking and communications, and even such mundane items as FAA certification for the vehicle.

In reality, he had spent most of the past five years making presentations to groups of potential investors. "Nothing like having a real-live astronaut talking to them about the future of spaceflight," Lanny Consoldane, Mark's immediate boss, said frequently. Mark appreciated the power of his position, and enjoyed the presentations, but he cringed whenever Consoldane suggested he wear his NASA flight suit, complete with its STS-100 mission patch. Since his annual birthday trip for a medical checkup last June, he had only visited the Johnson Space Center once. He wasn't current on the T-38 jets flown weekly by members of the astronaut corps; he wasn't in line for a future flight assignment, especially with the backlog in Shuttle launches after the *Columbia* disaster and the immense knot of unflown astronauts waiting for their first ride to orbit. The only indication that he was still considered an astronaut was that his official on-line biography called him "current," though on "management" status.

This morning Mark entered the office to find the latest in a series of temporary receptionists behind the desk. This young woman was a Latina, dark-eyed, a bit overweight, named Lupe. Mark introduced himself, learned that he had no messages, then headed for Consoldane's office.

He found him facing out the window, which looked east to the launch and test sites. Rumpled, bearded, and overweight, the X-39 program director was as far from agile as a human being could get. Mark had seen him drop a PalmPilot and walk away rather than try to pick it up. Yet this morning his feet were up on a cabinet and he was leaning back in his chair. "Five minutes," Consoldane said, in what passed for "good morning."

Mark sat down and glanced at the television monitor to the right of Consoldane's desk. It showed a fixed monochrome view of the hybrid's nozzle and pump structure. Wisps of cold steam rose from the piping. Consoldane had his back to the screen. "Is it that the Tularosa Basin is particularly lovely this morning," Mark said, "or that you can't bear to watch the test?"

Consoldane lowered his feet and turned to face Mark and the screen. "What do you think?"

"Three minutes," said the muted voice from the television.

Mark liked Consoldane; they had worked well together for almost four years without ever becoming friends. This was partly because Mark spent his first two years on X-39 taking every opportunity to go back to Houston, and partly due to Consoldane's utter lack of social life: no family, no friends, no dates. He was a celibate monk of spaceflight, a John the Baptist of the doctrine of single-stage-to-orbit vehicles.

And he was two minutes away from seeing his messiah rise from the dead.

"When do we flight-test?" Mark said, anxious to fill the silence with a human voice.

"We can put the motor on the airplane in six weeks." That was one of Consoldane's charming habits, referring to a prototype spacecraft as an "airplane." "We could make a hop in six months."

"And then go for a follow-on?" The X-39 was officially the X-39A; X programs were ideally designed in stages. You flew the A model until it broke, built a better B model, then repeated the process with a C or D model.

"The money's out there. We just have to get folks to give it to us."

"Thirty seconds." That was the voice from the control room at the test stand. "Motor is enabled."

Now even Mark found it difficult to talk, or even sit. He had noticed this quirk of his own while watching Shuttle launches—especially after he had experienced one of his own. It was as if sitting down equaled being confined, and being confined meant being unable to deal with problems. He was on his feet, leaning on the edge of Consoldane's desk, as the control voice counted down every five seconds to "ignition."

A jet of pale flame shot out of the nozzle base. The whole structure started to vibrate, shedding flakes of frozen condensate that vanished in the brutal heat of the exhaust.

"Plus five. All indications are good."

"Come on!" Consoldane said, leaning forward, as if the addition of his considerable bulk would help the test.

"Plus ten—" The test conductor paused. Mark sensed the problem before he saw it: on the screen, the engine began to vibrate with a frequency that just didn't look right.

A fuel line rattled off, and a second later the whole screen went white.

The test conductor uttered a single word: "Shit."

A dull shock jolted the building, like an earthquake lasting a fraction of a second.

To the east, in that beautifully craggy desert landscape, a single column of smoke arose.

Mark spent the next four hours driving back and forth to the test stand, including one trip with an army lieutenant colonel from the White Sands facilities squadron. "Boy," he said, "you guys really screwed up my stand," a statement that was as uncalled-for as it was true. Mark felt like punching him, but the heat and emotions of the day left him without energy.

From the outside, the test building appeared to be undamaged, except for some scorching on one side, where the ruptured line had spewed flaming fuel. The inside was another matter, however: it was not just burned, but its walls were scored with metal and glass fragments of the motor and the test instruments.

No one on the X-39 test team was injured, since the test had been remotely controlled from a building a hundred yards away. But to Mark's eyes the five engineers seemed wounded.

Then there was Consoldane himself, who had first taken the disaster calmly, riding to the test stand with Mark and plunging into the preliminary investigation of what went wrong. He was even polite to the sour-faced army lieutenant colonel, and proclaimed that while the damage to the test stand was significant, the cause of the rocket failure seemed to be easily fixable.

By early afternoon, however, after Mark had returned the obligatory phone calls from the local newspaper and radio about the "setback," and while he was watching KDPC's news team preparing for a stand-up in front of the Harriman/Pyrite building, Consoldane entered his office and closed the door. "We're done," he said, looking flushed and less healthy than usual.

"Done with what?"

"The program. That was the end of it."

"Come on, Lanny! We had a test failure! Every rocket program in history has had the same. You were just saying it wouldn't take much to fix it."

"It won't. That is, it wouldn't, if we had any money." He held out his hands, as if looking for answers—or cash—and finding neither. "Pyrite's pulling the plug, effective immediately."

"Doesn't that violate their contract?" Mark was sufficiently informed about the program's shaky finances to know how much cash Pyrite had committed, and for how long. They were nowhere near the breaking point.

"Yes. And they invited me to take them to court." Consoldane forced a smile. "Know any powerful attorneys who'd like to take on a losing cause for a contingency fee?"

Mark closed his eyes. "Did they say why? I thought their owner wanted to get into the space business."

"Oh, he's apparently found some other place to spend his money. That's why he wants to, uh, redirect the cash he was putting into the X-39."

"The anonymous owner. Have you ever met this guy?"

"Once, in a big crowd. I'm not sure I got the name. He was impressive, driven." Consoldane blinked. "The kind of man who is no stranger to litigation. So, my friend, if I were you—"

There was a knock on Consoldane's open door—Lupe, the temp. "Phone call for . . . you," she said, turning to Mark, obviously having forgotten his name.

"If it's another reporter, forget it—"

"All she gave was her name. Kelly Gessner. Do you need the number?"

Mark realized he had jumped to his feet. "I know the number."

Lupe ducked out as Consoldane grunted. "Astronaut Kelly Gessner. Calling to gloat, do you suppose?"

"That's not like her." Mark knew he sounded unconvincing. "What advice were you going to give me, Lanny?"

"Get out of Dodge, my friend."

THE WICKED WITCH

Kelly Gessner would later calculate that she was at angels seventy-five—7,500 feet—on the morning of Tuesday, October 4, when the great JSC Earthquake struck.

There was no visible sign, of course. No rippling of ground, no swaying buildings, no sundering of the temple curtain. Just the usual crawl of traffic on I-45. Not that Kelly had time to do more than glance at the view, as the T-38 bumped and burbled as it lined up on the runway at Ellington. "Got some thermals this morning," Bruce Howdek advised. He was the NASA instructor pilot in the front seat.

"I'm familiar with the concept," Kelly replied from the back. In thirteen years as an astronaut, not to mention another three years flying in NASA aircraft out of Ellington, she had logged almost two thousand hours of time in the sky over the area. And *every* flight had subjected her to thermals.

Of course, Bruce Howdek, a recent addition to the staff of pilots in Ellington's aircraft operations, didn't know that: he undoubtedly considered Kelly Gessner to be one of the dozen interchangeable women astronauts who wouldn't be within a mile of a cockpit if not for some misguided affirmative action law. His whole manner since preflight had been overly protective, a misguided attempt to be chivalrous. He had flown straight and level, with no wrenching aerobatics, offering plenty of warning about the most benign upcoming maneuvers.

Kelly wasn't eager to be flung around the sky, but Howdek's patronizing attitude made her want to rap her knuckles on his helmet. The impulse dissipated, however. Howdek was new to the operation, and there *were* a number of rookie mission specialists who needed gentle handling during their twice-monthly flights. Kelly just didn't happen to be one of them.

Another bump. The freeway flashed past below, I-45 clogged with the remnants of rush-hour traffic headed for the towers of Houston.

"Going in. We'll be on the ground in five."

"Thank you, Bruce," Kelly said. "It's been great." Protocol demanded that Kelly offer the praise. But she was telling the truth: blasting out of Ellington at dawn, flashing toward the operating area over the Gulf . . . if you didn't feel a rush, you should quit the business.

Kelly wasn't ready to quit. In spite of the worst NASA had thrown at her the past few years.

"Say again?" Howdek was on the radio to Ellington Tower, which had uttered some static-ridden burst that Kelly didn't understand.

"Just a friendly reminder to check with ops at first opportunity. Big doin's over at the Center. Earthquake."

Big doin's at the Center? Earthquake? In *Houston*?

Howdek, who seemed oblivious to this tantalizing announcement, took his own sweet time taxiing up to Hangar 276. It was all Kelly could do to keep from popping the hatch and jumping out.

She stowed her helmet and parachute in her locker, then went racing up the stairs to ops. There she found Diana Herron and Wayne Shelton talking to each other. Or rather, not talking; both of them affixed silent grins to their faces as Kelly approached.

"All right, what's this about an earthquake?"

Neither Herron nor Shelton took the conversational cue. Both were astronauts who had waited years for their first flights, still to come. That was all they had in common. The mere fact that they were communicating added to Kelly's sense that something special was in the wind. "Wayne," she said, offering Shelton further encouragement.

"This is big," Herron said. "Big news." She was an air force flight test engineer, blond, tan, with a dazzling white smile and the manner of a pro volleyball player. Herron was also a notorious tomboy who often proclaimed that she could out-drink and out-screw any of the astronaut office record-holders (there were several in each category), and had the reputation to match.

"Am I cleared for it?"

Shelton laughed. He was a shy, soft-spoken Ph.D. astronomer who had come to JSC from the Goddard Space Flight Center. He was also Kelly's significant other of the moment, a situation both of them were trying to keep secret. Hence the stilted nature of their conversation.

"It's about Fehrenkamp," Shelton said, clearly struggling with an unaccustomed conflict of emotions.

Lester Fehrenkamp was the deputy director of the Johnson Space Center. According to its official description, the holder of that job "assisted the center director." In truth, thanks to his previous lengthy tenure as head of flight crew operations, his unparalleled knowledge of the space agency, and his eagerness to exercise power, Fehrenkamp had been running the place for a decade and a half, not only performing the deputy's functions, but holding on to authority in other areas, including Shuttle and station flight crew assignments. He was known as the "director-for-life" among those few astronauts brave enough to speak of him openly. That group included Kelly. "Really? The tumor is inoperable, the aorta just burst, what? Good news can't wait."

It was a testament to Fehrenkamp's power over them that, as one, both Herron and Shelton glanced down the hallway toward the ops desk, as if afraid of being overheard. "Come on, you guys," Kelly said, losing patience. "He *never* comes to ops."

Herron recovered first. "He got fired this morning—"

Shelton was half a second behind her. "—Not fired, actually, but put on 'special assignment'—"

"Whatever, McEwen apparently showed up unannounced this morning and hauled Hutchings in with him. They told Les he was out, effective immediately." Michael McEwen was the newly appointed NASA administrator; Robert Hutchings was the head of JSC, a well-meaning space scientist who had been Fehrenkamp's puppet. "He's supposedly cleaning out his stuff even as we speak."

Kelly barely heard anything said after the word "fired." Even though she was still wearing her sweaty flight suit, even though her legs were weak with excitement, she was already running down the stairs toward her car, leaving Wayne behind.

She *had* to get to Steve Goslin.

The offices of the members of NASA's astronaut corps took up the entire sixth floor of Building 4S, and a bit of the fifth. As a senior astronaut Kelly worked on the top floor between the corner offices occupied by the chief astronaut and his deputy. Since she had been on the *Columbia* recovery team for the last two years, Kelly only shared her space with one other astronaut. (Those who were in active crew training bunked together, five or six to a single room.)

Kelly's officemate was Jinx Seamans, another veteran mission specialist currently supervising launch support activities at the Cape. Most Mondays he was on an airplane to Florida, not to return until Friday, so Kelly effectively had a private office.

Usually she was quite happy about that. Today she really wished she had Jinx handy, to connect her to the chat among the military astros. On the other hand, seeing clusters of active astronauts huddled in doorways, she realized she wouldn't have to troll for gossip. Three different astronauts asked her, "Have you heard the word?" before she reached her door.

She paused before going inside. "He's really gone?" she asked the nearest knot, which included a pair of secretaries.

"His office is bare," one of the secretaries said.

"They're moving him across the street," the other added.

Astronauts could be fooled by their own hopes, but in her tenure at NASA, Kelly had learned to trust the career secretaries: they had wires into every department.

Fehrenkamp gone. It was unbelievable. She desperately wanted to join the free-flowing debate in the hall to find out why. Why now?

No matter: Fehrenkamp was out. And there was one person who needed to know. She dialed a number in the 505 area code.

"Spacelifter."

"Hi. I'm trying to reach Mark Koskinen."

It felt strange to be making that call, since she and Mark had not spoken in weeks, not since he had phoned to wish her a happy birthday. Sweetness of the gesture aside, until this Tuesday morning, Kelly had no plans to call Mark again. Not because he had especially offended her: both of them had done whatever they could to screw up a promising relationship. Distance was the primary problem, of course. Mark had been exiled to New Mexico after his extremely controversial Shuttle mission, during which astronaut Cal Stipe died. Stipe deserved to die, but only Mark, Kelly, and a few select others in the program knew that. To the public at large, Mark was a failure as an astronaut.

With Mark's encouragement, Kelly had remained in Houston, in the astronaut office, in the hope that the exile would prove to be temporary, and that in a year or at most two, Les Fehrenkamp would conclude that Mark had done sufficient public penance and parole him. Mark was an EVA-experienced astronaut who had done a better-than-good job under extreme circumstances: he would be an asset to a station assembly crew.

But Fehrenkamp never made the offer. And outside forces had conspired against the couple. The International Space Station program had run into a variety of delays as the millennium turned, reducing the number of flight opportunities. During the late 1990s, NASA had loaded up on astronauts, selecting perhaps twice as many as ultimately needed, forcing Mark to the end of a long line.

Then the orbiter *Columbia* was lost, along with seven crew members, while returning from a routine science mission. The investigation into the accident, and subsequent modifications to the surviving vehicles in the fleet, had caused a year-long stand-down, further adding to the backlog.

Kelly had run into the same Cold Equations: her last flight was six years in the past, and she expected to wait another year or two before receiving a new assignment.

So Mark stayed in New Mexico. He and Kelly had visited faithfully for the first few months. Then she had been ordered to a six-month "rotation" at NASA Headquarters, a tour that stretched to more than a year.

Mark had asked her to turn it down, to give up her astronaut career and move to New Mexico. Stocks were booming: Spacelifter was flush and looking like a better career move than Shuttle and station.

But Kelly had said no. She wanted Mark to make the move, to either beg Fehrenkamp for a second chance in CB, or simply resign and take one of the available engineering support jobs in the JSC community, working for SpaceHab or United Space Alliance.

This time Mark had said no.

Alone in Washington, hurt and all too aware of the ringing on her biological alarm clock, Kelly had immediately fallen into a promising relationship with a congressional staffer, knowing Mark would inevitably find out, which he did.

They did not speak for a year.

Kelly eventually returned to Houston, leaving behind her Washington hill rat (an appropriate label, as it turned out). Soon after she made a surprise trip to Las Cruces to see if there was any chance she and Mark could pick up where they left off.

In Las Cruces Kelly discovered that Mark had a girlfriend named Ginger, a very attractive woman of perhaps twenty-five who was a medical student at the University of New Mexico. Or a waitress at Chili's. Kelly was never quite sure.

They did not speak for much of the *next* year.

Last June, Mark had returned to Houston for his annual physical. Kelly happened to encounter him entirely by accident in Building 9. After an exchange of awkward hellos, surprised-to-see-you-heres, et cetera, she heard herself say, "How's Ginger?"

"I call her Doctor Ginger these days—"

"Congratulations."

"—on the rare occasions we're in touch."

"I thought you'd be making wedding plans by now." Kelly's bitchiness surprised herself. Well, she was having a bad day for other reasons. Or so she rationalized.

"She might be. I wouldn't know. We broke up."

"Oh," she said, shocked at how happy that news made her. "Sorry to hear it."

"Chicks, go figure." He smiled to make sure she caught the irony. "She chose an internship in Tucson over life in Las Cruces."

"Like you say . . . chicks."

The ice had thawed a bit, but neither Kelly nor Mark found the desire to resume contact. She had since turned to Wayne Shelton. She assumed Mark had found another doctoral student or waitress.

But personal matters aside, she owed him this call.

She left a message for Mark at the Spacelifter office, then, knowing work would be impossible, strolled down the hall to Steve Goslin's office.

A former Marine test pilot, Goslin had served as chief astronaut for the past four years. The job was far less glamorous than the title suggested. The first chief astronaut had been Alan Shepard, the famous first American in space, who had been grounded for medical reasons and given the administrative job. Frustrated at having to watch less experienced, and in his opinion, less capable astronauts going on to glory in the Gemini and Apollo programs, Shepard had run the office like an ill-tempered scoutmaster. Later chiefs ran happier ships, but often inherited the dirty jobs that higher-ups such as Les Fehrenkamp wouldn't handle in person.

Goslin had presided over a massive and unwanted expansion of the astronaut team, followed almost immediately by forced attrition. Through it all he had remained open and accessible—perhaps with no choice, since his ruddy complexion easily betrayed his inner feelings.

This morning, for example, his face was split into a giant grin as he talked on the phone, and waved Kelly to a chair. "Yeah, yeah," he was saying, "a total surprise. The chief is always the last to know." At the same time, he also got to his feet, a charming holdover, Kelly knew, from days at a military school.

He hung up without sitting down, perching on the edge of his desk. "So what have you heard?" he asked Kelly.

"That the wicked witch is dead. The cowardly lion and the tin man found their courage—"

"Yeah, ding, dong," Goslin said, blushing with discomfort at Kelly's irreverence.

"You had no warning."

"*Nada.* A call on my cell phone this morning as I was driving in."

"Doesn't that bug you?"

"What?"

"The way they treat you, Steve!"

Goslin shrugged. "They pay me to take the hits."

"Has anyone from Building One talked to you? I mean, you *did* report to Les."

Reporting to Les was a euphemism: Fehrenkamp had used Goslin as a tool—sometimes a hammer, sometimes a scalpel. "Technically, of course, I report to the director of flight crew ops."

"LaFollet?" Jeff LaFollet was an air force astronaut who had somehow managed to become a NASA lifer, inheriting a bureaucratic empire that included the astronaut office as well as the fleet of aircraft based at nearby Ellington Field. Kelly had never been impressed with him.

"Okay, Jeff's more of a placeholder than a leader."

"He won't last a week without Fehrenkamp to protect him. It'll be like the Egyptians: the pharaoh dies, and his stooges go to the netherworld with him." Kelly knew she was making Goslin uncomfortable. "Look," she said, saving him the trouble of challenging that statement, "I just came to see how you were doing. And to ask about Mark."

"Koskinen? What about him?"

"Come *on,* Steve: what about bringing him back?"

Goslin got a faraway look in his eyes, and let out a breath. "I like Mark. I was his commander, you know." Kelly knew, of course. She had been part of the same STS-100 crew.

"He's stayed in touch with the office. Not just his annual physical, but other visits. And he volunteered for the *Columbia* recovery."

Goslin began to wither visibly under Kelly's attack. "Fine, fine. I stipulate that Mark deserves another shot here. But you know the numbers. What do I do with him? I can't put him on a crew anytime soon."

"You've got a ton of shit jobs nobody wants to do."

Goslin grunted. "True. But why would he give up his cushy corporate gig to go to the end of the line around here?"

Kelly wanted to laugh out loud. Cushy corporate gig, indeed: she knew about Spacelifter's shaky financial situation. She also knew that Mark was still being paid his civil service salary as a NASA astronaut. But now was not the time to educate Steve Goslin about the fine points of detailed assignments. "Just for the sake of argument, suppose he has a weak moment and asks for a job."

Goslin's intercom buzzed. A secretary's voice announced a call from Jeff LaFollet. "Speak of the devil," Goslin said.

"You better take that." Kelly stood. "I'll be back for a debrief later."

Goslin nodded. "Tell Koskinen to give me a call, before I change my mind."

TRIAGE

The "Shadowy Principle behind the mysterious Pyrite Corporation"—to use his favorite among the many ridiculous ways Tad Mikleszewski had been described in print—arrived at Konrad Hoeffler's Beverly Hills home in a bad mood that began eighteen hours earlier and two thousand miles to the east, with the news of the accident at White Sands. Then he had endured the challenges of rerouting himself from Chicago to New Mexico, and from New Mexico to Los Angeles. He had used his own Aero Commander 690B; nevertheless, going through an added sanitation protocol in Las Cruces made a long trip outright torturous. Especially when he finally elected to simply call Consoldane with the bad news from the airport, rather than make the sixty-mile round trip to White Sands.

And now he struggled with the terrible condition of the road to Hoeffler's home in the rural part of Beverly Hills, an isolated woodland a handful of miles north of the Beverly Hills Hotel, and south of Mulholland Drive. There were no streetlights, and the ancient road surface was ribbed with subsurface roots in the places where it wasn't worn to bare dirt and gravel. TM usually liked to drive himself, especially to events that seemed to reward the arrival of a wealthy individual behind the wheel of a Boxster. But having endured several jolts, at least one wrong turn, and the lack of valet parking, he realized he would have been better off booking a limo. Or taking a cab. Or catching a ride with Leslie, his ostensible date, who should have arrived ahead of him. But he didn't see her car among those squeezed onto the shoulder of the road.

He had reached the base of the impressive stone stairway up to the front door of Hoeffler's house when he was illuminated by headlights from another arrival. Leslie, in her Honda hybrid.

He watched with approval as she quickly negotiated the turn that had caused him so much grief, smoothly wedging the silver Honda into a spot that TM had not seen. Leslie emerged from her car, as always, at full speed, heels clicking on the pavement and hands busy jamming a cell phone into her purse. She was 26, almost thirty years younger than TM, small and dark-haired. She gave him a kiss on the cheek and practically turned him around. "How did it go today?"

"Let's just say I had to shoot the wounded."

Leslie laughed sharply. "No more X-39, huh?"

"No."

She hooked her arm in his as they headed up the steps. "Do you have any memory of me telling you it wasn't a good investment?" Leslie had no interest in his space activities.

"Your objections are on record. Not that you'll gain anything from it." There were thirteen steps; TM counted them, panting as he reached the front door. "Christ, I thought I was in better shape than that."

Leslie smiled as she waited for him to catch his breath. "I wonder if your host and his guests know that Spacelifter is dead."

"Oh, they know," he said. "News travels fast, and bad news goes at the speed of light."

"Pessimist."

"Just watch Konrad."

"How many of them even know that you are the money behind Pyrite?"

"Not many, but all you need is one."

The front door was open and a stranger—or home invader—could easily have believed the house to be empty. "Hello!" Leslie called up the stairs. "It's very brave of you to face them, under the circumstances."

"It wouldn't be a Hoeffler party if I didn't have at least one bitter argument." TM was, by nature, contrarian, which Leslie well knew.

"I wonder how much this cost?" Leslie said.

"Four million," he said, absentmindedly. "He spent a million on the garden alone."

"I mean *this,*" Leslie said, pointing to a mannequin standing inside the front door, as if greeting arrivals. It wore a white space suit. "I presume that's real."

"Oh, it's real." Hoeffler had bought the suit for ten thousand dollars at a Sotheby's auction. Much of the former Soviet space program was for sale.

A young man wearing a white dress shirt and black trousers appeared. He also had a tiny black headset and microphone wrapped around his face as he consulted a pocket planner. "Good evening," the young man said, hesitating only briefly as TM's face appeared on his electronic prompter. "Mr. Hoeffler and the others are upstairs. Enjoy the evening, Mr. Mikleszewski."

In the age of X-Pox, cautious citizens rarely gave big parties. At least, they didn't give big parties for strangers. But then, Konrad Hoeffler wasn't cautious. He had inherited a beneficial mixture of money and brains, and employed both in a variety of activities, from the whimsical to the daring.

Such as a party for forty people, perhaps half of whom he knew.

The guests were a typically eclectic bunch, linked only by an acquaintance with Hoeffler and an interest in private space efforts. Or so Hoeffler's invitation said. TM had recognized the names of a powerful Hollywood talent manager as well as a member of the Dodgers and an actress.

Perhaps they were all closet space enthusiasts. Or, more likely, Hoeffler was trying to impress the baseball player (he was a noted Dodger fan) and date the actress, in spite of the obvious fact that the actress and the Dodger were a couple. The presence of the manager was undoubtedly related to one or the other, or perhaps both.

TM and Leslie ascended to the living room, a vast open area lined with books on art and technology. Twenty people, more men than women, stood chatting and ingesting hors d'oeuvres offered by more servers in white and black.

"You'd never know there was a plague," Leslie said, her face radiant, but her voice low and savage. She worked for the Department of Water and Power, specifically in its emergency operations office, and lived daily with such issues as purity of water, its secure delivery, and the growing number of unpaid bills of the deceased.

"These people don't get X-Pox," TM said. "They pay others to die for them."

He was rewarded by the Leslie Look: a single arched eyebrow. "*These* people? *They?*"

TM was saved from having to justify his own wealthy existence by the appearance of Konrad Hoeffler. Their host was a pudgy man in his forties wearing a safari jacket and a red beard. By way of greeting, he kissed Leslie on the cheek and squeezed TM's shoulder. "I heard," he said in a bereaved voice, as if TM had lost a father, not just Spacelifter.

"It was a noble effort," TM said, glancing sideways at Leslie, who made a conciliatory, you-da-man gesture.

"Had it worked, it would have been a *Nobel effort,*" Hoeffler said. In addition to being a rich, technically trained eccentric, he was a tiresome automatic punster.

Leslie took this as a cue to announce that she was going to see what new culinary toys Hoeffler had added to his kitchen.

"I don't suppose you're going to change your mind," he said to TM.

"I was at White Sands this afternoon—"

"Before the body was even cold! Ouch."

"The deed, as Mark Twain used to say, is done."

Hoeffler closed his eyes, as if offering a moment of silence. He had been TM's original connection to Spacelifter, though he had managed to invest substantially less money in the project. "Well," he said, "on to the next."

"I'm not so sure about that."

He had managed to shock and surprise Hoeffler. "What do you mean?"

"I mean, I may be a slow learner, but I think I've finally realized that the best way to make a small fortune in the space business is to start with a large one." It was an old joke between them.

Hoeffler was about to launch into his Passionate Defense of a Private Space Future, Lecture #4, when one of the white-shirted servers appeared at his side with an urgent question. "Excuse me," Hoeffler said, turning away. "We aren't through with this subject."

"Of course not," TM said. He was braced for a whole wave of assaults, as if he were Normandy in June 1944, and the space activists the Allied armies. In addition to Hoeffler, who had invested in every private space program known to TM, from a contender in the X-Prize to a Russian-built commercial space lab, TM could see Ian Sedgwick of the Eternal Frontier Association, the movement's frequent talking head. Next to Sedgwick was Opher Elyan, the mysterious Azerbaijani who seemed to be part of every financial transaction between private parties and the Russian Air and Space Agency, aka Rosaviakosmos. No doubt there were unidentified others still lurking, waiting for an opening to pounce.

Whether it was the prospect of endless debate, or fatigue from a long day of travel, TM now wished he had stayed home. For years he had noticed that in certain circumstances he could predict with confidence every word he would hear or every action he would observe. It was, no doubt, a form of déjà vu. (Hadn't he read years ago that déjà vu was merely a symptom of a tired mind?) But he had been feeling it since awakening in his Chicago hotel room.

For example, he hadn't needed the depressing message from Consoldane to tell him about the engine failure: he had already heard the words. Not that he actually had a face-to-face conversation with the program manager: from the beginning, he had preferred to be the Anonymous Investor, the Shadowy Principle operating via e-mail and the occasional phone call.

Conversation was redundant, in any case. TM had the feed from the test stand on streaming video through his laptop as he waited for takeoff at Chicago Midway. He had a tremendous amount of experience with start-ups in a variety of technical fields, from dot.coms to biotech and medical imaging firms. He expected a certain number of failures.

The problem with Spacelifter was that in *success* it had no realistic chance of ever turning a profit. In a perfect world, it should have been a prototype for easy access to space, the twenty-first century's equivalent of the DC-3 aircraft. Cheap to build and operate, safer than Shuttle and Soyuz, it would have allowed businesses to make use of the the International Space Station: not just to perform scientific research, but to create new drugs, to film movies, to serve as an exotic honeymoon destination—to name just a handful of the ideas people like Hoeffler, Sedgwick, and Elyan had proposed.

For several years, on both sides of the year-long hiatus caused by the *Columbia* tragedy, Rosaviakosmos had sold open seats in Soyuz "taxi" flights to the occasional thrill-seeking millionaire. (In fact, TM was sure one or two of these "spaceflight participants" were present in the crowd tonight.) But relocating to Russia for months of technical training on the Soyuz, not to mention six months of Russian language lessons, were obstacles guaranteed to keep that market from growing.

What Spacelifter could have provided was a way for any responsible party to propose a mission, pay a fee, and see his mission launched within a reasonable time—on the order of months, as opposed to the years it took to get anything done on ISS. (TM had heard horror stories of scientific researchers waiting *their entire working careers* to fly experiments with NASA.)

There had been two flaws with the scenario: the first was that it turned out to be technically impossible to build that cheap, single-stage-to-orbit launch vehicle. The chemical fuels available for even the most advanced rockets had absolute limits to the amount of energy they could unleash. Given the weight of a vehicle robust enough to withstand repeated launch and landing, you were left with a minuscule payload. One of the Spacelifter team—Koskinen, the astronaut—called these figures the "Cold Equations."

TM had invested in Spacelifter rather than its competitors because its hybrid motor promised at least a theoretical improvement in the Cold Equations. They got warmer, at least.

The other flaw was the size and readiness of the commercial market. Anyone could write a magazine article touting the money to be made. But where were those investors hungry to take advantage of a cheap ride to ISS Alpha? What would they sell that would pay the freight? So far it was all fairy gold.

Hoeffler had returned, but he was not alone. With him was a blond, green-eyed woman of perhaps thirty who could only be the actress—

"Rachel Dunne, Tad Mikleszewski. And vice versa."

In what TM judged to be the sole example of X-Pox awareness among the evening's guests, Rachel Dunne did not offer her hand. "Hi," she said. "I'm Rachel."

"Call me TM," he said, as he had been saying to people for forty-some years. His fatigue vanished like a soap bubble, thanks to an inescapable euphoria triggered by proximity to Rachel Dunne. In low heels, she was model-tall. She wore a loose, tailored gray business suit much like TM's, but with a camisole-like shirt that barely contained a pair of Hollywood's finest, and most popular, breasts. TM had dated actresses; he had learned to be on guard against their sorcery. Nevertheless, he admired Rachel Dunne's presentation in the same way he appreciated a 1986 Groth or a fallaway jump shot by Jason Kidd. "So," he said, "what's it like?"

The question seemed to confuse her. "I beg your pardon?" Her voice was well modulated, too, a bit husky, far from the breathy, Marilyn Monroe purr adopted by most actresses.

"Having all this power."

She opened her mouth, then closed it and cast a glance toward Hoeffler, who was clearly happy to receive even fragments of Rachel Dunne's attention. "Connie, you didn't tell me that Mr. Mikleszewski was so *challenging.*" Her tone managed to combine genuine admiration with sarcasm, a neat conversational bank shot that caused TM to raise his estimate of her IQ.

"TM is *very* challenging," Hoeffler said, directing his words past Rachel Dunne. "He's the one man we all thought would make it happen."

Noting that Rachel Dunne seemed to know what "it" was, TM turned directly to Hoeffler. "Why me? This room is full of people who have more money." *And who have lost it on various space-related fantasies,* he thought, but did not add.

For a few seconds, Hoeffler seemed to forget that Rachel Dunne was shimmering almost within his grasp. "Because you live in the real world," Hoeffler said. "You deal with X-Pox—"

"So far, not with any success—"

"But you see an actual need and are taking concrete steps to meet it—"

Fortunately for Hoeffler, who seemed on the edge of a painful self-revelation, Opher Elyan pushed himself through the crowd and tried, with only momentary success, to attach himself to Rachel Dunne. "Beautiful Rachel!" he said, breathlessly, as the actress offered him a minimal kiss on his bearded cheek before expertly slipping out of his arms. Whether it was X-Pox caution, or, more likely, simple distaste for Elyan, TM couldn't tell.

Sensing that the single hug was all he was going to get from the actress, Elyan, as always, turned to business. He greeted TM with a more reserved embrace and a sorrowful shake of his head. "I'm sorry to hear about your setback."

"It's the nature of the business," TM said, appalled at his own ability to utter such automatic responses. "It seems America will have to leave commercial space to the former Communists."

Elyan nodded; again, it was not an original comment. "We are booking some business for Harmony." Harmony was a Russian-built commercial module being readied for launch to Alpha. Elyan handled the marketing with, from what TM knew, a certain amount of success. "If even a third of the leads turn out to be real, we should break even."

TM could only grunt. Leslie had been right: he should have avoided this party and perhaps sent in his place a life-sized doll preprogrammed with the lines the other guests wanted to hear. Where, in fact, *was* Leslie, anyway?

Determined to avoid further exchange of clichés and old news with Elyan, TM turned again to Rachel Dunne. "What's a smart young woman like you doing with men like these?"

"They're sending me into space in six months," she said, relishing the look of surprise on TM's face. Ah, that explained it! The idea of sending an actor into space wasn't new—six years ago a Russian actor had trained for a visit to the Mir station, before the whole project collapsed in a pile of unpaid bills.

But beautiful Rachel Dunne? TM was suddenly curious, but before he could craft a follow-up question, one of the white-shirted helpers announced, "Dinner is served."

TM wound up seated to the left of Ian Sedgwick, who anchored the foot of the table. The baseball player, whose name TM never did learn, sat across from him on Sedgwick's right, and paid an excessive amount of attention to Leslie, who was to his right. TM was vaguely aware that he had a female dinner companion to his left, but she seemed more interested in directing her conversation up the table, so TM's attention was inevitably demanded by Sedgwick.

Contrary to his usual spew of peppy sound bites, Sedgwick was depressed—not, to TM's surprise, about the space business. (True, if he had been capable of being depressed by failures there, he'd have killed himself years ago.) No—Sedgwick had just learned that his sibling in San Diego had contracted X-Pox.

TM closed his eyes. "When?" Meaning, when was the illness diagnosed?

"Saturday."

When the plague first appeared, and was first identified by a panicked America, it killed its victims within a week, two at the most. But the introduction of Merck's treatment had increased that to a month, then two. TM's own company had followed Merck into the marketplace with React-X, which increased survival time by 50 percent without, unfortunately, improved quality of life. "Have you got her on React?"

"Yes, since the weekend."

"How old is she?"

"Twenty-nine." Rachel Dunne's age.

"I'm very sorry," TM said. It was all he could offer.

One of the waitpersons distracted Sedgwick then, and TM felt himself slipping into a state he knew well: a meditative zone in which he was able to carry on basic conversation, and even respond facially with smiles and nods, all the while another part of his mind broke words, phrases, and ideas into distinct packets, then recombined them. His ex-wife had joked about it, calling him the "transcendental meditator" for several years, until he ceased to amuse her.

Packet #1: People were catching X-Pox and dying in increasing numbers. The search for an X-Pox antidote had hit a dead end, at least when it came to traditional processing methods.

Packet #2: The Russians were four months from launching the Harmony module to dock with Alpha.

Packet #3: Rachel Dunne was going to fly in space.

The answer arrived like a candy bar delivered by a vending machine. TM felt no emotion, even as he knew his life had changed.

After dessert, he went directly to Leslie. "Having fun?" she said.

"Not at first."

She looked into his eyes. She well knew the signs of TM's special state. "Oh, God, what now?"

He chose not to answer directly, since Opher Elyan was passing within reach. "Opher, my friend," TM said. "Tell me how I can book research space aboard Harmony and Alpha."

Now he faced Leslie, and could not help smiling at the horror on her face. "*I* want to go."

EMBRACING THE INEVITABLE

A Southwest Airlines flight from El Paso to Houston Hobby took less than an hour and a half. Even with security screening (add thirty minutes), X-Pox-related prophylactic measures (add another thirty minutes), and the usual lead time needed to secure an aisle seat on no-frills Southwest (minimum one hour), plus X-Pox screening on arrival in Houston (thirty to forty-five minutes), plus driving time to and from both airports, the entire trip could be accomplished in five hours, less than half the time it would take to drive the 800 miles from Las Cruces to Houston.

Nevertheless, Mark chose to drive. Arriving back at his condo at nine P.M., twelve hours after the engine failure, he packed for an extended trip, configured his computer, left a message for his landlord, and slept perhaps three hours before arising at four A.M. to get on the road.

He had not been able to return Kelly's call until five-thirty Tuesday afternoon, an hour after the close of business at JSC. Expecting to leave a message—indeed, hearing Kelly's voice saying, "You've reached Kelly Gessner at the astronaut office"—he had been startled when she picked up. "Sorry, I'm here."

"Hey. It's Mark."

A slight hesitation. "About goddamn time. I stayed late." Mark was startled again by the way the sound of her voice cheered him. Either he was having a truly crappy day, or he was not over Kelly.

"You may have heard we had a few problems today."

She couldn't help laughing, since she had long predicted failure for the X-39 hybrid motor. But when she claimed she hadn't known of the incident when she made the original call, Mark asked why she had picked this day of all days to get back in touch. "Because Fehrenkamp is *gone,* Mark-o." That news was so surprising Mark almost didn't hear what Kelly said next. "And I pulsed Steve Goslin about bringing you back."

Bringing you back! In spite of his years of exile, Mark had stayed informed on the workings of the astronaut office—crew assignments, changes in leadership, the two new groups of candidates selected after him—almost to an obsessive degree. In fact, after four years in New Mexico, he knew more about CB than he did during the three years he was physically present in the office. He told himself he was just being prudent—staying prepared on the off chance he would get a call from the chief astronaut or one of his deputies. In fact he was clinging to his former life, the same way a high school athlete might turn up at games long after graduation.

"And what did old Steve say?" he said, trying to keep it light.

"He said to call him."

Call him. "Anything else?"

"He was encouraging. Guarded, but encouraging. Of course, I think he'd only known about Fehrenkamp for maybe an hour by this time. He was still having problems adjusting to the new world order."

"Well, he *is* a Marine." The moment he said those words, he regretted them, not because Kelly would object: like most astronauts, she rarely passed up the chance to tease a colleague, and Marine astronauts had been the butt of jokes since the days of John Glenn. No, Mark regretted his words because his whole future now depended on Steve Goslin. From this moment on, no disloyalty was to be tolerated.

"Pick up the phone first thing tomorrow."

Mark already had a better idea. "Suppose I drag my sorry ass to Houston."

Silence from Kelly. "Oh, yes, the patented Koskinen Grand Gesture." There was just enough sarcasm in her voice to make Mark slide past the subject.

"Hey, I was just advised to get out of Las Cruces. A few days in Houston won't do me any harm."

"Then it's probably a good idea," she said, adding, "you can even stay with me."

Mark would have preferred to keep his professional situation separate from his personal relationship with Kelly. But he realized that was impossible. "Thank you" was all he could say. They agreed that Mark would drive directly to Kelly's house, and that a key would be in the mailbox.

In any case, he couldn't say no without jeopardizing his opportunity to return to the astronaut office. As his father used to tell him, when you don't have a choice, embrace the inevitable.

Mark had made a previous drive across the heart of Texas, in February 2003, shortly after the orbiter *Columbia* disintegrated during reentry, killing its crew of seven.

The orbiter broke up at an altitude of 207,000 feet over the Dallas–Forth Worth area, spewing debris for hundreds of miles to the east and south. Ad hoc teams of searchers had formed, spending weeks tramping through woods and fields in search of tiles, airframe, tanks, and other pieces of the vehicle, a grim task necessitated by the need to discover the cause of the breakup.

Mark had gotten up early that morning to watch *Columbia* streak through the predawn sky to the north of Las Cruces. He had barely been able to spot the thin line of plasma low in the sky; he was certainly far too distant to see what other observers noted: disturbing signs that the orbiter was shedding tiles as it flew across California, Arizona, and New Mexico.

So he had been shocked and horrified when contact was lost with *Columbia* ten minutes later . . . never to be regained. He recalled how complacent he had been about his own reentry aboard *Discovery* on STS-100. Of course, after his near-death experience on an EVA, flying through a three-thousand-degree plasma sheath struck him as only slightly more dangerous than a final approach aboard a 767.

Obviously he should have been more concerned.

That night he had packed enough clothing for a week, and driven to the recovery staging area in Nacogdoches.

He'd stayed for a month, until Spacelifter business dragged him back to Las Cruces. In all that time spent tramping through the woods of east Texas, he found one piece of metallic debris that could have come from an aircraft, or even a passing semi.

Yet just taking part in the recovery effort made him feel as though he had honored the memory of the *Columbia* crew.

He pulled into a truck stop near the town of Van Horn for breakfast at seven-thirty. In spite of the big wheelers roaring past, or jammed into its parking lot, the truck stop seemed lost in time: Mark saw copies of a magazine called *From Sex to Sexty* on sale near the checkout. Well, at least the meal prices were up-to-date.

Sitting in the parking lot, waiting for his coffee to cool, he left a message on Steve Goslin's phone, knowing the chief astronaut would still be at Ellington. "Steve, Mark Koskinen. Kelly said I should call you." He deliberately did not say why, since he could not decide which was the most productive approach: *"About begging for a job?"* Too pathetic. *"About moving back home?"* Too flip, and Goslin wasn't noted for his sense of humor. *"About returning to CB?"* Accurate, but dry.

"I'm going to be in Houston beginning Thursday morning. Maybe we could meet, either at your office or somewhere else. Coffee would be on me." He closed by leaving his cell phone number, knowing he would turn it off, forcing Goslin to leave a message.

Then the torture began. Mark judged that not only the content of Goslin's return message, but its swiftness, would be a vital clue to his status. The longer he had to wait, the less likely it was that Goslin really had anything to offer him.

His instinct was to check his messages every hour beginning at ten A.M., when Goslin would return to the office, but that proved to be difficult. The service area for Mark's cell phone simply didn't extend uniformly across the vast emptiness of west Texas.

For a while it appeared he would never be in range, as he and several dozen other vehicles were halted on I-10 north of Kerrville around eleven-thirty. A Texas highway patrol unit was parked across the interstate behind a line of flares and cones. Mark thought about walking up to the officer and asking what the problem was, but the new rules of social interaction caused by X-Pox forced him to keep his distance.

Instead he got out of his car and leaned on the hood, squinting in the bright midday sunlight. The driver of the car in front of him, a tired-looking BMW, emerged, too. He was a heavyset man in his late forties, with a fringe of long hair and a walruslike mustache. He, too, kept his distance. Mark spotted the X bracelet on his wrist, and understood why. "Any idea what's going on?"

"Not a clue," Mark told him, as they leaned on the grille of his Explorer. But he had suspicions: a few miles back he had seen a pair of helicopters swooping low across the highway, suggesting some sort of nearby military operation. (Launches from White Sands forced similar road closures on Highway 70.) After years of living near Ellington Field in Texas, and White Sands in New Mexico, Mark was used to the constant presence of aircraft in the sky.

Only now did he wonder what military bases were located in San Antonio. His vaunted trick memory called up the army's Fort Sam Houston as well as three air force bases: Randolph, Lackland, and Brooks. Brooks was the home of the air force's aerospace medicine operations, and an obvious site for X-Pox-related research. Fort Sam hosted army medical operations. And who knew what satellite facilities had been planted in outlying areas?

"We've been pretty lucky, so far," the other driver said.

Thinking of the bracelet, which signified loss of a family member to the plague, Mark wondered how this gentleman could make such a statement. Perhaps he was an optimist. "Where are you from?"

"Houston."

The mention of Mark's destination, with its obvious connection to X-Pox, gave him a chill. He had read *nothing* about plague deaths there, nor had Kelly told him of any. Was he being too hasty in returning? He wanted to ask the man about the death in his family, but before he could frame a suitable question, he heard cars starting up farther down the line. "Looks like we're back in business," the man said.

Before he had driven a hundred yards, Mark already had the answer to his question: it didn't matter if there were dozens of "secret" X-Pox deaths in Houston; for his own sanity, he *had* to return to JSC.

Besides, based on *Challenger* and *Columbia,* and any number of other close calls, it was still far more likely he would get killed on a spaceflight than die of plague.

It wasn't until almost one-thirty, when Mark had reached San Antonio, that he was able to connect with his service. He heard the magic words, "You have one new message," followed by Goslin's brisk voice: "Mark, Steve Goslin returning. Good to hear from you, man. Good timing on the visit. If you can, come by first thing. I'll be in at eight, and I'll have a badge waiting."

The content was reassuring, but what made Mark happiest was hearing the time of the message: 10:12 A.M. Goslin had returned at his first opportunity.

He had been right to drive, right to pack for an extended visit. The Grand Gesture was going to pay off; he was going back to the astronaut office.

The two hundred miles from San Antonio to Houston flew by.

Mark was late getting to Kelly's; a downpour that hit before Mark reached downtown Houston made sure of that.

On the telephone Kelly had also warned Mark that she might not be home until after eight. "I'm qualifying at the neutral buoyancy lab." Mark immediately suggested that Kelly was in line for a new crew assignment, something she quickly dismissed: "No way, not after four years on the sidelines. Do you realize I've *never* done an EVA sim in the tank?"

Mark, who had performed one of the most difficult EVAs in space history, had laughed and said, "Then it's high-fucking time you start."

He further delayed his arrival by performing a ritual visit to his former condo, just south of the runway at Ellington. For the first year of his exile in New Mexico, Mark had retained ownership, renting the place out. But there were annoying problems with the tenants, and when a broker made him a minimally profitable offer to sell the place, he took it.

He found Kelly's place without trouble, let himself in, and stashed his bags in the spare bedroom. There was, predictably, no food in the place, and he debated ordering a pizza or waiting until Kelly arrived home. He had just reached the point where he was searching for her phone—he still remembered the number of the nearest Domino's—when the door opened. "Hey, you made it!" Kelly said, setting aside her gym bag and giving him a hug that went on a few pleasant moments longer than necessary.

"Did your suit leak, or did you get caught in the rain?" Mark said, teasing her for her wet hair.

"Neither. I showered and ran. Overnight guest, you know." She disappeared into the kitchen for a moment. Mark could hear her opening the fridge, and easily imagined the look on her face.

"Goslin's going to see me first thing."

"That's great!" she called, then returned to the dining area. "I have no food."

Mark brandished the phone. "Do you want to cook, or shall I?"

She smiled and took the phone. "Let's go out."

This was an atypical suggestion from Kelly Gessner. "Are we celebrating something?" Mark said, jokingly.

"Goslin told me after the sim that I'm going to be on ULF-Three." ULF-3 was International Space Station utilization and logistics flight number three—a Shuttle mission scheduled for launch in the spring of next year.

Mark picked her up. "That's great!" He set her down. "What did I tell you?"

"Yeah, yeah."

"Well, we *have* to go out. And *I* have to buy."

"What do you think he'll do with me?"

Dining options in the Clear Lake/JSC community were as good as those in any American suburb, ranging from the expensively quaint down to the inevitable chain restaurants. But for Mark and Kelly, there were really only two choices: Le-Roy's, the famed Cajun joint near Ellington's main gate; or Adriano's, the pretty good Italian place by the Baybrook Mall.

Mark vetoed Le-Roy's on the grounds that the spicy Cajun specialties would be wasted on him after his day of truck stop food. Le-Roy's also held too many memories of his astronaut days; it was the one place Mark was likely to see his fellow astronaut candidates, which would trigger a whole chain of guilt-driven discussion—*When did you get in town? Yeah, meant to call,* et cetera—that Mark wanted to avoid. Kelly didn't argue. She was probably happy to avoid the certain sly looks of fellow astronauts who would assume she and Mark were once again a couple. Wayne Shelton, the new boyfriend whose name Kelly had finally divulged, .wouldn't be happy, either.

Adriano's was a safer choice, especially on a slow Wednesday night. Mark and Kelly had worked through the ritual of choosing a wine—more challenging than necessary, because neither drank except at parties or special occasions—winding up with the house Chianti, then ordering, all without talking business.

The wine hit Mark as most drinks did—quickly. Its major effect was to add romantic music and soft lighting to his view of Kelly. Well, it seemed as though it did.

Kelly had surprised Mark by insisting on "getting ready" before dinner. In their time together, he had learned how much tolerance she had for such activities as hair-drying, application of makeup, and clothes-changing, which is to say, not much. She would happily "doll up," as she called it, for an appropriate function, and even in her everyday NASA uniform of slacks and polo-style shirt, remained neat and groomed.

But to take half an hour, to change into a blouse and skirt and apply lipstick, on a rainy Wednesday night? Was this the Wayne Shelton influence? Mark had gone through astronaut candidate training with Wayne; he doubted it.

Was it because Kelly was older now? Mark felt cruel just allowing himself to consider the concept. True, an objective pair of eyes would note that Kelly was perhaps five pounds heavier and that there were a few more lines on her face. (Flying in jets was hell on anyone's complexion.) But Mark had put on weight himself. And there were more gray hairs on his head every time he bothered to look.

Nevertheless, her eyes were still vibrant, pale blue. Her smile was quick and warm. And her voice was still the same wonderful instrument, capable of shifting from self-mocking laughter to throaty sexuality in the space of a single breath.

Mark was midway through his plate of vermicelli when he could stand it no longer. He blurted out the question: "Is Goslin really going to take me back?"

Kelly, ravenous after the unaccustomed effort of an EVA sim, had already finished her meal and was eyeing the dessert tray. She smiled. "He'll take you back, or he wouldn't have been at all encouraging. You've been following the office. You know the challenges right now."

"I wasn't a math major, but I can count. I figure at least thirty-nine astronauts who still haven't made a first flight—"

"—And have, in some cases, been waiting eight years—"

"—Which is longer than the time since my flight. Have I said I could do the math?"

Kelly leaned forward and smiled. "Actually, you're wrong: there are only thirty-seven kiwis now. Two of them are going to be on ULF-Three with me."

"Kiwis?" Mark was momentarily stumped. "Oh, flightless birds." The term was a subtle reminder that he had been away from the astronaut office for too long: he was no longer current on its jargon. "See? Things are better already, and I've only been back in Houston for a few hours. Besides," he said, "I'm young, I've got flight and EVA experience, and I will make it clear to Colonel Goslin that I'm willing to start at the end of that long line." He smiled. "I'll even take over your old specialty." Kelly seemed blank. "Station cargo."

"Oh, God! I've been trying to forget." Handling station cargo matters was one of those vital but uninspiring jobs that astronauts did between flights. Each Shuttle flight to Alpha delivered a couple of tons of supplies (food, water, clothing, equipment), and returned a like amount of trash. Not only did this material have to be inventoried for launch, it had to be transferred from the Shuttle's cargo hold to various locations in Alpha in an orderly manner. And then stowed according to strict guidelines developed in Russia and the United States—otherwise the expedition crews would be wasting hours searching for a new washcloth. "A master's in aero engineering, fifteen years at NASA, six hundred hours in space, and I was spending my days dealing with a scanner for bar codes. It was like being assistant manager of a supermarket. Don't, Mark," she said. "Don't take that job. Flying in space isn't worth it."

"You don't mean that."

The one thing that separated astronauts from the rest of the human race was that, for them, flying in space was worth *everything*.

"Here's my prediction," Kelly said. "When I haven't been doing redesign, I've been lead for the OSP." The Orbital Space Plane was a new NASA program to develop a cheap crew transfer and rescue vehicle that could be launched to Alpha with a few days' notice. It was seen by Mark's private space associates as a typical fat, useless NASA pork project aimed at putting money into the hands of giant companies like Lockheed or Boeing. Mark's view was more benign: the orbiter fleet was down to three, and aging. NASA needed a new vehicle. "With a crew assignment, I'm going to have to give that up. If Goslin has any sense, he'll make you my deputy. Then, in three months, when I go into mission training, you take over. Cripes, your background with X-39 makes you a perfect choice."

Mark was so intent on convincing himself that this would indeed be the scenario that he almost missed seeing Kelly's eyes go wide and hearing her whisper, "Oh my God, look who's here."

Mark shifted his glance toward the door, then back. He probably had the entrance in sight for less than a second, but it was long enough to confirm that Les Fehrenkamp had entered. "My, my," was all he could say.

The former deputy director was alone as he was shown to a table for two.

"What are we going to do?" Kelly hissed.

"Getting the check would be a good start." With Fehrenkamp's back toward them, Mark felt safe in signaling the waiter. "What brings him out tonight, do you suppose?"

"He's out of a job," Kelly said, "so he's got to find some way to fill the hours he used to spend screwing up people's lives." Kelly was so upset that she made no protest when Mark paid the bill. "Is there a back door?"

"We don't need that." He pushed back his chair and stood up. Kelly looked at him with growing alarm. "What are you doing?"

He was rising and marching toward Les Fehrenkamp.

The former deputy-director-for-life had changed in the four years since Mark had seen him. His thinning hair was completely gray now. He had put on weight. One of Fehrenkamp's tricks had been his ability to glide silently into any room, overhearing any conversation. But Mark had seen him waddle as he walked slowly to his table; perhaps he was having knee trouble.

One thing that hadn't changed was Fehrenkamp's disarmingly passive response to basic human interactions. If you offered greetings, he often seemed not to hear you. And when he did finally respond, his voice was usually so low that you had to turn your ear toward him.

He seemed not to notice Mark's approach. Fine. Mark simply slid into the seat across from him. Without extending his hand, he said, in his quietest voice, "Hello, Les."

Fehrenkamp looked up from his menu. "Mr. Koskinen," he said, keeping the menu in his hands. "I didn't realize you were in the area."

In the old days, which is to say, any time prior to Tuesday, a statement like that from Fehrenkamp could have announced the end of an astronaut's career: *I didn't realize you were in the area* translating to *You're not supposed to be here.*

"Just visiting," Mark said, feeling bulletproof. "I heard about the director's decision." Mark had considered vaguer phrasing—*"your new situation,"* for example—but decided to be as direct as possible. "I just want you to know that I appreciate the work you've done for this agency for the past thirty years. We may have had problems, but with my experiences on Spacelifter, I have a better understanding for your style."

Now Fehrenkamp put down the menu. He actually seemed flustered. "Ah, thank you."

And now Mark put out his hand. "Good luck."

There was an instant of hesitation, but finally Fehrenkamp shook Mark's hand. "You, too." Now, in classic Fehrenkamp style, he was already gazing two inches to the left of Mark's face. "Or do I say, you T-double-U-Oh?"

Mark turned to find Kelly looming behind him. Her presence explained Fehrenkamp's labored attempt at a pun. "Hello, Les." She did not offer her hand.

Fehrenkamp brightened considerably at the sight of her. He had never hidden his pleasure in the company of most of the women astronauts, and Kelly had always been one of his particular favorites. "Hello, Kelly."

"Would you like to join us for coffee?" she said. The offer sounded smooth, but Mark knew she had to force herself to make it.

"Thank you, but I have a date," Fehrenkamp said, with just a hint of satisfaction.

Mark took that opportunity to say good-night; he led Kelly out into the muggy Houston evening. "That's two in two days," Kelly said, as they walked to Mark's car. "Don't make a habit of it."

"Two what?"

"Two Grand Gestures. First the surprise visit to Houston, now the easily avoided encounter with Fehrenkamp."

Mark had acted on impulse. "I guess I just wanted to show him I wasn't afraid of him anymore."

"Then why are your hands shaking?" Mark had to laugh. "Here's why," Kelly said. "You know that man won't be truly gone until they're zipping him into the body bag. And maybe not then."

"I'll burn that bridge when I come to it." Mark stopped and glanced up at the sky. Clouds obscured some of the stars, but not all.

"What are you looking for?" Kelly asked.

"Alpha. There's a pass tonight."

Kelly looked directly into his eyes. "Oh, God. You still check the schedule." She meant the agency website that told cities when the bright star of Alpha—third brightest object in the night sky, after the Moon and Venus—would sail overhead.

Kelly linked her arm in Mark's. "Alpha did a maneuver this afternoon, so it won't be over for a while yet. Which means that you, hotshot, don't know everything."

As Kelly unlocked the door, Mark could not help remembering their past times together. The touches, words, glances that would send them from doorway to bed.

Not tonight, not after Kelly's halting account of her unformed relationship with Shelton, after Mark's overly detailed telling of his father's decline. Romance had been replaced by fatigue, as Mark slipped past Kelly into the living room. "Thank you for dinner," Kelly said, closing the door.

"Thank you for letting me come back."

Their eyes met, and there was a momentary spark, more an acknowledgment of the past than an invitation. "Up at six?"

"Up at six."

She smiled as she headed down the hallway, leaving Mark wondering just where and how his relationship with Kelly—hell, his entire life and career—had slipped out of his control.

Mark was sitting on the couch outside Steve Goslin's office at 8:10 when the chief astronaut emerged from the stairwell at full spring. Goslin had not changed since Mark had last seen him. The ruddy-faced, sandy-haired Marine was still in shape and somehow slightly out of touch. "Mark?" he said, with such obvious surprise that Mark feared he'd forgotten their appointment—a very bad sign.

But Goslin recovered quickly, extending his hand. "Sorry, I expected you to be calling from the gate or something. Security is nuts these days."

True, access to JSC, especially to the astronaut offices in Building 4S, had gotten tighter since Mark's departure. First it was due to the presence of an Israeli astronaut; then, of course, it was due to the events of 9-11 and X-Pox. "You left a badge for me," Mark said, by way of explanation. "And Kelly escorted me."

"Ah, Gessner." He had his office unlocked. "Come in and let's see what we can do with you."

Corner offices in NASA buildings—like those in any organization—were highly prized perks, and usually decorated by their occupants to emphasize their power and importance. Mark had seen several striking examples during his many sales calls on behalf of Spacelifter.

Goslin's was the exception. Blinds obscured the view of the JSC campus. The desk was standard Government Service Administration metal. The couch and chairs had to have been left over from the Gemini program. Goslin had several photos, including one of the infamous STS-100 crew that included Kelly and Mark, stacked against one wall. The office could just as easily have passed for a Marine air ready room in Yuma.

Mark actually found the low-rent surroundings relaxing. He almost put his feet up on Goslin's desk as the chief astronaut unloaded papers from his briefcase and stacked them neatly on his desk. "Look at this." He tapped the papers. "Officer efficiency reports. Training schedules. Flying schedules. Memos from the leads. And I get a stack like this every day."

"The price of power."

Goslin laughed. "So you want to come back."

There was no point in pretending otherwise. "Yes, sir." Mark's time in the air force had been spent in engineering, with little in the way of military protocol. But now and then, in circumstances like this, he once again became a junior officer.

"You know the situation here. The long line."

"Yes. I'll start at the end."

Goslin grunted. "You know, you go back to civil service pay."

Mark was amazed yet again that Goslin—a Marine colonel with combat experience, veteran of three Shuttle missions, head of the astronaut office and almost two hundred personnel—seemed not to know basic financial information. Well, that was the Goslin he remembered. "Steve, Spacelifter's been paying me for the past four years. But only my civil service salary. I never actually left NASA; I was only loaned out."

"Really?" Goslin's face broke into a grin. "Then I guess I've got no choice but to take you back." He stood up and extended his hand. "Welcome home, Mr. Koskinen. When can you start?"

"Is this afternoon too soon?"

Goslin laughed. "I actually have a job that needs to be filled quickly, though not this afternoon. Next week should do it."

"Whatever it is, I'll take it." As commander of STS-100, Goslin showed that he valued the willingness to be a team player over almost every other trait. Besides, how bad could it be? Capcom? Support at the Cape? Avionics lab? Any job would put Mark closer to a return to space than the X-39.

"Is your passport up-to-date?"

"As far as I know," Mark said. He had renewed it for STS-100 training. "Why?" he said, suddenly knowing the answer.

"I want you to go to Russia for the next six months."

NASA STATION STATUS
Lyndon B. Johnson Space Center
Houston, Texas 77058
281/483-5111

International Space Station Status Report #13-14
3 P.M. CDT, Monday, April 17, 2006
Expedition 13 Crew/Taxi Crew 10

TOXIC SPILL ON ALPHA

Early this afternoon a toxic spill was reported in the commercial Harmony module while spaceflight participant Tad Mikleszewski was performing a materials processing experiment with the Eridan glovebox. As a result, Harmony has been isolated from the Unity node while Mikleszewski implements standard cleanup procedures.

The Expedition 13 crew of commander Viktor Kondratko, flight engineer Nate Bristol, and science officer Jasper Weeks, together with Taxi-10 crew members Igor Gritsov and Rachel Dunne, are assisting Mikleszewski. The crew is in no danger.

Further updates will be issued as events warrant.

X-DAY ZERO, PLUS FORTY-FIVE MINUTES

"Tango, what the hell's going on in there?"

Bristol was calling on the separate intercom frequency as TM frantically tugged a mask over his mouth. The action was almost certainly futile, since the air in this section of the Harmony module was now rich with pure X-Pox droplets. Nevertheless, it made TM feel as though he had made an effort to save himself. It also helped him speak clearly and frankly to Bristol, since there was no sense in trying to cover up the situation. "I've had a breach," he said, his voice muffled through the mask.

"How serious?"

"Well, I was working with X-Pox."

"Oh, *shit.*" TM's work had been classed as "proprietary"; NASA and the other international partners in the Alpha program did not officially know what he was working on—only that Rosaviakosmos had certified the procedures as "safe." Bristol's adjustment to the news that the deadly virus was loose in Harmony suggested that he at least suspected the truth. "All right. I show Harmony on internal power."

TM forced himself to look at the control panel to his right. Originally designed in the 1980s to operate as a single, free-flying unit, Harmony had its own independent power, propulsion, and life support system. That was one of the reasons the various international partners in Alpha had allowed it to be added to the station: it wouldn't be a major drain on the resources of the core. "Yes, all of Harmony's systems are operating."

"Okay, then, TM, just stay calm. We'll get everybody working on this. How do you feel?"

"I'm fine!" he snapped. "It takes days to make you sick."

Bristol ignored the outburst. "Any idea what happened?"

"No. I just got an alarm and a warning light."

"Was Moscow in the loop?"

"Only my team there."

"I've got to tell Houston."

"Please do."

"Meanwhile—"

"Meanwhile I've got a whole book of procedures to follow."

"I'll go through them with you. Wait one while I—" He never finished the statement. TM could hear worried voices in the background—Kondratko, Weeks, Gritsov, Rachel Dunne—no doubt battering Bristol with questions.

It took several minutes before Bristol spoke directly to TM again. By then Lanny Consoldane had come back on the line from Korolev, fighting for airtime with the Russian "operator" who was insisting that TM "Report, please!" The astronaut capcom in Houston had put in a call, too, in that studied, calm voice: "Harmony, Houston. Give us an update on your, uh, situation, when you have a moment."

Bristol cut in. "Okay, everybody, this is Bristol. Let *me* talk to Tango. The Harmony interface is secure, and we've got plenty of time to deal with our little problem."

The overlapping chatter ceased so abruptly that TM assumed Bristol had now isolated Harmony's communications as well as its environment. "Still with me, Tango?"

"Yes."

"We're gonna start running through that checklist."

"I've got it right here," he said, lying only slightly, as he fumbled for it.

"Just keep focused on the job, Tango. We've got procedures for an incident just like this. You've got air and water and power for weeks."

"Food, too."

"Good point. Wouldn't want you to starve to death." No, that would be the least of his problems. Within a week, at most, he would develop a rash on his face. Then it would spread to his arms. When, a week after that, the rash turned to pustules, he would no longer be interested in food, only death. "Ready for page one?"

"I feel like such a goddamn idiot."

"The idiot is the guy that designed your glovebox, Tango. Now . . . page one."

X-DAY ZERO, PLUS TWO HOURS

Lester Fehrenkamp hated Washington. It wasn't the notoriously awful weather of the nation's capital; the winter and spring of 2005–2006 had been lovely. It wasn't even the stress of living in the U.S. capital under conditions of war, with mysterious convoys rushing through the streets, blaring sirens, masks, and the earnest paranoia of the governing class.

It was that he believed he would die here.

Considered simply, the thought was undeniably melodramatic. Nevertheless, the evidence was convincing. First, there was his lapse into sheer carelessness. Since moving here from Houston last October, he had ceased worrying about his diet, consuming sweets and fats whenever and wherever offered. He had put on fifteen pounds, with no end in sight. He was adding to the caloric intake—and damaging his liver—by having that first drink earlier and earlier, too.

The drinking didn't interfere with work, probably because he had no real work to do. Yes, Administrator McEwen included him in staff meetings, but when it came time to parcel out the assignments, Fehrenkamp found himself with the tasks nobody wanted. Flying off to NASA Ames in Palo Alto to conduct the latest in a series of "reviews" of its value to the space agency. Or serving as the NASA representative to this year's World Space Congress. The worst was being loaned to the Department of Energy to advise them on ISO 9000 certification for one of their laboratories.

He was no longer involved in day-to-day Shuttle or Alpha matters, such as the hasty decision to allow the Russians and their commercial partners to add the Harmony module to the station. Well, probably for the best: Fehrenkamp would have opposed it with all his power.

Because of these and other indignities, Fehrenkamp had simply stopped wearing the mask that had become required wear for citizens of Washington, D.C. He told himself that if X-Pox broke out here, the mask would be of little use.

But his refusal to wear one—while facing the critical stares of fellow NASA workers and capital residents—only reinforced his feeling that he had reached the end of his life.

The breakdown extended to his conversation. For years, Fehrenkamp had essentially confided in no other person—not even his wife, during the time he was married. Yet one evening he found himself sharing a drink in a Georgetown bar with Terry Doolan, a former astronaut who was now the agency's associate administrator for manned flight. The fact that Fehrenkamp and Doolan were even on speaking terms was a miracle: years ago Fehrenkamp had banished the former Shuttle commander from Houston for the sin of outspoken independence, figuring a season of butting heads in Washington might be educational.

But Doolan, with a consistency of personality as admirable as it was stupid, failed to show that he had learned discretion, being quoted one too many times in *Aviation Week* and even the *Washington Times* on agency matters best left unaired. He seemed to relish his role as fighter-jock-turned-senior-manager, and probably felt grateful to Fehrenkamp rather than resentful.

In any case, there they were, several vodka tonics into a rainy night, when Doolan unwound sufficiently to express sympathy—sympathy from Terry Doolan!—for Fehrenkamp's situation. "Did you ever think this would happen to you, Les?"

Fehrenkamp was just drunk enough to say, "Of course." And it was true: he had always known the day would come when he, too, would be "promoted" to a job that had a title and no duties. He had arranged too many similar bureaucratic "retirements" for others to have any hope of avoiding the same fate. "I feel like Yagoda,

Yezhov, and Beria. Every one of them took over a job that killed his predecessor. Each one would have had to be stupid or insane to expect to dodge the bullet. Literally." One of Fehrenkamp's skills was to know his audience: Doolan's hobby was Soviet history, specifically that of the KGB. Doolan was the one American in a thousand who would recognize the names of the heads of Stalin's secret police during the worst of the Great Purge.

So Monday, April 17, 2006, was just one day closer to death when Administrator McEwen appeared in Fehrenkamp's office doorway.

"Les?" With McEwen were Terry Doolan and two others, Chris Gifford, the head of the Alpha program, and Melinda Pruett, the head of ISS commercialization. All of them looked sick. "Join us in the vault?"

The vault was a secure conference room in the HQ, a leftover from Cold War days. It was here that in the summer of 1968, George Low learned that the Soviet Union had the ability to send cosmonauts around the moon within the next six months. Low had promptly developed a radical plan to have American astronauts beat them—the Christmas 1968 flight of Apollo 8 resulted.

That was before Fehrenkamp's time. His first visit to the vault had been in 1975, when, as the newest intern in the building, he had been present as an officer from the National Security Agency played voice intercepts from a Soyuz launch abort for the administrator and several astronauts.

The place had not really changed. It was merely a windowless conference room without the usual photos of glorious moments from NASA's history. Just a table and chairs. Oh, one thing: Gifford brought a laptop in and unfolded it.

McEwen didn't waste time. He closed the door and nodded to Gifford. "Tell them."

Gifford indicated his laptop, which showed a small video clip of Alpha science officer Weeks talking to mission control. Arrayed around the picture on the screen were a number of Alpha status displays, plus a smaller window showing Alpha's position in relation to the surface of the Earth. At the moment, the station was heading into night over the Middle East. "An hour and twenty-five minutes ago there was a toxic release in the Harmony module."

Doolan immediately went into his operations mode. "What level?" The ISS manual for toxic releases had five levels, from zero (green), nonhazardous, up to level four (red), most hazardous and uncontainable.

"We're at three," Gifford said. Fehrenkamp had overseen the writing of that manual, reviewing every page. He knew that level three (orange) was for a release of hazardous-but-containable material. "They've got Harmony sealed off. Airflow positive." Harmony's air pressure was slightly lower than that of the Unity node, meaning that any leak would flow *into* Harmony, not out of it.

Melinda Pruett was the first to register alarm. Like Doolan, she was a former astronaut, though her original move to HQ had been a reward from Fehrenkamp, not punishment. Of course, Pruett's original job was chief scientist. She had since moved to commercial relations. Prim and intense, she was, in Fehrenkamp's judgment, the worst possible selection for that particular job. "Was it Mikleszewski's material?"

McEwen answered. "Yes."

"Oh, God."

Doolan was, as usual, half a lap behind when it came to the larger issues. "Sorry, I do Shuttle ops more than day-to-day station stuff. What was he working on?"

Fehrenkamp heard himself answer. "X-Pox. He had both prototype vaccines and samples of the virus itself on board."

"How the fuck—?" Doolan exploded, then just as quickly shut himself down. "Let me guess . . . the Russian hardware crapped out."

"The initial report implicates the Russian glovebox, yes," Gifford said.

McEwen leaned forward now. "There'll be plenty of time for

pointing fingers. It appears we have a contaminated module, and a crew member exposed to a toxic substance. What do we do?"

"Cut it loose," Doolan muttered.

"And doom a human being?" Pruett said, astonished. "We can't have reached that point yet!"

"Nor do we want a twenty-ton module filled with X-Pox circling the Earth," McEwen said, clearly foreseeing the public relations nightmare.

"Then command the fucker to reenter over France," Doolan said.

"That's not even *possible,*" Gifford said. "All of the Alpha modules have their pyros and other rockets disabled when they hook up. Even if you did somehow cut it loose, you can't control it. It might take off a chunk of the station as it goes.

"I can't see myself justifying either decision to the president or the American people. Look at *Columbia,* for God's sake. Did we learn anything from that?" The board investigating the *Columbia* tragedy had concluded that the orbiter was destroyed by a blowtorch of three thousand-degree plasma melting the structure of its left wing. The plasma was able to penetrate the wing because several protective tiles on the wing's leading edge had been damaged on launch when struck by debris.

The only way the *Columbia* crew could have survived was if NASA had realized the seriousness of their situation immediately—within hours of the ill-fated launch—and tried to rescue the astronauts with another orbiter, a process that would have taken two or three weeks.

Losing a crew was a tragedy. Losing a crew when there was some chance—however slim—of rescue was unacceptable.

The horrible memory forced everyone around the table into silence. Finally McEwen said, "Speaking of the American people, what information has gotten out?"

Gifford examined the laptop. "Only a standard press release about a spill."

"That will buy us some time," Doolan said. "What about the air-to-ground?" Most of the conversations between Alpha crew members and the various Earth-based control centers were conducted in the open.

"Word of the problem was transmitted in the clear," Gifford continued, rubbing his forehead. "That's why we had to come out with a release.

"But comm was immediately switched over to Channel B." Channel B was the catchall term for a secure, encrypted frequency usually used for medical consultations or family conversations. "Rosaviakosmos has taken steps to keep the gory details quiet."

"Christ, you can't trust those guys to do anything right," Doolan snapped.

The three-way argument threatened to go critical, so Fehrenkamp broke in. "Gentlemen! And lady," he said, including Pruett, "the issue isn't public disclosure. That's inevitable. We can deal with that, because we have a plan." Now everyone stared at him. "We have simulated this emergency. We have a kit for toxic cleanup and extraction that can be loaded onto an orbiter within a week. Launch follows as soon as you can put the orbiter on the pad. We can attempt a rescue of Mr. Mikleszewski within three weeks. *That* is one lesson we learned from *Columbia*."

"Do we *have* three weeks?" McEwen said. "How long will this guy last?" Nobody at the table seemed to know. McEwen turned to Fehrenkamp. "Les? Can we launch any sooner?"

"Depending on beta angles and cutouts, we might be able to move it up a week." He saw Doolan nod in grudging agreement. "But it will be tight, and we have to have life sciences making sure this guy can stay alive."

"Look," Gifford said, "say we leave the module attached and clean it up. What's the point of rushing a rescue?" Everyone looked at him. "X-Pox is *fatal*. We're going to spend a hundred million dollars to bring him back, and he's going to die, anyway."

Before McEwen could launch into one of his patented "rah-rah" speeches, Fehrenkamp rapped on the table. "We don't know that." He turned to Pruett for support. "He's been up there synthesizing a vaccine. Maybe he's got something that will save his life."

Pruett shrugged. "All that data is proprietary, but—"

Fehrenkamp moved on. "He's certainly going to be motivated to field-test whatever he's cooked up. I say we go for the rescue, and go quickly."

McEwen didn't wait for a sense of the table. He turned to Doolan. "What's the next payload?"

"ULF-Three on *Discovery*. It's already on the pad, scheduled for launch on sixteen May."

"Tell them to hold on for a change of plans." He stood up and nodded to Fehrenkamp. "Les, you seem to be a step ahead of everyone here. This one's yours." McEwen's voice was relaxed, but his expression was almost sly, as if signaling to Fehrenkamp that they shared a secret.

Seven years ago, Fehrenkamp had handled—there was no other word—the Cal Stipe affair. To the world, to all but perhaps half a dozen people who knew the truth, Stipe was a heroic astronaut who had died during a tragic EVA accident on the Mir space station.

In fact, Stipe was an unbalanced individual who had caused the death of a fellow astronaut prior to his mission. He had chosen death rather than a return to Earth.

Fehrenkamp had suppressed the real story with a skill honed by thirty years of bureaucratic maneuvering. He had threatened no one; he had merely cited the danger to the program if the real truth were known. Stipe's colleagues in the astronaut office—Goslin and Gessner, in particular—would never reveal the facts.

The only wild card was Mark Koskinen, the young astronaut who had uncovered Stipe's activities in the first place. Koskinen had proved resistant to Fehrenkamp's rewards. Yet he had also kept the faith.

What did McEwen know? Worst yet, what did he think he knew?

Fehrenkamp realized it didn't matter. He recognized the brilliance of McEwen's decision. In success, Fehrenkamp went into retirement in a blaze of glory, the agency's secrets intact. In failure, McEwen was insulated, and the thirty-year veteran of Apollo, Shuttle, and ISS—Les Fehrenkamp—took the blame. Any subsequent unpleasant revelations would be suspect, sour grapes.

He suddenly had a reason to live. Too bad it meant someone else had to die.

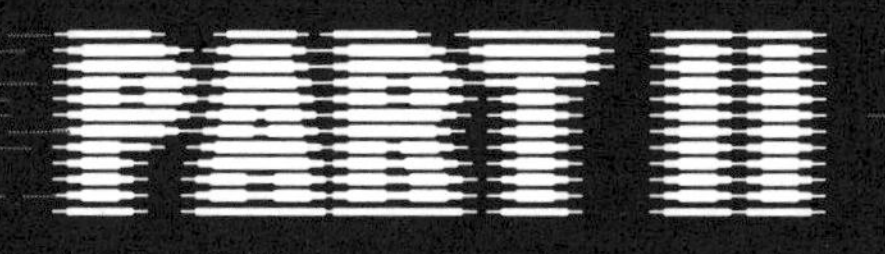

X-Minus Five Months
(November 2005)

Daily Variety, Monday, November 7, 2005

D'Works 'Recoil' Sends Dunne Spaceward

Actress Rachel Dunne is going to Space Station Alpha—courtesy of DreamWorks SKG and Aussie helmer Brad Beck.

Dunne will play Terry Drake, a NASA astronaut who is marooned aboard a space station with a mysterious secret.

The $100 million production, in association with Russia-based MosFilm, began principal photography in Texas on September 15. It will be the first dramatic production to include footage and scenes actually shot in space.

Beck, famed for music videos for Coldplay, Kylie Minogue, and Thrasher as well as the cable series *Spell Check,* is a former aero engineering student. "I always wanted to fly in space myself. But no one wants to see a scrawny, nearsighted white guy on film."

Dunne, who leaves for Moscow this week, is the star of numerous flicks, including *Overtime, Harley Girls*, and *Project All-Star*. She and Beck are both repped by Evolution.

THE PILOTS' MEETING

"All right, what am I forgetting?" Steve Goslin slowly shuffled the notes in his hand as if they were playing cards and he was trying to line up a flush.

He sat at a table at the front of a conference room on the sixth floor of Building 4-South. To his left, and slightly behind, was Harry Avedon, his deputy—"The power behind the throne," Kelly murmured as she and Mark took seats.

In the seats in front of Goslin were over eighty members of the astronaut office, plus another dozen members of the support staff. It was Monday morning, October 10, 8:15, and the chief was chairing the weekly pilots' meeting. Mark sat next to Kelly, toward the back and on the right, stunned at the realization that he knew less than half of those present.

"Quit teasing us, Steve-O!" somebody shouted, triggering a round of chuckling.

Mark knew that heckling the chief astronaut was a pilots' meeting tradition going back at least forty years. Legend said that the most fearless and skillful astronaut heckler was Pete Conrad, later to command Apollo 12 and the first Skylab. Heckling the likes of Deke Slayton and Al Shepard took real courage, since both men ran flight crew ops and the astronaut office with an effective combination of secrecy and ruthlessness, a tradition that continued through the long regency of Les Fehrenkamp. A hot pilot could get away with anything, of course, from violating aircraft flight rules (the troops at Ellington still told stories about Gus Grissom taking off in an F-106 with zero-zero conditions) to poaching one of the chief's girlfriends.

But it was risky.

This morning, Goslin had escaped relatively unscathed. It helped that the brief announcements coming out of HQ were benign, that the branch chief reports were routine. Goslin had been cunning enough to start the meeting with a call for volunteers for an X-Pox fund-raiser to be held over the coming weekend in Kemah. Being reminded of the plague simmering in the "real" world was enough to shift the gaze of even the most starry-eyed astronaut back to Earth.

The mood lightened after a few minutes, however. Now Goslin smiled and blushed. "You guys." Mark noted how happy and relaxed he seemed to be in his role as chief astronaut. It was a significant improvement over the often-humorless, easily exasperated first-time Shuttle commander he had trained and flown with six years back. "Okay, let me introduce the crew of STS-One-twenty-four, mission ULF-Three. Uh, please hold your applause until all the nominees have been named." More chuckles. "Commander will be Brad Latham—"

In spite of Goslin's plea for silence, a lone "Go, Barracuda!" could be heard—a fellow astronaut using Latham's nickname from navy days. Goslin elected to play the game, too. "Pilot will be Kevin 'Hoser' Ames, mission specialists—" Here it got trickier. "Diana 'D-Vine' Herron . . . Yung-Hun 'Hunster' Lai . . . Jeff 'Dagwood' Burnside . . . and, uh, Kelly 'Keyhole' Gessner."

The other astronauts applauded. Mark couldn't help laughing. He turned to Kelly, who sat next to him. " 'Keyhole'? Did you do some spying for Goslin?"

"As a matter of fact—" Kelly was unable to finish the sentence, as other astronauts reached over to shake hands and execute high fives.

"Okay, people," Goslin said. "I also want to announce a new addition to the team." It was as if the group of astronauts cleared their throats as one. "Actually, the return of a prodigal. Was lost, but now he's found. Our own Mark Koskinen. Stand up, Mark."

Mark got to his feet to what sounded like grudging applause. Well, he *was* another competitor for the finite number of seats. "Thank you, thank you, I'll be here all week." That earned a titter of laughter.

"Mark will be heading off to the Russian Front as the new director of operations at Star City." That comment earned a single enthusiastic clap from the darkness. "Mark, check in with Harry here after we break. We want you to be traveling next Monday." Harry Avedon was the deputy chief of the astronaut office; he would no doubt deal with the logistics of Mark's upcoming tour.

"Last item," Goslin announced, as Mark sat down and the bodies in the room began to shift with impatience. "The Multi-Lateral Crew Operations Panel has given tentative approval for two spaceflight participants—" The rest of Goslin's announcement was lost in an immediate uproar.

Goslin's face went red, and he actually rapped his knuckles on the tabletop. "Knock it off!" The room settled. "At least let me finish. Then you'll know why and what you're bitching about.

"As I was saying, before I was so crudely interrupted—two spaceflight participants for the E-Thirteen increment, on the taxi mission scheduled for launch in April oh-six." He waited, as if expecting an explosion from his left, where Jasper Weeks and Rich McCown sat quietly. Mark knew they were the two NASA astronauts assigned to the Expedition 13 crew. They would have to deal with the new spaceflight participants. Weeks had his eyes closed. McCown, who wore a walking cast on his left foot, seemed to be eagerly awaiting further information, like the good student in a class of fourth-graders.

"The assignments, of course, are routed through Rosaviakosmos." Goslin, who had no skill with languages, made the name of the Russian Air and Space Agency sound like a growl. "They are subject to approval by the main medical commission—"

"—And forty million dollars going *ka-ching!* in the old Swiss acount." At first Mark didn't realize who had spoken: it was Weeks, who still had his eyes closed. Goslin glanced at him, but chose to ignore the outburst. Weeks and McCown, who were scheduled to launch to ISS Alpha in less than two months, were the two people in the room with irrevocable, Pete Conrad–level immunity.

"—And subject to both conclusion of a financial agreement between the parties, as well as a safety briefing here at JSC prior to launch."

McCown's hand shot up. "Do we have names?" he asked politely.

"Yeah, I suppose names would help," Goslin said. "Spaceflight participant number one, under program *Recoil,* is Miss Rachel Dunne." Dunne's name had been floating around the office for weeks, so this was no surprise. It earned a genuine, old-fashioned wolf howl, which in itself earned the howler a reproving glance from at least two women astronauts.

Not Kelly. She turned to Mark and whispered, "I would pay money to be on Alpha when the actress shows up." Kelly's Shuttle mission was scheduled to follow a month after Rachel Dunne's visit would end.

"SPF number two, who will be conducting ops aboard Harmony, is named Tad Mik—" Goslin stopped dead on the Polish name. "Mik-le-sevski" was the best he managed.

"Who the hell is he?" an unknown astronaut asked.

"A guy who's rich enough to buy all of us," another voice answered.

"All right, people," Goslin said, getting to his feet. "That's the news. Be careful out there."

Astronauts usually scattered from pilots' meetings like quail at a gunshot. But several crowded around Mark and Kelly, offering congratulations or hellos as they exited. Among them was Jinx Seamans, a twenty-year veteran of the astronaut corps. Mark had not seen the air force mission specialist since making the move to Las Cruces, and was shocked at how much older he appeared. He had gone completely gray. Did *he* also strike people this way, like a ghost? "Good to see you back."

"Thanks, Colonel." They had never been on a first-name basis.

"It's just Jinx, these days. I've been retired for three years." This information did nothing to lessen Mark's feeling that too much time had passed. "Thanks for falling on the grenade, by the way."

"Grenade?"

"The DOR job. I was afraid they were going to stick me with that fucker."

"That bad, huh?"

Jinx narrowed his eyes. "Stop by and see me before you go." He slapped Mark on the back as he moved off.

Kelly moved up behind him. "Told you so."

Mark's acceptance of the DOR job had sparked an argument that flared up at various times over the next four days. Kelly first complained that since Goslin had *asked* (in Mark's account of the meeting), the Russia job was merely an offer. "That was your opening to *negotiate*! You know he's got the OSP job to fill. So you ask to work in SAIL or at the Cape, then he comes back at you with a job you can agree on!"

"It didn't feel like a negotiation. It felt a lot like begging."

"You're a civil servant, Mark. Absent criminal behavior or a complaint, Goslin *has* to take you back."

"I know. But he doesn't have to *fly* me."

"Which kind of astronaut does he want to fly? A confident self-starter? Or someone who operates based on fear?"

"Look, I'm a logical choice. I speak Russian—"

"—As if they've ever cared about that around here—"

"—I know the Soyuz inside and out—"

"Not to be too picky, but you know the Soyuz TM; they've been flying the TMA model for a couple of years now."

"How much difference can there be?"

"The point is, you *don't know*."

"I can manage, okay?"

"The way you've managed your NASA career so far?"

At almost any time in the past few years, an exchange like this would have triggered an eruption. But now Mark was able to take a breath and say, "Do we have to fight?"

"Not if you don't want to."

In a way, his new ability to avoid fighting with Kelly was troubling. Did it mean he no longer cared? That Kelly couldn't provoke a reaction? Then, after the third such argument, Mark realized that Kelly's anger had more to do with their past relationship than with his astronaut career. So Mark chose to avoid even the opportunity for further conflict by getting busy with the mundane, yet surprisingly complicated, business of renting an efficiency apartment—literally a glorified self-storage unit, since he would be resident in Russia for at least nine months—and closing out the condo in Las Cruces.

This required several shopping trips around Clear Lake, where the rents startled him, and numerous phone calls on his cell. (He shuddered to think of the bill.) It didn't help that the real estate market in Las Cruces was flat. He might not lose much on the condo, but he sure wasn't going to come out of the deal with a windfall.

Mark had not worried about money since getting out of college and entering the air force. As a single man in his twenties, the pay of a lieutenant and then captain was perfectly sufficient. He then spent three years at Hughes, where for the first time he found himself making more money than he could spend. So he had bought an expensive car, rented a nice apartment, traveled, and indulged in sailplaning.

Coming to NASA seven years ago, he had become a civil servant, specifically a GS-11, at a somewhat reduced rate, compared to Hughes. During his time in Houston, he had had no time for luxurious vacations or time-consuming hobbies; he was barely ever home to do grocery shopping. Money was simply irrelevant.

Spacelifter had paid him the same GS rate—that was how their memorandum of understanding worked with NASA. Since life in Las Cruces was cheaper than in Houston, Mark simply went on cashing checks and writing them, and putting a small amount of money aside.

It was during a visit home two years back, at the time the recession of 2002 was mutilating pension plans and stock portfolios, that he had agreed to help his sister Johanna pay for private school tuition. Johanna had moved to San Diego with her husband, Lewis, who was taking a job in a dot.com. The dot.com cratered, taking Lewis's job with it, and they were struggling to send their daughters Cayley and Madison to good schools.

Feeling expansive, thanks to three of his father's frozen daiquiris, Mark had offered to pay half of the $15,000-a-year tuition. But $7,500 a year was a lot when your GS pay was $68,687 per year and you didn't have many deductions. Normally he sent the checks, and didn't miss the money too much. But he had had to write out $3,000 worth in the month before the X-39 meltdown, and now he wondered when he would ever catch up.

It wouldn't happen in the astronaut office, where everyone, military or civilian, was paid by one government scale or another. Some astronauts came from wealthy families, of course, and at least one mission specialist had made a fortune on a patent prior to selection. In the early days, the Mercury astronauts had been blessed with a huge *Life* magazine deal for their personal stories. A generation later, however, there were no big media companies eager to pile up the cash for inside astronaut stories. Civil service rules had gotten stricter, too. Here in the early years of the twenty-first century, NASA astronauts lived a middle-class existence.

The astros who worried most about money were those going through divorces (always a few), and those with children approaching college age. In fact, before transferring to Las Cruces, Mark had observed that the single most popular reason for astronauts to leave

NASA was to find more lucrative jobs that would better pay for tuition.

Now, here he was, a single man with no family, and yet in the same situation.

By Friday, two days after his original reunion meeting with Goslin, Mark found himself sitting at Kelly's kitchen table about to fling his cell phone against the wall in anger and frustration, and not just at his financial challenges. He was irked that Goslin had no office space for him. "We're hot-bunked as it is, and you're gonna be shipping out in two weeks." He was also angry that he wasn't going to be allowed to return to currency on the T-38. The tight schedules—mission specialists were only booked for flights two days a week—meant Mark wouldn't even have a check ride. "There's no aviating in Russia, anyway," Goslin had said, "so what's the point? You can start flying when you come back."

Ah, yes, six months from now. In the middle of their trio of arguments, Kelly had scored a point concerning the term of the DOR assignment. "They're going to tell you six months, and then they're going to keep you over there for nine or ten or a whole year. Watch."

Mark knew that an extension was possible, which also complicated his rental planning. And added to his spending.

He leaned back and closed his eyes. What was wrong with him? Lack of sleep, lack of exercise, stress on the professional and personal fronts.

Take a breath. Evaluate. Do the kind of analysis NASA taught you.

The mantra helped. He had left his cell phone intact, and borrowed Kelly's dusty bicycle to go for a ride. He was smart enough to continue working out—and not thinking about money—and avoiding further arguments with Kelly—until this Monday.

Mark's follow-up meeting was with deputy chief astronaut Harry Avedon, reputed to be the smartest person in the history of the office. So Mark believed; even Kelly said so. He was Mark's age, yet had been an astronaut five years longer, racking up three successful missions to Mark's one.

Even Harry's selection bespoke his brilliance: most astronauts came to NASA with operational military backgrounds, usually in flight test or related engineering work (like Mark, with a tour at Air Force Space Command), or from other areas of NASA itself (like Kelly, from aircraft ops at Ellington). Occasionally a candidate would be selected from some aerospace-related business.

Avedon was one of the very few who came to the astronaut office straight from the university, in his case, MIT, where he had been one of the youngest professors of astronomy in the institution's history. He had no military background and no unusual athletic skills, either, unless you counted being a scratch golfer. The story was, Harry had earned straight-A grades all the way back to preschool.

He was also tall and good-looking, in a shambling, Jimmy Stewart way. He had managed the magical feat of becoming one of Les Fehrenkamp's pets while still remaining popular with his contemporaries.

He shut the door when Mark entered. "About time you got your butt back here," he said.

"I don't remember any calls from *this* office wondering when I'd be showing up," Mark said. As members of different astronaut groups, the two had never been close, but Avedon had the gift of immediate intimacy—you could say anything to him without giving offense. It was another arrow in the quiver.

"That would have required unusual courage on my part. Or have you forgotten the change in administration hereabouts?" Avedon didn't wait for Mark's confirmation. "I'm learning the science of bureaucracy."

"It seems you're well on your way to a Ph.D."

Avedon grunted. "What did Steve do to get you to take the DOR job? Threats, blackmail, bribery?"

"He *asked.*"

"Gee, why don't more people do that?" Avedon leaned forward. "Don't get me wrong, I'm glad you took it. You know enough of the language to get by, the Russians think you're some kind of goddamn hero—" This was news to Mark. "—you haven't been drinking from the poisoned well around here, either." He forced a smile. "You can bring fresh eyes and ears to the situation."

"What *is* the situation?"

Avedon looked at him while drumming his fingers on his desktop. "I don't want to prejudice you."

"Which means you want me to walk into this thing blind."

"Or I want you to walk into this thing blind, yes." He stared off into space, as if reading directions written on the wall, but visible only to him. "Okay, we've got big problems on the Russian Front. I mean, on our side. Too many of the folks we're sending over there are going native. Lots of drinking, lots of staying up late and running around. A lot of marriages are taking hits. We've also had people getting robbed and beaten. It's like the Wild West, man, and not just for astronauts, but the MOD support folks, everybody."

"How many of them are my responsibility?" Mark was hardly an expert on the NASA presence in Russia, but he knew that in addition to the DOR based at Star City, there was another official based in the headquarters of Rosaviakosmos who actually had much more power.

"Maybe a dozen of the forty, but yours are the most visible. They also tend to be catalysts: if one of the ISS crew folks is behaving badly, it tends to encourage the others."

Mark had spent two weeks in Russia seven years ago—not long, but sufficient to alert him to the temptations. "So I'm supposed to go over there and be a scoutmaster?"

"You catch on fast, Koskinen. Yeah, try to keep the troops in line."

Sensing that the briefing was over, Mark got up. "I'll try to leap a tall building while I'm at it."

"You may have to." Avedon was shaking his head. "You know, it's really too bad about Spacelifter."

"Why would you care?"

"Christ, Mark, I was *this* close to investing in it! NASA's way of doing business is obsolete. If we're going back to the Moon or anywhere the hell beyond low Earth orbit, it's going to be a commercial deal, like Spacelifter. Yeah, I was rooting for you."

Mark was shocked. If Harry Avedon, the rising star of the astronaut office, felt like that, maybe Mark had made a big mistake returning to Houston.

He grabbed his backpack and headed for the elevator. Just as it was about to close, Shannon, Steve Goslin's secretary, thrust her hand between the doors, jamming them open. "Sorry!"

"Come on in!" Mark said.

"No, I was trying to stop you." She handed him a pink message slip. "There was a call."

Mark glanced at the paper, and recognized the 505 area code for New Mexico.

He didn't need to return the call to know that it had come from his former office at Spacelifter, that the caller was his mother, and that it was bad news about his father.

THE VOMITORIUM

Rachel Dunne spent her first night at the Institute for Medical-Biological Problems throwing up. At the first warning rumble in her stomach, she feared she had caught the flu. In Los Angeles, the thought of any contagious illness would have sent her into serious panic. Here, however, in the grim suburbs of Moscow, with Russia not targeted by the terrorists who launched X-Pox, she was able to remain calm . . . to note the lack of fever . . . to replay her activities and eating since arriving at Sheremetyevo-2 airport early that afternoon, and conclude that she was suffering from food poisoning. Two officials from Rosaviakosmos had insisted on taking her out to dinner at a new restaurant in Korolev; one too many vodkas had made her too weak to resist the appetizer, some very tasty dumplings made of mystery meat.

Or perhaps it was just the stress of travel. The flight from Los Angeles had been exhausting—five hours L.A. to New York, then nine hours on Delta to Moscow. First she had tried to sleep, with no success. Then, in frustration, she had devoted three hours—well, one hour—listening to Russian language lessons on CD. That eventually did put her to sleep, which screwed up her internal clock. She was groggy when the plane reached Moscow.

It could have been worse. Instead of sitting in first class on a 747, she might have been packed into one of those Russian planes with smokers for the same amount of time.

She was traveling alone; Opher Elyan had offered to pay for a second first-class ticket in order to have an "assistant" accompany her. (That is, if Rachel somehow failed to invite Opher to make the trip with her.) But Rachel had never risen high enough on the Hollywood food chain to require, which is to say, afford, a personal assistant.

Rachel knew exactly where she ranked on the blond actress scale, since there was only ever room for one at the top, and then only for eighteen months. (This happened to be the time it took for a movie starring said blonde to be an unexpected hit, for the blonde to be cast in another movie, and have it be released, and fail.)

All through school in Arizona, through the dismal jobs she talked about (waitressing and modeling for department stores) and the frightening ones she didn't (stripping and phone sex), through small roles on television and in teen flicks, Rachel had watched other blond actresses come and go. Sharon Stone, Michelle Pfeiffer, Uma Thurman, Gwyneth Paltrow, Charlize Theron, Reese Witherspoon—each had taken her place at the peak, only to slide down.

Rachel knew that the slide was inescapable, like this evening's sunset. She only wanted the chance to reach that peak and enjoy those eighteen months.

Recoil was her means of ascent.

The film's gimmick—that the lead actress would actually have to fly in space, and even worse, train for several months to do so—had eliminated at least a dozen of the actresses on the hot blonde list ahead of Rachel. Some were terrified of the whole idea. One was pregnant; two others had children in school and did not wish to live in Russia. One had had an ugly experience with *Recoil*'s director, Brad Beck.

There was also the language problem. One of the blondes highest on the list was known for her skill with languages, but she was in the throes of a marital breakup, and not interested in adding Russian to her résumé.

These disqualifications still left a dozen hot blondes ahead of Rachel Dunne, but she had a secret weapon: she once starred in a low-budget movie called *Harley Girls* that had been cast by a man named Harry Griner. Because *Harley Girls* made money, Harry Griner's star had risen, and he wound up working on *Recoil.* Because

Rachel had put up with the horrendous nonunion working conditions in Mexico while doing her own stunts on *Harley*, Harry Griner remembered Rachel fondly when it came time to audition the blondes who were far down the list. (Rachel could imagine him telling Beck, "Look, she learned to ride a hog. Why not a Russian spaceship?")

Rachel knew that Sharon Stone became a star by being willing to discard her panties in *Basic Instinct*. Flying in space, while more time-consuming and dangerous, seemed classier, somehow.

Though not this evening, as Rachel staggered from her hospital bed to the toilet down the hall. Fortunately, thanks to a years-long struggle with an eating disorder, Rachel was familiar with the mechanics of purging. For an actress, having bulimia was almost a rite of passage, like turning your boyfriend into your manager (or vice versa). If nothing else, she told herself, she would be pleased when she stepped on the scales during her examinations tomorrow.

Assuming the Russians even used decent scales. Maybe they would load her into some kind of contraption better suited to weighing livestock.

She wiped her mouth, then padded down the darkened hallway to her lonely room.

Although originally unnerved by her relative isolation in what Elyan laughingly called the "Presidential Suite" of the institute—it had been remodeled for use by American astronauts and those who had preceded Rachel as "spaceflight participants," but still lacked lightbulbs in the hallways, fresh paint, and decent flooring—Rachel was happier enduring trips to the vomitorium without witnesses.

There probably weren't more than a dozen human beings in the entire IMBP complex, half a dozen concrete buildings spread over several acres of land in northern Moscow. The Institute for Medical-Biological Problems was not an actual hospital, but rather a research facility where Soviet (now Russian) aerospace medical specialists tested civilian candidates for spaceflight, and conducted various experiments of their own. Rachel had been told, upon arrival, that in the building across the muddy square, five European college students were confined to bed for three months as part of a study of the deterioration of human bone and muscle on long-duration spaceflight. Aside from those five, a scattering of guards, and a single night nurse, the institute was deserted.

So, about two A.M., when Rachel heard thumping through the wall of her room, she was alarmed. But her stomach took advantage of her momentary wakefulness to force her to hurry to the bathroom. When she returned to bed, she heard no more noises, and collapsed, finally, into a restful sleep.

She was awakened by Yelena, the dark-haired, dark-eyed IMBP staffer who had checked her in the night before. In halting English, Yelena said, "We must start with blood sample this morning."

"Does it matter that I was sick last night?" Rachel said.

Yelena didn't understand what was being said until Rachel performed a pantomime. Alarmed at the news, the white-coated woman said, "No. No. I will come back later." She gathered up her needles and vials and left.

Rachel showered, amusing herself with a study of the unusual flow of water out of the shower onto the floor. She used three of the very thin, small towels to sop up the excess.

Then, following Yelena's directions, she donned what appeared to be the standard IMBP client uniform—sweatpants, sandals, and a T-shirt. There was also a hooded sweatshirt bearing the logo of the Eternal Frontier Association.

She went out to the hallway, trying to remember whether the cafeteria was to the right, away from the bathroom.

The door to the adjoining room opened, startling her. "Hello!" she said, tentatively and automatically, hoping English was her neighbor's language.

It was. Her neighbor was the man she had met at Konrad Hoefler's party—Tad Mikleszewski. He, too, wore an Eternal Frontier jacket and sweatpants, though he added a Dodger cap to the ensemble, which made him look like a minor league baseball coach. The way he held out his hand and shook hers only reinforced the image. "Hello to you." He looked both ways down the hall. "Is there a place to get food around here?"

"Follow me," Rachel said, demonstrating a confidence she didn't feel. Well—she *was* an actress.

"So it's true. You're going, too?"

"If my check clears," TM said.

Rachel laughed. Why did rich men always pretend they didn't really have money? "Your check for your flight, and DreamWorks' for mine."

"Don't worry, they've got tons of cash." He smiled. "I'm a stockholder."

Rachel and TM were seated in the clinic cafeteria, the quietest breakfast place Rachel had ever seen, with the exception of a small hotel on the South Island of New Zealand when she guest-starred in some god-awful syndicated adventure show one rainy winter. There was a single attendant behind the counter, ladling out bread, potatoes, peas, and what appeared to be a limp, cold sausage. She then drifted over to the cash register to record not sales, but usage. Two other IMBP staffers, a man and a woman in the ever-present white coats, were having a cup of tea at a different table. As one of the thirty most desirable blondes in the world, Rachel was used to being recognized, and sure enough, she saw the man checking her out.

TM saw him, too. "There's that power again."

"Hmm?" she said, knowing perfectly well what he meant.

"Never mind." He smiled. "It's good for me to know I can be aboard that space station, and no one on heaven and earth will pay any attention to me."

Rachel hadn't much liked TM on that first meeting. His body

language screamed arrogance and power; his looks weren't good enough to compensate. This morning her opinion had climbed into neutral territory. But with that unwanted and, in her opinion, entirely unnecessary observation, TM's stock had fallen back into negative territory.

That was bad news, because every man she had ever been involved with had started out on the bad side of the dial. "Lucky you," she said quietly, pushing back her breakfast.

"Not hungry?"

"No more Russian mystery meat for me, thank you."

"Do you mind?" TM held his fork poised over her plate.

"Be my guest." As TM speared one of the sausages, Rachel said, "Do you have any idea what they're going to do with us?"

"Well, you had a physical in L.A.? And you passed?"

"Yes."

"So did I. If a show-stopper had turned up, neither of us would be here." He swallowed a last bite, then dabbed his mouth. "Nervous?"

"Yes. I mean, it's one thing to sign up for a movie that requires stunt work or just dealing with bad weather. So far that's what this has felt like.

"But I assume that today they start whirling us around on that machine—"

"The centrifuge."

"—and strapping us into tilting chairs, just to see whether we get sick or not."

"Oh, we'll get sick. Vomiting is inevitable. They just want to have some idea how long it's going to take us."

Perhaps it was the way she'd spent the previous night, but the prospect of test-induced purging merely made her feel tired, not frightened. "Well, then there's the whole business of being locked inside a little space capsule and blasted into orbit with two Russians I barely know."

"You've got five months to learn how to scream in Russian."

"Ha-ha."

"Besides, it won't be two Russians." He stood up and gathered his plates. "It will be one Russian you barely know, and me."

"How comforting." She made no effort to hide the sarcasm.

TM laughed. "Don't worry about these tests. You paid the money. If you can fog a mirror, you're flying."

She remembered TM's words when, four hours later, following an annoyingly leisurely schedule of routine tests, Yelena and Dr. Fedorov arrived in her room wearing terrified expressions. "Is there a problem?"

"Your chest X rays," Yelena said. "They are very disturbing."

For a moment, Rachel failed to understand the problem. Then she understood all too well. She yanked up the sweatshirt as if she were "showing the babies" in a straight-to-video audition. Fedorov's mouth fell open, and Yelena recoiled with disapproval. "Implants," Rachel announced. "Silicon gel, the best Beverly Hills can offer. They do leave a shadow on X rays, but I've been assured they are perfectly safe."

The Russians still seemed confused. "Like dental fillings," Rachel suggested.

That seemed to satisfy them. Soon both Fedorov and Yelena were laughing nervously.

And Rachel Dunne was one step closer to being certified as physically fit for flight into space.

THE RING ROAD

"Tell him if he doesn't slow down, he's fired!"

That's what TM shouted to Lanny Consoldane from the backseat of the Mercedes SUV as it swerved into oncoming traffic, then back, just in time.

"He speaks English!" Lanny said from his position in the front passenger seat. "He's our translator!"

The driver-translator, whose name was Andrei Salnikov, was hunched over the wheel, concentrating on his driving. TM approved of the concentration, but not Andrei's automotive manner. The Mercedes had pulled out of the IMBP parking lot at a reasonable speed, thanks to the potholes and mud puddles which made a fast getaway impossible. But then the young Russian had turned onto the Ring Road, headed north and east toward Star City, and opened up the throttle like an entrant in a Grand Prix.

Complicating matters was the lack of clearly defined lane stripes or, worse yet, *any* sort of barrier separating the northeast-bound traffic from the southwest flow. TM hung on through several unnecessary swerves and close calls, then chose to speak up.

"He doesn't *act* as though he understands English," TM shouted. Andrei had the window open, and the roar of other vehicles and the wind generated by eighty-mile-an-hour speeds made it difficult to be heard.

Lanny apparently agreed, because he slapped Andrei on the arm, and yelled several words in Russian to him. Andrei was the official, local translator, but TM always liked to have a backup. So he had rehired Lanny Consoldane from the Spacelifter project. Years past, pre-Spacelifter, Lanny had worked with NASA's Moscow-based, illogically named Houston Support Group. Lanny had met TM at Sheremetyevo Airport on Monday afternoon, dropped him at IMBP, then gone off to play. TM had only met Andrei this morning.

Uttering a flurry of protests, Andrei kept ripping along. He managed to point in the general direction of the rearview mirror, so TM turned and looked behind them: a green Ford Expedition was several cars back, pulling the same incredibly risky maneuvers. "It's probably the *militsiya,*" TM said, referring to the Russian equivalent of the highway patrol. "I'm surprised they're not shooting at us."

Of course, even TM had to admit that everyone on the Ring Road was driving fast and furiously today. The *militsiya* could stop anyone.

A looming bloc of merging traffic allowed Andrei—after sliding onto the right shoulder in order to pass several cars and their unhappy drivers—to bull his way into a lane, and slow to around sixty-five, still too fast for TM's nerves. Andrei then rattled off several sentences in Russian.

Lanny looked over the seat at TM. "Sorry. He says he thought you wanted to get to Star City by ten."

"I have an *appointment* at ten," TM said. "But being on time is less important than being *alive.*"

Andrei seemed to absorb this, then turned back to his driving, window still open. Lanny caught TM's eye: he had hired Andrei, and knew he was responsible for him. "He'll be fine."

TM did not meet Rachel Dunne again during those three days at the medical institute. He learned later that she had been rushed through a battery of tests, then taken off into the city for preliminary photography for *Recoil,* as well as a calendar shoot.

Just as well: Lanny and Andrei were both single men, and from passing comments, TM knew they were a bit too eager to get chummy with the actress. The only surprise in that was that Lanny

Consoldane—formerly TM's candidate for the world's oldest living male virgin—was openly lustful. Perhaps it was the lure of life in Moscow.

In any case, Rachel would have been a major distraction, and while TM knew that dealing with the actress issue was an inevitability, he was happy to postpone it for weeks or even months.

Lanny was a typical engineer, at least in appearance: thirty pounds overweight, indifferently dressed. Andrei was thin, almost gaunt, with a pockmarked face. He wore a black leather jacket, which made him seem like a candidate for the Russian *mafiya*. Maybe he was already a junior member. He certainly drove like a man on a fast getaway.

Yet Andrei had a degree from Moscow Aviation Institute, one of the best aerospace universities in the country. According to his résumé, he had worked for the past four years at the Krunichev Space Center, a massive facility in northwest Moscow where Proton launch vehicles and space station modules like Harmony were manufactured. TM was counting on Andrei to serve as his eyes and ears into the Krunichev organization, and into Harmony itself: thank God Andrei wouldn't be flying the thing.

TM had noted the change in the landscape outside the car. IMBP was located in the city itself, surrounded by towering, crumbling apartment buildings. But for the past few minutes TM had glimpsed open country, including cottages that looked as though they had been built in the 1700s. Off to one side were several huge tracking dishes. Next to them, a lake.

They left the highway and drove down a two-lane road. More cottages, and now some more prosperous-looking condos off in the birch trees.

At an intersection, Andrei came to a stop at a sign which, to TM's surprise, was the familiar U.S.-style hexagon—with the word STOP written in *English*. Right in front of them was a statue of an airman. "Valery Chkalov," Lanny said, playing tour guide. "There's a big air force base named for him, right through those trees." Sure enough, as the car drove on, TM caught sight of a chain-link fence, and through the trees, tail sections of aircraft.

Several more turns brought them to a security checkpoint—a guardhouse, a new-looking gate, and beyond these, a reception building. A young soldier in a blue overcoat approached them. There was no other traffic. No other people seemed to be about. Of course, the October day had grown cold and dark. Intelligent Russians were probably all inside.

"Welcome to Star City," Andrei said. The young guard took passports and a copy of a fax into the gate shack, presumably to examine or record them.

TM looked at his watch: it was 9:52. "Colonel Filippov is supposed to meet us," Lanny said. Pavel Filippov was the Star City official in charge of "international affairs"; TM had met him in Los Angeles just days ago. He had signed the document authorizing TM's initial training at Star City.

Now Andrei turned to TM. "Has the money been paid?" A blunt question like that would have triggered a sneer from most multimillionaires, but TM was acutely aware that he was in Russia, a foreigner hoping for admittance to a formerly classified facility. He had only a vague understanding of the rules involved.

"I authorized a fairly substantial wire transfer before I left Los Angeles."

"Then where's Filippov?" Lanny said. "He should be here with a big smile and a tray of snacks!"

TM's deal with the Russians required him to pay two million dollars by this date, something Andrei almost certainly knew. His office had already wired half a million to Rosaviakosmos, to cover the initial medical tests and first weeks of training at Star City.

But TM, wanting to keep the Russians off-balance, had chosen to pay less than the full freight—only one of the promised two million, out of an eventual forty. Playing games like this bothered him, but every single adviser he had talked to had said the same thing:

hold back some of the money until you are in space. It wasn't that Rosaviakosmos was crooked, it was just that there were too many people who would claim the money, then find a way to renege on the deal. "They'll discover some medical condition that will prevent you from flying," one veteran of the ISS program had told him. "And just in time for them to slip another paying customer into the seat."

So now TM played a game of chicken with Star City.

A caravan emerged from the birch forest, a pair of black Ford SUVs followed by a Lexus, all of them traveling at high speed. They pulled up to the guard shack, and with a flurry of slammed doors, half a dozen men in blue uniforms emerged. "Is this the reception committee," TM said, "or the bouncers?"

Pavel Filippov was the first to reach TM's car. "Good morning," he said in English, smiling broadly. "Welcome to *Zvezdny Gorodok.*" He used the Russian-language name for Star City.

Lanny said, "I guess the check cleared."

The negotiations that transformed Tad Mikleszewski from millionaire-investor to potential spaceflight participant moved with surprising swiftness, lasting less than a week. TM was not noted for being a tough dealmaker: he hated haggling, and either liked a price or he didn't. He knew full well that in his business career he had overpaid for various properties or even whole companies because of this; he believed he remained healthier and happier for the same reason.

Throughout that career he had relied on a series of attorneys and managers. At first he truly needed them, as the success of his patents forced him to incorporate. Then he formed subsidiaries, and sold them, each transaction spawning its own collection of attorneys in a process that struck him as biological, like cell division run amok.

At one point, shortly before his fortieth birthday, he realized he was responsible for the employment of two dozen managers, and a like number of assistants. And that was just to service the entity that was TM.

He spent the next fifteen years attriting those managers, to the point where he was able to enter negotiations with Rosaviakosmos and the Endless Frontier Association with a team of two: Dave Yarrington, his longtime manager, and Leslie, his consultant from, of all places, the Department of Water and Power.

Rosaviakosmos alone had more principals and lawyers than TM's side, beginning with a representative of the agency itself (a seriously overweight man named Shevchenko), an assistant, and two American attorneys. With that quartet were Col. Pavel Filippov from Star City (the Russian air force component), which trained cosmonauts and spaceflight participants, as well as negotiators from the Energiya Corporation, which was, in essence, the prime contractor for the Russian elements of the International Space Station. There were also representatives of the medical institute, which would have to legally certify spaceflight participants flying on Russian hardware, and finally the Krunichev Space Center, a former subsidiary of Energiya that was now independent.

The meeting had taken place in a conference room at the Century City office leased by TM's holding company, Pyrite. Leslie had insisted: "They need the money. They want to make this deal. So they come to us. Besides," she added, ever pragmatic, "Endless Frontier is in a storefront in Westwood. They'd have to rent a meeting room."

So Ian Sedgwick brought his four Russians and two attorneys to Century City. "Is there anyone left in Russia?" Leslie muttered, as she and TM approached the glass-sided conference room.

Yarrington was already with the Russians, glad-handing and offering beverages while performing his own brand of reconnaissance.

TM let Sedgwick, who was acting as middleman, do the intros. Then it was TM's turn, and he got directly to the point. "Your agency," he said, nodding at Shevchenko from Rosaviakosmos, "has a history of offering individuals the chance to fly in space. Whether

NASA likes it or not." He smiled, triggering nervous laughs from several of the negotiators.

"Rosaviakosmos and NASA, and all of the other partners in Alpha, have agreed on a set of qualifications for spaceflight paricipants," Shevchenko replied. For a moment TM feared the Russian would launch into a lengthy lecture on the subject, but he stopped there.

"Here's my proposal: I want to fly to Alpha for an extended period, at least two weeks, preferably twenty days, to perform some serious biological research in the Harmony module." Here he nodded, in turn, at the representatives from IMBP and Krunichev. "I understand Harmony is already at the cosmodrome awaiting launch."

"It's scheduled for January eighth," Filippov said, smoothly carving out a space in the conversation. That date was three months away.

"Good. Given the Proton launch history—" TM had, over the weekend, become a bit of an expert on the success rate of the giant Russian rocket. "—I expect Harmony to be docked to Alpha and checked out by mid-February.

"Here is the question: Is such a flight possible? How much laboratory time in Harmony has been booked, and when? Is there a seat available on a Soyuz taxi mission?"

"The whole question rests," Shevchenko said, breathing with obvious difficulty, like a man who has just climbed too many stairs, "on when you wish to fly."

Here TM smiled. "Next April." When there was no immediate reaction from the Russians, he added, "Six months from today."

Now he saw a reaction. All of the Russians tried to whisper to each other at the same time. Their American attorneys interrupted: TM noted that one of the Americans spoke fluent Russian.

Then Shevchenko folded his hands. "Impossible."

TM shot a glance over at Leslie, who was fidgeting, as if she desperately wanted to be somewhere else. "Why? You have one spaceflight participant tentatively booked." This was the actress he had met at Hoeffler's party. "But there's still one seat in play."

"That seat is committed to an astronaut from the European Space Agency," Fillipov said.

"Not from what we hear," Yarrington said. "Rosaviakosmos and ESA have a letter of understanding that only gives them an *option* on the seat—" This statement triggered a surprising barrage of crosstalk from men who were, as far as TM had been told, not English speakers. TM was able to understand two phrases: the IMBP man said, "It's more than an option!" while Filippov noted, "They've paid two million dollars against twenty—"

"—I'll buy it outright," TM said. He turned to Filippov. "And I believe their price was twelve million dollars, not twenty."

This produced a nervous silence. Yarrington looked as uncomfortable as the Russians did. Finally Shevchenko cleared his throat and said, "Twelve million dollars buys a ten-day mission. You are asking for twenty days—"

"Is twenty possible?"

More silence. Then Filippov spoke again: "Physically, yes. Politically . . . we have the option of extending the time our Soyuz remains docked to Alpha during the handover."

The Krunichev man had a point he wanted to make. Shevchenko and Filippov listened, then Shevchenko took over. "Use of the Harmony module will also bring a surcharge."

"How about this," TM said, enjoying the sight of Yarrington looking out the window toward Beverly Hills, and Leslie doodling on a yellow pad. "If we can agree here and now on a flight, I'll pay you thirty million dollars up front. Prior to launch, on a schedule to be mutually determined."

TM knew—and the Russians surely knew that he knew—that the funding for ESA's seat on the spring mission was uncertain, that the Hollywood studio paying for Rachel Dunne had only put up a fraction of the fee so far. Further, that the Russian government had drastically underfunded Alpha-related programs for the year. With the year-long interruption in lucrative tourist missions due to the *Columbia* disaster, the Russians were desperate for cash. They needed to pay salaries at Star City, Energiya, Krunichev, as well as at the Baikonur Cosmodrome and the Samara factory where the Soyuz spacecraft and its launcher were assembled.

"For thirty million dollars U.S.," Shevchenko said, "I think we can reach an agreement."

An hour later the Russians walked out carrying a letter of understanding from Pyrite Enterprises. Ian Sedgwick lingered, and offered his hand. "You had me worried when you shut down Spacelifter."

"Why?"

"I thought you were bailing completely out of the space business."

"Let's call it a repurposing," TM said.

"This will do more for private space than a dozen Rachel Dunnes."

"I don't believe that."

"You're actually going to do something productive. If you can produce *some* kind of medicine . . . well, you'll have opened a door."

"And done a good deed," Yarrington said.

Only now did TM remember that Sedgwick's sister was ill, possibly dead by now from X-Pox. "I'll do my best," he said. Sedgwick nodded and hurried to catch up with his Russian guests.

"I love it when you play hardball," Leslie told TM. She gathered up her notebook and purse and walked out, leaving TM with Yarrington.

"It's time to talk about life insurance," the lawyer said.

Now, on a cold November morning at the main gate to Star City, Filippov shook TM's hand with real warmth, as if greeting a lifelong friend. There wasn't the slightest sign of any resentment at TM's gamesmanship. In fact, Filippov said, "I'm sorry we weren't here to meet you. You're ten minutes early!"

"Thank Andrei for that," TM said, nodding toward the driver-translator just out of earshot. "A Soyuz launch can't be any more dangerous than riding with him."

"He drives too fast?"

"*Da*," TM said, utilizing 10 percent of his usable Russian.

Filippov laughed out loud and slapped him on the back. "Be grateful, my friend! Andrei has worked with us before. When he drives fast, he is only keeping you safe!"

"I don't see how."

"You're a rich, famous American traveling alone in Moscow. I'd be shocked if there weren't three or four groups of kidnappers trying to grab you and hold you for ransom!"

TM remembered the green Explorer, how it struggled to keep up with them. *Militsiya?* Or kidnappers.

Good God, what had he signed up for?

MARSHALLTOWN

On the day he should have been starting the long, tiresome flight to Moscow via NASA's fleet, nicknamed "Air Lester," Mark Koskinen made a shorter but equally tiresome flight from Houston to Minneapolis–St. Paul, then south to Des Moines, where he rented a car and drove the last fifty miles to his hometown of Marshalltown, Iowa.

Even though he had not lived there in almost twenty years, Mark liked Marshalltown, its houses, its streets, its people, his friends, his memories. He would have happily remained there all his life, except for one thing: he couldn't have stayed in Iowa and still become an astronaut.

Not that the other options were totally compelling: his father spent thirty years as a high school guidance counselor, while his mother worked as a secretary at an insurance company. Neither job gave Mark or his sister Johanna a career path, unlike most of their contemporaries, who always seemed aimed at the family bank or service station, or toward the furniture plant where Dad worked.

Like Mark, some friends had left town for college or the service and never returned, enough so that a stop at the Sports Club, the Main Street tavern he frequented during summers home from college, or the Dairy Queen, or even a high school football game, would fail to turn up any familiar faces.

Well, occasionally there would be one acquaintance, usually a friend of Johanna's, female, pushing a stroller or trying to herd three children into a Vanagon. Or Mark's best old friend, Jay Pollack, on his way to or from, but most likely to, the Sports Club. Jay had become a full-time musician, playing hits from the sixties, seventies, and eighties at weddings and class reunions. He had never married, a state which formerly struck Mark as a bit unusual. But, then, Mark had never married, either, though in his defense he could point to a trio of serious relationships.

There was no time for the nostalgia tour today, however. He pulled off the highway and headed directly for the house on Frasier Street.

It was not the home Mark and Johanna had grown up in: that was a much smaller split-level several miles away, in what had since become a less-desirable part of the city. The Koskinens had moved during Mark's junior year in high school, giving him a much nicer room on the top floor—he finally had enough shelf space to display all his science fiction and space books as well as his *Star Wars* and Space Shuttle models. The new house never felt like home, yet his parents had owned it now for two decades: it was the last home his father would ever know.

As he pulled up in front, it was already after four P.M., and the sky was the color of lead. No rain yet, but it was on its way. Mark's knuckles ached as he reached for his bag, a side effect of EVA training. He approached the front door, and felt, strangely, that the worlds of NASA, JSC, Spacelifter, and certainly Russia were nothing but fantasies: this was his house, wasn't it? Hadn't he just come home from seventh period at Marshalltown High? His father wasn't inside, dying, he was still at the office and planning to watch football tomorrow—

His mother opened the door. "I saw you drive up." A plump woman who always seemed cheerful and enthusiastic, she looked tired this afternoon. Nevertheless, she smiled broadly as she hugged him. "You're in time for dinner."

"Good. I'm starved." He was being truthful: he had not eaten since breakfast. "Where's Dad?"

"Taking a nap," she said, putting on her brave face. "He had a good day." Before Mark could utter a word, "Come inside! It's cold out."

Yesterday's message had been short, but powerful: "They've given your father six months." Apparently Glenn Koskinen had fainted Wednesday morning during one of his regular breakfasts with fellow retirees at the DQ. He had revived quickly, but his cronies had driven him to the nearest hospital. His doctor had been called in, tests had been run, and the news was as obvious as it was bad: not only had the original tumor on Glenn's liver returned, but the cancer had spread elsewhere, and was judged to be inoperable.

"You're getting a second opinion, of course," Mark had said, automatically. His mother's hesitation—another sign of her genial timidity when it came to authority figures like doctors—infuriated Mark, but fortunately he didn't express it.

"We'll talk about it," she had said, sighing. Mark realized he needed to make a quick trip home. He had hesitated only long enough to phone his sister in California. She had just had an identical conversation with their mother. "I'd get on a plane myself, but I can't, not till next week."

Now Mark was here, in the warm dampness of the house, smelling the aroma of cooking lasagna, hearing the sound of the television from the kitchen. Something was missing—his father's presence in the living room, his television tuned to either Fox News or ESPN and winning the volume war with *Oprah*.

Mark couldn't help thinking that this was what the house would soon be like. *Stop that.* "Where is he?"

"In the bedroom."

"Can I—?" Take my bag upstairs, he meant to say.

"Go ahead. If he's asleep, you won't wake him."

Dreading the encounter more with every step, Mark dragged his bag up the stairs and past his parents' bedroom. Thankfully, the door was closed. He dropped the bag in the last of three bedrooms, turning on the light and seeing the fine layer of dust that had gathered on his possessions. Well, he had always been the one to dust his models—he should be grateful they still had a home here in Marshalltown.

What disturbed him most was the vague odor of mildew. Midwestern houses always smelled that way in the winter. But he had been away in the dry southwestern states for so long he had learned to notice it.

He was stalling. He went down the hallway and gently knocked on the door to his parents' bedroom. "Dad?"

"Hey," his father's voice said, surprisingly strong. "Come in." As Mark opened the door, he could hear the rustling of sheets.

Glenn Koskinen had been an amateur athlete in his youth—not big. None of the Koskinens was big. But wiry and muscular. In middle age he had gotten heavy and slower; his reddish hair had gone white. But he had still radiated strength and authority—handy traits in dealing with high schoolers on a daily basis.

The man who now struggled to his feet, grabbing for a cane, was not the same man. He had lost forty pounds from a too-heavy 180. The full head of white hair was now completely gone, thanks to chemo. The ruddy face was pale and drawn. To Mark, his father looked like a skeleton. He had prepared himself mentally for the sight; he had seen his father recently enough to accurately foretell his condition.

Still, it took all his effort not to close his eyes or shake his head, or give some other sign that he didn't want to see what he was seeing. Instead he offered his father a hug—an action not often shared among Koskinen males—and was surprised to find it returned.

He was shocked to feel a sob shuddering through his father's body. That was all it took, of course. Mark's eyes filled with tears and he found himself sobbing, too. "God, Dad," was all he could manage to say.

The mutual breakdown passed quickly, with both men at arm's length, wiping away tears. "Sorry," Glenn said.

"What do you have to be sorry for?" Mark said, knowing the

answer. A strong Finnish man didn't allow emotional displays. He wasn't the center of attention.

He didn't get cancer.

"Oh, I don't know," Glenn said, as he seemed to regain strength and color. "Your mother . . ."

"Well, Dad, something like this is hard on everybody. But I think we can all agree—your situation is a little tougher than Mom's."

Mark had always been able to make his father laugh—Glenn would accept irreverence from his children and almost no one else. And this time the old magic worked. Glenn laughed so hard he started crying again. "Yeah," he said. "Yeah, I think I drew the bad hand here."

He gave Mark a fatherly punch to the shoulder. "Let's go downstairs and see how much dinner I can handle."

The rain started as Mark set the table. He didn't realize it until he happened to glance out the front window, and noticed that his car was wet, gleaming in the dim street and house lights. Combined with the situation inside the house, the view outside was now thoroughly depressing.

Nevertheless, the dinner went well. If not for the fact that the man across from him looked like the police sketch version of his father, and that his mother, who usually had an hour's worth of family updates, neighbor news, and local color to offer, was usually subdued. As Mark helped clean up, his mother said, "Are you going to see Jay?" Jay was Mark's friend since age five, the kid across the street in the old neighborhood. On Mark's previous trips, once or twice a year, it would be Jay who gave him the guided nostalgia tour.

"I don't think so," Mark said. "I didn't tell him I was coming." This was unsurprising, since Mark hadn't known he would be in town until midday yesterday. "Why don't I just stay around tonight?"

It was fine with his mother, of course, though the presence of another human being in her part of the house clearly disrupted her habits.

So Mark grabbed a beer and sat with his father in front of the television. A golf tournament was on—Mark hadn't followed sports since college, but mid-week seemed like the wrong time for this sort of event. He was equally confused to learn that the tournament was taking place in Dubai. When had pro golf penetrated the Middle East? He said as much, which prompted his father to tease him, which made the otherwise-grim evening feel a little like old times.

After a while Mark went upstairs to finish unpacking. He had brought his laptop along—he had loaded the latest Station ops book on it; homework. He scrolled through the pages for perhaps ten minutes, then gave it up. Lying on his old bed, hearing the dribble of cold rain on the roof, he traveled far back in time. Christ, all he needed was some disco music on the radio.

For a moment he leaned back and looked up at the ceiling. A planetary mobile still hung there, just as it had since 1981. Jupiter was faded. Someone had torn one of Saturn's rings, then taped it. The whole solar system was out of date, of course: current astronomical theory held that Pluto was no longer a planet, but a planetesimal, one of hundreds (and possibly thousands) of similarly sized icy rocks in the darkness beyond Neptune.

It was dreaming about the planets—about red Mars and big Jupiter—that took him to college, to the air force, to the Aerospace Corporation, to NASA.

To space. To an eleven-day mission to Mir in late 1998, in which Mark made a spacewalk like no other in history. A troubled astronaut died, and almost took Mark with him. For an hour Mark had found himself floating free in space—untethered to Shuttle or station—and never once did he think about Mars or Jupiter, or anything but *not* fucking up.

Even after his failed rescue of Cal Stipe, after the orbiter departed from Mir with one fewer crew member than planned, Mark could not remember looking out the window at anything but the blue Earth below.

He stood up. He was still on Mountain Time, an hour ahead of the good people of Marshalltown, and probably three hours ahead of Glenn and Carol Koskinen.

He went back downstairs and found his mother on the phone in the kitchen, his father complaining about poor play by Tiger Woods.

In fact, before Mark sat down, the match was over. With speed belying his condition, Glenn snatched up the remote and clicked over to the news.

Mark knew there was supposed to have been an EVA aboard Alpha today—swapping out some parts on the station's robot arm—but if so, it didn't make the news. Or not the news Mark and Glenn watched.

He had a second beer, then elected to use the downstairs bathroom, since his mother now seemed to be occupying the upstairs facility.

On his way back, he stopped to peer at the familiar set of pictures lining the hallway, which was the Koskinen family museum. (Mark had been known to call it the "Hallway of Fame.") Here were the baby pictures of Mark and Johanna, along with hideous school portraits and such treats as Mark in a Little League uniform and Johanna on the parallel bars. Mark and Jay in their first garage band—what was the name again? Oh, yeah, the Soul Syndicate.

With these images were shots of Glenn and Carol in younger days, memories of family trips to Yellowstone, Lake Superior, Gettysburg, and—a giant concession to Mark's wishes—Edwards Air Force Base in California. (The temperature had been 107 degrees that day.)

One of the more recent additions, sandwiched around Johanna's two children, was a framed photo of Mark's STS-100 crew, their mission patch and a shot of the orbiter roaring into the sky on its twin solid rocket motors. The matte frame around the three images had been signed by the crew after landing. Mark's inscription read, "To Mom and Dad, who made it all possible." He had wanted to write "Don't worry, I'll clean up my room when I get home," or something equally facetious, but even if he hadn't realized that his parents might be offended by defacing of a permanent monument, the circumstances of the flight demanded a more dignified approach.

He was still staring at the crew of seven—commander Steve Goslin (chief astronaut these past five years), pilot Jeff Dieckhaus (who had rotated from STS-100 to his own Shuttle command, then left NASA to fly for Southwest Airlines), mission specialists David Freeh (flew one of the early Alpha missions and then returned to the air force), Donal O'Riordan (back in Europe now, waiting for a chance to fly to Alpha as an ESA astronaut), and Kelly Gessner. Mark was in an EVA suit, along with Russian cosmonaut Viktor Kondratko—his good friend Viktor, now assigned as commander of the next Alpha mission.

Not only did they all look younger, but the picture had actually faded! Was it the harsh environment of Iowa? Or the fact that the flight was really several years in the past?

"Ever see any of those folks?" his father said. Mark had not heard his approach.

"I was just thinking that." Apparently Glenn Koskinen had developed telepathy and teleportation along with cancer. "Not until just this week. Uh, Spacelifter is closing down. I'm going back to NASA." Mark wasn't sure how up-to-date his father was on his career moves—the man had had more serious matters to consider. Mark pointed to the crew in turn, running through their fates, leaving out Kelly.

Too conspicuously for his father. "What about your gal here?" Mark had brought Kelly to Marshalltown on two occasions, once for Christmas, once for a parental wedding anniversary. She had seemed to fit right in—not only with the various Koskinens, but even the town itself, knocking back brews with Jay and the gang at the Sports Club. One night they had gone out to see Jay and his group play: Kelly, under the influence of no more than a beer, perhaps two, had gotten up and sung a creditable version of "Honky Tonk Women."

"I was with her all this week."

"That mean you're getting back together?"

"I don't think so." He had thought about this subject a lot during his flight north. The wounds were too deep, the differences too great.

"You love her, though."

It was strange, possibly unthinkable, to hear Glenn Koskinen talking like this. "Yeah. I suppose I do."

"Then what's the goddamn problem with you two? Get married. Have kids. You're going to be forty."

Mark didn't like to argue personal matters with his father in the best of times. He certainly didn't want to fight *now*. So he chose a different approach. "Hey, Uncle Ilpo didn't get married until he was forty-two."

Ilpo Koskinen was actually Glenn's uncle, Mark's great-uncle. "Ilpo lived on a farm and didn't see people but one night a week."

"True," he said, trying to be conciliatory. "But living in Las Cruces is pretty close to being on a farm."

Glenn grunted and turned away, heading back to his chair. As he went, reaching for support on wall, cabinet, furniture, with Mark following, he said, "You're back in Houston?"

As they sat again, Mark explained his situation, ending with, "So, yeah, they're taking me back. Of course," he added, wondering how this news would be received, "they're sending me to Russia for the next six months."

His mother entered the room at that point, hearing enough of Mark's statement to be alarmed. "Russia?" She sat down close to Glenn and took his hand.

"Everybody who's going to fly to the space station needs to spend some time in Russia."

"This mean you're on a crew?" Glenn asked.

"Not yet. I'm just going to be in charge of training. It's a step toward getting back on a crew." He could sense their alarm. "But, look," he said, lying slightly. "So far it's just an offer. If I tell them about . . . what's going on, they'd understand."

The look on Glenn's face reminded Mark of the time he had told his father he was quitting track. Glenn had refused to allow it, delivering a long, heated lecture on living up to commitments, being a team player, et cetera. "What do you plan to do? Hang around Marshalltown and drive me to the doctor?"

Mark couldn't help glancing at his mother. He had been thinking that very thing. Telepathy again. "Maybe."

"Christ." Glenn leaned forward. "I know the news isn't good, but one thing I've seen with these doctors: they aren't very effective fortune-tellers." He smiled, completely without amusement. "The last guy I went to told me I was good for five years.

"I'm going to be around for a while, Mark. I'm going to fight this thing and beat it. I don't need you moping around here, pissing away your astronaut career."

Typically, Carol commented on Glenn's language. "Glenn, do we really need to use words like that?"

Glenn leaned toward his magazine rack and started digging. To the left of his chair, it held nothing but multiple, years-old issues of *TV Guide* and *Sports Illustrated.*

And now, apparently, a paperback book. "Ever heard of Robert Louis Stevenson?"

Mark looked at his mother again, searching for a clue she could not give. "He wrote *Treasure Island,*" Mark said. "*Dr. Jekyll and Mr. Hyde.*" And, he now remembered, a famous poem called "Requiem." Oh, God, where was this leading?

Glenn flipped through the pages, found what he wanted, and handed the book to Mark. He saw a well-worn page with a passage marked in pencil. "That's an essay called 'Aes Triplex,' and it's about the attitude Stevenson had when he was . . . in the same fix I'm in. He died of tuberculosis young, you know." Mark didn't know, but didn't dispute it. "Read that." Glenn sat back. "Read it out loud."

Mark cleared his throat. " 'By all means begin your folio; even if the doctor does not give you a year, even if he hesitates about a month, make one brave push and see what can be accomplished in a week.' "

He closed the book. Glenn had taken Carol's hand. "Okay," Mark said. "I guess I'm flying back to Houston tomorrow."

"And getting your ass to Russia," Glenn said.

"Language," Carol said, though she did not, to Mark, seem at all cross.

X-DAY ZERO, CONTINUED

MCS TELECON 17 APRIL 2006

Participants:

at JSC: (DF/Terry Doolan, Les Fehrenkamp and others, TT/ Larisa Kuchina)

at MCC-M: (RSC-E/Vladimir Sharov, DF/Darin Chambliss, OK/Carol Baer)

Minutes:

1. GMT 0035 Toxic Spill

In an attempt to make sense of the spill from the MCC-M perspective, Vladimir Sharov recounted Monday's events commencing with the RGS pass at 2320 on 16 April. It was during this pass that MCC-M realized that ops in Harmony had still not begun; they were receiving no Eridan telemetry, only voice ATG between TM and Consoldane, which was on a dedicated channel.

Vladimir then noted that Harmony/Eridan ops began shortly after 0010 on 17 April, quickly degenerating into loss of Eridan control.

Les Fehrenkamp asked for clarification of the "loss of Eridan management" statement. Vladimir explained that, as far as MCC-M knew then and knows now, several levels of toxic containment associated with the Eridan glovebox failed, due to a suspected combination of equipment problems and possible operator error.

Fortunately, Harmony was isolated from the rest of Alpha at the time, and remains so. Mikleszewski is alive and supportable for at least three weeks under current circumstances.

The toxic situation aboard the rest of Alpha is still Level One; pending updates from Houston and MCC-M, the crew has been advised to resume normal activities.

The telecon ended with Les Fehrenkamp's order to prepare STS-124 *Discovery* for a possible rescue, and to explore the feasibility of using Soyuz TMA-8 as a backup.

X-DAY ZERO, PLUS FOUR HOURS

"Viktor, what the hell are we going to do?"

After ten years of training and flying in space with American astronauts, Viktor Kondratko's English was excellent, almost fluent, yet he failed to understand Nate Bristol's words. Or maybe he just failed to hear them.

Viktor was in his shorts and T-shirt, strapped into a standing position atop the TVIS, which was the exercise treadmill aboard Alpha. He had been jogging on the unit for ten minutes when Nate Bristol swam in front of him, his gray eyes wide in his sharp-featured face.

"What did you say?"

Bristol, easily exasperated at the best of times, shook his head and shut down the TVIS. "I said, what the hell are we going to do about this situation?"

Again, Viktor wasn't quite sure of the question. But now he realized it wasn't his own lack of English. He really was having problems hearing Bristol's words.

The TVIS was bolted to the floor of the Zvezda, the forty-foot-long module that had been one of the key building blocks of International Space Station Alpha. Originally known as the Service Module, it served as living quarters as well as all-purpose storage room, what an earlier crew member had called the attic.

Soiled clothing, old food wrappers, broken tools, and other discarded material were to be dumped overboard in an empty Progress supply vehicle, or returned to Earth during Shuttle resupply missions, but human nature won out; it was just easier to stash something in Zvezda than to spend forty-five minutes scanning it into the system (assuming the item even possessed a bar code), then moving it to the desired location.

The TVIS contributed to the sense of Zvezda as a dumping site, since it was in use six hours a day by the resident crew. (Each long-term crew member required two hours of treadmill work per day, to postpone or at least minimize the muscle atrophy and osteoporosis that awaited every space traveler.) The treadmill made a horrific racket.

Even with the TVIS stopped, the Zvezda hummed with the too-loud drone of fans and pumps. Viktor pointed toward the far end of the module, where the e-mail station sat upside down. It was slightly quieter here. "Where are the others?" Viktor asked.

"Jasper and Igor are trying to get Rachel to calm down. They're all in Destiny." Destiny was the giant U.S. built laboratory module. Bristol didn't have to mention TM, of course.

"She's still upset?"

"She stopped crying," Bristol said. "I'm *this* close to giving her a sedative."

"Let me talk to her first."

"What are you going to tell her? And the rest of us? Viktor, it's been four hours! No one's doing anything!"

Viktor had known Bristol for several years prior to the mission, but due to a series of personnel changes, they had not worked as crewmates until three months before their launch to Alpha. Rich McCown, the second American astronaut in Viktor's crew, had suddenly been replaced because of some last-minute worry about cumulative radiation exposure. McCown had suffered a broken leg in a touch football game in Houston, and undergone a series of X rays. The injury itself was relatively minor, and merely cost the astronaut a week of training.

But the set of X rays added to McCown's previous exposure to radiation on three prior Shuttle missions. There was a new chief medical officer at NASA HQ who took a by-the-book approach to such matters, and over Viktor's protests, McCown was judged to be no longer eligible for a long-duration Alpha mission.

Bristol, who had been training as a backup crew member for a different mission entirely, had been shifted to Expedition 13. He had proven to be completely knowledgeable about Alpha systems, and far too excitable by Viktor's standards. (Viktor realized that he had the relaxed Russian approach to life in space. For example, he had no idea of his own cumulative radiation levels. True, he had only spent eleven days on orbit, on a single Shuttle mission in 1998. But he had undergone dozens of X rays in his career as a fighter pilot, test pilot, and cosmonaut. He was mortally certain that only a fraction of them were recorded. And equally certain that the subject was not worth worrying about.)

"What do you have in mind, Nate? TM is sealed inside the module. There are no leaks. We have our own masks at the ready. The only way to deal with a crisis is to keep your head, and keep to your routine. I'll be done here in an hour. Then you should do your exercises. Give Houston and Korolev the time they need to figure this out."

Bristol seemed satisfied for the moment. Sometimes he only needed to feel he was being listened to. "Do you think the word is out?"

"On the accident? I doubt it."

"How can they keep this secret for long? It's not as though it's one of us," he said, meaning a professional astronaut, "it's a fucking passenger!"

As Bristol raged, Viktor tapped keys on the computer. The station was linked to an Internet portal—suitably firewalled, so the station's database was not instantly accessible to anyone on Earth—and a handful of mousepad clicks showed no news stories and, better yet, no rumors on the various newsgroups (which, in Viktor's experience, seemed to scoop professional news organizations by at least fifteen minutes). "Nothing so far," he told Bristol, allowing the astronaut to look at the screen.

"Fine. But you know the word is going to leak out, and sooner rather than later."

"Hopefully, by then NASA will already have a contingency plan in place."

"Hopefully that plan will be something better than simply closing the hatch, putting on masks and waiting."

Viktor smiled. "Have faith," he said. "My team managed to save Mir on several occasions. Your team saved Apollo 13."

"Apollo 13 was thirty-six years ago, Viktor. And we've managed to fuck up two other missions on a fairly large scale since then." He meant *Challenger* and *Columbia.*

Bristol's pessimism, never welcome, was now starting to bother Viktor. "Nate, why don't you do your hour now, hmm?" Viktor's manner was casual, but after six weeks on orbit together, he and Bristol—and Weeks—had learned to read each other. Bristol was about to protest that he usually didn't do his second TVIS workout until later in the day. But he correctly read this as an order.

Viktor went looking for the rest of his crew.

International Space Station Alpha, in its Phase 13 configuration, resembled a train made up of cylindrical cars: starting at the aft or minus-X end you had the fresh Soyuz that had brought Igor, Rachel, and TM to the station. The Soyuz was docked to the rear of the Zvezda module, which contained two crew cabins. Zvezda docked to Zarya's spherical after-chamber, which held a number of ports: the old Soyuz was attached here, on the nadir, as well as the Pirs airlock module, on the port side, and the Progress supply vehicle on the zenith.

Then came Zarya itself, the station's closet and gymnasium. Zarya linked to the Unity node, which had the Quest airlock module on one side, and Harmony on the other. Swimming through Unity, an Alpha crewmember found the spacious Destiny lab. At the front or plus-X tip was a pressurized mating adaptor, suitable for a Shuttle docking.

There was more, of course: on Destiny's plus-Z exterior, also known as the top, there was a boxlike truss that supported radiator panels, a photovoltaic module and the winglike solar arrays. From the outside, the whole structure of the station reminded Viktor of a robotic insect. Nate Bristol, in the single poetic moment he had shared with his commander, claimed that the station suggested an ancient sailing vessel, and called her "the good ship *Alpha*."

Good ship or robot habitat, Viktor was Alpha's commander—an unlikely one, even though he was a veteran cosmonaut, with a Shuttle mission and a difficult spacewalk to his credit. Certainly his colleagues at Star City thought so: to them the only spaceflight that counted was on a Soyuz. (The Russian government also seemed to share that judgment, awarding the valuable "Cosmonaut of the Russian Federation" degree to Kondratko only after a delay of months.) But Kondratko had flown his Shuttle mission to give NASA and the other partners a chance to get to know him. Only then would he be acceptable as an Alpha crew member, capable of being entrusted with the lives of other astronauts, not to mention the one-of-a-kind, $40-billion station.

And he had passed the test.

Besides, Viktor knew that he *had* relevant command experience. He had served as a flight leader in the Russian air force and as deputy commander of a test squadron on the godforsaken salt flats of Aktuba. True, with the fuel shortages that hampered the Russian air force in the early 1990s, Viktor actually served in command for perhaps six hours a month. And he had no say over the pilots assigned to him. This was, of course, exactly like his situation on Alpha, especially with regard to Bristol. And as a flight lead he'd had very little freedom except the speed with which his flight responded to orders from ground control—again, not so different.

His work in the test squadron had more direct relevance. There he had worked as part of a team that included a dozen pilots, a like number of flight test engineers, and tens of other people, all engaged in what was, even then, seen to be the fruitless job of refining the latest (last?) generation of Russian fighter plane. Viktor had interacted with that team every day, motivating slackers, rewarding those who showed initiative—showing initiative of his own when it came to securing housing for his people. Or money. Or food.

Or medical treatment.

"How is TM?" he said, as he reached Unity. In front of him was the open hatch to the Destiny laboratory; to his right was the closed hatch to the Harmony module.

Jasper Weeks handed Viktor his headset. "He's staying pretty cool, given the situation."

Viktor took the headset. "Tango? Viktor."

"Hey, Viktor."

Viktor noted, with approval, that TM's voice was calm, his breathing steady. "We still don't have guidance from Houston."

"There's a surprise." Sarcasm. A good sign.

"Yes. We've handed them a complex problem." As soon as he said it, Viktor regretted the statement. It was true, but it put TM on the defensive.

"Complex? I'll show them complex, Viktor. I'm sitting here in a cloud of X-Pox with no hope of rescue. How much air do I have? How much water? Is there any food? Forget medicine—I know nobody's going to come up with that. I'll probably just suffocate or starve to death first!"

TM's outburst, overheard by everyone else in the crew, provided Viktor with a chance to exercise calm leadership. "You raise an excellent point," he said. "Harmony was originally designed as a free-flying module, you know. It is almost identical to Zarya," he added.

"I spent five months hearing that stuff, Viktor."

"Then you already know that because of the work you were doing, Harmony was configured to operate on its own oxygen system for at least two weeks. There is also an emergency supply of food and water."

"Not to mention *my* food supply," Weeks said. True, many of the boxes carrying Weeks's preplanned menus were stored in Harmony.

"You make it sound like a great little vacation cabin, both of you. All I need is cable TV and a fucking toilet."

"I can't help you with the TV right now, but there should be plenty of bags for the stowage of waste," Viktor said. There were, in fact, dozens of bags aboard Harmony; they had been placed there for the transfer of the samples TM was supposed to have produced. "At least you'll have some privacy." There was a Russian-built toilet aboard Alpha (the NASA-built unit had failed years ago) that functioned well, but provided little in the way of privacy to Americans who, in Viktor's eyes, were ridiculously self-conscious.

Viktor didn't expect TM to be in a joking mood, and he wasn't. "Fine, I've got everything I need for two weeks. What happens if I manage to live longer than that?"

"You misunderstood me, Tango. Harmony was equipped to support a crew of three for two weeks. You are only one. So your consumables should last three times as long. That should be plenty of time for NASA to arrange a rescue."

There was a moment of silence on the line. Viktor stared at the gray metal hatch, and wondered where Tango was in the other module: floating freely, or huddled against the metal, not a meter away. He considered tapping on the hatch, but didn't. "Finally, some good news," Tango said.

"Yes. A lot can happen in six weeks. You have a Shuttle mission already scheduled to launch within that time."

"You make it sound as though I'm not going home on the Soyuz."

At the moment, there were two Soyuz spacecraft docked to Alpha: TMA-6, which had launched in late November 2005 as the ninth ISS "taxi" mission, and served as the assured crew rescue vehicle for Viktor, Bristol, and Weeks.

The other was the fresh vehicle TMA-7, which had brought Igor, Rachel, and TM to Alpha. The latter trio was scheduled to return to Earth in the older TMA-6 in nine days, leaving the fresh craft for the expedition crew. (The on-orbit lifetime of a Soyuz was around six months: too much longer in the harsh environment of open space, with extremes of freezing and heating, and its fuel began to evaporate, electronics became suspect, and vital surface materials deteriorated.)

"It's too early to say that, Tango. We can extend TMA-Six for a little while." Viktor was angry with himself. He had not anticipated Tango's question, had not thought far enough ahead to the time when Igor and Rachel would have to return to Earth *without* Tango. Because if he were still alive at that point, it would mean there were four crew members aboard Alpha—and room in the rescue craft for only three.

It did not matter then if Tango was sick, or infectious. Viktor could not imagine abandoning him. If anything happened aboard Alpha, and an evacuation was required, it would be *Viktor* who stayed behind.

If today's events hadn't impressed him with the burden of command, *that* thought did.

"The next Soyuz, TMA-Eight, is already at Baikonur, anyway," Viktor said, hoping he was telling the truth. Rosaviakosmos had made a deal years ago to carry winners of a game show on a free-flying trip to space—a week on a Soyuz, no docking at Alpha. That flight had been delayed, but enough money had been paid to raise the rate of Soyuz production from two per year to two-and-a-bit. Which meant that Soyuz TMA-8 was nearly assembled and awaiting checkout. "Look, it's long past lunch. Why don't you open the emergency kit—it's in the lab portion of the module—and get yourself some food and water? By the time you've eaten, we should have heard from Houston. If nothing else, we should have the medical team on-line."

Another wait. Viktor could not believe that TM was remotely hungry. But he said, "All right, sounds good."

Viktor disconnected, and turned to three members of the crew.

(He could still hear Bristol ratcheting away on the TVIS.) Igor had the camera in his hands. Weeks held a procedures book. Rachel Dunne, her eyes red and her face blotchy. "All right," Viktor said, realizing he needed to get control of the situation now. "Jasper, let's get lunch started. Igor, stow that camera and check the teletype. Then get back here." Both men were in motion before he finished giving the orders, Weeks heading deep into Zarya, followed by Gritsov.

Rachel looked at him with a mixture of fear and confusion. She sniffed. "*Mnye ochen zal,*" she said, in her passable Russian. "I'm so sorry."

Viktor inclined his head toward Destiny, and pushed himself into the giant laboratory module with a fingertip. A moment later, Rachel swam through the hatch, and into his arms.

"Poor baby," he said, brushing her hair back from her face.

X-DAY ZERO, PLUS FIVE HOURS

"I think this goddamn thing is broken."

Kelly Gessner turned her head inside the fishbowl-shaped helmet, and saw the bulky white human-shaped figure of Diana Herron actually tapping the power wrench on the side of the orbiter's payload bay, raising a cloud of bubbles.

"Careful," Kelly said. "It's only a mock-up, but you don't want to start learning bad habits."

"They gave me a mock-up *wrench*." Herron was still turning the tool over, struggling to make it come to life. "I might as well have a paperweight."

"Stand by, Diana." That was the voice of Swim-Two, who floated over from the mock-up of the P6 truss to take a look at the wrench. The diver was even more ruthless with the tool than Diana as he dissembled it. Of course, since his hands were bare, Swim-Two actually *could* disassemble the tool.

Swim-Two was one of the team of divers who accompanied spacewalking astronauts during sims in the giant water tank known as the Neutral Buoyancy Laboratory, which is where Kelly Gessner and Diana Herron floated. The astronauts were snug and dry inside their I-suits, but the divers wore swimming trunks, masks, tanks, and flippers. Toward the end of the four-hour sims, Kelly had noticed the divers getting impatient, and who could blame them? They got completely pruned each session.

"Doug," Swim-Two called to Swim-Four, "get us a new wrench down here." And he kicked toward the surface in order to shorten the delivery time.

"Don't you just love the view of the Earth from orbit?" Herron said sarcastically, since the astronauts could do nothing for the next five minutes.

Kelly didn't answer. She was a little worried about Herron and her learning curve. Launch of STS-124 was less than a month away, and her EVA partner was still making rookie mistakes—like thumping a malfunctioning tool on the side of the orbiter, as if she were trying to kick-start a balky flashlight in her garage.

Kelly's unease with Herron was partly due to her own inexperience. She had never performed an EVA on her three Shuttle flights. The one EVA she had supported, on STS-100, had been a nightmare, with Cal Stipe lost overboard, and Mark Koskinen flying after him in a futile attempt at a rescue.

For years NASA had typically assigned a veteran spacewalker with a rookie, but by now, with a score of Alpha assembly missions in the books and dozens of EVAs successfully accomplished, there was no difference between veteran-rookie teams and those consisting of first-timers. The underwater training could prepare any astronaut, it seemed.

But the astronaut had to be trainable. Herron, who had come to NASA from the air force, where she flew as a tanker pilot, had always struck Kelly as a little too impressed with her own operational experience. The rookie astronaut's attitude had not improved during four long years of technical assignments, including a year in which Herron had worked under Kelly. Herron was smart and able, just not as smart and able as she thought.

She also tried too hard to be one of the boys.

The presence of two women as the EVA team had triggered a certain amount of teasing, not all of it good-natured. Some of the EVA support staff had actually labeled Kelly and Diana as the "Kotex Team," which Kelly hadn't realized until the second sim, in which she kept hearing the call signs "K-1" and "K-2" on the loop. At first she had assumed *K* stood for Kelly, until she actually overheard Herron called "Kotex-2."

"Did you know about this?" she had asked Herron as they were cleaning up in the NBL locker room.

"Yeah, Jay Silver told me." Silver was the EVA lead for their mission.

"And it didn't bother you?"

Herron wadded up a towel and fired it toward a hamper. "It's a joke," she said. "And we do use them, Kel. At least, *I* still do."

Kelly couldn't decide which pissed her off more—Herron's blithe acceptance of the sexist label, or the insinuation that Kelly was old enough to be menopausal. She chose to respond to the former insult. "The day the staff calls a male team 'Trojan-One' or 'Prostate-Two' they can call me 'Kotex.' Not until then." And she had told Silver, as gently as possible, that she would prefer a different call sign.

"Whatever you say, Kel." Herron's tone was still so insolent that Kelly wanted to slap her. She calmed herself by imagining the rookie astronaut about four hours after the STS-124 launch—spacesick, green-faced, wrapped in a blanket on the mid-deck.

That encounter had taken place three months back. Herron had been doing well in ascent and entry sims; she was assigned as the MS2 for the mission, the flight engineer who assisted the commander and pilot during ascent and entry. Her air force background served her well when it came to offering updates to Brad Latham, the commander, and Kevin Ames, the pilot, getting to the right cue card at the right time.

But she had continued to struggle with EVA training. Latham had noted the problem. "Jesus, Kel, how are we gonna get her up to speed?" Latham had been pilot on a pair of Shuttle missions, but this was his first command, and like many first-time commanders, he leaned heavily on his most-experienced mission specialist—Kelly. "Have you talked to her?"

"Yes," Kelly had said. "Have you?" She knew the answer: no. Latham was a little intimidated by the big, blond Herron and her flashy air force credentials. (The word was that Herron had done flight test at the super-secret Groom Lake facility in Nevada.)

"I just want everybody to be happy. And ready to fly, of course." He sighed. "I don't understand this. On paper, she should be gang-busters."

Kelly knew exactly what Latham meant: in her years in aircraft ops and the astronaut office, she had noted the inexplicable struggles of any number of supremely qualified individuals: hotshot pilots who made bonehead mistakes with airplanes, computer whizzes who kept crashing their own PCs, operational veterans like Herron who seemed unable to function as members of a team.

"She's an astronaut now, Brad." She smiled as she said it. Every astronaut went through it—the period in which a rookie astronaut manages to believe that he or she is bulletproof. Kelly had gone through it herself. So had Latham.

"How are we going to convince her she's mortal?"

Kelly suggested that Latham send a message to Herron through Phil Mendez, the astronaut who was head of the EVA branch. "It can be a little tag-up, or even a little more pointed. You know, 'the NBL team thinks you're falling behind. Do you need help?' She'll get the message without freaking out."

Latham had followed the suggestion, and Herron's EVA work improved. Until today, with the launch fast approaching.

Swim-Two floated down to them just as the training capcom said, "Kelly, Diana, we're going to call it a day."

That was unusual: they still had several squares to fill on the chart. "We can work around the tool, if that's a problem," Kelly said. Swim-Two had a new wrench in his hand.

"Orders from the top," the capcom said.

Cocooned in their I-suits, it was impossible for Kelly and Herron to exchange looks. They could only wait as they were hauled to the surface and hung on hooks. (The suits were so heavy that they needed to be supported in order for astronauts to get out of them.)

Herron looked pale, and even apologetic. "Kel, I, uh . . ." She struggled with the words. "Can I buy you a drink?"

Before Kelly could say yes, Silver came up to them. "Kelly, Goslin wants to talk to you."

Kelly was still wriggling out of the I-suit. "I'll call him in ten minutes."

"He's here."

The chief astronaut, here in the NBL? Had he witnessed Herron's attack of attitude? Herron seemed to think so. "Oh, God," she said, and looked stricken.

Feet up, eyes closed, Goslin was at the desk in Silver's office when Kelly entered. "Close the door," he said.

There was barely room for the two of them here. Goslin, knowing how bone-tired Kelly must be after four hours in the I-suit, stood so she could collapse in the chair. "What's up?"

Goslin slumped against the wall, eyes closed for a painful moment, then met Kelly's gaze. "We have a giant fucking problem." Kelly's first reaction was surprise at the use of profanity: Goslin was notoriously strict in his personal behavior. No drinking, no screwing around, definitely no swearing. "Have you been paying attention to the station lately?"

"Uh, it was still up there, last time I looked." She immediately regretted the jocular tone. "No."

"Me neither, frankly." Goslin sighed and forced himself to offer a smile. "You know, they're going round and round, everything's fine. I haven't even checked Rachel Dunne's Space Diary."

"I hear there are some interesting pictures."

"So they say."

"Has she caused a problem?"

"I wish. No, it's Mikleszewski."

Kelly was surprised. "He seemed pretty stable to me."

"He is, for a rich, arrogant prick. It's his work and that module." He sighed. "They had an outbreak today."

"A dangerous one?" Kelly felt her stomach turn over.

"As dangerous as it gets." In the space of seven sentences, Goslin briefed Kelly on the horror aboard Alpha. "And here we are: a contaminated module, a sick crew member, and a horribly contagious and dangerous virus."

"Cut him loose," Kelly said, almost without thinking.

"Believe me, if we could, we probably would. Though it will make it tough to sign up future tourists."

"Yeah, wouldn't want *that* to happen." She was too tired to keep the sarcasm out of her voice.

"The Russians need the dough, Kelly."

"Yeah, yeah, and if they don't sell the seats, we don't have a Soyuz to park there. I just wish they sold better equipment."

"Even if they *could* cut Harmony loose, with Mikleszewski dead, what happens to it?"

Through her fatigue and worry, part of Kelly's brain was imagining the scenario. "That's right: in a few weeks, it comes down—"

"—Burns up—"

"—It's full of X-Pox—"

"—Which reproduces with heat."

Kelly was the first to say it: "It would spread that stuff all over several hundred square miles."

"That's the worry. Even if we command Harmony to dive into the emptiest part of the Pacific, the spores will multiply in the heat, spread during the breakup, and be carried God knows where by the winds."

"Whoever designed this thing was an evil bastard, Steve." She was now officially too numb to speculate further. "I suppose ULF-Three is off."

"Not off. Changed."

"How?"

"We've got extraction and cleanup equipment. The 124 crew is going to take it up there, seal the module, and try to get this guy out alive." The chief astronaut had a curious look on his face, part disbelief at what he was proposing, part childish glee.

"Okay." That was being an astronaut, Kelly realized: make a decision quickly. "Do Brad and Kevin know?"

"They've been shooting landings all day." He glanced at his watch. "I'm on my way to ops to break the news to them."

"I'll go with you."

"Thanks." He opened the door. "You're okay with this?"

"Why wouldn't I be?"

"Well, this is the closest thing to one of those World War Two suicide missions we've got here in the astronaut office."

Kelly hadn't thought of it like that: it was just a more challenging mission. *More exciting than bolting new solar arrays onto a truss outside Alpha!* "You sound like you want to come along, Steve."

"Oh, I do. Believe me."

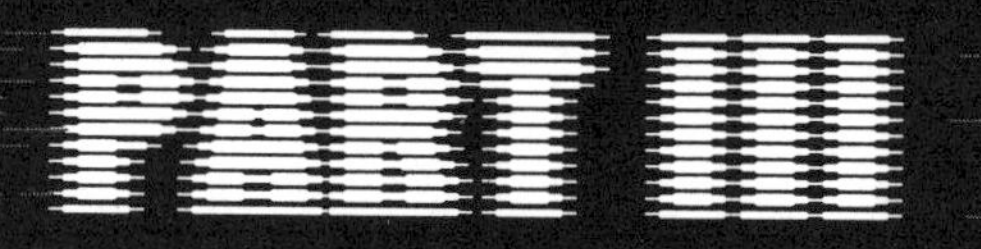

X-Minus Five Months
(November 2005)

"Confirmed"
Director of the Cosmonaut Training Center
named for Yuri A. Gagarin

Ye. Ovsyannikov

28 October 2005

TRAINING PLAN FOR GROUP ISS EP-10 (IG, RD, TM, GR, VK)
For Period 31 October–04 November 2005

Time	Training	Instructor	Site
	31–10 Monday		
	RD TM		
9.00–12.50	Russian language	Gulyayeva	2-215
14.00–15.50	K57-Kh module (TM)	Mezenov	KMU-315
14.00–15.50	Alpha modules (RD)	Bobirev	KMU-315
16.00–17.50	Physical training	Kirilenko	10
	IG GR VK		
9.00–9.50	Independent study	Levitin	2-416
10.00–12.50	English language	Dolgova	2-317
14.00–15.50	Soyuz simulator	Yegupov	KMU-315
16.00–17.50	Physical training	Kirilenko	10

<u>01–11 Tuesday</u>

RD TM

9.00–12.50	Russian language	Gulyayeva	2-215
14.00–15.50	Alpha modules	Bobirev	KMU-315
16.00–17.50	Physical training	Kirilenko	10

IG GR VK

9.00–10.50	Scientific experiments	Kolesnikov	2-416
11.00–12.50	English language	Dolgova	2-317
14.00–15.50	Sky study	Kryukov	Planet.
16.00–17.50	Physical training	Kirilenko	10

<u>02–11 Wednesday</u>

RD TM

9.00–12.50	Russian language	Gulyayeva	2-215
14.00–15.50	Soyuz spacecraft	Svirin	KMU-311
16.00–17.50	Physical training	Kirilenko	10

IG, GR, VK

9.00–12.50	EVA training		Vlasov Hydro
14.00–15.50	Independent study	Levitin	2-416
16.00–17.50	Physical training	Kirilenko	10

<u>03–11 Thursday</u>

RD, TM

9.00–12.50	Russian language	Gulyayeva	2-215
14.00–15.50	Sokol suit	Rudnev	KMU-200
16.00–17.50	Physical training	Kirilenko	10

	IG GR VK		
9.00–12.50	Independent study (GR)	Levitin	2-416
9.00–12.50	Flight training (IG VK)	Masslenikov	Airbase
14.00–17.50	RMS lecture	Senkevich	KMU-204

04–11 Friday

	All		
9.00–9.50	Independent study	Levitin	2-416
10.00–12.50	Meet with RKK Energiya	Levitin	KMU-315
14.00–15.50	Soyuz simulator	Yegupov	KMU-315
16.00–17.50	Physical training	Kirilenko	10

Deputy Director for International Training Cosmonaut Training Center

P. Filippov

STAR CITY

"This is unacceptable," TM said, sliding the three-page schedule back across the table to Filippov and his twin deputies. He turned to Andrei the translator and said, "Phrase that any way you want."

It was shortly after seven on Monday morning, October 31. According to Filippov's schedule, TM and Rachel Dunne were to commence Russian language lessons in less than an hour. TM, Andrei, and Lanny had spent the night in the Hotel Orbita—roughly the equivalent of a Motel 6 in, say, Amarillo—and were blinking sleepily as they sipped Russian tea. TM desperately wanted coffee, and from the look on his face, so did Lanny.

But what TM wanted more was at least *nominal* control over his schedule for the next five months. And the first week's sample was not promising.

"Oh, we all understood you," Filippov said, nodding right and left. "Even those of us who don't speak English. Would you care to tell us what's wrong with the schedule? Keeping in mind that we have been training cosmonauts for over forty years."

"To begin with," TM said, "I have numerous other commitments. With all due respect to your, uh, extensive experience in training candidates for spaceflight, most of them didn't have outside business interests."

"I believe Mr. Tito did." Filippov had been involved, in a junior way, in the training of Dennis Tito, the California millionaire who had become the world's first paying spaceflight participant.

Now TM had the advantage, because he had spoken with Tito as recently as last week. "Mr. Tito certainly had outside business interests. He also had *total control* over his training schedule, something you are not offering me."

Filippov and his deputies conferred again, but TM knew that he would prevail. Star City still needed the money. Nevertheless, he didn't want to appear to be a bully. "Colonel Filippov," he said, assuming his most conciliatory voice and posture. "This schedule *does* strike me as well thought out." He nodded at the deputies, who seemed to accept the compliment. "It would just be better, for me, if I had one day a week free, or at the very least, a half day. And more direct input into future schedules."

Filippov smiled. "I think we can accommodate both wishes." He retrieved the pages and handed them to the deputy on his left. "Whom shall I contact regarding your schedule?" He seemed to be expecting TM to point to either Lanny or Andrei.

"Her name is Leslie Seldes. I'll be picking her up at Sheremetyevo in—" He glanced at his watch. "—about three hours."

The last four days in Russia had driven TM to a mental and physical breaking point.

First there had been the tour of Star City. For two hours, TM, Lanny, and Andrei were shown around the installation by Filippov and a different pair of deputies. TM had been briefed on the basics—that Star City was a military village that combined a research and training institute with a residential community. The closest analog in the United States was Los Alamos, originally built as a combined nuclear research center and town in the mountains north of Santa Fe.

Star City's present population was around four thousand. The residents included around a hundred current and retired Russian air force cosmonauts (the civilian cosmonauts lived elsewhere), plus their families, plus the several hundred technicians, engineers, instructors, bureaucrats, and secretaries who worked on the staff of the center itself. Then there were the inhabitants of the village—schoolteachers, janitors, auto mechanics, and shopkeepers. Under the leaden sky, hidden away here in the birch forests, Star City, to TM, felt like a rundown junior college campus in the wilds of Iowa or Wisconsin.

Nevertheless, Russian cosmonauts, NASA astronauts, and dozens of international space travelers—including all space tourists—had trained here for forty years. So he paid attention as the entourage visited the centrifuge building—"You will have to take a spin before you are certified for flight," Filippov said, with apparent relish—then the hydrobasin building, where a pair of ISS astronauts were simulating a spacewalk in the thirty-foot-deep water tank.

The next building was a huge hall in which a mock-up Soyuz TMA sat hooked up to a series of consoles. Beyond that, mock-ups of four different Alpha modules waited, each one cradled in scaffolding. "Is one of these Harmony?" TM asked.

"No," Filippov said. "We can't afford a mock-up of the new module yet." Then, as if about to launch into a tirade, he added, "Perhaps when your next payment arrives—"

Before Filippov could comment further on TM's financial treachery, there was an interruption. A tall, dark-haired man in a flapping trenchcoat rushed up. "Hi, there!" he said, in what even TM could recognize as American English, colored by an accent that suggested Oklahoma or Texas.

"Gene Struve," Lanny said, moments before the man reached them. "The chief NASA guy in Star City."

"You must be Mikleszewski," Struve said, planting himself in front of TM, slightly too close for TM's taste.

"How's your Russian?"

"Nonexistent," TM said, immediately irritated by Struve's manner and body language. "Thank you for asking."

"Defense Language Institute in Monterey says it takes eighteen months to get fluent in Russian. It took me a year just to reach minimal competence." He turned to Filippov and rattled off a phrase in Russian that could only have translated as, "Ain't that right, Pavel?"

Filippov, whose diplomatic skills were beginning to impress TM, shrugged and smiled at the same time, saying, "That's right, Gene." He nodded at TM. "Of course, our pilot-cosmonauts are fluent in English, which happens to be the operating language on Alpha. Mr. Mikleszewski starts language lessons on Monday at eight A.M." This was news to TM, and the first sign that he would have to take control of his schedule soon. "In four months he should be capable of reading instruments and understanding basic commands."

"So that's what cosmonaut training has come to," Struve said, not bothering to hide his contempt. " 'Understanding basic commands.' "

"I may not be the most perceptive person on the planet," TM said, unwilling to let Struve's rudeness go unremarked, "but I sense that you're unhappy that I'm flying."

Struve sighed, like a man getting ready to dive off a high platform. "I'm unhappy any time a nonprofessional—no matter how qualified—puts himself in a situation that could kill him—"

"You mean, like a Shuttle launch or landing?"

"—and kill someone else," Struve said, ignoring TM's point.

"Your station must have pretty piss-poor safeguards if it's that easy for someone to get killed on it."

"I'm guessing you don't really know what you're talking about, Mr. Mikleszewski."

"Since we're being antagonistic, why don't we make it 'Doctor Mikleszewski'?"

"Gentlemen!" Filippov had been trying prevent this exchange from turning into an actual fight. He literally stepped between the two of them. "Let's save this debate for another time."

"That's a date," Struve said, heading toward the parking lot in front of the administration building. "Enjoy your time in Russia," he added, with just the barest hint of sarcasm.

The moment Struve was out of earshot, or nearly, Filippov said, "We also have officials who speak without thinking. In our case, of course, they are usually drunk."

"I don't believe Captain Struve has enjoyed his time in Russia," TM said. That, at least, was the word from TM's growing list of spies at the Johnson Space Center: Struve was about to be recalled.

Filippov chose not to comment further on Struve, gaining more diplomatic points with TM.

The tour continued for another hour, past the Profy or Profilactorium, originally built as Hotel Kosmonavt for the Apollo-Soyuz mission of the 1970s, then remodeled as a sort of spa where space station crews could recover from long-duration missions.

"Isn't that where NASA has its offices?" TM had spent several hours of his flight learning what he could about Star City.

"Yes, including Commander Struve," Filippov said. "I doubt you will have much desire to visit."

TM laughed, as Filippov directed him to a new hotel, called the Orbita. "We've reserved three rooms for you," Filippov said, including Lanny and Andrei with a look, and making TM wonder who would have to be evicted if they chose to take the rooms.

"We'll be staying in Moscow through the weekend," TM said.

Filippov accepted this news without comment, leading the trio on to the block of residence flats—four twenty-story towers, two old and crumbling, two newer. Beyond them sat a cluster of two-story condos. "The NASA astronauts and other long-term visitors stay in the condos," Filippov said. "We have no vacancy at the moment, but you can stay at the Orbita or in Dom Fifty-four," he said, indicating the newest apartment tower.

"I'm sure that will be fine."

Lunch followed in the Star City canteen, with TM and his party seated in what appeared to be the VIP section, separated from the general residents (many of them in blue Russian air force uniforms) and a few men and women who were obviously NASA types.

Three hours of meetings followed, this time in the administration building. TM was used to meetings; sometimes it seemed as though he'd spent the last ten years trapped in a conference room. He tried to limit them.

His powers didn't extend to Star City, however. He and Lanny and Andrei spent the entire afternoon facing a stream of briefers in twos and threes. They heard about the language lessons. TM hoped to shorten that process by using Andrei as much as possible. "I'll be hiring at least two other translators to stand by," he said. This, of course, resulted in another lengthy discussion concerning the source of the translators, and whether they would be cleared for admission to Star City.

There was a presentation on the overall events TM would face on his road to space (to use the words of one briefer): TM's preliminary clearance by the physicians at IMBP would only allow him to train. To fly, he would still need formal certification by the Grand Medical Committee approximately a month prior to flight. Filippov, glancing through the report of the Star City medical team, noted that TM still had his appendix and his tonsils, that he wore glasses, that he was ten kilograms over desired weight. "Any one of these would exclude a typical cosmonaut candidate," he said, his entire manner and expression saying quite the opposite.

"I'm not going to have corrective surgery," TM announced, "but it would probably do me good to lose twenty pounds. I think I can manage that in five months."

"I know these strike you as arbitrary restrictions," Filippov said. "But, let us take the weight issue: you need to be fitted with a Sokol ascent and entry pressure suit." TM was familiar with the white garment and its soft helmet: every photo of cosmonauts ascending the gantry for a Soyuz launch showed them. "Simply manufacturing a Sokol takes almost five months. You will have a fitting in the next two weeks; that suit will be sized to your larger frame."

"Maybe I should keep the weight on."

"The physical training will take it off, I can promise you that."

This was troubling news. But before TM could question that point, Filippov went on: "The suit can be resized to accommodate a few extra pounds, of course. We have had . . . stout cosmonauts in the past. It will require an adjustment before launch, however.

"I cite this as merely one factor behind our rules."

"I understand," TM said, liking none of it.

There followed a discussion of the examination schedule—all Russian space crew members, even spaceflight participants, were subject to a series of periodic tests as training progressed. "Mr. Tito compared this to going back to your first semester at college," Filippov said.

"Fine," TM snapped. "I got straight A's my first semester at college."

Finally, Filippov announced that TM was being assigned to ISS Visiting Crew 10 along with Rachel Dunne and three Russian cosmonauts, including Lieutenant Colonel Igor Gritsov, who would be the pilot of the Soyuz TMA-7 spacecraft. "You three will train in a group with two other cosmonauts, Colonel Grigory Rynin and Vyacheslav Karpov, who will be your backup crew."

With that announcement, the meeting broke up. The last set of Star City briefers left, and Lanny and Andrei practically fled from the conference room in search of bathrooms. TM was alone with Filippov. "May I ask you a personal question?" the Russian said.

"Sure."

"Why are you doing this?"

"What do you mean?"

"I've spent my whole military career at Star City. Twenty-three years, working my way up through the Second Directorate. I'm an aerospace engineer by training; I'm in good health. Yet I never considered applying to become a cosmonaut even though the former commander here asked me to apply."

At first TM had dreaded Filippov's question, which, like that of an ill-informed television reporter, seemed designed to elicit an embarrassing sound bite. But now he was curious: why *would* an otherwise qualified aerospace engineer pass up the opportunity? "Okay, why didn't you?"

"Because I've seen forty crews come and go, at least eighty different cosmonauts. And not one of those people—not a single one—was a better person for the experience of going into space. Many of them were worse off. They became unbalanced in their personal lives, arrogant, impatient. They lost friends and hurt their families. I didn't want this."

TM was tired and hungry, never a happy combination. He grew short-tempered and too often said exactly what was on his mind. "I grew up watching astronauts and cosmonauts from a distance. I would see these spacewalks and moon walks on television and want to do the same thing.

"In fact, once, when I was about fifteen, I had a—I don't know what to call it but a vision, since I was awake. This vision of myself floating inside a spacecraft. I was wearing a blue flight suit of some kind, not a space suit, and I had these cables all around me . . . it was a television picture, too, all grainy.

"It was as if I'd been shown a piece of my future, especially when I got older and saw the first videos of Shuttle astronauts in orbit: they were wearing the same blue suits I'd seen in my vision.

"Of course, by then I had gone to college and started working in biochemistry. It was always in my mind that I could apply to become an astronaut, but I started making money, then I had some personal problems, and I was over forty—famous—rich. NASA wasn't going to be able to fit me into their group of anonymous team-player astronauts.

"So I started using some of my money to invest in other ways to get to space, because I still had this vision of myself floating in that spacecraft.

"And here came this . . . I don't want to call it 'opportunity,' and you guys have this module ready for launch—"

TM stopped talking. He and Filippov were both looking out the conference room window, at the early dusk of a Russian October afternoon. Cars were snaking out of Star City's rear gate. Uniformed officers hurried along sidewalks with shopping bags in hand. A quartet of what could only be very hardy teenage boys played soccer on the dead grass next to one of the residence doms.

"Well, I guess I'm fulfilling a vision. Does that answer your question?"

"Yes. Thank you."

"And unlike these other fine astronauts and cosmonauts," he said, "I can't be ruined by the experience. I'm *already* unbalanced and arrogant."

Filippov laughed out loud, and extended his hand. "Congratulations, Dr. Mikleszewski! I think you are the forerunner of a new generation of space traveler!"

The long day at Star City, along with its brutal realities, wasn't enough to make TM wish he hadn't agreed to spend $30 million fulfilling a youthful vision.

An October weekend in Moscow almost did it. Wanting to experience first-class living conditions in the Russian capital between stays at IMBP and Star City, he had allowed Lanny to book the two of them into the Penta Hotel.

The arrival and check-in Friday night was promising, like a visit to the Four Seasons in Georgetown, TM's ideal hotel. He was given a suite on the top floor, and Lanny a suite only slightly smaller on the floor below.

When it came to furnishings, the suite had everything TM could have wanted: a huge bed, nice sheets, telephone and fax machine, Internet port, a television with several hundred satellite channels, most of them from the United States. (For a man who believed he did not watch much TV, TM desperately missed the chatter of CNN or Fox News, if only as background noise.) At nine-thirty, with a hot shower behind him and a fabulous meal yet to come (so Lanny had promised), TM placed a telephone call to Leslie in Los Angeles, where it was nine-thirty in the morning . . . the start of a workday.

He reached her in her car, a bit of twenty-first-century communications magic that should not have astonished him, but did. "Tell me it's sunny out there," he said.

"I'll tell you anything you want, but you should know that we've got a thick marine layer, I've got the wipers going, and I feel as though I'm coming down with a cold." Typical Leslie: direct to the point of brutality.

For a moment, TM felt a stirring of panic at the thought that she might not get on the plane Saturday. "Have some Thai food. I need you here."

"I'm sorry, you're breaking up." He was doing no such thing, but he let it go.

They chatted about business, then he really did start breaking up—or she did: the signal was lost.

He finished dressing, reassured that Leslie would be at the airport sometime Monday midday, and was about to leave to meet Lanny and Andrei when his phone rang.

Assuming it was Lanny, or even Leslie calling back (from her car in Beverly Hills?), he answered with a friendly "Talk to me."

"We can do more than *talk,* Mr. Tad," a female voice said.

"Who is this?"

"I'm Nataliya, and I'm eager to meet you." The caller was young, spoke English with only a slight accent, and was trying very hard to be sexy.

"I think you have the wrong room."

Nataliya laughed. "I don't think so. I'll be there in two minutes—"

Then TM remembered . . . even the best hotels in Russia were essentially staffed by call girls. Very aggressive call girls.

TM enjoyed the company of beautiful women, and there had been times in his life when he had indulged in the fantasy of paying a substantial amount of money for the attentions of a beautiful, high-priced prostitute.

But not for years. And from what he had heard about the rise of AIDS in Russia, certainly not *now*. "Sorry, Nataliya, I'm leaving. We won't be talking further."

He hung up and grabbed his jacket.

As he let the door close, he heard the phone ring again.

It was ringing again when he returned, shortly before midnight, feeling bloated and overserved. (Had he *really* needed that last toast with a Georgian liqueur?) Being this tipsy had, at one time in his life, been a dangerous state: that's when his prior experiences with paid sexual companionship had taken place.

But he was older, wiser, and ever more fearful of the horror of a sexually transmitted disease, not to mention X-Pox and its rumored cousins. He amused himself by picking up the phone, saying "No, thank you," or even "*Nyet, spasibah.*" Every five minutes, a different girl. What did they expect? That he would eventually find a voice he liked?

He thought about phoning Lanny and putting him to work solving the problem, but feared he would find him occupied.

Finally he phoned the front desk and insisted that they block his calls.

After half an hour of blessed quiet, there was a knock at his door! He knew better than to open it: a glance through the peephole (in this case, a very appropriate name) showed a statuesque blonde wearing a fur coat and little else.

He didn't bother to answer. He merely made sure the door was bolted and chained. He turned the TV on, filling the outer room with the sounds of a badly dubbed version of the movie *Pulp Fiction*, then closed himself in his bedroom.

Bright and early Saturday morning, he took Lanny and went in search of a manager, who turned out to be a harassed-looking man of thirty named Alexei. Alexei apologized for the annoyance and claimed that he had no control over the infestation—his word—of prostitutes. "They bribe my doormen. They pay the maids."

Alexei offered no solution, however. When he excused himself to take a phone call, Lanny turned to TM. "Maybe we should move to another hotel?"

"If it's a big hotel that caters to rich Westerners, it will have the same problem," TM said. "I have an idea."

When Alexei returned, TM counted out a thousand dollars and set it on the desk in front of the Russian. "This is to show my appreciation for your sympathy and concern about this problem," he said, as Alexei's eyes widened ever so slightly.

Then he stood, shook Alexei's hand, and walked out. In the hallway, Lanny said, "If that works, I'm going to have you handle all our deals from now on."

There were no more calls from prostitutes for the rest of TM's stay.

The rest of the weekend was not as successful. TM found that all his business e-mails had bounced, and he was forced to spend Saturday afternoon resending messages as faxes. Saturday night's dinner, with a pair of representatives of the Krunichev Space Center, was unsuccessful; the too-rich food and excess alcohol finally caught up with TM, and he spent most of Sunday night awake with what he suspected was a gall bladder attack.

He could not get Leslie on the phone. Maybe she was out shopping for her upcoming visit.

So it was a sleep-deprived, frustrated, and thoroughly grouchy TM that arrived at Star City on Monday morning to have it out with Filippov. By lunchtime he was at Sheremetyevo Airport, the survivor of yet another of Andrei's wild rides, waiting for Delta 303 from New York. The fact that he would soon have Leslie around to help had improved his mood; so had an encounter at the Tsiolkovsky train station at Star City.

Before leaving for the airport, TM had accompanied Lanny and Andrei in search of lunch. There was a line at the Star City canteen, but Lanny knew of a kiosk at the nearby train stop.

All three men were happily downing tea and Russian sweet rolls when TM chanced to look to his left, to an alcove between kiosks. There, in the shadows, a man and a woman were kissing so energetically that actual stand-up, outdoor intercourse could not be far away.

TM nudged Lanny. "I didn't know Russians played public tonsil hockey like that."

The sound of his voice might have interrupted the happy couple's activities, or perhaps it was the arrival of the train. In any case, they disengaged, and TM was surprised, then amused, to realize that of the eight million inhabitants of Moscow, perhaps five of whom he knew on sight, here was one:

The man making out with the woman was NASA director of operations Gene Struve.

What was it the NASA spies had said about Struve? That he hadn't enjoyed his time in Russia?

It seemed to TM that Struve was enjoying it a little *too* much.

The flight had arrived, but experience told TM that it would be some time before Leslie cleared Russian customs. He desperately wanted to read an American newspaper, and remembered that there was a kiosk on the second floor near the Delta lounge.

He had only to reach the top of the steps, however, to see that the kiosk was closed. Shit. He returned to the spot where Lanny and Andrei were standing.

Before he reached them, he saw Leslie emerge from the gate—

she wore a T-shirt, khaki slacks and sneakers, and looked like a film star traveling to a location. In fact, her very manner reminded TM of Rachel Dunne.

It apparently reminded Andrei of Rachel Dunne, too. Without realizing that TM was standing behind him, he said to Lanny, "That's TM's girlfriend? I think she's too hot for him."

It was Lanny who happened to see that TM was five feet away. He took Andrei's arm, hoping to shut him up, but TM was already laughing.

Now Andrei saw him, realized he had overheard, and began to offer an apology.

"Don't worry," TM said. "I get that all the time." He smiled at Lanny, then waved at Leslie. "Leslie is not my girlfriend. She's my daughter."

THE RUSSIAN FRONT

During his former career as a scope dope, that is, as an air force lieutenant at Space Command's mission control center in Colorado, Mark Koskinen had witnessed half a dozen change-of-command ceremonies. They ranged from the emotion and pageantry attendant on the replacement of a three-star general (who also happened to be ending a thirty-two-year career in the air force) to the comparatively casual ceremony due a lieutenant colonel taking over a small detachment.

Mark's new command in Russia gave him responsibility for a score of astronauts assigned to upcoming prime and backup Alpha crews as well as their "bubbas" (support crew members), plus a comparable number of training specialists on rotation from Houston. There was also a small administrative staff.

In sheer numbers, the DOR office was between a platoon and a company. In importance, it was more like a small embassy, or a program office.

So when Mark arrived at his office in the Profy at eight A.M. on the bright, clear morning of Tuesday, November 1, after a torturous two-day trip from Iowa to Houston to Alabama to Moscow, he expected to meet the outgoing DOR, Gene Struve, and take part in *some* kind of handover.

Struve might have been available; it was impossible to tell, because the office wasn't even *open.*

It was only due to Mark's previous experiences—now five years past—that he was able to gain access to the building in the first place. Following a record twelve hours of sleep in his room in the "new" wing of the Orbita, he had presented himself at the rear gate to the training center, which was separated from the Star City living complex by a brick wall. He had been advised to telephone the NASA office and have one of the Americans meet him there. But he woke early—shortly after four A.M. local time—devoured his stash of peanut butter and crackers, showered, shaved, exercised, reviewed all his paperwork yet one more time, and still found himself waiting, waiting, waiting for seven A.M. to arrive.

So he brandished his Johnson Space Center identification, a piece of official-looking fax paper (two copies, one in English, one in Russian, of the letter from Goslin to Colonel Nesmeyanov, the chief astronaut's counterpart at Star City, confirming Mark's appointment), Mark's old Star City pass, and fifty dollars U.S.

He also put on his dealing-with-Russia manner, which could only be compared to that of a feudal lord to serfs. He had learned the attitude during his first visit to Star City, while training for the STS-100 mission. It had taken him a single week of observing post-Communist Russia to realize that pushing to the front of lines, bulling past old women and children, and treating subordinates (including waiters, shopkeepers, and bus drivers) like shit was the only way to get anything done.

When Mark arrived at the gate, he marched directly to the young guard in blue, presented his papers and passes, and announced, in fair Russian, that he was the new "*glavny* NASA *rukovitel*" ("big NASA chief").

He had given the guard perhaps five seconds to examine the papers before demanding, also in Russian, "Is there a problem? Let me in or telephone Colonel Nesmeyanov immediately."

The guard, noting the early hour, weighed the likely punishment due for allowing Mark into Star City against that of waking Colonel Nesmeyanov for what was probably a trivial matter, and stood aside with a salute.

Mark knew better than to smile or even say "Thank you." And he returned to Star City feeling like an ass.

He had made it to the Profy with no further difficulties, enjoying the walk from the gate, balancing his laptop and briefcase. The air was cold and brisk. The chill breeze rustled the branches of the birch trees and stirred the few leaves still on the ground.

At one point he stopped and looked down the main street—the Alley of Cosmonauts—toward the administration building, and the statue of Yuri Gagarin, first man in space. A quarter moon hung in the sky, looking down on Gagarin, and a lone man in a blue track-suit jogging toward Mark. An American or European astronaut, no doubt: Russians did not, as a rule, jog.

It still struck Mark as ridiculously unlikely that he could not only look on Star City with his own eyes, but could do so while on his way to work here. When he was growing up, building models of the Space Shuttle, Mark had known of Soviet spaceflights only from brief mentions on television newscasts, and fuzzy, black-and-white photos in space-related magazines. Soviet cosmonauts were mysterious, their vehicles and activities largely unknown, their very existence classed as top secret. The race to that quarter Moon, won by the Americans, was still a fresh memory.

Here, less than thirty years later, Mark Koskinen was the veteran of a flight in space that had docked at a Russian space station . . . he had a close friend who was a Russian cosmonaut . . . and he had just talked his way into Star City.

The moment of reflection made him wonder about his friend and former crewmate, Viktor Kondratko. Mark would have telephoned him immediately upon arrival at the Orbita last night, but he knew that Viktor was in Canada for training on the ISS remote manipulator arm.

Mark reached the Profy and found it to be substantially less secure than its equivalent at the Johnson Space Center, Building 4S, where you had to produce a badge, then walk through a metal detector just to reach an elevator. When you reached the sixth floor, you were scrutinized again by a different guard.

Here Mark noted signs in English and Russian warning of "quarantine." It had nothing to do with X-Pox, but with the presence here of the next Soyuz taxi crew, scheduled for launch in a few days. One crew member was a Russian pilot-cosmonaut, another was an engineer from the European Space Agency (the jogger?), and the third was, of all the goddamn things, the winner of a German game show!

Mark rang the doorbell and waited. No answer. So he pushed on the door, and it opened. The reception desk, a holdover from the days when the Profy was the Hotel Kosmonavt, was unoccupied, though it offered a selection of facemasks for the safety of the taxi crew. Mark hoped that no one with a bad cold happened to be following him into the Profy this morning. . . .

To the left was a glass door that led, he remembered, to a bar that had been built specially for American astronauts back in the 1970s, when they were in residence at a much more security-conscious Star City during the Apollo-Soyuz Test Project. (According to one veteran flight controller, who worked the ASTP program, "The Soviets built the Hotel Kosmonavt to keep the American team from wandering loose all over Moscow. Then they built the bar to keep the Americans from wandering loose all over Star City!")

Mark opened the glass door. "Hello?" he said in English, following with a *"Dobry den?"* ("Good day?") No answer. He looked into the bar, and saw that it was now a gym. From booze to aerobics in a single generation: the room could be considered a symbol of the evolution of the astronaut office.

There was an elevator in the lobby, but Mark had had bad experiences with Russian elevators. He chose to use the stairs, and entered a stairwell that was completely dark. The only light came from one floor up, where the door had been propped open.

After no more than a couple of missteps, he emerged on the second floor, and found a door marked "NASA DIRECTOR OF OPERATION." No *s*.

It was locked. He knocked. No answer. He put his ear up to the door, expecting to hear voices or music or some sign of human occupation.

Nothing.

For a moment Mark wondered if he had simply lost track of the day: suppose this was Sunday, not Monday? Or was it a holiday, like Canadian Thanksgiving?

Think, Mark. You're an astronaut. *A pioneer. How could you expect to deal with an emergency in orbit, or on the surface of Mars, if you can't deal with a closed office in Russia?*

In years past, Mark's temper would have ignited; he would have kicked the door, then stomped up and down the hall. The first person he met would have been subjected to a tirade.

But no longer. He was older, wiser, slower to anger. Besides, he had learned, in his NASA training and spaceflight experience, not to mention years of frustration at Spacelifter, that such outbursts were counterproductive. Worse yet, in a world threatened by X-Pox, unjustified.

And, nasty as Russia could be, it was not Mars. Or even Alpha. He could breathe here. There were natives to deal with, and many—possibly most—weren't openly hostile.

So he took a breath. He shouldered his laptop and briefcase again. He had rubles as well as dollars in his pocket; he hadn't eaten a proper breakfast. Maybe he should simply visit the Star City canteen. If nothing else, he might find some other Americans—

He was making his way down the darkened stairs when he met another human coming up. "*Privyet!*" he called. ("Hi!")

A voice from the darkness said, in Texan American, "Hey. You must be Mark!"

Only when both figures emerged into the pale yellow light of the second-floor hallway did Mark have any idea whom he was talking to. It turned out to be a man in his early thirties, round-faced, cheerful, wearing glasses and a T-shirt from the famed Ron Jon's Cape Canaveral Surf Shop under a down jacket. He stuck out his hand. "Darin Chambliss. I'm your new deputy."

They shook. "Not that I want to be Regular Army about this," Mark said, "but where the hell is everybody?"

Chambliss made an apologetic face as he struggled with the office door. "You ever heard of the Dniepr Apartments?"

"Yes." Before Mark had left Houston, he had been offered the choice of living quarters in Moscow—the NASA cottages at Star City, or the Dniepr, which was downtown near the headquarters of Rosaviakosmos. Rumor had it that life in the Dniepr resembled *Animal House* on toga night, so he had opted for Star City. He traded hours of commuting for isolation and exile from the bright lights.

"Well, we had a big party last night. Jasper Weeks's birthday." Weeks was one of the astronauts assigned to the next Alpha expedition crew. "It was sort of a going-away for Gene Struve, too."

"A good time had by all?"

"Don't get the wrong idea: it's not like everybody's hung over or something. It's just that a lot of the folks who live out here decided not to risk the train late at night. And this morning there was some kind of problem—Chechen terrorist threat or something. Nothing was moving from Mytishchi on. Cars, either. That's why everyone's late."

It was a valiant excuse, and possibly even true. Mark decided to let it pass as he looked around his new workplace. It was a bullpen filled with half a dozen desks and surrounded by eight smaller offices. "You're going to be in the corner here," Chambliss said.

As Mark entered, he passed a row of photos of familiar faces—his predecessors as DOR. There was no Gene Struve, however, just a Post-it with the words, "Wild man photo to come."

Mark's new office was barely big enough for a desk, chair, and guest chair. A Tinkertoy model of Alpha in its current configuration used up a quarter of Mark's desk space. The walls held portraits of all the flown Alpha assembly and expedition crews, at least thirty of them, adding to the sense of crowding. Fine; he planned to spend a minimal amount of time here. He was going to get to know Star City, and get himself back up to speed, even if it had to be on Russian spacecraft. "Hey," Mark called, "who do I see about training on the TMA?" The TMA was the latest model of the Soyuz. Mark had a good working knowledge of its predecessor, the TM, but the new version had been in use for the past couple of years. It had improved electronics and displays as well as a completely rearranged interior.

"That would be Nesmeyanov," Chambliss said from his desk, right outside Mark's door. "Your counterpart."

"When do I see him?"

Chambliss was playing back telephone messages, most of them left by Houston late Friday, and reading e-mails. The door opened once, twice, and other members of the team arrived. "He's expecting you at nine."

"Great. Is Struve going to be part of that?"

There was no immediate answer. Suddenly Chambliss appeared inside Mark's office, closing the door. "Uh, Geno is on his way to the airport."

"Under guard?" Mark said, half-joking in reaction to Chambliss's secretive manner.

"Practically. One of the guys from downtown basically perp-walked him out."

Mark had learned one trick of exercising power from his time at Spacelifter: creating a silence that had to be filled. He waited; sure enough, Chambliss continued: "I don't know how much they told you in Houston, but Geno got himself into some deep personal water here." Mark fiddled with his laptop. Chambliss was forced to keep talking. "These Russian assignments are tough on marriages. There's a lot of single Russian women around. They like American men. And there's a lot of drinking."

Only now did Mark speak. "A formula for trouble."

"Yeah. Geno got seriously involved with a woman here. His wife found out. She ratted him out to Steve Goslin."

"Ouch."

"Oh, it gets messier. For one thing, Mrs. Struve is still here, which is why you won't have a cottage to live in. She and Geno have two kids in grade school, and she refuses to move them in the middle of a semester."

"Even if it means getting out of Russia and going back to Texas?"

"I'm guessing her desire to avoid being in the same country with Geno outweighs any inconvenience she faces here."

"Is that it?"

"Oh, no: that's not messy, except on a personal basis. Geno's new love in life is Tanya Vladimirovna Filippova . . . the *wife* of Colonel Filippov."

Oh God. Mark knew that Filippov was one of three military deputies to the civilian director of Star City. "This may seem like a stupid question, but does Filippov know this?"

Chambliss's smile grew broader. "No! Everyone in the American office knows—well, with a few exceptions—and probably half a dozen people in Houston. And Geno and Tanya haven't been remotely discrete. But as far as anyone can tell, Filippov has no idea."

"So Goslin and JSC yanked him back there at the first opportunity." No wonder Goslin had seized on Mark as the first available body to throw into the breach here: he didn't have to disrupt other assignments or make explanations. Mark wished his chief astronaut had been a bit more frank about the situation in Star City. "Will that be the end of it?"

"Not a chance. Geno was going around the party last night—with Tanya—telling everybody who would listen that she was going with him to Houston, and they were going to get married."

"That's not going to make the Russians happy. When they find out."

"No. Filippov is very popular. He's basically the Russians' point guy with the U.S. He's right in the middle of negotiations to get more Soyuz for the station." NASA's deal with the Russians to provide a pair of Soyuz "taxi" or rescue vehicles annually was about to expire. NASA's horrible experience with *Columbia* had made it clear that the agency had no backup for the Soyuz—no "assured crew return vehicle" to park at Alpha, giving the Russians a seller's market. The price they had quoted NASA for continued Soyuz production was too high: NASA couldn't pay it even if the agency wanted to. There was no money in the budget, and with X-Pox and other related disasters eating up the federal budget, no chance of getting it from Congress. NASA was facing an impossible choice: find money it didn't have to buy more Soyuz, or let Alpha return to the partly manned status of the *Columbia* hiatus, or even worse, with Shuttle crews visiting for perhaps a total of three months a year. A partly manned Alpha would have zero value as a research platform, and would have even less support with the public and Congress.

Mark wanted to laugh. The situation was absurd! The hopes and dreams of two nations, not to mention fourteen other international partners, for a permanent, valuable human outpost in orbit were in danger because one astronaut couldn't keep his dick in his pants.

"What else do I need to know, Darin? Seeing as how I'm theoretically in charge around here."

Chambliss rose from the chair. "Let me get my list."

Two hours later, Mark had met ten more members of his staff, eight of them in their thirties, or younger. Only two were over forty, veterans of the Mission Operations Directorate. None of them were fellow astronauts. Only half of the dozen assigned to crews or support were actually in Russia at the moment, and they were off at early morning training activities. (These schedules were detailed on a set of pages Chambliss provided.)

Mark knew none of his staffers; he assumed they were competent. Nevertheless, he felt overwhelmed, even depressed. He blamed the feeling on jet lag and worry about his father.

Chambliss's list of open issues had also been heavily weighted toward personal problems. Not just the Struve affair . . . there was the flirtation between two support astronauts that was distracting the pair from their work; the fact that another expedition crew member was so unhappy with his separation from his pregnant wife back in Houston that he was on the verge of quitting the program; vandalism and anti-American graffiti on the cottages; JSC was having a tough time finding new volunteers for the Star City office—the "Russian Front"—to allow the current staffers to rotate home.

There was a simmering resentment by NASA and ESA astronauts toward the "spaceflight participants" the Russians kept bringing into the program. "I can understand that," Mark said, truthfully, "but it's like complaining about the weather. It ain't gonna change."

"Spoken like a man from Spacelifter," Chambliss said, taking a big chance by teasing his new boss. It showed confidence, arrogance, or stupidity. Perhaps all three. Mark chose to act as though Chambliss had used just the right amount of levity, smiling without comment. "Then there are the actual technical problems," Chambliss said.

"Thank God for them," Mark said, with some relief. He was less relieved when Chambliss reached the end of the second list, which ranged from maintenance problems on simulators and the horrible financial shortages at Star City (which were forcing Russian staffers to work part-time jobs outside the training center) up to confusion in the whole program over the shape of Alpha six months or a year hence. "For example, it appears they're going to launch this Harmony module after the first of the year, and no one at JSC or Boeing seems to know when we're going to have a review of the hardware."

"Even if we had a review tomorrow, would we be able to make any changes?"

"That's what's bothering everyone at the program office. They say it would be 'very difficult.' "

"Adding Harmony would make the stack asymmetrical, too."

Mark reached for the Alpha model on his desk. "They're going to have to put it on the node, aren't they?"

"Yes. Where it will also complicate EVA assembly activities on Fourteen-A and ULF-Three."

Mark realized that he had a lot of work to do. "All right," he said, his head starting to throb, "anything else I should know?"

"Well," Chambliss said, "in world space news, the Chinese launched their second manned flight this morning." The Chinese had spent a decade developing a manned space capability of their own, though it leaned heavily on technologies and designs licensed from Russia.

"Shenzhou-Six?" Mark said, having heard rumors that a launch was pending.

"Correct, with a crew of two '*yuangyuan*.' Shenzhou-Seven is supposed to launch tomorrow with another couple of crewmen. Everyone thinks they'll rendezvous and dock."

"I wonder if they have the problems we do," Mark said, more to himself than to Chambliss.

Mark could only hope that the ten-minute walk from the Profy to the admin building would pump endorphins into his system and lift his spirits. The start was not promising. The sky had clouded over, dropping the temperature, both real and apparent, by ten degrees Fahrenheit. The Moon had disappeared.

He could see small groups of people—twos and threes, most of them young Russian air force officers in blue greatcoats—hurrying from one building to another. No one stopped to talk. All of it reinforced the feeling that Mark was almost alone in a strange land.

Then Chambliss said, "Oh, Christ. Not them."

"What?"

Chambliss indicated a group of five people emerging from the main simulator building. Three men, two women. The men were stocky, almost overweight, like most Russian males. But they wore civilian clothes, not uniforms, much like Mark and Chambliss. The women wore slacks, ski jackets, and baseball caps. As Mark approached, he realized, with amusement, that both hats bore the log of the Spacelifter team.

And that one of the wearers was none other than Lanny Consoldane, his former colleague. "The new spaceflight participants," Chambliss said, unnecessarily.

"I'm guessing Tad Mikleszewski and Rachel Dunne," Mark said, as each group paused for the inevitable encounter.

"Correct."

"Hey, Lanny!" Mark said, as cheerfully as he could, to a broadly smiling Consoldane. Then he held out his hand to TM. "Mark Koskinen from NASA. You must be—"

"Your former boss," TM said. "Nice to meet you, after all these years."

"Who'd have thought we'd all wind up here?" Mark couldn't help sizing up the head of Pyrite. He was Mark's height or a bit taller, perhaps five-nine. Bearded, almost scholarly looking, and supremely confident.

"Yeah, where did we go wrong?"

Mark was about to introduce Chambliss, but TM already knew him. "How's it going, Darin? Is Jasper Weeks still bitching about me?"

"Who?" Chambliss said, prompting a laugh from TM.

TM pushed Andrei forward. "Mark, this is Andrei Salnikov." Mark shook hands with the young Russian, though he barely registered his presence. He had come face-to-face with a dark-haired woman who, even in boots, barely came up to eye level. "My daughter, Leslie. She doesn't bite."

"But I do nibble," Leslie said.

"And you have probably already recognized Miss Rachel Dunne."

In fact, while Mark recognized the name of the actress, he could not remember seeing one of her movies. "I, ah, loved you in *Citizen Kane.*"

His reward was the tiniest possible look of doubt on that perfect face, followed by a genuine laugh. "Thank you! Working with Orson Welles prepared me for all this."

As the other five walked off, hurried to their next class by Lanny, both Rachel and Leslie turned and waved. And Mark was torn: blond and beautiful Rachel Dunne was not only a cover girl come to life, she was clearly intelligent and had a sense of humor.

Yet he found small, dark Leslie, Mikleszewski's daughter, the most fascinating and attractive woman he had ever met.

The sun came out, the temperature rose—or so it seemed. Mark began to believe he might just enjoy his tour on the Russian Front.

X PLUS THREE DAYS

NASA NEWS
National Aeronautics and Space Administration

April 29, 2005
Shannon Crosby
Headquarters, Washington
(Phone 202/358-4504)

Lou Wekkin
Johnson Space Center
(Phone 281/483-5111)

Release: H05-32

CHANGES IN DISCOVERY LAUNCH DATE, PAYLOAD

Launch of Space Shuttle Discovery to the International Space Station on mission STS-124, formerly set for May 25, 2006, has been changed.

Discovery's new mission—Utilization and Logistics Flight 3.1—will launch no earlier than May 10, 2006, and will carry a special payload designed to assist the Alpha Expedition 13 crew in cleanup of this week's toxic spill.

A new launch date for Discovery's liftoff will be announced early next week. A precise time will be announced about 24 hours prior to liftoff.

Discovery's crew will deliver special sanitization and extraction equipment to Alpha aboard the Rafaello Multi-Purpose Logistics Module.

Brad Latham (Cmdr., USN) will command STS-124, and Kevin Ames (Lt. Col., USAF) will serve as pilot. Mission specialists will be Jeff Burnside (Col., US Army), Kelly Gessner, Diana Herron (Maj., USAF), and Yung-Hun Lai. Gessner and Herron are the EVA crew members.

Discovery is scheduled to land at the Kennedy Space Center approximately six days after launch. This flight will mark the 35th flight for Discovery, and the 120th for the Space Shuttle Program.

end

ALL HELL BREAKS LOOSE

Kelly rolled out of bed before the alarm, showered, made a cup of tea, and was heading south on El Dorado Boulevard before six A.M. It wasn't worry that did it, but excitement.

True, she had a mission for the first time in years. But even during the roll-up to her first mission—God, eleven years ago?—she hadn't felt nearly as pumped up. Maybe it was the layoff. Maybe it was that she was older and better able to appreciate the opportunity.

The hell with that. It was the fact that there was a problem on Alpha, and she was going to be part of the team to solve it. The meeting in Building 30 last night, with the commander and pilot of mission ULF-3 (which was already changing to ULF-3.1), Steve Goslin and his boss, Jeff LaFollet, as well as the senior management of the Shuttle and Alpha programs, had run to midnight. What was really impressive was that Les Fehrenkamp stayed linked as part of the telecon from Washington, meaning he had stayed up until three A.M.

The issues had been talked upside down and sideways, as Kelly's late father used to say. There were procedures for sealing a contaminated module on Alpha. (Done.) There were also procedures for cleaning up a contaminated module. (Being looked at, though they did not address a substance with the lethality of X-Pox.) The affected crew member was comfortable, but isolated. The other crew members were safe, though obviously concerned and eager to get on with the cleanup.

The kit had already been flown to the Cape and would be installed in the Multi-Purpose Logistics Module (MPLM) already mounted in the orbiter *Discovery*'s payload bay. The MPLMs were built by the Italian Space Agency, and had names. This particular one was Raffaello. "We'd prefer to use SpaceHab for an extraction like this," said Scott McDowell, ULF-3's lead flight director from mission operations. "We could outfit it for medical support. But the thing we need most is an outright cargo carrier, and Raffaello fills the bill."

"What we need *most,* Scott," said Les Fehrenkamp on the speakerphone, "is *speed.* I don't care if we pile the extraction kit in the airlock. It's got to be on orbit within fourteen days."

"Les, I would think security is pretty high on the list," LaFollet said.

Kelly could easily picture Fehrenkamp's eyes rolling to the ceiling. "Jesus Christ, Jeff, the leak took place thirty hours ago. I'm surprised we don't have CNN and every reporter on the planet climbing up our ass right now. We aren't going to be able to keep this secret for weeks. We aren't going to be able to keep it secret until this time *tomorrow!*"

Fehrenkamp's statement spread a cloud of gloom around the room. "You really think so, Les?" McDowell said. "I know the crew has multiple comm links and even Internet access, but they *all* run through us. I'm confident we can control this information—" Like every flight director Kelly had known, Scott McDowell was so confident in his own brilliance that he sometimes forgot that others were just as smart. Or, in the case of Fehrenkamp, smarter.

And much less patient. "Wake up, Scott! I know you can censor all the downlink. But what you can't do is *replace* that missing material. People will notice immediately that the crew isn't talking, and once they get the scent, they'll get the fox. The story is coming out. Prepare to deal with it. And let's move on!"

"They're going to crucify us," LaFollet said, almost to himself. Unfortunately, everyone heard him.

"Who?" That was McDowell, happy to have Fehrenkamp's attention directed elsewhere.

"Everybody. Not just the press, but the public. Half of them don't believe we went to the Moon. The other half think we fucked up on *Columbia*. How hard is it going to be to convince them we're not unleashing a new X-Pox vector on the planet?"

"How would we do that?" another controller said. "I mean, for the sake of argument—thinking like these dumbshits out there. How would we unleash X-Pox?"

"On a returning Soyuz crew," Kelly said. She usually preferred to stay in the background in these telecons. But it was clear that her colleagues from the MOD needed a bit of real-life perspective. "We're pushing the lifetime of the old Soyuz now. Even if Mikleszewski has to stay on Alpha in some kind of quarantine—"

"—Until we get him with the Shuttle." That was Goslin, helping out.

"—Gritsov and the actress are going to have to come back. They're going to thump down in Kazakhstan somewhere and pop that hatch. Are the Russians going to be able to throw a plastic bubble around the spacecraft before they do?"

"That's not a realistic threat, Kelly." Now McDowell was challenging her. Well, they had a history of butting heads. "The Soyuz has been completely isolated from the, uh, outbreak."

"*You* know that and *I* know that, and all of us *here* know that. But the public won't be so confident. And then you've got the Shuttle's return."

"Kelly's right," Fehrenkamp said from the box. "We've already been in touch with the Russians and their recovery forces. They're searching for some kind of bio-insulation tent they can transport to the landing site and erect quickly."

"It's the least they can do," McDowell said. "It was their equipment that failed."

For the first time, a troubling thought formed in Kelly's mind. *Was it the equipment that failed? Or was it the operator?* Ultimately it made no difference: they were in trouble either way.

The meeting had continued for another ninety minutes, veering into a discussion of Russian techniques for "venting" contaminated space station modules. Fehrenkamp reported that the Russians had actually performed such an operation back in the 1970s, on one of their military space station flights, which was encouraging news to Kelly. Goslin, never an enthusiast for the Russians, reminded everybody of the "accidental" venting of the Spektr module on Mir twenty years later. "Of course," he said, to general laughter, "I don't think we want to ram a Progress into Harmony like they did that time."

Even Fehrenkamp had seemed amused, adding, "I think Mr. Mikleszewski would object to that procedure."

"Not to mention his lawyers," McDowell added.

But soon the meeting degenerated into what Kelly called "alphabet stew," in which various department heads began speaking almost entirely in acronyms: C&W, CR, IMMT, ECLS, CoFR, IMBP, ASI, RKK-E. Even Kelly wasn't sure what all of them meant, and by the time things broke up was feeling tired, confused, and not at all confident that they had made progress.

By morning she had regained her energy and enthusiasm. In daylight, the problem aboard Alpha seemed solvable. It helped that she could visualize her moves. Carrying its replacement payload of isolation chamber, haz-mat suits, extra oxygen and drugs, the ULF-3.1 core crew (they would fly with four, not six) would dock with the station at pressurized mating adapter-2 on the plus-X or nose end of the stack. The resident crew would be herded into their Soyuz at the rear. The hatch from the Unity node to Zarya would be dogged shut; the Soyuz would be powered up and prepared for emergency undock and return to Earth.

X-Pox detectors would be placed along the route from the orbiter's mid-deck through its docking module into the PMA pressurized mating adaptor into the Destiny lab, then into the Unity node.

Kelly and either Diana Herron or Burnside (she would ask Brad Latham to assign Burnside) would don pressure suits, seal off the Unity module from Destiny and the airlock, and move into Harmony, where they would then place TM inside a full-pressure suit.

They would vent Harmony's contaminated atmosphere into space. One of the few weaknesses of the X-Pox virus was that it could be killed by cold. Space, of course, was both cold and hot, depending on whether you were in direct sunlight or not. The operation would be timed to take place when Alpha was in the Earth's shadow.

A new atmosphere would be pumped back into Harmony, though the module would not be fully pressurized. (If there were leaks, the air would flow from Alpha into Harmony, and not the other way around.) They just wanted Harmony sufficiently pressurized to allow cleaning chemicals to work properly.

Kelly and Burnside would first isolate the glovebox and any other contaminated equipment. They would scrub the interior, as well as the three pressure suits, then egress from Harmony, transferring TM to the isolation chamber on the *Discovery*'s mid-deck.

The hard part would be getting TM into a pressure suit in the first place. They had to assume he would be ill, possibly unconscious. But they could sim that operation on the ground. (It would be more difficult in zero-G, but they could carry restraints.)

So far, so good. The list of open issues was still too long, beginning with the overdue decision about downsizing the crew. Two mission specialists who had now trained for six months were about to be kicked off their flight. Yes, they would be quickly assigned to downstream missions, but it would be a blow. Kelly had no desire to be chief astronaut, and when it came to decisions like this, she wanted it even less. She could easily imagine the tantrum Diana Herron would throw: she had already proven herself to be an astrodiva, and from what Kelly knew, she operated on the assumption that all men, including the very-married Steve Goslin, were happy to do her bidding.

She realized that her thoughts had shifted from operational matters to gossip. Bad form. But even disappointment at her own inability to stay focused didn't really diminish her excitement. She had a mission.

She also knew a secret only a handful of people in the entire world shared.

There was, as usual, a line of cars backed up at the north entrance to JSC, even at 6:15 in the morning. As Kelly waited, she flipped on the all-news radio: "—sources have not said whether this problem will force the abandonment of the station. NASA has made no official comment. This is Peter King at the Kennedy Space Center."

Kelly punched up another station, and heard a bit more. Then a third station was just breaking the story, noting that the "incident" was "far more serious than NASA reported."

For an instant, Kelly felt a stab of disappointment that her secret was out. But it was replaced by a stronger emotion, a rising excitement much like the growing thrill of riding up in a roller coaster headed for the top—

Here we go.

She had barely locked her car before her cell phone rang. "Kelly?" It was Goslin. "Where are you?"

"Heading into Four-South."

"I'm on the road, ETA ten minutes. Go to my office and wait. We've got problems."

Goslin had obviously heard the broadcast. Was it the cell phone connection, or did the chief astronaut sound rattled?

Wearing sweatpants and a naval academy T-shirt, Brad Latham was already sitting at one of the secretaries' desks, feet up. "Goslin reached you, too?" Kelly said.

"Yeah." He rattled his pager. "I know we're under the gun, but, jeez. A guy can't even take a twenty-minute jog anymore."

"I take it you haven't heard the news." His face gave her the answer: no, he hadn't. "Word is on the street."

"Oh, shit."

"It'll make life easier, Brad. Really. Now we can work in the open."

"I hope you're right." He was already rising as Steve Goslin appeared from the stairwell, almost at full run.

"Come in," he said, unlocking his office door.

Kelly and Brad entered, closing the door behind them as Goslin flipped on lights and otherwise bled off nervous energy while waiting for them to take their places in front of him. "Okay, item one: the X-Pox story hit the news this morning."

"We already know," Latham said, appropriating Kelly's information without even a courtesy nod.

"Item two, you're flying with four, not six. That's definitive."

It was Kelly's turn to speak for her command. "We should break the news to Diana and Hunster ASAP." She offered Latham the barest nod of apology.

Goslin blushed. "Well, yeah, Hunster's gotta stand down, but Burnside's gonna be the other one to stay home. You're talking Diana Herron."

Latham and Kelly both looked at each other with alarm. Kelly was happy to let Latham speak. "No slur on Diana, but if I've got a crew of four, Burnside's the guy I want."

"Turns out Herron has a nursing background, and she's also been through some special-ops biowar training. Can anybody else here say the same?" Goslin sat down behind his desk without waiting for a demurral, which wasn't offered.

Kelly would have preferred working with Burnside, but her astronaut training took over: Herron's background would be invaluable. She would actually learn from her junior crewmate. Or so she told herself.

She realized that Goslin was holding something back. Latham sensed it, too. "Is there an item three?" he said, carefully.

"They're looking at a problem at the Cape." Neither Kelly nor Latham asked the obvious question—what kind of problem?—

forcing Goslin to offer it up. "Weather. There's a tropical storm off the coast and it looks as though it's turning west."

"Toward the Cape?" Kelly said, knowing that these storms often changed direction.

"Right now Pad Thirty-nine-A seems to be its target. We might have to roll back."

"Shouldn't we be rolling back anyway?" Latham said. "How are we going to put the rescue equipment on the orbiter?"

"At the moment, the plan is to do the change-out on the pad." Kelly was horrified; the orbiter and the logistics module would be vertically stacked and sealed. One worker would have to be slung inside the vehicle to unload supplies and insert new gear—all while working in a harness. "But I agree: the smart decision is to roll back now, while we still can.

"Which is why I was thinking it might not be the worst idea in the world for you guys and the whole crew to get down to the Cape. Remind the troops what's at stake." He smiled at Kelly. "It's not as though you need any more EVA sims. All the haz-mat equipment will be in Florida, anyway."

"Yeah, if the weather's gonna be bad, we'd better get down there by lunch," Latham said, standing. "I'd better get hold of Kevin and Diana."

"I'll give Hunster and Burnside the bad news first thing."

Latham turned to Kelly. "Meet me at ops in two hours." "Ops" meant Ellington, for the flight to Cape Canaveral.

"See you there." He went out.

Kelly lingered. "What do we do if we can't launch the orbiter in time?"

"Plan B is the Russians. We launch a Soyuz with a smaller kit and do the extraction that way."

"Who flies that mission?"

"I'm thinking Mark Koskinen. I just saw him in Russia. He's stayed current on Soyuz. God knows he's done stuff like this before."

Mark would have been first on Kelly's list, in spite of her simmering pique at the lack of contact between them. Well, what did she expect? She was still involved with Wayne Shelton, at least as far as Mark knew.

And as far as *she* knew. Wayne had spent most of the past three months at the Cape, and seemed increasingly distant when he and Kelly were together.

"People will give you a hard time if you do that, Steve. I mean, there are half a dozen expedition crew members who have varying degrees of knowledge of the Soyuz—"

"I know. But they're scattered all over the world at the moment—"

"—While Mark is in Moscow—"

"Yes. And, let's face it, Mark's training for the Cal Stipe thing parallels what you're going to be doing in the next two weeks." Cal Stipe had required what NASA and the FBI called a "hostile extraction" from the Mir space station. Mark had trained for the dirty work at Quantico, along with Viktor Kondratko. Goslin had commanded the mission.

"All he would need is to get read up on the haz-mat part of the program," Kelly said.

"The Russian haz-mat plan is pretty minimal. Soyuz can only carry a couple of hundred kilograms of material. It will be three bio-insulation garments and not much else."

"Let's hope we don't have to go to Plan B, then."

"Copy that," Goslin said. He looked at his watch, prompting Kelly to do the same. Good Lord, it was barely seven A.M. "Dinnertime in Moscow. I should call Mark and get him up to speed—"

"—Just in case."

"Just in case. And then start ruining people's days here in Houston."

"And I've got a plane to catch."

As Kelly left Goslin's office, she saw two of her ULF-3 crewmates, Yung-Hun Lai and Jeff Burnside, talking down the hallway.

Judging from his gestures, Hunster was agitated. Well, both he and Burnside had to know some sort of decision loomed. And knowing they were being excluded from the conversations, it was not likely to be good for them.

Kelly sympathized, but had no time for comradely commiseration. She had to pack for a mission scheduled for launch—she hoped—in less than two weeks.

TROPICAL STORM ALLIE

"We're going to have to go around."

Les Fehrenkamp pronounced his judgment less than five minutes after the rental Buick came to a stop in the line of traffic. He could not even see the west gate to the Kennedy Space Center ahead of him; too many cars. Rolling down his window, he heard the distant, by-now familiar chants of "Let it go!" and "No Pox from Space!" Opening the passenger door and standing up for a better view, Fehrenkamp could see the problem: a collection of television news satellite trucks filled the small parking lot while dozens of other vehicles jammed the shoulders and the road itself.

Blocking the highway, right in front of an unnecessary number of television cameras and crews, sat a row of protesters. Beyond the gate was a jumble of KSC security, prowl cars with flashing cherries, and the usual blue-uniformed agents talking on cell phones and, no doubt, wondering just what the hell they were supposed to do with these people. They were obviously obstructing access to a U.S. government facility.

Just as obviously, KSC did not, to Fehrenkamp's knowledge, have a jail. (In years past, he had often wished it did, in order to teach a few of his more rambunctious astronauts a lesson.)

"What do you want to do?" his driver said. The young man's name was Curt Freitag; he was an administrative assistant in headquarters, sent by the KSC director to fetch Fehrenkamp at Orlando, where he had flown in on Delta.

Fehrenkamp had not wanted to fly commercial; the sanitation procedures alone doubled the travel time and quadrupled the annoyance. This particular flight had gone just as badly as he had expected, with the added attraction of a rough ride the last half hour, as the pilot worked his way through a storm front off the coast.

McEwen had originally offered Fehrenkamp the HQ Gulfstream, which would have taken him directly onto the facility, landing at the skid strip—the runway next to the Vehicle Assembly Building that was used for Shuttle landings, among other activities.

But then McEwen had withdrawn the offer of the NASA corporate jet: the approaching storm front of protest over the "accident" on Alpha had caught the attention of a White House normally too preoccupied with war and X-Pox to think about spaceflight. McEwen had been summoned for a face-to-face presidential meeting. Unfortunately for Fehrenkamp, the president happened to be in Colorado at the time. "Here are the choices," McEwen had said. "Fly commercial to the Cape, or come with me to meet Mister Wood." Mister Wood was one of McEwen's folksy expressions; this one was the rhetorical equivalent of "get yelled at." The theoretical third option—wait another day until McEwen returned with the Gulfstream—had not been offered, not with a launch readiness review pending.

So Fehrenkamp had come stumbling out of the jetway to find a hulking young male in a short-sleeved white shirt holding up a sign with Fehrenkamp's name on it. "Put that away" were Fehrenkamp's first words. "For Christ's sake, I've got reporters trailing me day and night."

Realizing the gravity of his error, the young man went pale, and quickly folded up the sign. He tried to take Fehrenkamp's bag and was told, "Get me to the car."

Only when they had reached the 405 toll road heading across the palmetto flats did Fehrenkamp learn his driver's name. Curt offered nothing more—wisely, given Fehrenkamp's preoccupation with the car radio, as he switched from station to station, hearing nothing but the Alpha story (with generally supportive spin, thanks to the presence of the NASA team in the area) and the weather.

Tropical Storm Allie had already received a name. It was one of the earliest storms of recent years, so the reports said, and not expected to threaten the Orlando area. Nevertheless, Fehrenkamp listened to the reports, looked out the windshield at the dark clouds directly ahead, and worried.

The STS-124 launch was still two or three weeks away; Allie would be a memory by then. But should she grow in strength, and turn north and west, she could do tremendous damage to NASA's plans for *Discovery*. Right now the orbiter was on Pad 39A, ready for the installation of "rescue" hardware. *Discovery* was relatively safe at the moment, but the orbiter would not be safe on the pad in a hurricane. Its delicate ceramic tiles could not survive the impact of rain; subjecting them to a torrent of drops blown sideways at a hundred miles an hour would be like shooting them with a machine gun. After *Columbia,* no one took any chances with the orbiter's thermal protection system.

No. Bad weather would cause a week's delay, possibly two. Fehrenkamp knew he didn't have the extra time.

More to the point, Tad Mikleszewksi and the crew of Alpha didn't.

Weather, of course, was a long-term threat to the schedule. This traffic jam and protest was in Fehrenkamp's face. "Let me ask you something, Curt. Have you lived around here long?"

"Actually, I grew up in Titusville," the young man said, obviously relieved to be asked a question he could answer. "My dad worked for Rockwell."

"Good. Then I'm betting that if I tell you to turn this car around and get us across the river somewhere north of here, you can handle it."

Curt hesitated. "Uh, sure, but the north gate is closed."

"You get us there, Curt. I'll worry about the gate." Curt needed no further encouragement. As if he could make up for his prior mistakes by showing excess enthusiasm now, he almost violently wrenched the car out of its position in the first eastbound lane and guided it along a very narrow shoulder to a shallow spit of grass. (There were no turnarounds that Fehrenkamp could see.) Then it was across, up and over a low curb, and onto westbound 405.

Without further instruction from Fehrenkamp, Curt took the ramp to northbound Highway 5, headed into his old hometown. He wisely made a detour to the west, finding a less-traveled side road that paralleled 5.

Fehrenkamp had been visiting the Cape and environs for thirty years. He had caught it at the end of the Apollo boom, when it seemed that every home had a "for sale" sign on it, and you found laid-off space center workers taking your order at McDonald's.

He had seen the Shuttle-fueled rebound in the early 1980s, as developments sprawled again and high-rise hotels and cruise ships invaded—apparently to stay. But Titusville, the old Florida community that lay across the Banana River from Merritt Island and the Shuttle launch pads, had always seemed immune. It never built up, and so never had to cut back. The houses were old, by Florida standards, faded, situated on sandy, scrubby lots, shaded by trees. Every third lot had a pickup truck parked in it. The streets were narrow and, fortunately, given how fast Curt was driving, little traveled.

Fehrenkamp couldn't completely relax and consider his options. It wasn't Curt's fault; he could have had Steve Goslin or any of the very capable "drivers" in the astronaut office behind the wheel, and he would still have tensed at every turn. It was age. It was being in a situation he couldn't control.

Much like the growing horror that was Alpha. The original story of a minor-but-manageable "toxic spill" aboard the station had held for no more than two days, half what Fehrenkamp had hoped when he had originally leaked it to the reporter from CNN. A print reporter based in Russia had blown the whole thing wide open. *X-Pox! Harmony module contaminated! Mikleszewski trapped!*

Fehrenkamp was angry at himself for underestimating the boredom of an American reporter based in Moscow; why else would he have picked up the NASA spin on the incident in the middle of the night, and gone right to work adding to the story?

Fortunately, aside from the need to avoid protesters, the firestorm of public outrage never singed Fehrenkamp. Space reporters were either too beholden to him, or too afraid of him, to make him part of the story. Those who didn't regularly cover the space program had never heard of him; when they aimed at NASA, the crosshairs would center on administrator McEwen, or possibly, the head of life sciences.

So far, if what Fehrenkamp had seen on television and his laptop was any indication, the news coverage was, for the moment, focused on specialists from the Centers for Disease Control, the Department of Homeland Security, and some science fiction writer who had written about a deadly virus from space some years back. One former astronaut had popped up to note that the situation on Alpha was "serious," but that the crew was in "no immediate danger," that "existing contingency plans" were perfectly capable of dealing with "toxic events." Fehrenkamp approved even as he marveled at the ability of Shuttle-era astronauts to act like professional athletes whenever the camera was on, uttering stock phrases that all sounded like "We really came to play."

The car emerged from a quiet, almost lifeless residential area into a strip of ramshackle storefronts. Auto parts, liquor, pawn, and the Florida special, a "gentleman's club." More ominously, rain began to spatter the windshield. "How far from the river are we?" Fehrenkamp asked, thinking more about the weather than the distance to the Cape.

"I'll cut over to the Brewer Parkway up ahead."

"Not that I want to encourage a federal employee to break a law, but I'd appreciate it if you could pick up the speed here."

As if on command, Curt made a right turn, and Fehrenkamp saw trouble ahead. A small number of protesters clogged the roadway leading onto the Brewer Parkway. Several marched along the side of the road, carrying signs. Others were weaving in and out of traffic, forcing cars to slow down. "Shit." That was Curt, showing some life. "What do you want me to do?"

Fehrenkamp had already gone miles out of his way. There was no access to the Cape north of Titusville; going around to the south, via Melbourne, would take an hour, probably two in this weather. And there was no guarantee that gate wouldn't also be blocked by protesters. "Keep going."

There were no police and no television crews here, another worrisome sign. But traffic was being allowed onto the bridge.

A protester suddenly loomed in front of the car. Curt stopped without hitting the man—barely. He was, Fehrenkamp noted, burly, bearded, with a gas mask around his neck. And angry. He pointed right at Fehrenkamp and shouted, "These are NASA people!"

"How the hell do they know that?" Fehrenkamp said, knowing he could not possibly have been recognized—not in Titusville—and amazed that he could hear the man through the closed windows.

"Sticker on the car," Curt said, resigned. Of course; this was a NASA vehicle.

"Run him over if you have to!"

"But—"

"Goddammit, young man, do as I say!" Fehrenkamp snapped. "He'll back off!"

Curt angrily stomped on the accelerator. The car lurched forward, and the protester, after a moment of disbelief, stepped out of the way. "You fuckers!" he shouted. "No X-Pox!"

Something thumped behind them. A rock or a fist, Fehrenkamp couldn't tell. "Keep going!" The rain was falling harder now, a good old tropical shower that seemed to dishearten the protesters swarming the car. Curt swerved into the oncoming lane long enough to pass two slower vehicles, then edged safely back where he belonged.

They were across the parkway before Curt spoke. "Did I hit anybody?"

"No," Fehrenkamp said, sounding more certain than he felt. He had been looking out the rear window, searching for signs of pursuit. Now he turned and slapped Curt on the arm. "You did a good job."

"This is crazy! We're trying to help them, aren't we?"

Fehrenkamp thought about the boarded-up houses he had just seen in Titusville. Several had the black *X* sprayed on the door, their inhabitants dead from the plague. "Of course we are."

Then he felt the car braking, and losing traction.

He turned just in time to see the tail end of a tractor trailer swinging toward them.

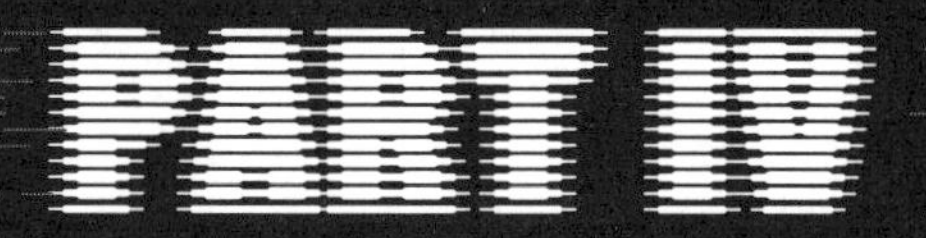

X-Minus Three Months
(January 2006)

RUSSIA LAUNCHES HARMONY MODULE

(Text of report by Russian news agency Interfax)

Korolev, 8th January: A Proton rocket carrying the Harmony module was launched from Baikonur Cosmodrome to the International Space Station Alpha at 2229 Moscow Time (1829 GMT), the Russian Aviation and Space Agency Rosaviakosmos has told Interfax.

The commercial scientific-experiment module was lifted into space by Proton in accordance with launch calculations performed by the agency.

This is the first flight of a commercially funded module to the Alpha station. Mission control in the town of Korolev has been instructed to control the Harmony's docking maneuvers in order to achieve a docking on 10th January.

The parameters for the Harmony's predetermined working orbit are 410 by 460 kilometers.

"Your man does not want to fly the mission."

Mark Koskinen opened his eyes in time to see a naked Viktor Kondratko tossing yet another cup of water on the heater. The sauna was filled with the hiss of fresh steam. To Mark it sounded like a horde of snakes preparing to strike, but then, after almost two months on the Russian Front, most sounds still struck him as harbingers of attack. "Viktor Viktorovich, you are full of shit," he said, in Russian. It was one phrase he had mastered.

Viktor laughed, wrapped himself again in his towel, and returned to his seat on the well-worn bench. The first few times Mark visited the sauna here at the cosmonaut gym in Star City, he had been a little awed to think of the heroes of the cosmos whose bare asses had polished this wood. Alexei Leonov, first man to walk in space and Star City's deputy commander, certainly. Vladimir Shatalov, the first Soviet cosmonaut to pull off a successful docking. What about Yuri Gagarin, first human in space? "He died before it was finished," Kondratko had informed him, when Mark first asked the question. "But he had approved the design and was a great enthusiast for saunas as a way to bake the rocket fuel out of the system. So Gagarin's spirit is here."

Talk of Gagarin and rocket fuel led to a discussion of cosmonaut drinking habits. "This was long before my time, of course," Kondratko said, "but my neighbors knew him and his comrades. For example, Gagarin himself came from a world where it was common to have a shot of vodka to start your day. That was how they did things in this little village where his father was a carpenter. He grew up during the famine and terror of the 1930s. When he was a little boy, the Nazis occupied his house." Mark could only imagine. "On a scale where the difficulty of Gagarin's life would be a ten, mine would be perhaps a four." In their earlier time together, training for the STS-100 mission, Mark had learned something of Kondratko's life. Father an officer in the rocket forces, commander of a missile unit in central Russia near Kozelsk. He was killed in an auto accident when Viktor was five. ("I used to tell people he died in a rocket explosion.") Mother worked as an elementary school teacher. ("When my father died, we were trapped in the military village attached to the base.") Young Viktor was smart, physically fit, and ideologically sound ("Only because I had never troubled to ask questions. I was too busy playing football and chasing girls"), which helped him win acceptance into the Soviet air forces at the age of eighteen. ("A civilian university was out of the question. I had good grades, but no connections.")

"And my American degree of difficulty is about zero."

Kondratko had smiled. "Oh, no, my friend. You are what my former instructors in Marxism would have called a member of the bourgeois class. You inherited no money or property to speak of. Like me, you had to pay for higher education by joining the military. You grew up in Iowa, which, from my travels in the USA, is not much more inspiring than Kozelsk. I would rate you at least a one, one and a half."

"You're generous."

"I see things that you do not. Such as . . ."

"Such as Rich McCown not wanting to fly? This afternoon he was in my office packing up a whole bunch of pictures and lesson plans for this classroom-in-space he plans to teach during the mission."

"McCown is an honorable man. I would like to fly with him. He will do everything he is supposed to be doing right to the point where he stops dead. Which will be in about a week."

Over the past couple of months, Mark had gained confidence in his ability to run NASA's Star City office, successfully mediating disputes between astronauts and training personnel, between Americans and the apparatchiks of Star City, between NASA and Tad Mikleszewski's ever-changing personnel and hardware. He wasn't ready to apply for a NASA Distinguished Service Medal, but he believed he knew what was going on.

Yet here was a Russian cosmonaut telling him that a member of the next Alpha expedition crew was on the verge of quitting! Rich McCown was a model astronaut: forty years old, with eight years in the astronaut office and three Shuttle missions to his credit. He was a NASA lifer, a Ph.D. in geophysics who had worked on Mars probes at the Jet Propulsion Laboratory prior to selection. While in college he had taken part in a couple of sea voyages for geoscience research, giving him the perfect operational background for a five-month tour as science officer on Alpha.

Better yet, he was funny, articulate, at ease with the public, a perfect science officer. McCown was also a Mormon, with a pretty, outgoing wife and four children—the youngest born in September, just before Mark's arrival at Star City. All of them lived in a cottage at Star City; there was no chance McCown would "go native," and he had been among the first to volunteer for an ISS mission years back. So what was the matter? "Is he having problems with training?"

In a tradition going back to the Project Mercury days, NASA astronauts were not officially graded or tested during classes or exercises; their performance was judged in more informal ways. At least, that was the practice at the Johnson Space Center.

Russians had different methods. Cosmonauts were not only graded on their work in each training session, but they were tested every few weeks on specific systems. And because the Russians had twenty years of hard-earned experience in preparing human beings for extended stays on orbit, at Star City NASA used their methods: trainers filed reports to Mark and those above him in management.

"He gets more fives than I do," Kondratko said. "On technical grounds, he is completely familiar with the modules. He works well with Jasper and me.

"But he is increasingly moody and critical. He has lost his discipline regarding nutrition." If true, that was a disturbing sign: McCown was famous for eating special meals designed by his wife, and at very regular times. "He's suffering some kind of somatic crisis." Here Kondratko used a word from the lexicon of Russian aerospace medicine that had no real equivalent in English.

"But you have no idea of the reason."

"No." At that point, Kondratko reached for a handful of birch switches. He started whacking his bare back and legs, then indicated he was happy to do the honors for Mark.

"No, thanks." Mark was happy to do as the Russians did, but only to the point where the birch switches came into play. Thinking of physical actions caused his memory to serve up another item about Rich McCown. "Is Rich still limping or favoring his ankle?" During a stay in Houston back in July, the astronaut had broken an ankle making a bad slide in an astronaut office softball game. It had been a complicated break, requiring McCown to use crutches for two months. Both accident and recovery predated Mark's tenure as DOR; Mark hadn't spent enough time in the same room with the astronaut to know whether or not he was still favoring the injury. That was another item for his list of improvements: *get to know the crew members!*

"No. Physically he's in better shape than Weeks or me."

"Well, what would you do if you were me?" he said. "Confront him?"

"No. If you act too early, McCown will either quit, or feel he has to soldier on—with a bad attitude. Worse yet, it will hurt my relationship with Jasper. He'll know I was reporting to you, and that will be the last time he trusts me." Mark did not make the obvious point: that neither McCown nor Jasper Weeks *could* trust him to keep secrets. Then again, as Mark had already learned, the greater good often outweighed an implicit commitment between crew members. Viktor Kondratko was also in the difficult position of being a Russian mission commander over a pair of Americans.

"So I should do nothing."

"For the moment. But thinking about which of the doubles should fly in McCown's place."

That wasn't necessarily an automatic decision: the Expedition 13 crew of Kondratko-McCown-Weeks had a trio of "doubles" or backup crew members: a civilian cosmonaut named Taras Ravshanbek and two NASA astronauts, astronomer John Essington (a fellow member of Mark's 1997 astronaut candidate class) and Commander Charlene Hart, a navy flight surgeon. "You'd like me to assign Charlene, wouldn't you?" Kondratko was a traditional Russian womanizer, and Charlene Hart—while cold and almost asexual in Mark's judgment—was an uncommonly attractive woman.

Kondratko tilted his head, a very Russian gesture. "If offered female companionship for a long voyage, I'd be a fool to say no."

"Too bad she's only trained as a Soyuz researcher." Each pair of prime and backup ISS crews had to contain two Alpha commanders, two Soyuz pilots, and two Soyuz flight engineers in some combination. An Alpha commander could be a Soyuz flight engineer. The Soyuz pilot could also be the Alpha commander.

One member of each crew had minimal Soyuz training, and was qualified only as a "researcher." On the E-13 crew, that was McCown. His counterpart on the E-13 backup crew was Essington, not Hart. "There's too much delta between Essington and Hart," Mark said. "And not enough time to get her qualified as a flight engineer."

"Then give me Essington. Just give me someone who wants to fly."

Who wants to fly. One of the misconceptions about astronauts—when the public thought about them at all these days—was that they were so eager to fly that they would say yes to any assignment. (Come to think of it, it wasn't only the general public who had this mistaken idea—NASA management shared it.)

But Mark knew from his own experience that astronauts frequently turned down flight assignments, and had since the Gemini days. Personal incompatibility was the most frequent reason, though career issues and family pressures also played a role. "Maybe I'll go," he said, jokingly.

"Is that possible?" Viktor thought Mark was serious.

"Not yet. I've been training on my own, mostly on Soyuz. But I'd need another year to be up to speed on the modules. I've never been to Japan or ESA. I'm still earning my way back into Goslin's good graces."

"I could talk to him." Kondratko knew Goslin well, thanks to their shared experience on STS-100.

"Thank you, but the best thing I can do is work hard for the rest of my tour." He slapped Kondratko on the shoulder. "Maybe we can fly together on your next Alpha mission."

Kondratko crossed himself. "Like you, I will concentrate on what's before me."

"Is Rachel Dunne before you?" Mark had noted Kondratko's use of the term "long voyage" when speaking of female companionship. The actress-model–spaceflight participant would only be a short-term answer to Kondratko's needs—in theory.

Kondratko laughed loudly. "Miss Dunne is very beautiful and sexy. I look forward to her visit to Alpha. I look forward to her morning jogs. But Igor will kill me." Igor Gritsov was the relatively young pilot-cosmonaut assigned to command the taxi mission that would take Rachel Dunne and TM to the station. "He has fallen deeply in love with Miss Dunne."

"What does Galina Gritsova think of this?" Galina was the cosmonaut's wife; Mark had met her. She was in her early twenties, a secretary in the Star City headquarters building. Moral questions aside, Lieutenant Colonel Gritsov was going to have a tough time keeping an affair with Rachel Dunne from his wife.

"She knows nothing. And there is truly nothing to know. Igor is in love with Rachel Dunne. So are most of the men working with her. She has favored none of them."

"You sound disappointed."

"I am a practical man, Mark. A famous Hollywood actress can have whomever she wants. It's not likely that she wants me."

"And even less likely that she wants Igor Gritsov."

"I just hope she can handle his attentions without hurting the mission."

"Look at it this way, Vitkor: if she can handle agents, producers, and directors in Hollywood, she can handle your cosmonaut."

It was dark when Mark left the gym—no surprise. January days in Moscow were the shortest Mark had ever known, and he had lived through Iowa winters, where the sun rose around eight A.M. and seemed to set in mid-afternoon.

Kondratko stayed behind to take a swim, so Mark was alone as he picked his way through the treeless birches, heading toward the Orbita Hotel. He looked forward to a light, home-cooked meal, and catching up on e-mails from the United States, especially from his father. (Johanna had bought Glenn Koskinen a laptop computer. To Mark's astonishment, his father had become quite proficient with it, not only sending his own meticulously typed and punctuated letters, forwarding the usual jokes and stories from *Chicken Soup for the Soul,* but also uploading family photos.) Since Mark was still struggling with the Russian language, he might even watch television.

It was a quiet life, but not much quieter than the life he had lived in Las Cruces.

He broke out of the trees within sight of the gate to the residential block, and saw another figure emerging from the woods twenty yards to his left. In the dark, it was hard for him to tell if the short, bundled-up figure was Russian or American. Then he heard a female voice. "Boo."

"Leslie?" She was close enough now. It was indeed Mikleszewki's daughter. Mark had hoped to see her after that first meeting on the Alley of Cosmonauts, but she had returned to the United States on TM's business—or so Rachel Dunne had said. (Not that he'd seen much of the actress, either. But her training was controlled by Star City, and they were rarely in the same place at the same time.) "It's Mark Koskinen," he said, assuming she would not remember him.

"I remember you," she said. "You were the daring young man with the deer-in-headlights look."

Mark laughed. It was undoubtedly true. "Guilty, officer."

"Oh, you weren't the only one. My dad and the actress were pretty wide-eyed that day. I think you had some idea what you were getting into. They didn't. Still don't."

"How long have you been back?"

"Since Sunday."

"Quick trip?" They were now walking together, slowly approaching the gate.

"Alas, no. My father seems to think he needs me by his side."

"You know how fathers are."

"Well, I could tell you stories about this one. Another time."

"Tell me one thing," Mark said: "What's your name? Or is it just 'Leslie'—"

"Like Madonna?"

"That's one option. You might also have three names, like Catherine Zeta-Jones."

She closed her eyes and lowered her head, as if waging the world's quickest debate with herself. Then she smiled. "My name is Leslie Seldes. For three years I was married to a Mr. William Seldes of Beverly Hills, California. To save you the next set of questions, we're amicably divorced, and no, I don't have plans for this evening here in Star City, and, yes, I will have dinner with you."

"How can you stand it?"

"Stand what?"

"Working for NASA. Living in Russia. Either one."

Mark and Leslie were seated in the window of a small restaurant just off the main street of Shchelkovo, a grim industrial suburb less than ten kilometers north of Star City. The name on the door was *Almaz,* Russian for "Diamond." The décor was upscale: subdued lighting, dark wood, white tablecloths, a selection of wines. There was only one other couple in the place. Well, it was a Monday night in January. Snow had started falling even as Mark and Leslie had boarded the train at the Tsiolkovskaya Station near Star City.

He had considered checking out one of the NASA cars and simply driving to Shchelkovo, to the restaurant recommended by Darin Chambliss. At least Russians drove on the same side of the road as they did in the United States. But the weather, his lack of knowledge of the route, and his general fear of Russian traffic forced Mark to propose that they take the train. "How very East Coast," Leslie had said. Before he could feel at all affronted, she had added, "Good. I was afraid you were going to insist on taking a car."

Star City did not have restaurants in the sense that a town of similar size in the United States did: no McDonald's (though there were now a score of the fast food places in the Moscow area), no Denny's, no cozy Mom and Pop diner, no Italian joint that brings in the customers from miles around. There was the Star City canteen. There was a dining room at the Orbita. That was it.

The area around Star City was dotted with villages that were as small, if not smaller: Leonikha, Bakchiavanji, Chkalovskaya. Mark had no hope of finding an eating establishment there. It was Darin Chambliss who reminded him of Shchelkovo, a ten-minute train ride away, and who also recommended the Almaz. "It's like a little bistro. Expensive, especially for Russians, but nice. Just try not to look too closely at the rest of the neighborhood as you walk there. And keep moving."

Chambliss had been right; the Almaz sat on a darkened street of blank gray buildings—not even closed storefronts. Signage in Russia had improved mightily since Mark's first visit to the country in 1998, but only Moscow itself had enough bright lights, billboards, and street signs to make an American feel at home. Shchelkovo still looked like Eastern Europe before the fall of the Berlin Wall: gray, grimy, blank, and crumbling.

Except for the Almaz, and Leslie Seldes sitting across from him in her sweater and necklace, like a graduate student in French history or possibly semiotics, out with one of her teachers on a dare.

"Working for NASA isn't that difficult. I'm a team player. That's what seems to work," Mark said. "But living in Russia? In the winter? I'm not liking it much. I mean, I've always hated the cold. If being an astronaut meant I'd have to move to Alaska, I'd never have applied in the first place."

Leslie laughed.

A waiter who couldn't have been older than eighteen took their order, which Mark feared he would have to give by pointing at the menu. Translating the menu was, in fact, his first challenge, since Mark's knowledge of Russian was still relatively light on the names of foods. He recognized *bifstek,* but hoped for something, anything else. Fortunately, the waiter spoke passable English, and seemed entirely unimpressed by the presence of two Americans here in Shchelkovo. He recommended a dish neither Mark nor Leslie knew, describing it as "stew" while pantomiming its warming effect. With no options, Mark and Leslie went along with his suggestion, adding a bottle of Burgundy.

"Isn't it tough being back at NASA after five years on Spacelifter?"

"I don't really feel as though I'm back at NASA. I was in Houston for about two days before they shipped me here. And working here is a lot like working for Spacelifter—"

"—Except that here you can actually *fly.*"

Mark was surprised by Leslie's apparent disloyalty to her father's concept. "That's a little harsh. True, but harsh."

"I tried to talk my father out of the project from day one. But I was busy getting married, and I must have let that distract me."

"Does your father usually do whatever you tell him?"

She made a face. "Not as often as he used to. It's hell getting older."

"Talk to me in ten years." Mark wasn't sure of Leslie's age—he had only been sure of her *name* for two hours—but knew she had to be under thirty. And he was, as he realized more often, closing in on forty.

Their food arrived, and proved to be satisfying, if not memorable. Mark was too busy debriefing Leslie—not that she needed much prompting. He heard about growing up in Beverly Hills as her father became rich. ("He turned into an asshole. My mother finally left him. I wasn't very nice, either.") About going to school and dropping out. ("My father insisted that I stay out of the Ivies, because he hated what they produced, and sent me to Northwestern. Which I hated. So I managed to get myself thrown out by not attending classes for a semester.") About running away for a year, then hitting bottom. ("I managed *not* to get pregnant and *not* to get beat up and even avoided getting a tattoo. But that was all you could say.")

Then it was back to college, this time at UCLA, then law school. Then marriage ("He was a partner at the same firm I joined as an associate. Smart, huh?"). Then a divorce (no comment) and a newfound yet informal ("I have a real job with the city") association with Tad Mikleszewski and his empire.

The outline of Leslie's life was not shocking, though Mark knew her worlds of Beverly Hills, law, and high finance only from a great distance. What intrigued him was her attitude.

And her voice. Somewhere between the time Leslie dropped out of Northwestern and ran off to Florida, Mark realized he was falling in love with the way her words sounded—smart, funny, fluid.

As for Leslie herself . . . he was enchanted. Pushing forty, of course, he recognized the signs. He had played this game before. But never, he had to admit, with such intensity or velocity.

Maybe it was being in Russia. Maybe it was the growing realization that Kelly was definitely lost to him. Maybe—

"Your turn." She was smiling at him, waiting.

"Where do you want me to start?" Mark said.

"Just skip to the reason why a man as handsome as you is still single. I don't get the gay vibe, so . . ."

He had not planned to discuss his relationship with Allyson, or her shocking death, or the long, torturous emotional ride with Kelly. But he did, enough of it so that the reappearance of the waiter almost shocked him, as did his largely untouched dinner. The cook wanted to go home, the waiter said. "Slow night."

True. The other couple had already departed. So Mark and Leslie went out into the cold, heading for the Shchelkovo station four blocks away. Without making a conscious decision, Mark offered Leslie his arm, and she took it. "I didn't realize NASA employed gentlemen."

"Have you heard otherwise?"

"I've *seen* otherwise."

Mark left it at that. He felt drained, the way he imagined patients did after a session with a psychotherapist. But also happy.

Too happy, perhaps. It wasn't until he and Leslie had gone two blocks that he realized they were being followed from the restaurant.

Mark didn't have to be trained in military special ops or law enforcement to see the problem: there was no one else on the snowy street. A single truck, one of those European models with the high cab and box, passed, drawing his eye, and he saw a figure in black appear from between two buildings, headed toward them.

He was still a block behind them, and the station two blocks distant. "Let's hurry," Mark told Leslie.

"Okay, but—"

"This neighborhood creeps me out." Mark had been warned about the dangers facing Americans on the loose in Russia. Americans had been killed in gang-style murders; even NASA staffers had been beaten and robbed. Mark had taken the information seriously, but added his own discount, since he was not in business or hanging out at nightclubs, or buying controlled substances or sexual services. He was in a small Moscow suburb on a quiet winter night.

He further discounted the threat because he had never been mugged, and never known anyone who had.

But that was in America, at home. Here he could barely communicate with a member of the *militsiya*—the police—much less a robber.

The figure walked faster than they did. When Mark picked up the pace, Leslie glanced back, saw the man, and correctly judged the situation. "Let me know if you want to run," she said.

"It's not going to do us much good if the train is late." Russia's infrastructure was crumbling; its trains were ancient, almost dating back to the days of the tsars, but here in Moscow District, they ran frequently if not always on time.

They reached the platform and found it deserted. Worse yet, no train.

Mark turned. Their pursuer was thirty meters away and closing. "Maybe you should run," he said to Leslie.

"Maybe I should stay right here."

Fine, Mark thought angrily, maybe she's a fifth-degree black belt. He concentrated on the man, impulsively deciding that the aggressive approach was the best one. "What do you want?" he said, his best, most belligerent Russian.

The figure stopped. It was a man of thirty, bareheaded like Mark, and wearing a worn black leather jacket. His hands were in his pockets.

"Don't fuck with me!" Mark snapped. Viktor Kondratko had made sure he was current on Russian profanity.

The man pulled his left hand out of its pocket. In it was a scrap of wine-red cloth. "My scarf," Leslie said.

The man's hand trembled. Mark reached out, took the scarf, and said in his most gentle voice, "I'm sorry. Thank you."

The man laughed. "I cook for you tonight. Restaurant Almaz. *Ya Sergom.*"

That's why they hadn't recognized him. He was the cook, Sergei. "Tell him the meal was excellent," Leslie said. Mark rattled a phrase in Russian, then added one more.

The train arrived at that moment. Sergei waved and got on, moving to the back of the car as Mark and Leslie went to the front. "You added something," Leslie said.

"Yes. After I told Sergei that his meal was excellent, I said, 'I am an American asshole.' "

It was 10:30 P.M. by the time they reached the Orbita. The ride back from Shchelkovo, and the brisk, stumbling walk on the unshoveled pathway from Tsiolkovskaya Station to Star City, had allowed Mark to calm down.

Leslie seemed less bothered. On the train, she had glanced at the meager collection of students, *babushkas*, and couples, all of them carrying worn plastic shopping bags from their day in Moscow, most of these bearing logos from Western stores, and said, "How come Russians don't wear glasses?"

"They don't?"

"Do you see any?"

Mark took inventory. Of the twenty-odd people in the car, only a single elderly woman wore glasses. "Oh, you know the laser surgery they do for eyes in the States?"

"God, yes. One of my first jobs was handling a LASIK lawsuit—"

"They started it in Russia twenty years ago. Only they didn't use lasers." He smiled, relishing the goriness of the image. "They would line patients up and the surgeon would go from one to the other, literally slicing the eyeball to reshape it—"

"God! Remind me not to ask you any more medical questions." But her voice made the admonition into a love song.

The Orbita seemed unusually busy for this time of night. Several Star City staff cars and a minibus were parked out front as Mark and Leslie entered. There was no crowd at the desk, however. "Someone's having a party," Mark guessed.

"And didn't invite us."

Like Mark, Leslie was booked into the "new" wing of the Orbita, one floor below his. "Daddy's right over there," she said, pointing to the room across from hers.

Mark could hear a television playing through the door. "I'll try to keep quiet," he said, as Leslie fit herself into his arms.

"A modest moan of pleasure would be appropriate," she said, as she kissed him. Her lips were cool and soft. Her down jacket was open, and Mark could feel her surprisingly substantial breasts pressing against his chest.

The kiss lingered several moments past the first date point. Lack of oxygen forced them both to break it. "Oh my God," Leslie said, blinking.

"Too much for you?"

She flashed a smile, and punched him in the shoulder. "You wish." She looked at him for another delicious moment, then said, "Were you expecting to sleep with me tonight?"

"I wasn't even expecting to have *dinner* with you."

She laughed. "A true NASA gentleman."

At that moment, Mark knew he *could* sleep with Leslie. She had the room key in her hand. Her posture was inviting.

But there were voices in the hall. Loud voices coming their way. "It's a little late for a parade, isn't it?" Leslie said.

Around the corner appeared Filippov, one of his deputies, and four Asians. Three were pulling suitcases. One of the Asians was desperately trying to translate Russian into Chinese and vice versa, without much success.

"Good evening!" Filippov announced, a bit too loudly. To Mark's knowledge, Filippov didn't drink, but tonight he seemed tipsy. "Mark Koskinen of NASA! Leslie Seldes of America! Meet our new friends from China! They just arrived!"

Filippov rattled off a series of syllables that apparently added up to four Chinese names. Mark clearly heard "Wang" and "Yu," and not much else. Handshakes and bows were exchanged all around. "We have business to discuss tomorrow," Filippov announced. "First I must direct our guests to their rooms."

The parade moved down the hall. The entire encounter could not have taken more than five minutes. But it was sufficient to allow Mark and, he suspected, Leslie, to reconsider their rush to bed. "I am going to say 'good-night, and thank you for a lovely evening,' " Mark said.

"Probably wise," Leslie said, offering a more chaste kiss on the cheek. She opened the door. "Oh, who were those unmasked men? The Chinese, I mean."

"I could be wrong," Mark said, "but I think two of them were Chinese astronauts."

THE CENTRIFUGE

Mark Koskinen was starting to annoy TM.

It had nothing to do with Mark's manner, which had been consistently friendly throughout their three months at Star City. They had had breakfast on several occasions, rehashing the Spacelifter experience, for example. Mark had managed to be honestly critical about Pyrite's (and thus TM's) lack of realistic planning and support without being offensive. To TM's relief, the astronaut seemed to have no desire to somehow latch on to a piece of TM's millions—unlike 98 percent of the people he met.

TM believed his annoyance had nothing to do with Mark's interest in Leslie. Or, more to the point, with Leslie's inexplicable interest in Mark. It was just a feeling that he risked some sort of loss by talking to him. Information, perhaps, or the status that came from being the richest man for miles around. (Rich men had entourages; they weren't accessible to everyone.) Whatever the reason, whenever TM saw Mark approaching, he wanted to run the other way.

This morning, as he left the Orbita headed for the centrifuge building at the training center, Mark happened to be walking out, too, and TM was trapped. Neither Lanny nor Andrei was present; they were supposed to meet him at the center. And he had already zipped up his coat and started crunching through the snow, folder full of graphics under his arm. He could hardly claim he was waiting for his "team."

They exchanged greetings, then Mark said, "So it's the centrifuge today." Mark was copied on all the training schedules, so he obviously knew TM's destination.

"Yes," TM said. "They tell me it's the last phase of medical qualification."

"I wouldn't count on that. You'll be facing tests right up to the time you get wedged into the Soyuz."

"True." TM smiled. "But I can't seem to fail them."

"*True,*" Mark said, gently mocking his tone. "You have universal immunity." He didn't need to further identify this immunity, which was the fee TM was paying. (Another half a million dollars had recently been wired from his accounts to Rosaviakosmos.)

"Which makes me wonder why the Russians even bother with these tests."

"Ask your insurance agent." They were passing from the residential area into the training facility. Both were so familiar to the guards at the gate that they no longer needed to show badges. TM wasn't even sure he carried his. "The Russians are covering their collective asses, in case something happens. I'll guarantee that the day before launch, right around the time you sign the guest book in the hotel at Baikonur, you'll be confronted by a waiver that notes any deviation from their 'norms.' Even if you refuse to sign off, your refusal will indemnify them."

"Probably. The whole subject tires me."

"It's not keeping me awake nights, either."

TM made a left at the main street of the center, heading toward the centrifuge building. So did Mark. "Don't tell me you're going to have a run on the big wheel, too?" TM said.

"Would that shock you?"

"Yes."

"Well, technically, all my medical testing is supposed to be performed in the U.S. by NASA."

"So I hear. It seems kind of funny that astronauts are considered more fragile than spaceflight participants."

"How so?"

"We get tested up to eight Gs, like the Apollo astronauts. But none of you do."

"Well, the orbiter only gives you three Gs at worst. But all the expedition astros have to qualify on the centrifuge, just in case they have to come home on Soyuz."

"And you're not an expedition astro. How fortunate."

"I don't get to fly, I don't get to do EVA training, I don't get any fun." Mark held up a hand, then said, in a quieter voice, "Let me ask you something."

"Okay. But make it quick; it's cold." TM shifted the folder under his arm. He could see Lanny and Andrei stamping their feet in front of the building entrance. Deliverance was within sight.

"What would it take to get you to drop this?"

"Drop what?"

"This flight. Your flight."

"You've got to be kidding me."

"I'm serious. I think you ought to walk away, now. Let one of our folks do your experiments in Harmony."

"Who? McCown? Essington? Or are you bringing Bristol in?" TM made no special effort to pay attention to NASA's constantly changing astronaut assignments, but the rumors regarding the replacement of Rich McCown on the next expedition crew had become so loud and insistent that he couldn't ignore them.

"Everybody on the E-crew is trained to handle scientific equipment. Some more than others, yes. But even Gritsov could run Eridan for you."

"Better than I could, you mean." Mark didn't correct him. "At least you aren't suggesting Rachel Dunne as my replacement."

Now Mark smiled. "I think she'll be busy with her own experiments."

"Yeah. 'Does mascara run in zero-G the way it does on earth?' " TM was angry now. "Why don't you ask her and her movie company to give up their idea? At least *my* flight has a purpose!"

He got so excited he dropped the folder. Pages scattered on the icy pavement. Mark stooped to help him pick them up. "That's the point. Using microgravity for medical processing is the one space-related business someone is going to make money on. Unless it starts to look as though it's more trouble than it's worth."

"Meaning that if I screw up, no one else will want to try? That medical research in space is too important to be left to amateurs?"

"Something like that."

"Oh, bullshit." His momentary anger vanished. Now he was just cold, and even a bit sorry for Mark Koskinen. Perhaps their past association with Spacelifter—however impersonal—had lulled TM into believing that Mark was more imaginative and flexible than the typical NASA astronaut. Apparently he was just another errand boy. "Who told you to do this?"

"Nobody."

"Double bullshit. You're a smart guy; something like this is way too lame for you. It smells like your bosses at JSC."

"I can be lame, believe me."

"Well, tell whoever it was, I'm going. I've bought my ticket and I'm packed. And the next time I have a conversation like this, I'll be telling CNN or Fox News that NASA is throwing its weight around." He headed for the door. Mark kept up with him. "Don't you have somewhere else to be?" he said.

"This is where I'm supposed to be today." Mark opened the door. "I'm taking a run on this thing, too. Besides," he added, "you forgot these."

Mark handed TM several pieces of paper. They were samples of artwork for a mission patch, something every space traveler seemed to require. "It's getting kind of late to be picking graphics, isn't it?"

"We've got a couple of good designs," TM said. "We just haven't settled on a name. You know, like 'Odissea' or—"

"—Or 'Antares' or 'Marco Polo.' " Mark rattled off the mission names selected by past spaceflight participants. He smiled. "How about 'Icarus'?"

TM stared. "Very fucking funny."

TM's turn on the eighteen-meter-long "arm" had to wait: Rachel Dunne was first. "They spent all morning lighting the gondola," Lanny explained, meaning the film crew that had lately been following Rachel Dunne wherever she went.

Rachel herself seemed oblivious to the constant primping (a makeup artist was part of the film entourage). TM was more willing to tolerate the delays caused by the crew on this morning, however; instead of being wrapped in bulky fur coats or baggy flight suits, today Rachel was dressed in a black, skintight uniform that seemed to have come off the rack at the Starship Victoria's Secret. TM had not consciously avoided Rachel up to now; their schedules kept them apart, except during training sessions.

Maybe it was time he changed that.

Of course, Rachel looked a little less inviting when she emerged from the gondola—pale, sweaty, unsteady on her feet. She still wore a smile, but the crew was no longer filming.

TM saw only moments of this. He was busy having his blood pressure taken and sensors taped to his chest. (Had Rachel Dunne worn the same sensor rig? It would certainly have spoiled the look. . . .) The trio of technicians was also at work on Koskinen as well as a European astronaut and the pair of Chinese pilots TM had seen around Star City for the past couple of weeks.

Finally a technician named Sasha, a man in his sixties wearing a white lab coat, said, "We're ready, Dr. Mikleszewski." (One thing TM liked about Russia—perhaps the only thing—was that people pronounced his name correctly.)

Moving carefully, since he trailed several lead wires, TM stepped into the spherical gondola, where he was immediately sickened by the smell of sweat and vomit. Forty years' worth?

He was strapped into a seat reportedly identical to those in a Soyuz command module. Flight couches would be shaped and sized to their users; this was one-size-fails-to-fit-all. There was a rudimentary control panel in front of him, and spherical windows to either side.

Sasha explained the procedure. "You will have three runs. Two Gs, four Gs, then, if things are going well, eight Gs. Each run will be sustained at peak load for two minutes."

"How much time in between?"

"The same."

"No tumbling?" TM knew that in some "advanced" centrifuge tests, the gondola was tumbled end-over-end, forcing the subject to endure a rapid shift from plus-two-Gs to minus-two-Gs. TM used to get sick on a tilt-a-whirl; he never wanted to feel anything like that again.

"You will only experience G-forces through your back."

TM nodded as Sasha handed him a small electronic unit, like a 1950s television remote, but with a single button. "Hold this. When the red light appears on the panel, squeeze it. This shows the operator that you are still conscious."

TM had been briefed on this half a dozen times by now. One of the cosmonauts called it a "deadman switch." "Okay."

Sasha patted him on the shoulder, then climbed out of the gondola. It took a moment for the hatch to be swung into place and dogged down. TM wondered why it was so robust—did subjects try to escape?

"Ready?"

"Ready."

With a groan and a shudder, the gondola began to move.

Tad Mikleszewski liked to tell people he came from a long line of hardheaded Poles. "Look at my name, for Christ's sake. All the other relatives who came over here at the same time changed it to 'Mitchell' or 'Mickleson.' " Like most stories he told, this was only true in a very narrow sense. True, his father, Jan, had gone through three years of naval service in World War II defiantly confusing chief petty officers with the spelling of his name. But the Mikleszewskis—then—

lived in Chicago's Polish community, where the odd *z* never looked out of place.

But, late in life, Jan confessed to TM that he had almost changed it in 1950, shortly after the birth of the son who would be known as "Todd Mitchell." He felt his business—manufacturer's representative for plumbing supplies—was suffering.

"I had married an Italian girl, you see," he said, naming TM's mother, the former Marie Monteleone. "I had to find *some* way to keep my family happy." By then, of course, TM knew it hadn't worked: the Mikleszewski-Monteleone marriage failed in the 1960s, Jan and Marie separating the moment young TM went off to school at Champaign-Urbana.

The fact that the couple had stayed together that long was a testament to stubbornness on both sides, TM felt. It would certainly explain many of his decisions—to major in biochemistry when his grades and background pointed him to business. To take a clerk's job at Eli Lilly in Indianapolis when that hard-won degree would have given him a white-collar position at a different company in a more impressive city.

To leave Lilly after ten years and a series of increasingly promising and lucrative promotions to start his own company in the awful economic climate of the recession of 1981.

To start an affair with Catherine Greer, a married secretary at Lilly, in spite of warnings from several other men at the company that she was unstable. (If nothing else, the resulting scandal made it easier for him to leave the company.)

To walk away from Catherine when she cheated on him repeatedly, taking their daughter, Leslie, with him. To direct his company's research into cures or treatments for herpes and AIDS because of his own fears that his middle-aged sexual frenzy made him vulnerable. (He was forty when he separated from Catherine, a single father, not remotely handsome or charismatic, yet his millions apparently made him movie-star handsome.)

TM knew that his first instincts had proved to be the right ones, no matter how wrong they seemed. And that he would prevail by stubbornly waiting for the rest of the world to recognize that.

His first instinct, in the centrifuge gondola, had been to relax. *Get tense,* he had been told, *and you'll start to see the gray curtain closing in—the approaching blackout.*

So, as the arm swung faster and faster, as he began to feel as though a large animal was sitting on his chest, he stayed relaxed.

Two Gs came and went. Easy.

Four Gs—a little worse. He had trouble moving his arms, though no trouble responding instantly whenever the red light blinked.

Eight Gs—more than he expected to face on a Soyuz launch or reentry. Hard to breathe. The gondola seemed to vibrate, as if it wanted to take off and fly. Red light; squeeze.

Then it was over. For a moment, TM worried that he had blacked out and missed a minute or more. But he still held the deadman switch.

The gondola stopped. It took several minutes to edge it back up to the platform, much as it always took several minutes to disembark from a Ferris wheel.

Sasha unstrapped him and offered a hand. TM found, to his immense pleasure, that he could stand without feeling faint. In fact, if anything he felt twenty pounds lighter.

Koskinen was up next. TM gave him a cheesy thumbs-up as he was led off to have the medical sensors removed. The ESA and Chinese astronauts were being wired up. TM gave each the smug smile of a patient who has already survived his visit to the doctor, and was midway through a pantomimed four-way conversation in as many languages when he heard a muffled siren.

Sasha rushed out of the room, leaving the four test subjects alone. "Something wrong?" one of the Chinese said, in perfect English.

The four of them went out to the hallway just in time to see a gurney being rolled past by another lab-coated tech.

TM managed to get ahead of the other astronauts and followed the gurney into the ready room for the centrifuge gondola.

There he saw a pair of doctors at work on Mark Koskinen, who was unconscious on the floor. TM grabbed Sasha, who was standing by, helpless. "What happened?"

"His heart stopped."

The two Star City doctors had unzipped Mark's flight suit, baring his chest, tearing off medical sensors taped to it, then applying the most ancient set of cardiac paddles TM had ever seen. *Thump!* Rapid-fire Russian from the doctors, as one listened to Mark's chest.

TM could already see that the procedure had worked; Mark spasmed, then began to move an arm.

"Slava Bogu!" Sasha said, crossing himself. "Thank God."

One of the doctors sat back on his heels, overcome at the close call. The other continued to minister to Mark, taking his pulse, speaking to the astronaut, who managed to nod.

There was pounding on the door to the ready room. Someone had closed it on the other astronauts. "Do we open that?" TM asked Sasha.

Sasha spoke to the doctors in Russian, and received a harsh series of *nyet*s, which Sasha translated as "Not this minute."

Mark was conscious now, though still flat on his back.

Sasha and the doctors had continued their conversation in Russian. TM caught very few words: centrifuge, wires. It was too fast. Finally he asserted his authority, telling them to "Slow down," then "shut up." Which they did. "Tell me what happened to Mark," he said. "Did he pass out from the G-loads, or what?"

It took a moment for the question to be made clear to the doctors, and for the answer to be agreed on. "There was a short in one of the leads," Sasha finally said. "He received a very serious shock when he pressed the deadman switch."

"How long was he unconscious?"

More words, shrugs. "Thirty seconds to a minute." That was a long time to starve your brain of oxygen. TM's expression must have communicated the thought, because one of the doctors added, and Sasha translated, "He was not in cardiac arrest that long. We believe his heart stopped when we took him out of the gondola. He must have received a second shock at that point."

TM wanted to believe them, for Mark's sake. But how could you trust people whose medical gear was so primitive? That malfunctioning lead could have been taped to his chest! Would he have come through an electrocution as well as Koskinen?

More muffled thumps on the door. "What do we tell people?" TM said.

"Nothing." The voice was Mark's, weak and wheezing, from the floor.

TM knelt by the astronaut, whose color had returned. "Well, I guess we can rule out serious brain damage, if you're already planning a cover-up."

Mark rose on his elbows. TM helped him sit up. "Shit like this happens all the time," Mark said, then added a similar, shorter phrase in Russian.

"Yes," Sasha said, answering for the others. "We have had such accidents in the past."

"Do we want an investigation that will shut down the centrifuge and suspend medical tests for weeks or months?" Mark offered the question to everyone, helped by Sasha. Now it was TM's turn to read responses by expression: no, no, and no.

"Then we need some kind of story for our colleagues," TM said, hooking a thumb at the door. "They know something happened here." The morality of covering up Mark's electrocution didn't concern TM; that was an issue for Mark and the medical teams at NASA and Star City. TM had no love and small respect for both entities. He just wanted to avoid any delays in his flight.

There was also the bonus of knowing that he now had a weapon to use against Koskinen the next time NASA tried to force him to do anything he didn't want to do.

"Tell them I bumped my head getting out of the gondola," Mark said. He looked around at the doctors, who seemed conditionally willing to accept this. "Shouldn't one of you put a bandage on my forehead?"

RESCUE TRAINING

Of all the horrors and indignities Rachel Dunne had feared during her training at Star City—language lessons, flight simulations in the cramped Soyuz spacecraft, the tilt-table and centrifuge, the Russian "vomit comet" aircraft, sea training in a bobbing descent module on the Black Sea—none worried her as much as winter rescue training. She and two other crew members would be dropped in a remote area with a Soyuz descent module, and left on their own to survive for forty-eight hours.

The location for the test wasn't the Arctic Circle or Siberia, though those had been used in years past, she had been told. No: winter 2006 cosmonaut rescue training would take place in the birch woods perhaps twenty miles north of Star City, somewhere beyond Shchelkovo. She could *walk* back to Star City if she needed to.

It wasn't even the cold or discomfort she faced over the forty-eight hour test. She had done location work for a low-budget film on New Zealand's South Island; she knew what it was like to be cold, wet, and hungry.

No, what frightened Rachel was the thought that she might be left alone with Igor Gritsov.

The schedule called for the whole Taxi-10 crew, Gritsov, Dunne, and TM, to do the training together. But the day of the test she learned that TM was flying back to California for some "urgent" business meeting having nothing to do with his upcoming flight.

Fine for TM, but nowhere near fine for Rachel.

In her years of work in film and television—not to mention her daily existence as a beautiful woman—Rachel Dunne had developed a broad spectrum radar to judge the intensity of male attention.

(There was always *some* male attention, even from gay men.) From their first meeting in a classroom at Star City, Igor Gritsov had pinged the meter, as the astronauts like to say. He had stared at her. He had stammered when talking to her. He had started showing off in training. He had brought her presents of candy and flowers.

All of this quasi-adolescent flirting would have been tolerable—God knew it was familiar territory for Rachel—except that Igor accelerated his efforts to make himself into her "ideal man."

He spoke nothing but English in her presence, and had picked up a number of her catchphrases: "Could have fooled me." "You've got to be kidding." "Yeah yeah yeah." He started wearing "American" clothing, polo shirts and jeans, to the obvious amusement of Grigory Rynin, the backup commander.

More seriously, the young pilot had left his wife, and his two-year-old daughter, moving out of their flat in one of the residence doms and into a Hotel Kosmonavt suite with an engineer cosmonaut from Energiya, who was away from Star City most weekends.

Leslie Seldes told Rachel that such behavior had gotten cosmonauts fired in the past. "All you have to do is complain to Colonel Filippov."

"Then what? Start all over with the next horny Russian they make commander?" The idea that a Russian pilot would treat her like a normal crew member didn't occur to her. She realized she had been slightly unfair to Rynin, the Taxi-10 backup commander, who had treated her with much-appreciated indifference. But Rynin, at age fifty-one, was more settled than the other pilots. And considered to be something of an old fogey doing a thankless job.

Rachel had no female Russian friends—if her reputation as a snooty American actress hadn't been sufficient barrier, the news of the Gritsovs' separation isolated her from the cosmonaut wives and daughters, medical assistants, and secretaries as completely as if she had a giant black *X* painted on her forehead. Even the Americans in the NASA office at Star City were cool. The three female astronauts were usually not present; the support staff seemed to have been warned to keep its distance from the spaceflight participant.

This was especially unfortunate because Rachel's best weapon against unwanted male attention was not resistance, contempt, indifference, or humor (she had tried them all), but redirection. The ideal trick would be to get Igor interested in a Russian woman, but Rachel suspected that the cosmonaut had worked his way through the pool of Star City candidates.

This left Rachel looking at the American women in Star City. But the female astronauts were out of the question, and the women in the support group also seemed to have judged, and dismissed, the cosmonaut.

There was Leslie, of course, but TM's daughter shared her view that Igor Gritsov was, at best, borderline in terms of physical attractiveness ("Those Asian eyes make him look like a Hun") and substantially over the border of strange when it came to deportment.

The *Recoil* film crew, which had the annoying habit of showing up just when Rachel wanted them least, such as that ridiculous day at the centrifuge, was not interested in footage of Rachel Dunne swathed in a bulky snowsuit. The director, Brad Beck, had apparently become entranced with a new special effects process, and was spending all his time at a lab in San Jose. (He had also taken on several "fill-in" directing jobs, and was said to be rewriting the *Recoil* script for the third time. Whatever the reason, he was not in Russia at the moment and hadn't been for weeks.)

In any case, Rachel had not complained. And with Leslie going off with her father, Rachel was completely alone.

She knew exactly how it would go. (It had gone like this before, on two—or was it four?—movie sets.) Igor would be the perfect gentleman for the entire first day, and into the night.

About two in the morning, a time when (Rachel believed) male sexual aggression was at its peak, he would reach for her. In the cramped interior of the descent module—which had as much room as the front seat of a small automobile—he wouldn't have to reach *far*.

And she would not only submit, she would make it memorable, because that was part of being an actress, because she wanted to make the film, and because she had done all this before.

But from that point on, from the first uninvited touch, she would not merely pity Igor and his weakness, she would *hate* him. And the rest of her time at Star City, not to mention the flight to Alpha itself, would be far more difficult than necessary.

She was supposed to go to the administration building to meet the bus that would take her, Igor, and a pair of trainers out to the woods and their "spacecraft." Her orders were to bring nothing—not even a purse or a bag. She would be using the standard Soyuz survival kit for all her personal supplies. (Thank God her period was over.) Walking alone, hands free, through the crunchy snow made her feel like the doomed heroine of a fairy tale. There were wolves in the woods—

And a wolf in the spacecraft.

A short woman in a blue down vest and other winter gear was waiting on the steps when Rachel arrived. "You must be Rachel," she said, in American English. "Charlene Hart." She offered a mitten for Rachel to shake.

"You're one of the astronauts." Rachel knew Hart's name, and little else. She was sure they had never actually met.

"Yeah, backup for E-Thirteen. I haven't been around much. I was home in Houston learning the modules." If nothing else, Hart was cheerful and energetic, especially for this time of the morning. She was pretty in a perky, wholesome way, the kind of woman who gets cast as a soccer mom.

"Why in God's name would you come back? Before the snow melts, I mean."

"Oh, they're going to turn me around on the prime crew for E-Fifteen. Lots of crew shuffling going on. With luck I'll be on Alpha by Thanksgiving."

"Hello, hello!" Igor Gritsov announced his arrival, a smile on his face that froze the moment he saw Hart. "Charlene."

Hart gave the cosmonaut a friendly hug, kissing him on both cheeks, talking to him in what seemed to Rachel like flawless Russian. She took the stocking cap off his head and ruffled his hair. "We did sea training together last summer," Hart told Rachel. "Igor was sicker than shit."

"You had the advantage," Igor said, a bit grumpily. "You were in the navy."

Hart punched him in the shoulder. "I'm *still* in the navy, *tovarishch*."

The bus pulled up then, loud, smoking. Igor excused himself to run back into the admin building. "I wish we'd get this show on the road," Hart said.

"Are you going, too?" Rachel said, confused.

"Yes."

"I would have thought you'd done rescue training a long time ago."

"I did, back in 2004."

"Why on earth would you do it again?"

Hart laughed. "Because my boss told me to look out for you."

"I imagine he's all over you," Charlene Hart announced five hours later, after the "crew" had been delivered to its Soyuz, inserted in the freezing couches with the hatch closed, then told they had "landed."

As instructed, Rachel and Charlene were spreading the orange-and-white parachute to make it more visible against the snow and trees. Igor had taken the survival kit's axe and had moved off to cut firewood, leaving the women alone for the first time since the bus ride.

Rachel was so surprised at Charlene's statement that she almost couldn't answer. "He wants to be."

"Well, if the cold doesn't slow him down, my presence should do the trick."

"Thank you."

"No problem. Koskinen found out that TM was jetting off to Los Angeles, and got me back here from St. Petersburg."

"I didn't know he cared. Actually, I didn't know *anybody* at NASA was paying any attention to my activities."

"You'd be surprised."

Over the next forty hours, Charlene Hart proved to be supremely competent, constantly amusing, and—at least as far as Igor Gritsov was concerned—totally intimidating. It couldn't have been her age, since she was barely forty, or her military rank, which was equal to Igor's, nor her looks, which didn't compare to Rachel's on any scale. "How do you keep him in line?" Rachel finally asked, after much speculation spread over the hours of tedious "survival" work.

"I've flown more than he has," Charlene said. "Not just in space, but in the air. Three Shuttle flights to his one Shuttle flight, and seven hundred hours of cockpit time to his five hundred. With some Russian men—not all—it's all about measurements. Mine," she said, with great satisfaction, "are bigger."

The two-day session ended with no incidents: at night, Charlene didn't even stake out the center seat in the descent module, but took the left-side "flight engineer" seat while Rachel camped out in the one on the right. Igor snoozed between them, the perfect professional.

Rachel's worst injury was chapped skin.

The first thing she did when back in her rooms at Orbita was to set a personal record for long-duration hot bath. Only then did she think about food, and accumulated mail and phone messages.

The mail was disheartening. As a beautiful blond female actress, Rachel was used to receiving great amounts of fan mail, much of it strange, even though the truly odd (or dangerous) was filtered through her agents, managers, or various studios.

She was unprepared for the material that reached her directly through Star City. In addition to the usual requests for autographs (if polite, Rachel had, in the past, been happy to sign), she now received everything from nude photos of herself to proposals of marriage or less formal arrangements, to business offers to death threats! At least, she *thought* some of the material was threatening: half of the correspondence was in languages other than English.

Now she was also faced with photos of the Taxi-10 crew (only one had been taken, weeks ago, but with Photoshop and other software, it was easy for any space fan to create his own team portrait) and various logos or other space-related memorabilia to sign.

Rachel had asked Colonel Filippov to put a hold on the mail, and for weeks she received nothing. Apparently the Star City post office had taken her two-day absence as an invitation to empty its filing cabinets.

She made an attempt to sort it, then simply dumped it all back into the cardboard box it came in.

The Orbita room, with windows that could not be opened, was always too hot or too cold. Most winter nights it was definitely too hot. On this particular night in mid-February, Rachel loved it. She pulled on a pair of panties and socks and sat down to a TV dinner.

No TV.

She was halfway through the meal when there was a knock at her door. She wrapped herself in her fluffy robe, a Christmas gift from her agents that she actually appreciated.

It was TM himself, wearing a white shirt and slacks, looking every inch the millionaire-businessman-at-leisure. He was holding a fax page as well as a heart-shaped box of candy and a bottle of champagne. "New schedule," he said, holding out the paper.

She glanced at it. "Oooh, Soyuz TMA training with Igor first thing in the morning. I won't sleep." TM laughed. "Who gets the rest of the loot?"

"Well, the champagne is for you. Apologies for skipping out on rescue training."

"You'll never know what you missed," she said, glancing at the bottle. Schramsberg, a name she didn't recognize. Not that she knew wine; an ex-boyfriend had tried to educate her, and she had progressed to the point where she could, with great confidence, tell red from white. "Apology accepted."

"This candy is also for you. Valentine's Day is next week."

She had forgotten. "Does this mean we're sweethearts?"

She was rewarded with a look that dropped years from TM's face. "I should be so lucky."

Rachel Dunne was used to performing the multidimensional math of sexual encounters, weighing the lure of physical release against the risk of disease or unacceptable kinkiness, and counting the power to be gained—all in the time it took to raise an eyebrow.

She stepped back to let him into the room. The moment the door closed, she undid the fluffy robe. TM reached for her with gratifying speed.

"What will Leslie think?" she said, looking into his eyes. They were bright blue.

"She is not her father's keeper."

"Could have fooled me." She raised her face to his. After a few moments, she said, "It's been a long time."

"Since you kissed a man with a beard?"

"Since I kissed *anyone.*"

Within minutes they were together in the narrow, hard queen-sized bed, making love with a speed and ferocity that surprised her. Well, given the fact that she had not made love in three months—her longest spell of celibacy in ten years—the ferocity wasn't the surprise.

It was that she *enjoyed* the speed.

Apparently TM was thinking the same thing. "Sorry."

"I'll let you know if you need to apologize." She fumbled for a sheet. The bedroom seemed cold.

"I did feel bad about leaving you alone with Igor."

"NASA arranged for a chaperone."

"I gave Koskinen a big fat hint that you might need one."

"He took it. They sent Charlene Hart."

TM raised himself on an elbow. "I hope you didn't need protection from *her*."

"Arc you saying she's gay?"

"I have no personal knowledge. I can't say I've even heard rumors. She just has—"

"A dykey manner? She's got two kids and a husband. They're not in Star City, but—"

"I shouldn't even have raised it."

She kissed him again, not necessarily because she felt affectionate. It just seemed to be the quickest way to signal TM that additional activity would be welcome. With a few brief stops along the way, she had worked her way down his chest.

"Well," he said, "*that* will raise something entirely different."

"You are one lucky bastard."

"Because I'm here with Rachel Dunne? Believe me, I am completely appreciative. As I hope I'm demonstrating." He had started using his mouth on her, with positive results.

"Because I should be having sex with Mark Koskinen. He was my true savior."

"He's too busy," TM said. "Besides, he has a crush on my daughter."

Rachel found this comment disturbing—another surprise. Was she jealous?

Then her attention was convincingly diverted.

"Really, I feel fine," Mark said, for the fourth time this morning. He looked up at the lights of the Krunichev Space Center's giant assembly bay, noting with approval that all of them seemed to be working.

The first three questions about his health had come from TM. This time the questioner was Leslie Seldes, who stood beside him in the cold, open space. "My father said your *heart* stopped."

"They *think*. You know Russian doctors," he said. "All right, maybe I missed a couple of beats."

"Missing a couple of heartbeats is excitement, my dear. The sort of thing someone like *you* is supposed to feel for someone like *me*. Having to be revived with those electric heart-starting thingees is much more serious, don't you agree?"

"Theoretically." He was only worried about his momentary electrocution to the extent that the story had spread beyond the small circle of witnesses: TM would have told Leslie, obviously. But the Star City doctors and technicians were just as happy as Mark to keep the accident quiet. Mark's run on the centrifuge had not been formally scheduled; there was no official record of the test, and thus no investigation into the faulty sensor harness.

Deceiving NASA, its doctors, and his superiors in the astronaut office troubled Mark only slightly. Reporting his accident would be like calling Steve Goslin and asking to be grounded. He couldn't risk it, not until he had finished his tour in Russia.

Besides, other astronauts routinely covered up or ignored medical problems. He told himself he wouldn't be a real astronaut *unless* he lied to the doctors.

"You're not going to give any ground on this, are you?" Leslie said.

"How was your flight?" Mark said, hoping to change the subject from his recent "spell" on the Star City centrifuge. He was also genuinely interested. Leslie had had to return to the United States for the past two weeks to deal with TM's businesses, returning only this morning. They had not been alone together since the evening of their dinner in Shchelkovo, a situation which aggravated Mark because he was fascinated by Leslie and wanted to spend more time with her. But the lack of opportunity had also been a bit of a relief, because he had realized that he was still thinking about Kelly Gessner.

"Once I got to the airport, it was fine." She lowered the volume of her voice so completely that Mark had to lean closer to hear her words. Not that he minded. "There's a bad outbreak of X-Pox in L.A. All kinds of streets were blocked. It took me two hours to get to the terminal, and that trip usually takes twenty minutes from the office."

"I haven't heard anything about it." Not that he necessarily would: while in Russia, his sources of information were far more limited than they were in the United States. Yes, there was CNN—but CNN would sit on a story like this, if Homeland Security made the request. It almost certainly leaked on the Internet, but Mark's Internet access was either through NASA (very restricted) or a very old, very slow, very unstable Russian provider. "Are many dead?" Mark thought of his map of the United States with its growing pink infections. When had he last updated it? Where, in fact, *was* that map?

"No one seems to know. No one in L.A. even talks about it." She frowned, then made her own attempt to change the subject. "The flight itself was trouble-free." It must have been, Mark realized, because Leslie had, miraculously, been able to rendezvous here at Krunichev with TM's party with minutes of the appointed time.

(Krunichev was a logical place to meet, since it was much closer to Sheremetyevo Airport than Star City.)

Leslie had arrived shortly after TM, his crew, and Mark (representing NASA as an "observer") had completed their briefing on Harmony training in the conference room. When told that Leslie was at reception, TM turned to Mark. "Would you do me a favor and be her escort?"

"Love to."

"If you feel all right, that is." (That had been TM's third reference to Mark's supposed ill health.) "And no fooling around, you two."

Now Mark and Leslie walked across the white floor of the assembly bay. Above and around them were long white sections of giant Proton launch vehicles in various stages of assembly. During his time in Air Force Space Command, Mark had visited the Denver plant where Titan IV launchers were put together, but that facility was laid out more like a classic assembly line.

In contrast, the Protons used the rotisserie method. The cylindrical core of the vehicle was mounted on a structure much like a spit, then rotated as fuel tanks were added to it. Mark counted six of the beasts in different stages of work, from one bare core to one complete and ready to be rolled through the gigantic doors at the far end of the hall, to be put on the train for Baikonur.

The assembly hall was so large that it had room for odd bits of flight or mock-up hardware, from prototype upper stages to a working model of the Harmony laboratory. TM, Lanny, and Andrei, as well as a quartet of instructors, were already at work in and around the module, which sat in a corner of the hall, surrounded by a support structure and ladder. There was also a console equipped with television monitors, allowing the instructors to observe the activity inside the module.

"Why don't they have this thing out at Star City with all the other stuff?" Leslie asked.

"Because Krunichev doesn't want anything to do with Star City."

"Aren't they part of the same space program?"

"Historically, no. Politically, only at the point of a gun."

"Is *anyone* in charge of the Russian space program?"

Mark smiled. "Only theoretically."

"Careful. That sounds like your word of the day."

"Wait 'til you hear tomorrow's word."

She offered an amused snort. They had now arrived at the shiny module. "It still boggles my mind that my father is going to be working in that thing when it's, what, two hundred miles out in space?"

"Two hundred and forty, but who's counting?"

She took his arm. "Mark, tell me he's going to be safe."

He looked her. "Leslie, I'm not going to lie to you: it's *not* safe. Flying in space is like being a coal miner. Do it long enough, and it's going to *kill* you. I lost six colleagues in *Columbia*." Thanks to his exile from Houston, Mark had not known the six NASA astronauts of STS-107 well. None were members of his candidate group. He had never met the Israeli payload specialist at all. Nevertheless, he had attended meetings with them . . . played in softball games against them.

And thanks to a thousand-to-one accident—a piece of insulating foam breaking off the external tank and hitting *Columbia* directly on the leading edge of a wing—they were gone. "We face a one-in-ten chance of being killed in our career. And that's the level of risk a professional faces.

"Your father is a smart guy, but he's a rich smart guy, and rich smart guys tend to believe that the laws of the universe bend as easily as the laws of finance."

Leslie looked at him with a mixture of concern and amusement. "And this insight is based on your extensive knowledge of rich smart guys?"

Ordinarily a challenging comment like that would have triggered an angry response. But Mark liked Leslie too much to lose his temper with her. He also saw her point. "All right. Speaking strictly from my own hands-on experience, my own hard-won knowledge, your father is going into a deadly environment without proper training. It takes NASA, the Russians, the Europeans, and even the damn Chinese at least two years to take an engineer or a pilot and train him to operate a spacecraft. Then you add at least a year for mission-specific tasks. That's just for a routine flight to space, not a space station science mission.

"Your father, who is not a pilot or an engineer or even an experienced lab technician, will have six months of part-time training, most of which has been spent learning a few words and phrases of Russian." Mark pointed at the control station, where he and Leslie could see television images of TM and Lanny inside the module. TM was trying out the Eridan glovebox.

"Is that why you tried to talk him out of the flight? Dad thought NASA was leaning on you."

"Look, NASA has an institutional resistance to tourist flights. If they have to happen at all, the agency would like them postponed for another couple of years, until Alpha is operating with crews of six or seven. But they lost the PR battle years ago, so they don't even raise the subject.

"Besides, your dad made his deal with the Russians. The Multi-Lateral Crews Ops Panel approved him. He's going and NASA will try to make it happen. The objections were all mine."

"Well, on behalf of Pyrite Enterprises and Dr. Mikleszewski, thank you for your concern."

"I might be slightly less concerned if I knew what the hell your dad was working on."

"I don't know." She waited for Mark to challenge her honesty, but he believed her. "It would be proprietary in any case."

"NASA has policies to protect that kind of information—"

"Oh, come on, Mark. Your people can't keep a secret."

"The National Reconnaissance Office would disagree." She had no idea what he was talking about. "Between 1985 and 1992 NASA launched half a dozen secret spy satellites. No leaks."

"Koskinen, you're making me feel bad."

"Sorry." He smiled. "You can feel better by convincing your dad to step aside."

"Let me tell you something about Tad Mikleszewski. He is a man who is convinced he is smarter than everyone else and that his decisions are right more often than everyone else. And, in spite of the way it looks, he does not actually listen to me on important matters. He's happy to have me do his scut work; I'm his daughter, and thus slightly more trustworthy than the usual hired guns. That's it."

"Well, then, since he won't back out, I should be paying close attention to his training."

"Do that. Meanwhile, I'll try not to nod off."

Leslie failed; she was asleep five minutes after getting comfortable in one of the director's chairs set up for the Harmony support team. Mark envied her. With the exceptions of occasional flights in aircraft or the first few EVA sims in water, and possibly maneuvers with a Shuttle or station robot arm, most training for spaceflight was repetitive and tedious. Astronauts and cosmonauts sat in simulators for long hours working step-by-step down checklists, flipping switches, and listening to chatter on the comm loops. The training, of course, was not just for the flight crew members, but also for the flight directors and their teams. It was not designed to be exciting, merely thorough and educational.

By mid-afternoon, TM had spent three hours working his way up and down his checklist, and he was obviously tired. Lanny called a halt to the training, to the general relief of all concerned. (TM did not possess the usual astronaut deference when it came to dealing with hardware and support personnel. Mark had heard more open complaining about equipment from TM in one afternoon than in all his hundreds of previous test hours.)

Leslie was awakened, and the crew dragged themselves back to their Star City minibus for the return trip. Leslie chose a seat next to Mark, and fell asleep on his shoulder, a gesture Mark found charming and, when he caught TM frowning at them in the rearview mirror, troubling. What did the father think about his daughter's new suitor? TM didn't particularly care for Mark, that was clear, but Mark believed the conflict was professional. They didn't *know* each other well enough to truly dislike each other.

For that matter, how well did he and Leslie know each other?

When they arrived back at Star City, it was almost dark. In spite of the March date, the weather was still cold and the ground covered with filthy snow. It reminded Mark of the deepest pit of an Iowa February.

Leslie was fully awake now, even chipper. "That flight couldn't have been very smooth," Mark said, helping her pull her wheeled luggage toward the Orbita.

"Oh, it was fine. I just haven't slept for twenty-some hours. I did watch three movies, including one starring . . ."

She let Mark guess, not that it was a challenge. "Miss Rachel Dunne?" She tapped a finger to her nose, as if he had just made a point in charades. "It must have been *Project All-Star,*" he said, naming the actress's last lead role before signing up with *Recoil* and the Alpha flight. Out of curiosity, and plain old habit, Mark had committed Rachel Dunne's filmography to memory.

"That was the one. Have you seen it?"

"No. I know it's about cloning, that's about all. Does it end with a dozen Rachel Dunnes?"

"You wish."

"She's attractive, but . . ."

"But what?" She stopped and faced him. "You're the handsome, single male astronaut around here. You've got that whole air of tragedy and mystery about you." Mark assumed Leslie was talking about his notorious STS-100 flight. "She's the hot blonde from Hollywood. You two should be all over each other."

"God, now that you mention it, I should give her a call." Leslie slapped him on the arm. "I don't know why I haven't taken a run at her. She's attractive. I think she's even pleasant." He took Leslie's hand. "Maybe I just met someone better."

The moment demanded a kiss. Mark was looking into her eyes, and twenty years of experience with women told him she wanted him to kiss her.

But nothing happened. Leslie dropped his hand, grabbed her bag and started walking.

Mark hurried, catching up with her. "Something I said?"

She kept walking. Finally, as they reached a curb buried under a mound of ploughed snow that forced them to back off and retrace their steps, Leslie came to Mark. She slid her arms under his open jacket and around his back, resting her head on his chest. "Did I ever tell you why my marriage broke up?"

"Did I ever ask?"

"Another woman," she said.

"Sorry to hear that." He stroked her hair.

She pushed back, looking up at him. "You don't hear that right, Mark. *I* was the one with the other woman."

"Oh." It was a reflexive response. Leslie and another woman? "So, then . . ."

"So then, what's the deal with you and me? I've been asking myself that." She rubbed his chest, as if to reassure herself that he was still physically present. "This will sound like something from *Oprah,* but most people aren't all one thing or another. All straight, all gay. It's kind of a spectrum."

"Okay."

"I'm just . . . realizing that I'm more toward the gay end of the spectrum than the straight."

"You don't have to apologize."

"I think I do. I like you. I could very easily fall in love with you." Mark found the idea both pleasing and appalling. "How stupid is this? I'm standing here thinking *this* is the way to, uh, let our relationship progress."

Both of them laughed with nervous relief. "So, you're saying, Miss Seldes, that it would have to be an open relationship."

"Yeah. Both of us can sleep with other women."

"Though not the same women."

"Just not with each other." Suddenly she was serious. "Actually, I guess that was the point of this . . . painful revelation. To explain why we haven't slept together."

"And here I thought it was lack of opportunity."

"You're taking this news suspiciously well." Leslie's voice was still self-mocking, but there was a hint of reproach.

Mark realized, with some embarrassment, that it was deserved: he *was* taking this news too well! He was certainly surprised, but also relieved. "I have a lot of outstanding issues of my own."

"Not in this general area, though."

"No."

It had gotten colder in the last few minutes. Or so it seemed. Leslie seemed to sense it; she shivered visibly. "Aren't we a kooky couple?"

"Can't argue with that," Mark said, wanting to be somewhere else. "Let's get this stuff inside."

Even though it was after seven P.M. in Moscow, Mark stopped by the NASA office to check in. The ten-hour time difference meant that the workday in Houston was just beginning. After the bizarre conversation with Leslie Seldes, he was *grateful* for any kind of distraction.

The first thing Mark did was check his e-mail, where he found a message from Viktor Kondratko, who was in the crew quarters at the Cape, awaiting the launch of the orbiter *Endeavour* carrying his

Expedition 13 crew, which now included Weeks and, as a replacement for Rich McCown, Nate Bristol. That swap had been handled by Steve Goslin with all hands in Houston. "Hello, Mark!" Kondratko wrote. "Tomorrow we take off, if the weather permits. I remember our flight six years ago. You should be here, too."

On this particular evening, Mark would happily have traded places with anybody on the *Endeavour* crew. "As one comrade to another, I have left a package for Miss Dunne with your office. Would you please see that it is delivered, once we have reached orbit?" Mark got up from the computer and looked through the accumulated packages on Chambliss's desk.

This had to be it: a Victoria's Secret package, bought in Houston and pouched to Moscow. Mark laughed. Viktor was, as they used to say in the air force, setting the table for an orbital encounter with Rachel Dunne.

He had just e-mailed best wishes for a successful launch along with a cryptic acknowledgment—"Shipment received and logged"—when his Houston phone rang.

"Koskinen," he said.

"Mark, it's Valerie at Steve Goslin's office." Mark was surprised; he usually talked to Goslin a couple of times a week, but the chief astronaut should be at the Cape helping prepare for tomorrow's launch—"Thank God I found you."

"What is it?"

"You had a call a few minutes ago, from your sister."

Johanna. Dad had died. Mark didn't want to hear the rest. "Did she leave a message?"

"She simply asked you to call her as soon as you could. She's in Iowa."

"I have the number."

"She sounded upset . . ."

Mark found himself telling Valerie about his father's health, and heard a similar story from her, with an equally unhappy ending.

Eventually he tapped out the long string of numbers that would connect him to his parents' kitchen. He paused over the last digit, foolishly hoping that he could somehow change the facts by delaying the connection.

Ultimately he pressed. Listened to the electronic pulses, the hiss of a carrier wave. The ring, ring, ring. His sister's voice, thick with grief. "Hello?"

"It's Mark," he said, feeling himself giving way to sadness and tears. "When did he go?"

"It's not Dad," she said. "He's fine! It's *Mom.*"

In later days, Mark would feel ashamed of the relief he felt on hearing that Johanna's call concerned their mother, not their father. He would try to tell himself it was because his father had been so ill for so long, but he knew the truth: he loved his father more.

His emotional betrayal only lasted a moment. Then he became again the dutiful son. "What happened?"

Carol Koskinen had been trying to carry a chair down the stairs when she stumbled. "She broke a leg, she broke a hip, and they're still monitoring her," Johanna said.

"She's in the hospital, then."

"God, yes."

"Okay, it'll probably take me a couple of days to get there—"

"No, wait." Then Johanna turned to speak off-mike, presumably to their father. "It's Mark." More conversation Mark could not quite hear.

Then: "Dad says to stay where you are. Mom's stable, he's fine. There's no need for you to come all the way from Russia. I'm quoting." From the changes in Johanna's voice as well as in the sound presence, she was walking to a different part of the house.

"Okay, Dad's message received. What about *you*?"

"I can handle things here for a while yet. Lewis has the kids at home. They've still got school."

School? Had he sent the check yet? Dealing with money in Russia was insanely difficult. Paychecks went to Mark's account in Houston by direct deposit, but getting money out and sent around required such old-fashioned techniques as wire transfers or simply stuffing several thousand dollars into your luggage when entering Russia. "I meant your health, kiddo."

Johanna had had a troubling breast examination several weeks ago. "It looks as though I've got cysts, nothing more," she said, then lowered her voice. "Although with Dad and now Mom—you know how God decides to close down a family? Like the Borcherts?" These were neighbors of the Koskinens at the old house. In one six-month period, a grandmother, two uncles, and the father had died, all of different causes. "It's feeling a little like it's our turn."

Mark's belief in God was not strong, certainly not strong enough to allow for the Deity's personal involvement in the day-to-day fortunes of the Koskinens or, for that matter, the poor Borcherts. Yet Johanna's words struck him with almost supernatural force, as if he had just seen Moses draw water from a stone.

Fortunately, Johanna's tone lightened, and with it so did Mark's spiritual dread. "I'm sorry. It's cold, it's dark, and I miss the girls. How are you feeling?"

"Just fine," he said. "Living a life of unprecedented purity."

Johanna laughed, and Mark knew he could never tell her of his near-electrocution.

X-DAY PLUS FOUR DAYS

USOS DAILY SUMMARY
GMT 1574, Friday, 21 April 2006

Alpha Crew,

Good morning, Alpha! Hope you slept as well as circumstances allow. Prep for STS-124 is moving ahead, though rollback is in progress today. (Mission management feels this will make installation of the SAE equipment easier.)

An extra docked day for Taxi-10 is still a possibility; decision to come by end of business today.

Now, as for today . . .

State of the Station

- Reboost—postponed until after Taxi-10 departure
- N2 troubleshooting—will uplink procedures

Today's Plan Comments:

- none

Three-Day Look Ahead:

- Saturday, GMT 1575: VK/NB medical checks
- Sunday, GMT 1576: Rest
- Monday, GMT 1577: Pack for Taxi-10 departure

Today's Mail Sync Times:
- Midday: 1574/1550–1640
- Pre-DPC 1574/2250–2330
- Sleep: 1575/0819–1000

Questions/Answers for the Crew:

Q: Could you check power usage levels on Harmony over the past 24 hours?

A: For Jasper Weeks: yes, you can return your laptop with you on TMA-6.

End of Operational Content

Quote for the Day:

"Failure is not an option."
—Gene Kranz

SANITIZATION AND EXTRACTION

"Good morning, Harmony."

Nate Bristol's voice crackled from the headphones that floated to TM's left. The sound startled him; he had not heard a human voice in eight hours, not since the rest of the Alpha crew had gone to bed—or rather, to use one of those NASA phrases he had grown to loathe, "started its sleep cycle."

If he'd wanted to chat with a live human being, TM could have called to Lanny or one of the Russian operators at Korolev: he had a secure loop that could not be overheard by reporters hanging around the Russian control center. But he hadn't gotten any help from Lanny in two days, and expected none.

Maybe he was just getting testy. Of course, he had now spent four days living alone in a smelly, contaminated module, eating food from a Russian survival kit or Jasper Weeks's personal stash, then crapping into plastic bags and wiping his ass with pages torn from a checklist. Well, his food would run out soon, so crapping would soon be a theoretical activity.

At least Harmony was quiet. Living in the other Alpha modules, especially the Russian Zvezda and Zarya, was like having an apartment next to a Chicago El, without the interruptions. But though Harmony's aluminum shell had been machined years past, the module itself had not been outfitted until after Alpha was on orbit, and the first expedition crews began to suffer hearing loss. So baffles had been added; equipment had been replaced. TM was aware only of the hum of ventilators, and the odd, disturbing creak of Harmony expanding and contracting as it moved from sunlight to dark.

During the first two days of what he chose to call—quite fairly—

his crisis, TM had held on to a schedule, eating, exercising as well as he could, talking to the other crew members, securing the glove-box equipment and updating his processing notes.

But he had not really slept that first night, nor the second, and soon grew bored looking out Harmony's little round window. The only excitement was watching a swirling tropical storm grow as it approached the Florida coast.

By the third day he was completely off schedule, intermittently angry, and determined to take action.

Meanwhile, his fellow crew members were going about their routine business. Rachel Dunne was probably preening for a camera aimed by Igor Gritsov—well, the backup camera, since the primary one was sitting here with TM. Bristol and Weeks were doing their exercises and fixing each day's quota of broken equipment, while Viktor Kondratko no doubt spent most of his time on the loop with Houston or Korolev trying to figure out what the hell they were going to do with Harmony.

TM easily grabbed the headphones and slipped them on as Bristol made his second call. "I'm here." If nothing else, this momentary crisis had taught him to feel at home in space. True, his hands and feet still felt cold and his head continued to feel stuffed up. But his head had been stuffed up during five months in Russia; here he still found childish pleasure in propelling himself the entire length of the module with only a finger. He was now completely used to the idea of setting a checklist or his glasses or the headset afloat, within reach, as if he had been doing so all his life.

"Up early, I see."

"Yeah. I could smell bacon and eggs."

Bristol laughed nervously. "Not from here, I hope."

"Why?" he snapped. "Worried about a leak?"

"That's not what I meant," Bristol said. He managed to sound wounded, then compounded his error by adding, "We're still working off our usual menus."

"You're breaking my heart, Nate. I can't seem to access the menu."

The line was silent. Then: "Can I start over?"

"Sure, Nate. You said 'Good morning,' and I said, 'Good morning, how are you guys?' How are we doing so far?"

"Better. Uh, we're fine here. Rachel and Viktor are going to be doing their last day of filming. Jasper and Igor are checking out the Soyuz. I'm talking to you."

"Baby-sitter, huh? Wait, NASA probably has a name for it. 'Confined Crew member Diversionary Support. CCDS.' "

Bristol laughed. "Glad to see you're holding on to your sense of humor."

"It's just one big party in here."

"Speaking of parties," Bristol said, before pausing. TM could easily imagine Bristol's face as he carefully rehearsed every phrase he was about to say, knowing that TM would pounce—as he had twice already this morning—on any deviation from the correct tone. TM suspected that Kondratko was not off "filming," but floating right next to Bristol, watching and Listening. "Uh, we've noted a high drain on the power flow to Harmony . . . what do you have running in there?"

"Well, there's the foot massager, then there's the microwave oven, the blender and the television. What do you mean, Nate?"

TM heard a rustling on the comm, followed by the stern voice of Viktor Kondratko. "TM, it's Viktor. Are you running the glovebox?"

"Yes."

"Even though you were supposed to shut it down?"

"I shut it down, Viktor. Three days ago." He floated close to the clear cabinet. In the containerless processing unit, a blob of gray goo was being spun by sound waves. "But I started it up again last night."

"It's not safe!"

"I'm already swimming in X-Pox here, Viktor. I can't make this place any *less* safe." It wasn't funny, but he wanted to smile. "I did put some gaffer's tape on the tear in the glove. I taped some cardboard over that crack, too. So I'm not making things worse."

"You don't know that."

"You know, Viktor, fuck you. You guys have had three days to come up with a plan—"

"—We are!"

"Well, great, but you sure as shit haven't told me! So I am doing whatever I can to save myself. I'm finishing the work I came here to do. I'm making a goddamn vaccine."

The line was silent again, though TM heard Viktor and Bristol arguing. Finally Kondratko spoke: "You're right. This is my fault. Here is the plan."

And for the next ten minutes, he laid out a perfectly rational series of steps, beginning with the departure of Soyuz TMA-6 the day after tomorrow. "Igor is going to take Rachel and Jasper back with him. It was decided that the station should not have more crew members than it has seats in a rescue vehicle. You should find that encouraging," Viktor had added, unnecessarily.

The Shuttle *Discovery* was to be launched late next week with a crew of four, who would dock with Alpha and begin a planned three-day "sanitization and extraction," in Viktor's words. "As a result of the SAE, you will be transferred to a special chamber on *Discovery* and returned to Earth."

It sounded good, in Viktor's presentation. But during his long, semisleepless nights, TM had also been looking out Harmony's window. "What about this hurricane off the coast of Florida?"

Another pause as Kondratko and Bristol conferred. "Good point," Bristol said. "*Discovery*'s on the pad. If they have to roll it back to shelter, it's going to cost them two weeks."

"By which time I could be symptomatic."

"There is a backup plan, TM," Viktor said. "A second set of SAE hardware has been delivered to Baikonur. It can be launched within that two-week period aboard Soyuz TMA-Eight—if it appears necessary."

"What determines necessity?" TM said, allowing himself, for the first time in four days, to believe that his crisis might have a happy ending.

"Well, the next item on our agenda is asking you how you feel. As long as you're asymptomatic, the countdown clock doesn't start ticking. You might get hungry, but—"

"I'm already hungry, Nate."

"We're sorry about that. But you realize you have more air and water than you need. A human being can survive quite a while on reduced caloric intake."

"I get it. I'm on a diet."

"If you can hang on for ten days or so—"

TM laughed. "A few years ago, back in Los Angeles, there was a guy who wanted to stop developers from cutting down some old oak tree for a highway. He climbed up in that tree and lived there for seventy-four days, I think. I can hang on, Nate. Really."

"Then quit fucking around with X-Pox or that vaccine," Viktor said, regaining the voice of command. "You will only make the cleanup more difficult."

TM looked at the glovebox. "Okay. Give me a minute to save and close up here."

TM powered through the morning with renewed energy and commitment, caching the latest attempt at a vaccine and transferring it to the safety cabinet. He even reestablished contact with Lanny, who seemed pleased to hear from him. "We were getting worried."

"Come on, you could have talked to the rest of the crew."

"We did. *They* were getting worried, too."

He learned that his "situation" was a major news story, driving the African famine, Florida storm warnings, and an American military strike against Yemen out of the top spot. TM was flattered, then horrified. "This can't be good for our stock," he joked.

"Actually," Lanny said, "it's been great. Analysts are saying you risked your life to come up with an X-Pox vaccine."

TM knew better than to correct Lanny over a comm loop, even one that was supposed to be secure. Besides, he *might* have a vaccine here on Harmony. Certainly he had one that had been processed more smoothly than anything yet manufactured on Earth. Over the next week or two weeks, he might be able to make real progress there.

He asked if Lanny had heard about the various contingency plans. "Oh, yeah. There was something on CNN last night about the Shuttle crew that's coming to get you. The only hang-up is the weather—"

"I just looked down at Florida," TM said. "That storm is heading right for Orlando."

"Well, the Russians say they are standing by to launch a Soyuz."

Something in Lanny's voice troubled TM. "What are you hearing around Korolev?" The Russian mission control center was staffed by employees of the Energiya organization, which designed and oversaw the construction of each Soyuz spacecraft. Located literally across the street from Energiya's headquarters, it was a great place to pick up gossip—or real information as opposed to the "pravda" put out by Rosaviakosmos to keep NASA happy.

"Just that the integration on TMA-Eight may not be as advanced as they're saying."

"There's a surprise." TM knew that the Russian space program was a loose collection of different types of organizations, each with its own institutional agenda. None of them wanted to bring ants to the picnic. "How far away?"

"Three months."

"Jesus." TM had expected a discrepancy of a week or two. It was easy to see how it would happen. The team integrating Soyuz at Baikonur, knowing the spacecraft would not be ready for launch until August 1, told Energiya that July 1 was possible, if enough money started to flow and crews could work double or triple shifts. (They had in the past.)

Energiya's managers, applying the fudge factor they had used for years, told Rosaviakosmos that June 1 was the ready date.

When the Harmony crisis occurred and NASA called looking for help, Rosaviakosmos figured—rightly—that a little extra cash would cut a month off that launch date.

But not *three* months.

"Well, hell," TM said, sounding perkier than he felt, "even if the orbiter has weather problems, it should be up here in a couple of weeks at the outside."

"Yeah, you don't want to come home in a Soyuz," Lanny said. "Shuttle's the way to go." This was still the feeling, in spite of the *Columbia* tragedy. Astronauts returning to Earth in the orbiter rode through a maximum of three Gs in airline-style seats in a vehicle that touched down like a faster DC-9.

Soyuz crew members were jammed into couches with their knees forced toward their chins, then subjected to six Gs through a fiery reentry, before free-falling in terror while waiting for the parachute to open. Once that opened, the momentary relief would give way to nausea as the descent module began to spin and wobble. (The access hatch on the nose of the module meant that the parachute had to be attached off-center.) Finally, you had to hope the solid-fueled descent rockets lit one second prior to hitting the ground, or you were going to hit the ground hard. Then the whole spacecraft would tip over on its side, so you could hang in the straps while waiting for rescuers to arrive.

TM clicked off and resumed his routine: exercising, eating, making notes on his work. He decided to give himself a sponge bath, even though the available water was cool if not cold, and soap and towels nonexistent.

He stripped off his blue polo shirt for the first time in three days, and then forgot all about a bath.

There was a rash on his chest.

Harmony had no mirror, but a reflective surface wasn't hard to find. He flew toward the smooth, silvery facing of the bioreactor.

The rash was on his neck and his face.

He had X-Pox.

ROLLBACK

"It's almost locked up, Les."

Kelly Gessner clicked off the cell phone, which she was using in violation of hospital rules, and turned toward the bed where Les Fehrenkamp sat up. "Good," he said, looking pale and thin.

Not that Kelly looked much healthier. In spite of her raincoat, she had gotten soaked on her way into the hospital. Her hair, overdue for a preflight trimming, was lank and wet, dripping on the smooth tile floor of the hospital room. She was also cold and tired. Maybe that was why she also felt a nagging sense of dread, as if she had forgotten to perform some important task.

Fehrenkamp calmly rubbed the condensation off the window near his bed, trying to improve visibility. "I can't see a thing from here."

They were on the east side of the three-story community hospital, looking in the general direction of the Vehicle Assembly Building at the Kennedy Space Center. On a clear day you could have seen the white and black bulk of the VAB, even from a distance of twenty miles. But not today: with low clouds and rain squalls, you were lucky to see the trees bordering the hospital's parking lot.

Assuming you could keep the window clear.

Kelly had reported to Les on the status of the Shuttle *Discovery* stack, which was being rolled back to the Vehicle Assembly Building on a massive crawler-transporter at its top speed of one mile per hour.

Wayne Shelton was at the VAB, giving her the play-by-play. It was the only conversation they had had since Kelly's arrival at the Cape. She was trying not to be angry about it, since she had a space rescue mission to train for. And apologies to make to her younger brother, Gerard, who had wanted to attend the launch and now, with the uncertainty of dates, couldn't.

The crawler-transporter had needed every inch per minute of its speed today, since NASA had been slow to make the decision to shelter the ten-million-pound stack. In fairness to the director of KSC, and to Fehrenkamp, Kelly knew that the air force weather forecasters had predicted that Tropical Storm Allie would miss the area to the north.

But late last night the storm had turned, and the crawler crews went into action. Fortunately for everyone, Allie's leading edge tended to switch between wind and pouring rain: a combined high wind and rain might have resulted in damage to the delicate silicate tiles on *Discovery*'s exposed surfaces, increasing the potential launch delay from two weeks to months.

And dooming Tad Mikleszewski.

Kelly had driven over to Titusville in order to brief Fehrenkamp in person. It had been Brad Latham's suggestion, on the grounds that it never hurt to offer respect to a powerful man. She had agreed, for that unstated reason, and because she wanted to judge Fehrenkamp's condition for herself.

The news of his accident had shocked the STS-124 crew and their support team. All of them had finally begun to believe that Fehrenkamp was no longer a threat to them, when they learned that the dark lord of NASA had been put in charge of the Tango Midnight rescue op. Then, as soon as they had resigned themselves to his presence, he was banged up in a crash. Broken collarbone (his right arm was in a cast from fingers to neck), punctured lung, and assorted lesser injuries, all sufficient to take Fehrenkamp out of the loop.

Or so people said. Brad Latham, with the skepticism of a professional pilot, wanted reliable eyes aimed at Fehrenkamp—preferably Kelly's.

They were, and what they saw was a man in his sixties who had trouble breathing, much less operating his shadowy empire within the space agency.

"What are they saying about Allie's ultimate strength?" Fehrenkamp asked, another sign of weakness.

"Force four, no doubt. Maybe five," Kelly said, remembering this morning's air force weather briefing.

"That's not a tropical storm, that's a hurricane."

"She may have been upgraded already."

Fehrenkamp closed his eyes. Kelly suspected that he was medicated. Certainly he was not actively working Shuttle matters: there was no assistant present, no pile of faxes and pink message slips, none of the litter of management. "I think we can still launch in fourteen days," he said, just when Kelly feared he had fallen asleep.

"Hopefully, we'll still be in time."

Fehrenkamp opened his eyes and raised his head. "What have you heard?"

"Me? All I hear is what *you* tell me, Les. I'm an astronaut, remember. A puppet?" She smiled to dull the edge of the remark.

"That's right, I keep forgetting." He returned the smile, for the same reason. "But I'm on the disabled list. So . . ."

Kelly said, "Mikleszewski had gone to ground for a couple of days, understandably. Kondratko told Houston this morning that he was bouncing back—but now, nothing. He's not even answering the phone."

"What do *you* think that means?" Fehrenkamp didn't wait for Kelly's opinion, because the answer presented itself. "Oh, God. He's sick." He cleared his throat. "Which really, truly puts a clock on us."

"Yes."

"Then, if we want to save him, we need to have the SAE package on board today, and be heading back to the pad tomorrow."

"I don't see that happening," Kelly said. It would take a minimum of three days to get *Discovery* headed back to its pad.

"Then we can shorten the countdown. And with a lighter payload, we can make a quicker rendezvous with Alpha."

"The old Gemini M-equals-one?" Kelly said, referring to the classic (and fuel-intensive) maneuver from the 1960s, when Gemini 11 made rendezvous—M—with an Agena upper stage within ninety minutes of launch, on orbit number one.

Fehrenkamp laughed off the example. "Only with no payload and no crew, and thus of no use. But we can cut the chase in half, or better. Maybe M-equals-four orbits."

Kelly felt thrilled at the thought. *It would be an exciting seven hours.* "How ready are the Russians?"

"That's still an open question. I'm cautiously optimistic."

The window rattled as the storm gusted. Kelly desperately wanted to get back to the Cape, but hesitated. Personal time with the Wicked Witch was still a rarity.

"Even if the Russia option is what we chose, *Discovery*'s still going to launch with your crew to do a thorough cleanup on Harmony. Management will also want one of you five to stay aboard Alpha, replacing Jasper Weeks."

"For how long?"

"Undecided. It could be the whole increment."

Spend four months with Nate Bristol and Viktor Kondratko? Kelly admired Bristol's doggedness—the man worried problems to death—and found the Russian's "hussar" act amusing, but both in small doses.

But an astronaut who said no to a flight was violating the prime directive. "I'll do it," she said.

"I leave that to you and Goslin."

As Kelly waited by the elevator, she saw that both cars were stuck on the second floor. After five minutes of waiting, she elected to take the stairs. She was an astronaut, after all: she should have taken the stairs in the first place.

But the door was locked. "Hey," she said to the nurse at the desk, a tired-looking African-American woman. "How am I supposed to get out of here?"

"Oh, you can't," the nurse said. "Not for the next fifteen minutes."

"Any reason why?"

"Second floor." Kelly's face must have shown her confusion. "The X-Pox cases. They're moving new ones in, so we're isolated up here."

X-Pox. Kelly was sometimes appalled at how infrequently she thought about the crisis—especially since she was going to be dealing with the virus in space. But why obsess? People were exposed; a high percentage contracted it; a frightening percentage of those died.

You took precautions. Avoided potentially infectious people or situations, or wore the mask when contact was inescapable.

Kelly had been in high school when everyone, it seemed, started talking about AIDS. She was not yet sexually active, so she had escaped the immediate fear that she might have been exposed to the deadly disease.

It loomed over her college days, however, and her life as a single woman. For years, she never went on a date without taking protection; in fact, for a couple of years she rarely went on dates, simply to avoid the whole problem.

But that fear had diminished over the years, as the shock wore off, as new drugs began to prolong lives. Kelly's generation grew numb to AIDS.

Then came 9-11 and soon after, bioterror. Maybe it was a function of age: she was already numb to X-Pox. "Uh, how many do you have here?"

"Usually about a dozen," the nurse said. "Once they come in, it's two, three weeks at most. Ten will die, one will recover okay. One will live with scars. It's nasty."

Kelly had never truly known the odds against recovery. Awful. "And no vaccine."

"You got one? I don't. They've been trying. Nothing seems to work well."

The bell over the elevator dinged. "Make your break while you can," the nurse said.

When Kelly arrived at the crew quarters lounge, Brad Latham was pacing, talking on his cell phone, as Ames waited. While Latham, the commander, practically twitched with obvious nerves, Ames was so laid back he seemed sleepy.

"Where's Diana?"

"She wanted to check something in Processing," Ames said.

"Why? Our payload's on the orbiter."

Ames shrugged. "One of the C-squares called, that's all I know."

C-squares? That team included Wayne. Kelly's sense of dread sharpened. Why hadn't he called *her*? "What are we supposed to be doing?"

"If it were up to me," Ames said, "I'd be filling sandbags. The levee's breaking." The STS-124 pilot was from New Orleans.

"There isn't much else to do," Kelly said. "I suppose we had to get down here, because nothing's flying in this weather. But the hardware's on the pad, and I'm about simmed out."

"I'm waiting for the eye," Ames said. Kelly wondered what he meant. The pilot was noted for a dry, offbeat sense of humor that was, in Kelly's opinion, going to make his life difficult as he rose higher in the space agency.

"What the *hell* are you talking about?" Latham said, just off the phone. He had a full-blown case of prelaunch jitters, the same tension that Kelly had seen in all three of her earlier commanders. Who could blame them? Even the most confident pilot eventually faced the staggering truth that he was responsible not only for the lives of his crew, but for an irreplaceable two-billion-dollar vehicle as well. It wasn't lack of faith in their own abilities; by this point in their careers, Shuttle commanders had flown at least two previous missions and had gone through thousands of hours of simulations. They knew their jobs.

It was the unknown factors, the cold weather, the cracked flow liners, the tanking error, the chunk of foam, the mystery design flaw that terrified them.

Ames, who should have known better, pressed forward rather than changing the subject. “Remember that movie, *Marooned*?” Kelly knew it, but chose not to get in the middle of what could easily become an argument. “Come on, Brad, it was about a Skylab crew stranded in orbit. The Russians are going to rescue them, but they don’t get there.”

Now Latham was staring with open hostility, the cold-eyed “Barracuda” of his call sign. “Your point, Hose?”

Kelly realized the moment required a softer touch. She leaned toward Latham, touched his arm, and said, “The Cape was threatened by a hurricane. So they wound up launching a rescue vehicle *through the eye of the storm.*” She tried hard to do an imitation of Rachel Dunne at her girliest.

Latham grunted. “That’s crazy, even if you had the bird on the pad. The RTLS options . . .” Latham realized that the others were staring at him, barely able to keep from laughing. He finally got the joke. “Time for the commander to hit the gym—”

“—Or switch to decaf,” Ames said.

Latham stood and stretched. “I need to be doing something other than sitting on my ass, that’s for sure.”

Ames said he was going to brave the storm and drive down to the weather office at Patrick Air Force Base and see a buddy who was working with the Forty-fifth Space Wing.

“I’m going to find our MS-Two,” Kelly announced, meaning Diana Herron. “Maybe we can have a pillow fight or get our nails done while we wait for blue sky.”

She was only half-kidding. Kelly got along well with men, always had, but there were times, like now, when she just couldn’t stand the thought of being around them.

Even a tomboy like Diana Herron would be an improvement.

The rain and wind had let up a bit as Kelly got out of Ames's car in the VAB parking lot, but it was still coming down worse than the typical Houston storm. And those would soak you in thirty seconds. "Run!" the pilot ordered. She needed no encouragement, splashing through the puddles toward the entrance.

She spent the next twenty minutes wandering through the cavernous VAB and the many offices and shops in search of familiar faces.

She also signed a few autographs. The United Space Alliance and other contract workers at the VAB had launched more than a hundred and twenty Shuttles going back to 1981. The teams had met three times as many astronauts, yet in Kelly's experience, they never became blasé. Almost everyone she saw wore a jacket or polo shirt with the STS-124 mission patch (which the crew had not had time to alter: it still showed the truss segment Kelly and Diana were to have installed on Alpha). Those she spoke to were uniformly encouraging about the weather and the prospects for rescuing "the rich guy."

Her sweep through the VAB was a sobering reminder of the gigantic effort involved in manned spaceflight. For every one of the dozen techs she saw here, there were a hundred others. It was said that it took a workforce of thirty thousand people to maintain and operate the three-orbiter fleet. Was it too many? When would NASA or USA, the giant partnership that operated the Shuttle for the agency, evolve toward more efficient airline-style ops?

It was that very question that had brought Tad Mikleszewski into the space business in the first place.

Kelly often wondered herself. But then she looked at the complexity of maintaining a vehicle that flew into orbit, that used almost no "off the shelf" technology, and was happy that there were thirty thousand people on the job. After all, she was riding the beast.

She finally located Jerry Juin, a European astronaut who was a member of the six-person Cape Crusader team. Juin was carrying a bunny suit and heading toward the elevator up the *Discovery* gantry. "Going inside?" she said.

"Yes. We have lots of boxes to put aboard. It will be easier here than on the pad."

"I bet." She looked up at the orbiter, where one payload bay door had already been cranked open and braced. "Have you seen Wayne?"

"He is here, somewhere." He made a vaguely Gallic gesture that could have meant inside the VAB, outside the VAB, or possibly just somewhere else in Florida.

"Thanks," Kelly said, not really meaning it. She decided to call off the search for Wayne. With chaos caused by the weather and rollback, he could be anywhere at the Cape right now.

She clutched her keys and steeled herself for a run to the car she and Diana Herron shared, out in the lot. After a few minutes, the rain only came down harder.

So she bolted.

As she reached the Ford, she saw, strangely, that the windows were fogged. Was it her imagination, or was the car *moving*?

She unlocked the door. "Kelly," Wayne said, immediately running out of words.

Diana Herron was with him. Neither was wearing pants. "Excuse me," Kelly said, as savagely as she could.

She threw the keys deep into the lot, turned and walked off in the pouring rain.

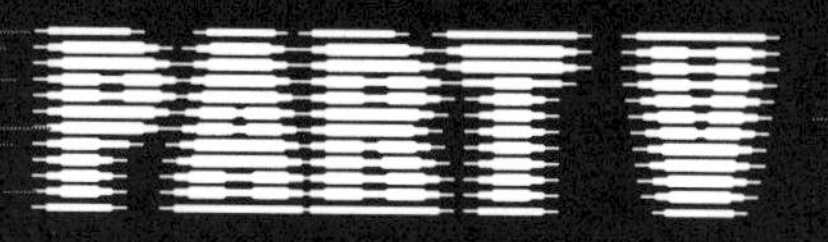

X-Minus One Month
(March 2006)

ENDLESS FRONTIER ASSOCIATION
1757 Gayley Avenue
Los Angeles, CA

For Immediate Release, March 9, 2006

TWO PRIVATELY BACKED SPACEFLIGHTS SET FOR LAUNCH APRIL 8

Two privately financed manned spaceflights, one to perform commercial biochemical research, the other to film a major Hollywood motion picture, have been officially scheduled for launch on Friday, April 8, 2006, according to the Endless Frontier Association.

"Actress Rachel Dunne and entrepreneur Tad Mikleszewski are proving again that manned spaceflight is no longer restricted to a small group of government-approved professionals," EFA President Ian Sedgwick said.

EFA facilitated the Dunne and Mikleszewski agreements with Rosaviakosmos, the Russian Air and Space Agency.

Dunne and Mikleszewski are to be presented to the Interagency Commission in Moscow today, along with their Soyuz TMA-7 commander, cosmonaut Igor Gritsov.

STATE EXAMINATIONS

"The Cosmonaut Training Center nominates as commander of Soyuz TMA-Seven, Lieutenant Colonel Igor Vasilyevich Gritsov."

Mark Koskinen sat, arms folded, trying to stay awake as Yevgeny Ovsyannikov, the director of Star City, made the formal announcement of the prime crew for the upcoming mission. Mark's chair was too comfortable, the conference room was too large and too well-heated. He had no official function to perform. Thus the fatigue.

All around him were representatives of half a dozen Russian space organizations—not only Star City, but the Institute for Medical-Biological Problems, the Energiya Corporation, Krunichev Space Center, and several from something called the Center for Biological Machine-Building, which provided the Eridan glovebox and other lab gear for Tango and the Harmony module. Mark knew without asking that this center was a former bioweapons lab. The fact didn't especially disturb him: *every* other organization here today had a history as part of the Soviet weapons complex.

Rachel Dunne's presence had tripled the number of journalists—at least when compared to those who showed up for the Expedition 13 examinations. Mark recognized the handful of Russians who covered space matters for American and European publications. The others looked—and acted—like paparazzi.

The occasion was the final State Examination session for the first and second crews for Soyuz TMA-7, now scheduled for launch in ten days. It was, by and large, a formality, though undoubtedly stressful for the five space travelers involved. One by one, each had been led to different offices in the headquarters building, to face a panel of questioners.

Mark knew that already, of course, but in case he didn't, Rosaviakosmos's increasingly efficient press office had provided the attendees with a brochure for Soyuz TMA-7, also known as ISS Alpha visiting mission 10. A colorful mission patch—a NASA tradition adopted by the Russians—decorated the cover. Inside were color portraits of the crew members, biographies, and ten pages of data on the various experiments to be performed.

Not one word, of course, on *what,* specifically, spaceflight participant Tad Mikleszewski, aka Tango Midnight, planned to produce during his work with "Experiment Pyrite A."

None of the journalists present seemed interested in finding out. Even those on the space beat were busy ogling the set of glossy photographs of Rachel Dunne in *Recoil* costume that had also been included in the brochure. Mark didn't expect to hear informative answers from today's presentation, but it would have been refreshing to hear *some* mission-related questions.

Ovsyannikov continued with his presentation, introducing "Spaceflight participant number one, Tad Mikleszewski"—Tango Midnight himself, sleek in a dark business suit, his beard trimmed, fifteen pounds lighter than the day he arrived at Star City—and "Spaceflight participant number two, Rachel Dunne"—who looked demure in a dark blue skirt and jacket, wearing a blouse with a Peter Pan collar. Or so it seemed; Mark's knowledge of feminine attire started with bustier and ended somewhere around black cocktail dress. It was only the fabled Koskinen memory that recovered "Peter Pan collar" from deep storage. His sister, Johanna, had undoubtedly mentioned it once.

The second crew—Colonel Rynin and flight engineer Karpov—were introduced. They smiled gamely for the crowd, comforted by the knowledge that they would surely rotate to the next taxi mission.

The head of Rosaviakosmos got to his feet at that point—a bit of a trick, given his bulk—and spoke for an uncertain amount of time (uncertain because Mark did doze off), summarizing the results of the exams. Rachel Dunne had actually outperformed not only Tango but professional cosmonaut Gritsov in at least one category—knowledge of emergency survival techniques.

Or so Mark thought. He might have dreamed it.

Mercifully, the ceremony ended. Stifling a yawn, Mark approached Tango and Rachel to offer his congratulations. The actress actually hugged him and seemed genuinely pleased to receive congratulations from a friendly American. (Mark had only spotted half a dozen other Americans at the presentation, and all of them were downtown types whom Rachel wouldn't know.) Then she was swept away by a sea of Russian space people, each one wanting to have his picture taken with her.

Mark turned toward Tango, but collided with a swarm of men under the guidance of Colonel Filippov. It was the two Chinese astronauts, Wang and Yu, with their handlers. Mark had seen them exactly twice since the brief meeting in the hallway of the Orbita Hotel. Once at the centrifuge building, once at the old Soyuz simulator. They were always together, the four of them.

"Dr. Mikleszewski," Filippov said, in Russian, "Our Chinese colleagues wish to offer their congratulations."

All of the Chinese were Mark's height. The stockiest of the group—Colonel Wang, a crew member on the first Shenzhou flight—stepped forward and, in passable Russian, wished Tango a successful launch on behalf of the Chinese *yuangyuan* team. Tango uttered some phrases in his wobbly Russian. Happy to be the genial host, Filippov made grammatical corrections to both speakers.

The second astronaut, Major Yu, thin and wiry like a gymnast, looked sideways at Mark and whispered, "Why don't we all use English, hmm?"

Mark laughed, and reminded himself, for the hundredth time, never to make assumptions.

Yu and the others moved off, leaving Mark alone with Tango. "Okay," he said, "I surrender. You're going. Have a good flight." He held out his hand.

Tango shook. "If you'd have told me, six years ago when I bought into Spacelifter, that I would wind up here . . ." He seemed genuinely humbled by what he was about to attempt.

"Well, when in doubt, remember the astronaut's prayer."

"Which is?"

" 'Dear Lord, don't let me fuck up.' "

Even though he had undoubtedly heard it a dozen times, Tango laughed. "I'll probably be repeating it all the way to orbit."

"It's when you get on orbit that you'll need it. Whatever it is you're working on." Mark was offering Tango the chance to tell him.

"Mark, my boy, you worked in the commercial world for us, didn't you? Remember all those nondisclosure agreements you signed?"

"You mean, for all those nonfunctional proprietary concepts and hardware?"

Tango seemed stung, but only for an instant. "Yeah, well, whether they work or not, I've got stockholders, and they deserve first look at what I'm working on."

At that moment, Mark realized *exactly* what Tango was going to be doing aboard Harmony. What did the world need most? What accomplishment would best satisfy the ego of Tad Mikleszewski?

Something that would erase the spread of pink death on Mark's map of the United States . . . "Fine, don't make any revelations," Mark said, as quietly as he could, "but remember that you're only leasing Harmony for a week, and that it's part of a forty-billion-dollar, one-of-a-kind facility." Then he smiled. "It's not the place to be casually fucking around with X-Pox."

Tango stared back with the full weight of hundreds of millions of dollars, thousands of employees, dozens of eager lawyers, and years of absolute authority. Mark was prepared for a blast that would launch him through the wall of the conference room. What he heard, instead, was a calm, possibly even friendly voice, say, "I knew you were a smart guy when I hired you, Mark." Then he smiled, gave him a fatherly clap on the shoulder, and spoke to someone directly over Mark's left shoulder. "Hello!"

Mark stepped aside to let Tango face the journalistic horde. He watched the millionaire's body language—perfectly balanced, moving side-to-side like a prizefighter—with admiration. He was not afraid of the writers.

Nor was he afraid of Mark and the organization he supposedly represented. Tango had not only not blasted him, he had not even *hinted* at the very good reason Mark wouldn't make public any information that would cause the millionaire spaceflight participant unhappiness. The message had been sent subverbally, possibly telepathically, but it could not have been clearer:

I know about your accident on the centrifuge. You want to fly in space again.

Mark actually blushed. Far from being smart, he was an idiot. A dishonest idiot, at that.

He looked for Leslie Seldes; she was part of the permanent cluster of humanity centered on Rachel Dunne.

He realized that he had no reason to remain here, except as a spectator. So he returned to his seat and retrieved the Rosaviakosmos promotional material, complete with TM's Harmony mission logo—no mention of Icarus. He was about to depart when he heard his name called.

Steve Goslin was flanking the shapeless mob gathered around Rachel Dunne, heading Mark's way. What was the chief astronaut doing in Moscow? More important for Mark, *why* had he come to Moscow *without* telling his director of operations? It couldn't be good news.

"They told me you were here," Goslin said, after an exchange of greetings that left Mark unenlightened. He looked around at the crowd, which seemed to be growing more raucous. "This sounds like a damn fraternity party," the chief astronaut said.

"It's a Russian event. Someone within throwing distance is drinking."

Goslin yawned. "I'll never get used to this."

"Do you have to?"

Goslin looked directly at him. "They want me to do a tour here."

"Is that why you dropped in?" Mark saw no reason to delay the delivery of bad news—if that's what Goslin brought.

"Yeah. Well, I'm not really dropping in. More like passing through."

"Where else do you go in Russia?"

"Baikonur, my man. The cosmodrome." He nodded at Tango, Rachel, and Igor, who had been collected for one more set of group photographs and congratulatory toasts. "Officially, I'm representing the program office at the launch."

"And unofficially?"

"Just doing the usual recon. We hear very conflicting things about how far along the next taxi bird is."

"This is all very sudden, isn't it?"

"No kidding. Last Friday, LaFollet called me in to say he was moving to engineering, finally." LaFollet had surprised Mark, and 90 percent of the staff at JSC, by surviving Fehrenkamp's transfer to HQ by five months. "The new director of flight crew ops will want a new chief astronaut."

"Sorry to hear that," Mark said. "I think."

Goslin shrugged. "It's a tour. When I got the job, they told me it would be three years. It's been over five. I'm ready to move on."

"To Russia?"

"Well, this is one of the options." There was a crash from another part of the conference room—a photographer had knocked over a display. "Turned out there was an opening on Air Lester, so here I am." He smiled. "Unannounced."

"When do you go to Baikonur?"

"Day after tomorrow. I'm supposed to bunk at Star City until then."

"So you haven't been out there yet." Mark didn't like the idea of his boss wandering around Star City unescorted. If nothing else, Goslin needed to be briefed on dealing with Darin Chambliss and the rest of the staff.

"No. My plane landed ninety minutes ago. I came straight down here with the other folks from DL." Code DL referred to members of the Houston Support Group in Moscow—the other passengers on Air Lester.

"Then let me give you a ride. We can talk on the way."

If asked, five months past, Mark would have harshly dismissed any suggestion that he would ever pilot a motor vehicle in Moscow. He had heard too many horror stories of unmarked roads, potholes the size of Volkswagens, and corrupt *militsiya* who were not deterred by the sight of an American passport.

In five months, he had only confirmed the worst impressions. But as his own skill with the Russian language grew, and as he learned the highways and byways of the northeast Moscow area, he gained confidence, much as he had learned to extend his range beyond a few familiar streets in Marshalltown, Iowa, after earning his driver's license.

Today Mark had booked one of the official NASA cars to make the drive into the heart of Moscow, parking at the Metropol Hotel five blocks away. (Moscow street parking was still too daunting.)

The decision required a walk, but it turned out to be the first truly warm, sunny day of spring. Mark felt the heat of sun for the first time in months, and looked forward to the walk back to the Metropol.

That is, until he and Goslin—the chief astronaut tugging his bag—reached the ground floor of the headquarters building and saw the flashing blue lights of three *militsiya* patrol cars parked sideways in the street. Siren howling, a paddy wagon was working its way slowly through a sea of other vehicles, some moving, some bumped up against each other. Several drivers were out of their cars, arguing. "What's going on?" Goslin asked, still dazed from his long flight.

"Police activity, I think," Mark said. "There's a back way out. I suggest we take it."

"You're the pilot."

The back way out opened on an alley that had not been paved since before the Bolshevik Revolution. The mud was so thick that Goslin had to carry his wheeled suitcase. "Is this some kind of bizarre 'Welcome to Russia,' Koskinen?"

"If only I could have arranged it," Mark said.

"Kelly says hello, by the way."

Mark had thought of Kelly frequently—several times a day, in fact, especially since the cooling of his relationship with Leslie Seldes. But they had no direct contact. Phone calls were impossible, of course, given the ten-hour time lag and the insane hours worked by astronauts in the final weeks of flight training. They had exchanged e-mails every few days, nothing more than a line or two, usually about work or astronaut office rumors.

Kelly had not commented on her relationship with Wayne Shelton. Mark hadn't asked. "How's she doing?"

"You know Kelly: she's all over that mission. I wish the other five were as good."

"Yeah, well, most of us aren't as good as Kelly." That was a judgment Mark could voice with absolute objectivity. He had worked closely with two dozen astronauts, and not one of them knew as much about the job, or did it with such skill and enthusiasm. Thinking about Kelly and the astronaut office reminded Mark that he had not lived up to its ideals. "Steve, I've got something to tell you—"

His confession was interrupted as they emerged from the alley into more gridlock. "Where do we go now?" Goslin said, happy to be able to set his luggage down.

"That way," Mark said, pointing east.

"You know, I've got something I've been meaning to ask you—"

A *thump!* from the closest cars caught Mark's attention, Goslin's, too. Two men were fighting; one man, wearing the black leather jacket that was the uniform of Russian thugs, had slammed another man onto the hood of a late-model Jaguar that had collided with a Volvo. Mark realized, with horror, that the man sliding off the Jaguar, stunned and bleeding, cowering against the next blow, was Wang Xianxiao, the Chinese astronaut.

Yu Guojun, his partner, was struggling out of the driver's seat of the Volvo as another pair of black-jacketed men tried to slam the door on him.

"Shit," Mark said to Goslin. Without asking Goslin's permission, Mark raced toward the two cars, screaming in Russian, "Stop what you're doing!"

He elbowed one of the black jackets aside, allowing Yu to get free of the Volvo. Everyone seemed to be yelling, the three black jackets in Russian, Wang and Yu in Mandarin, and half a dozen onlookers in as many other languages. Wang was battling his assailant. Mark continued to shout at the two facing Yu: "Fucking hooligans! Back off!" He took Yu by the arm and dragged him toward Wang.

Goslin had joined the fracas, abandoning his luggage to throw a football-style block on Wang's attacker. Both he and the black jacket hit the car, then slid onto the pavement.

But Goslin was up first—helped when Mark shoved the first black jacket back to the street. Switching to English, Mark yelled, "Get the bag!" to Yu, who grabbed Goslin's abandoned luggage with admirable speed.

"All of you, this way! Leave the car!" Goslin, Wang, and Yu immediately began to hustle toward the Metropol, which loomed a block away like a medieval castle.

Mark lingered long enough to throw what he hoped was a convincing scare into the black jackets, who were almost to their feet and preparing for pursuit. "Don't you fucking dare!" He patted a nonexistent weapon inside his jacket. "I'll fucking kill you all!"

They wouldn't be slowed for long. But Mark, Goslin, and the Chinese astronauts needed only a few seconds to clear the area, and cross busy Pervomayskoye Shosse to the protection of the Metropol, whose bellhops were quick to side with foreigners against local street thugs.

Mark gave the attendant the ticket for his car, along with a pair of twenty-dollar bills, then turned to Wang and Yu. "Are you all right?"

Wang was bleeding from a cut on his cheek, but he nodded convincingly as Yu translated the question. "What about the car?" the Chinese astronaut said.

"It'll be spare parts in Lyubertsy by sunset. Forget about it."

"We need to get back to Star City."

"You can ride with us." That seemed to satisfy Yu, who pulled a cell phone out of his pocket and stepped off, no doubt to inform the other members of the Chinese team—wherever they might be.

Mark was left alone with Goslin. "Jeez, Mark, I didn't know you had all that . . . savagery in you."

"Live in Russia for five months. You'll have it, too."

But he was shaking and his knees felt weak.

The drive to Star City was a difficult one; at the best of times, Moscow's highways were clogged with too many cars. At rush hour, they were a nightmare. Even Goslin, a veteran of ten years in Houston's congestion, was stunned by the number of cars trying to go both directions, as well as several that seemed to flow sideways into side roads, alleys, and dead ends. "It's a good thing we never tried to invade," he said. "We'd still be looking for parking."

Mark was always made uncomfortable by Cold War references, especially in the presence of people like the Chinese astronauts, who could, by some standards, still be considered potential enemies. He tried to take the curse off Goslin's statement by asking Yu and Wang, "How does this compare to Beijing?"

Yu translated the question for Wang, who rattled off a sentence in return. "My friend says, 'What makes you think we know anything about Beijing?' " Yu said.

"Your own newspapers have said that the *yuangyuan* team lives at a facility called 'Aerospace City' in the suburbs."

Yu repeated Mark's statement to Wang, who responded with a look that might have been a smile. He uttered more words in Mandarin. "He says, 'Good. Since you know so much, please tell us why *we* are at Star City.' "

Even Goslin laughed at that. "Welcome to the life of an astronaut."

"Why do *you* think you're here?" Mark asked. "They didn't just march you onto an airplane a month ago." He nodded toward Wang. "After all, you're one of the first *yuangyuan* in space."

"Our trip was to be phase two in the development of our training program. Some years ago, two of our team lived at Star City, learning the basic tests for orbital flight. We were supposed to be studying more advanced techniques, for longer-duration missions." Mark knew, of course, that the Shenzhou had the capability of remaining in space for at least two weeks. He also knew, just from reading news reports, that the Chinese were considering the construction of a rudimentary space station of their own by docking two Shenzhou orbital modules together.

"We started to study the Soyuz orbital module, as well as old plans for a small Soyuz station." Mark knew that the Russians had developed half a dozen space station concepts, going back to the 1960s. It didn't surprise him that they would be charging the Chinese for access to obsolete data. "But then it stopped," Yu said. "For the past two weeks, Colonel Wang and I have been doing physical training only. We were given the chance to fly an airplane at Chkalovskaya, I think to keep us busy."

"What about your two colleagues?" Goslin said, unable to resist intelligence-gathering.

"They have been talking to the Rosaviakosmos."

"They're probably talking to NASA, too," Mark said, earning a look from Goslin. "It's why you've been shipped here, Steve.

"NASA would like the Chinese to be part of the Alpha program. The Shenzhou has now proven itself as a manned flight vehicle—its design is based on Soyuz." Mark waited for a patriotic protest from either of the Chinese astronauts; none came. "I think your docking module is identical to the one Soyuz TMA uses now." Again, no argument from the Chinese. "We could fly taxi missions with Shenzhou."

"You know this for certain?" Yu said, without waiting for guidance from Wang.

It was Mark's turn to share the humiliation of being out of the loop. "No, not officially. But I've noticed that several key Star City people have been spending a lot of time down at Rosaviakosmos over the past couple of weeks. Then you have these mystery arrivals like Colonel Goslin. What else would they all be talking about?"

"Besides," Goslin said, "joining Alpha would save your country billions of dollars reinventing the wheel." Mark took Goslin's comment as tacit approval of what might have seemed to be indiscretion.

The Chinese talked this over in Mandarin for several minutes, as Mark negotiated the final approaches to Star City. Finally Wang announced, through Yu, "We look forward to flying with you."

"Again," Yu said. "I think this ride would count as our first flight with astronaut Koskinen."

When the car reached the Orbita, the Chinese went one way while Mark and Goslin went another. Once Goslin was checked in, Mark said, "What were you going to ask me?"

"Out there on the street? Before you kidnapped two Chinese astronauts, then told them classified information?" Mark knew Goslin well enough to recognize the Marine astronaut's tortured attempt at humor. "I was asking about your parents."

"My dad's doing as well as can be expected, but he faces a limited future. My mom had that fall about a month ago. She's bouncing back, but she won't be really up and around until midsummer."

Goslin's father had died during the time he and Mark were in the astronaut office. "I'm sorry that we've just left you out here on the Russian Front. If you need to take a trip home, just ask."

"Thanks," Mark said. "I'm in touch with them. And my sister's been staying there." Mark felt guilty about that. He had, in fact, offered to fly home on several occasions, earning an unprecedented phone call from his father forbidding him to jeopardize his Russian assignment. Even Johanna had sounded convincingly positive about their parents' situation.

Or so he selfishly chose to believe. It was, Mark told himself, just another of the moral compromises he had made since returning to the astronaut office.

"You've done a good job here. I'm going to recommend you for the next available assembly flight."

Well, there it was: the reward of the second flight, the one that proved to the rest of NASA—and the world—that you weren't a failure as an astronaut. That you weren't afraid. So why did he feel so uninspired? "Will the next chief honor it?"

"Oh, yeah. It'll be like one of those 'recess' appointments a president gets to make. That's the good news. The bad news is that the change in management means you won't be getting relieved on schedule."

"Was I scheduled for relief?"

"Well, your six months are up now."

"Hell, Steve, the usual DOR tour is closer to nine months." They had reached the door to Star City's NASA office. "Besides, when you hear what I have to tell you, you may want to leave me here." Goslin actually straightened up and stepped back. "Last month I sniveled my way into a turn on the big centrifuge here."

"Mark, you wouldn't be an astronaut if you didn't snivel your way into everything they have. Airplanes, simulators."

"Oh, I've done all of that." By charm, and occasional disbursements of personal cash, Mark had actually logged thirty hours of Soyuz simulator time. "But there was a problem with the centrifuge. The medical harness had a short."

"And you got hurt."

"Electrocuted, in fact. My heart stopped."

Mark had expected a typical Goslin twitch of surprise. But the Marine just stared, a look of what could only be amusement growing on his face. "Well, did it start up all right?"

"Yeah."

"Have you told any of the doctors here?"

"Not the NASA guys. I've had one of the Star City folks run a couple of EKGs." No appointment had been necessary, merely a phone call and the promise of a fee, in cash. "All the waves are normal."

"Hey, how many Gs did you take?"

"Six. I completed the same set of runs everyone else was doing."

"I'm glad you told me." Goslin thought for a moment. "Okay, here's what you do: send me a memo that contains the same information—unofficial run on the Star City centrifuge, accident with the harness, later EKG tests by Russian doctors. It doesn't need to be more than a couple of paragraphs. Don't give the *date* of the event.

"That way you'll be covered, and I'll be covered." He sighed. "It's going to be tricky."

"I'm sorry about all of this."

"Mark, you won't be the first astronaut to hide a medical situation. You might be the first to come clean voluntarily."

ROCKET-SPACE CORPORATION ENERGIYA
named for S. P. Korolev

Official Press Release
On the 10th ISS International Visiting Crew

April 26, 2006, Korolev, Moscow Region

The Soyuz TMA-6 landing module returned to Earth today with two members of the tenth International Space Station (ISS) visiting crew (VC-10)—Russian commander Igor Gritsov and spaceflight participant Rachel Dunne. The third crew member on Soyuz TMA-6 was ISS science officer Jasper Weeks, replacing spaceflight participant Tad Mikleszewski, who remains aboard the ISS due to a medical emergency.

Soyuz TMA-6 undocked from ISS Russian segment Zarya module at 22:09 Moscow Time on April 25 following a command from the Moscow Control Center (MCC-M). The vehicle descent was performed in the automatic mode.

The landing module set down in the target zone near Arkalyk, Kazakhstan, at 04:09 Moscow Time on April 26. Air Force rescue service reached the module within minutes, aided by representatives of the Russian Ministry of Health.

The landing coordinates are 51.14 degrees north latitude, 66.48 degrees east.

Seventy percent of the research tasks of VC-10 were completed successfully, including filming of the feature film *Recoil* and medical experiments under the program Harmony Pyrite A.

Cosmonauts Gritsov, Dunne, and Weeks feel well and are undergoing medical examination at Baikonur.

The ISS Expedition 13 crew of commander Viktor Kondratko and flight engineer Nathan Bristol continue limited onboard operations in support of the emergency situation involving spaceflight participant Mikleszewski.

CONTAMINATION LEVEL FOUR

Soyuz TMA-6 backed away from Zarya to the accompaniment of a ringing ship's bell, one of Alpha's practices.

Viktor Kondratko had no love of boats or nautical traditions, unless these included drinking and womanizing. But as a pilot, he was also superstitious enough to be sure that the ship's bell rang loudly as Igor Gritsov announced that the Soyuz docking module had separated from the station.

Alpha had suffered enough bad luck. Viktor could easily imagine how it could grow worse.

The farewell ceremony had been brief, and surprisingly emotional. Igor Gritsov had hugged Viktor and kissed him. This was a common form of contact between Russian men, but Viktor knew that cosmonauts tended not to do it when Americans were present. Igor had said to Viktor, "I'll be on the ground in six hours. What do you want me to do? What isn't being done?"

"Igor, you'll be puking for the rest of the day."

"Then I'll puke on somebody." He glanced down the length of Alpha toward the node that led to Harmony. "Maybe the crooked bastards that built that piece of shit."

"Just tell everyone to hurry up. We need the rescue mission."

By contrast, Jasper Weeks was so subdued that Viktor wondered if he had taken a sedative. Unthinkable, of course: the NASA astronaut had to assist Igor during retrofire and reentry. It was probably depression: Weeks had trained for three years to complete this expedition to Alpha, and now he was being shipped home a third of the way through the mission. Yes, NASA would make a good-faith attempt to send him back to the station.

Assuming, of course, that Alpha survived the present crisis. Viktor knew what mission controllers in both Houston and Korolev were saying: that a Shuttle rescue mission was on the pad in Florida, awaiting clearance for launch. That a backup rescue vehicle was standing by at Baikonur.

They were all very matter-of-fact, supremely confident that Tango could be safely extracted from Harmony, that the module could be safed, and that Alpha's missions could continue.

But from long experience in the Soviet military, and years of dealing with NASA on the horror that was STS-100, Viktor knew the darker side of both entities: someone, somewhere was considering a worst-case scenario.

For example, what if Harmony could not be sanitized? Some means would be found to undock it, and Tango would die. Then the world would be faced with the eventual reentry of a twenty-ton spacecraft filled with highly concentrated X-Pox.

It was true that Harmony could be deorbited over the remote Pacific, and even if the X-Pox spores multiplied ferociously in the heat of reentry and breakup, as claimed by several self-appointed biowar "experts," the nearest potential victims would be thousands of miles away.

But what if Harmony's reentry was uncontrolled? What if it came down over Washington, London, Paris? Alpha and Harmony orbits crossed all of those cities. Only Moscow was too far north to be threatened. (That last factor was also being discussed by the craziest websites, whose proprietors claimed that the outbreak aboard Alpha was some kind of deliberate sabotage—die-hard Soviet Communists in league with Al Qaeda?)

In such a case—Harmony breaking up in the sky within sight of a major city—the population faced the same threat posed by a single terrorist with a jar of anthrax dumped into the water or released into the air. Yes, a dozen people might be infected, and possibly one or two would die. Many more people would die of drug overdoses or gunshots or suicide in that same city that day.

Viktor knew that rationality did not apply. Governments often reacted hastily and stupidly when populations were frightened, and five years of low-level chemical and nuclear war had frightened even the strongest.

If Harmony was cut loose, it would be seen as a threat. What were the options then? Shoot it down? Launch a nuclear antisatellite weapon to vaporize it in orbit?

What would *that* do to the Alpha crew?

There was an even darker scenario that was causing Viktor to wake each night:

Suppose the whole station became contaminated? Would the nations of the world abandon their forty-billion-dollar outpost in space? What of the crew?

There would be a terrible accident, Viktor feared. A tragedy.

Jasper Weeks knew this. Viktor hoped that Weeks's innate decency and idealism would make him an ally of the Alpha crew when he returned to Houston.

Then there was Rachel Dunne.

This morning, after the "farewell" breakfast, Viktor had joined Rachel in the orbital module of Soyuz TMA-6, to help her don the Sokol pressure suit she, Gritsov, and Weeks would wear through reentry. Rachel was cool and distant, as if she were a movie star and Viktor an assistant costumer.

"I hope you got all the footage you wanted," he had told her.

"They're never going to finish this movie."

"Why not? It's been even more dramatic than the script. You and Igor were able to record it."

"A lot of our footage is locked up in Harmony. What's left will have to go to NASA. Nobody wants to make a movie out of stuff everyone has seen. Not Brad Beck. Dammit." She raised her hand. A tiny bubble of blood floated away from it. "I cut myself on the stupid zipper."

"Hold on." Viktor quickly twisted through the hatch into the cramped Soyuz descent module, searching for the emergency kit.

Viktor had had several dozen casual sexual relationships ranging in duration from one hour to a couple of months. The affair with Rachel Dunne had spanned two weeks, putting it in Viktor's upper quarter in terms of sheer duration.

To Viktor's surprise, and pleasure, it had started almost immediately—and with Rachel the aggressor. He had flirted with her at Star City, of course. Every breathing male over the age of twelve had done the same. But Viktor had learned from a shattered Igor Gritsov that Rachel was sleeping with Tango, a move that made perfect sense for the actress—personally, professionally, financially, even politically. The millionaire spaceflight participant was the one male on the planet who intimidated Igor Gritsov. The cosmonaut's obvious and ridiculous passion for Rachel Dunne seemed to vanish, replaced by a cool professionalism that made the directors of Star City much happier. Gritsov and his estranged wife were even seen together.

Soon after this, Kondratko, Weeks, and Bristol flew off to the United States for launch aboard the orbiter *Endeavour*. The stress of getting to orbit and taking up command of Alpha had totally consumed Viktor's energy and time. The subject of Rachel Dunne and her affair with Tango ranked far below the matter of Zvezda decibel levels or the nagging problems with the Vozdukh air system, or the checkout and inventory of materials aboard Harmony.

On the second night after the arrival of the taxi crew, Viktor found Rachel alone in her "stateroom"—which happened to be the orbital module of the Soyuz she arrived in. The hatch had been partly closed. He had actually knocked on the metal, calling "Hello! It's Viktor!"

The hatch moved just enough to allow him to pass through. Then Rachel closed it behind him. She was wearing the standard uniform of an Alpha crew member: a polo-style shirt and shorts. But no station astronaut in Viktor's memory ever filled those garments in quite the same way. Perhaps because no station astronaut chose clothing that was two sizes too small.

"How are you feeling?" Viktor asked. Many space travelers suffered occasional bouts of vomiting during their first forty-eight hours in microgravity. Viktor himself had been green with nausea during the first hours of the STS-100 mission. For his second launch he had dosed himself with Scope-Dex as soon as the Shuttle reached orbit, and felt better more quickly.

"I urped once," she said, making a face. "But that was when we were all trying to get out of our suits in here. Nothing since." She pushed herself back and forth with only her fingertips. "It really is an amazing feeling."

"After a few days, you can't imagine what it's like to live in gravity."

"What do you do for fun up here? I mean, there's work and meals and exercise and sleep . . . but that still leaves an hour or two every day."

"It's personal time," Viktor said, in all seriousness. "You read e-mails, talk to family and friends on the video. Sometimes we get together and watch movies."

"I was afraid of that."

"Well, what do they do in Hollywood?" he said, jokingly.

His answer was a kiss. The momentum of their embrace carried them against the storage lockers on one side of the module. Viktor's head hit, making an audible *bump!*

"God, I'm sorry." She put her hand to the back of his head.

"I forgive you." He snaked an arm around her, pulling her close, but slowly. "You must anchor yourself," he whispered.

"Tell me you haven't done this before, up here."

"I am not a member of the Hundred-Mile Club."

"But there *are* members."

"Over a hundred and twenty people have visited Alpha," he said, his hand finding Rachel's breast. It felt hard and cold—but then, so did he. Microgravity at work—blood remained in the trunk or in the head. The extremities were starved. "Two dozen of them have been women. The opportunities for such . . . explorations have been many." He smiled. " 'Those who say don't know; those who know don't say.' "

He was prevented from uttering additional maxims by the struggle to help Rachel Dunne out of her very tight Alpha shirt.

She was not wearing a bra underneath it. Well, in microgravity, a bra was not necessary. "What will your boyfriend think?" Viktor said, acutely aware that while Alpha was roomy, it was not remotely private.

"If you're thinking of Dr. Mikleszewski, we are no longer an item." She writhed about, bracing herself in a corner where the lockers met the spherical wall of the module. "In fact, we are barely speaking." Then she wriggled out of her shorts. Again, she was wearing nothing underneath them.

"I'm sorry to hear that," he said, feeling not remotely so, as Rachel helped him tug down his shorts. They wrapped around his left foot, but provided no distraction as he entered her.

He quickly found that he needed to use both hands and feet to brace himself, leaving no way to hold her. Rachel sensed the problem, however, and wrapped herself around him, drawing him closer. For an instant, he wondered how they would look to a visitor floating through the hatchway, since they were on the plus-X axis of the station . . . the ceiling.

Whether it was the novelty of the setting, or fear of discovery, or six weeks with no sex at all, he climaxed almost immediately.

Too quickly for Rachel, who was left panting and not satisfied. "Sorry, sorry," he said.

"It's all right." Her face was flushed. For that matter, all of Rachel Dunne was flushed. "You'll just have to try harder next time."

"I don't think I can be harder."

She laughed as she slid out from under him, scooping up shirt and shorts from the midair. "I wish we'd had the chance to practice back on Earth," he said, trying to get dressed himself.

Now Rachel switched to her charming, barely passable Russian. "You left Star City."

"I had a mission to fly."

Back to English. "Your priorities are screwed up, Colonel."

The next night they had a much more successful rendezvous and docking while the other four crew members slept. It occurred inside the Harmony module, among the mass of boxed equipment and storage bags that had yet to be properly stowed.

Two days later the accident took place.

At first Rachel had been visibly upset about Tango's situation, and seemed to require constant reassurance and comfort. But as the initial shock of the accident passed, and the "crisis" evolved into a weary game of wait-and-see, she grew more distant. Viktor wondered briefly if she had simply collected him as a souvenir of her trip to space—*here's where I made love to the commander!*

Then he cursed himself for the stupidity of the thought; Rachel Dunne was a famous American actress, desired by thousands of men. Of *course* she had collected him. And made him her ally in the bargain. Sexuality was a tool for such a woman.

As it was for Viktor.

Once the Sokol suit had been zipped tight, however, and the last gear safely stashed in the Soyuz descent module, Rachel began to weep. She was not sobbing, just floating in the Zarya docking module with tears bubbling from her eyes. Knowing she would be photographed, Rachel had made herself up this morning. But the combination of wet eye liner and zero-G tears made her look like a zombie from one of the black-and-white horror movies Bristol had in his library.

"And the Oscar for most unnecessary emotional display goes to . . ." So Bristol whispered as he and Viktor pushed themselves down the length of Zarya toward the docking module. Bristol was operating the video camera, sending a feed to Korolev mission control.

Viktor carried two small plastic bags, one holding a slice of bread, the other a small quantity of salt. He almost lost them both when Rachel launched herself at him and tried to kiss him.

Bristol tactfully kept the camera aimed at the Soyuz hatch, where Igor Gritsov lurked. Jasper Weeks floated at the top of the module, silent.

"We'll see you soon," Viktor told Rachel, in what he hoped was a soothing voice.

"I know, I know," she said, sniffling. "Just, save him, will you? It all got so weird."

Viktor gave the actress a reassuring hug—assuming she could feel anything through the suit. Then he handed Gritsov the bags of bread and salt. "As a Russian commander, I keep to Russian traditions," he said, knowing the camera was on him. "Especially in this difficult time. Before setting out on a voyage, we must all sit. Or, since we are in microgravity, hold still." All five were silent. "Then we slap thighs—" He demonstrated. Everyone but Bristol repeated the action. "And say, '*Bog pomugayu,* God help us.' "

Ceremony over, Igor grabbed a strap on Rachel's suit and tugged her into the Soyuz. Weeks followed. There was no last-second eye contact.

Bristol closed and dogged the hatch, then pushed himself back. "Well, it's just you and me, Viktor."

"And Tango."

"Oh, yeah. Have you talked to him this morning?"

"I said hello. He was already hard at work."

"Speaking of work, the Vozdukh's acting up again." More maintenance! It seemed that was all the crew had time for! And now there were only two to bear the load. "Let's see."

The Vozdukh took longer to fix than Viktor planned. By the time he and Bristol broke for lunch, Soyuz TMA-6 was miles away, maneuvering to the proper attitude for retrofire, and Tango had been silent for three hours.

Leaving Bristol to rummage for the meals, Viktor floated into Unity and snatched the headset for a direct link to Harmony. "Tango, it's Viktor, good afternoon."

No answer. He called again, and again. Nothing.

The fixed video cameras inside Harmony fed to Korolev mission control. Viktor had asked Korolev to reroute the comm back to Alpha. So he was able to call up a view inside the module.

Wearing his T-shirt and shorts, Tango was sleeping—or unconscious. It seemed to Viktor that the millionaire shuddered or twitched. A bad dream? Or fever.

Then Tango's body rotated, giving Viktor a clear view of his face and neck. There was the telltale red rash of X-Pox.

"Houston, Alpha, channel B," Viktor said, trying to keep his voice calm.

"Switching to B," the astronaut capcom said. Thank God they were always standing by. "Go ahead."

"We have a problem. Our condition is *worse* than red."

PART VI

X-Plus Five Days
(April 2006)

MARSHALLTOWN (IOWA) *TIMES-REPUBLICAN*
SUNDAY, APRIL 23, 2006

KOSKINEN, CAROL ELAINE (DOAN)

Died Wednesday, April 19, of complications from an injury suffered in a fall.

Born July 30, 1938, in Waterloo, Iowa, she graduated from Upper Iowa University in 1960. Married Glenn Koskinen of Marshalltown on June 13, 1962.

Beloved wife of Glenn, mother of Mark and Johanna, grandmother of Cayley and Madison.

Services were held Saturday, April 22, at Grace Community Lutheran Church.

Memorial donations may be made to the Marshall County Medical Center.

THE RESURRECTION AND THE LIFE

"And now Carol's son, Mark, would like to say a few words."

Mark stood up in the pew and stepped past his father, Glenn, careful not to stumble over the cane that Glenn had hung on the armrest. Then he had to maneuver around the silvery coffin.

The Koskinen family had attended Grace Lutheran Church for thirty years, though this building had been built in the last ten—long after Mark left Marshalltown. Mark, in fact, had been inside this church less than half a dozen times, all during family visits at Christmas. Holiday services were crowded, the winter light streamed brightly through the stained-glass windows, and there were trees, poinsettias, and a crèche on the altar.

Now it was a rainy day in spring. The church was a third full and the altar bare. The place felt more alien to Mark than the exterior of the Mir space station. Certainly he had felt more confident floating out of the airlock of the Shuttle *Atlantis* than he did now, making his way to the pulpit of Grace Lutheran.

All during the flight from Moscow to New York, New York to Des Moines, the drive across central Iowa, then the two-day vigil at the hospital, Mark had dreaded this moment—how was he supposed to sum up his mother's life? How did *anyone* sum up another life? When Johanna first raised the question with him, one hour after Carol's heart stopped beating, he had said, "Do I have to?"

"Do you *have* to?" she said, almost shrieking with disbelief. "Are you five years old, Mark? Mom's *dead*. Dad is sick. I'm going to be sitting there sobbing . . ." In fact, she *had* started to sob. "You're the *oldest child,* for God's sake. Why don't you act like it?"

Was he a bad son? His mother had had an accident in February, and he had not found time to visit her. True, he had spoken to her on the telephone twice a week. And he *was* based in another country—hell, on another continent.

The excuses sounded good—until you realized that your mother was in a box, and the last time you saw her conscious and alive was October.

The word of Carol's relapse had reached Mark early on Sunday the 16th. He had immediately found a flight to New York, and was still in transit on Monday when the accident occurred on Alpha.

But Mark knew nothing of it until late that day, after reaching Marshalltown, when his brother-in-law Lewis happened to mention it. By then Mark was keeping vigil at his mother's bedside. He had not seen a newspaper or looked at a newscast or logged on to his computer for two days. He merely shrugged and said, "They'll handle it without me." Chambliss had the authority to address matters on the Russian Front.

Carol never regained consciousness, passing away early on Wednesday morning, and Mark embraced the role of grieving son, enduring visits from friends and family, discussions with the funeral director, and awkward silences with his father.

He felt his already-tenuous connection to his astronaut career growing thinner with every mile he traveled from Moscow. Johanna's rebuke was like a blade slicing that thread.

"Thank you all for coming today. Mom would have been proud to see how many of you wanted to say good-bye. Of course, she would never have let on that she was proud." He heard a ripple of muted laughter. Thank God.

He recounted the facts of his mother's life—birth in Waterloo, school, first job, marriage—as if on autopilot, much as he had delivered standard NASA presentations to high schools and civic groups as an astronaut.

He was looking at the faces in the church, many from his own past, like good old Jay Pollack. Faces and bodies grown heavy. Hair gone gray—or gone altogether. Gravity at work.

Maybe that was what he had tried to escape all these years. Gravity.

Well, he had slipped the surly bonds, floated for days at a time, seen the Earth round and blue. His Shuttle flight had even taken him over this part of Iowa during a daylight pass. It had been cloudy, though. Marshalltown and all of central Iowa had been hidden under a blanket of gray.

Yet here he was—approaching forty, unmarried, childless, almost homeless. (How many nights had he spent in his condo in Houston in the past six months? More than one?) His career was stalled; his most notable action to revive it involved lying to his boss about an accident.

If he ever for a moment felt that he was somehow smarter or more successful than these florid, sniffling, obscure people, he certainly didn't feel that way now.

"My mother never flew in space. I don't suppose that anyone outside of Marshall County other than relatives and friends ever heard of her.

"But it's those friends who are important. All of you here," he said, extending his hands toward the congregation. "I believe that your lives were better because you knew Carol Koskinen, and I know for sure that her life was better because of you.

"As for her relatives—our family—"

Suddenly he could say no more. An all-encompassing sob was filling him, weakening him, robbing him of his voice. "We thank you," was all he could manage.

He groped his way back to the pew, to take his place between his grim-faced, dying father, and his quietly sobbing sister.

The rest of the ceremony passed swiftly. Soon the coffin had been carried to the hearse, and the bereaved family transferred to a limo.

Mark walked with his father, whose step was surprisingly strong and steady. Behind them came Johanna, her face smeared with tears, clutching Lewis's arm as each parent tugged a daughter.

The drive to the cemetery took ten minutes. Sitting quietly in the plush limo seat, Mark felt himself growing sleepy. Well, it was four in the morning by his scrambled biological clock.

The cold spring rain that had been falling most of the morning let up briefly. As the minister offered a final blessing at the gravesite, Mark happened to look to his left. There, among the familiar faces of his parents' world was one from Houston: a red-haired woman in a dark coat and, strangely, aviator sunglasses.

Kelly.

Mark had not heard from her since returning to the States earlier in the week. He had not expected much contact: he knew Kelly was at the Cape preparing for a launch. Her crew was almost certainly sleep-shifting and going into quarantine. He knew there were issues with the weather—some tropical storm—but for the first time in years, he wasn't paying any attention to the current mission and the Alpha crisis. Tango Midnight was on his own.

He took a step toward her, and she met him, arms out. "Mark," Kelly said, "I'm so sorry."

All he could do was nod.

The minister was finished. The mourners made one last pass by the casket, then scattered to their cars. Mark approached his father, planning to help him back to the limo. As he did, he heard Glenn say, "I'll be here soon, darling. You won't be alone for long."

There was more, of course. The ritual welcome of mourners to the house. Johanna regained sufficient strength to serve as hostess—a natural role, since she had spent more of her life in Marshalltown, and much of the last six weeks reacquainting herself with the community.

Mark worried that Glenn was wearing himself out, but found

himself turned away when he said, "Dad, do you want to take a rest?"

Kelly had followed the limo back to the Koskinen house, though it was an hour before Mark had a chance to talk to her. He found her making herself useful to Johanna in the kitchen. "So it was a blood clot," she said.

"Yeah. A complication from the fall. Nobody saw it coming. She was starting to get up and around."

"That's so unfair. With your father—" Kelly's father had died of cancer, too.

"Thank you for coming, by the way. In case I haven't said so."

She smiled. "I would have gotten here earlier. I've been down at the Cape since everything changed." She saw confusion on Mark's face. "The Alpha problem."

"I don't know any details."

"Oh, God!" She took a breath. "Well, this isn't the time to tell you. I'm just glad someone remembered that we . . . were close."

"Who *did* tell you?" Mark was more than a little curious who knew of his former relationship with Kelly.

"Goslin."

Mark was strangely relieved. Goslin knew, of course. And Goslin, their former commander, their boss, was still looking out for them. "When are you supposed to launch?"

"It was *supposed* to be two weeks. Now it's two weeks plus weather delay."

"Feel ready?"

"I feel weird. I mean, I've been living in the NBL."

"How's the rest of the crew?"

"It's a good group. Well, Herron's driving me nuts."

"There's a surprise." Diana Herron had been a member of Mark's astronaut candidate class, and would have been voted Least Popular. "How's Wayne?"

Kelly's eyes narrowed ever so slightly. "Wayne who?" she said, sweetly. "The name sounds familiar. Is he in the program?"

Mark laughed for the first time that day. "Wow. Another badly behaved man. We are a constant source of disappointment to you."

"Not *all* of you."

Kelly left soon after, though she made Mark promise to visit her at the Holiday Inn Suites if he needed a break. "There's no minibar," she said, "but I think there's a 7-Eleven across the highway. Room two-twelve."

"Don't you want to get some sleep?"

"Highway noise always keeps me awake. Remember?"

Mark returned to his duties as a bereaved son, but found, to his surprise, that by eight P.M. the last visitors had departed. Glenn had finally gone upstairs to sleep while Johanna and Lewis started the process of getting the kids bathed and ready for bed.

He should have crawled into bed himself. He was tired enough. But he had given his room to Johanna's kids, and there was no way he would be able to bunk down on the living room couch this early.

So he got in the car and drove south to Highway 30, then turned west.

Kelly was still in her funeral garb—blouse and skirt—and had obviously been napping when Mark knocked on the door. "So much for highway noise. I'm going home now."

"No, no, no! It's this damn sleep-shifting! This is the middle of the night to me."

"I feel as though I'm endangering your crew by waking you."

"We might not be launched for a month. So shut up and get in here."

As the door closed, Mark noticed a pair of Coors beer bottles sitting in the plastic ice bucket, like champagne at a five-star restaurant. "Nice," he said. "For me?"

Kelly removed both bottles, wiping them off with a bathroom towel. Then she handed one to Mark. "For *us*. For auld lang syne. And in memory of your mom."

"Should we twist off the tops before we toast?"

"The rules of etiquette are silent on that."

Neither Mark nor Kelly actually drank much; a sip or two. Mark flopped onto the bed while Kelly curled up in a chair. All around them were the sounds of a small motel on the outskirts of a small town in midweek. The shuddering rattle of the elevator. Thumps and voices of travelers checking in. The blare of a television. And, yes, the growl of a single semi heading up Highway 30.

Mark and Kelly talked about his mother and father, about her mother and brother. Goslin and Fehrenkamp. Tango and Viktor.

Rachel Dunne. "Not that it's any of my business, but did you . . . ?"

"Did I what?" Mark said. "*Sleep* with her? No. *No way.*"

"Off your game?" Kelly said, smiling, but obviously eager to know. "Or too much competition?"

"Both, I suppose. I never got to know her. Then she was Tango's girlfriend."

"Ah."

A day later he would remember few specifics of their conversation, just a growing sense of connection, as if he were warming himself by a fire.

Around ten Kelly rose from the chair to stretch. "It's hell getting old."

"You're not old."

She smiled. "Older than you."

Mark took her hand. "Stay with me."

She leaned toward him and kissed him, lightly, on the lips. "Mark, Mark, Mark . . . you're already in *my* room."

"Good point." He tugged her down on the bed.

"This better not be pity," she said some minutes and a good deal of kissing later.

"I could say the same."

They were both still asleep the next morning when the phone rang. Always quick to awaken, Mark was reaching for the phone when Kelly stopped him.

"Right," Mark said. "Your room."

She smiled. "Kelly Gessner." She was halfway through a yawn when her expression changed and she stood up. "Oh, hello, Steve," she said, making sure Mark heard who was calling. She pointed Mark to the television.

He found the remote and turned it on, earning a blast of sound from the preset hotel channel. He clicked over to CNN and saw stock footage of Alpha in orbit, as seen from a recent Shuttle undocking.

Kelly was still saying, "Okay, okay." Then she sighed and said, "Oh, shit. How did that happen?"

On screen, the shot of Alpha had been reduced to a box in the corner, replaced by a bigger shot of the Vehicle Assembly Building, its bay doors open to reveal a Shuttle stack. The CNN space beat reporter, John Rebholz, was talking to a retired astronaut named Scott Kevles, who had been on one of the early assembly missions. Kevles was saying, "—We're *already* facing a delay caused by the weather."

"They had to roll the orbiter back to the assembly building," Rebholz said, unnecessarily.

"Correct. That delayed any rescue launch by at least a week. But this—I mean, who knows?"

Eventually Mark realized that there had been an accident in the VAB. An operator using a crane to position SAE hardware in the payload bay had accidentally rammed the Raffaello module. The damage was slight—or so it seemed. But it would be days before it could be assessed, meaning more delays.

Mark turned to Kelly, who was still holding the phone. She held up a finger, forcing him to freeze. On the television, Kevles was being reassuring, noting that the station crew had all sorts of training and procedures in place for "toxic situations."

Toxic situation aboard Alpha? Mark tried to envision the station and the data files, but his focus quickly shifted to Harmony, and Tango, and X-Pox. The chat on CNN was still concerned with the accident in the VAB.

"He wants to talk to you," Kelly said, handing Mark the phone.

"Steve? Why?"

"Why don't you find out."

Mark said hello. Goslin immediately expressed condolences on the death of Mrs. Koskinen. Then he apologized for intruding on Mark's grief. Then there was more aimless chat about Goslin's recent trip to Moscow and Baikonur.

Finally Goslin stopped circling his point. "We already have a rescue flight in the works for Alpha. It's going to use Kelly's crew, assuming we can ever get them off the ground."

"Okay." Why was he telling Mark this?

"Management has also put a backup mission in place using the Russians—"

Now Mark saw some slim rationale for the conversation. "I'm sure they could handle it, assuming the next Soyuz is ready."

"Well, that's the problem," Goslin said. "I was just out at the cosmodrome, and I don't believe that Soyuz is going to fly before June. Which is not when we need it."

"Okay."

Goslin hesitated. "How quickly could you get yourself to San Francisco?"

"I could be there this evening, I suppose, but—" Now he was truly confused.

"Good. My office will call back with the details. There's an Air China flight at eight-twenty P.M., Pacific Time."

"Going where and why?"

"To Beijing, Mark. We're going to use that Chinese spacecraft as our backup."

"I'm not a payload integrator, Steve."

"We're sending an integration team. You're a contingency crew member."

Mark had made love for the first time in months; he had had a full night's sleep. He felt great—but he still had problems understanding what Goslin was telling him. "Crew member for what?"

"For the flight engineer seat on Shenzhou-Eight, if we need to launch it. I promised to recommend you for the next available mission, didn't I? Now get packed and get to Des Moines."

OPTION C

"They're down."

"Good," Fehrenkamp said, staring at the speakerphone by the side of his hospital bed. Who was on the other end? Chambliss in Moscow? Or someone else at the Korolev center? "How is the crew?"

"Weeks is wobbly, Gritsov threw up. The babe is already posing for pictures." *Babe?* Oh, yes, Rachel Dunne, the actress and spaceflight participant. Such irreverence could only mean the speaker was Chambliss. "But the doctors say everything is in the zone. The crew should be in Baikonur within three hours."

"Thank you, Moscow," Fehrenkamp said. "That's one item off the list."

"Only forty-nine more to go," a third speaker said, to general laughter. Fehrenkamp recognized that voice: Scott McDowell in Houston, the lead flight director for STS-124.

Les Fehrenkamp had been doing teleconferences for thirty years. His feelings about the procedure had evolved from awe and wonder at hearing decisions made by such legends of Apollo as Glynn Lunney and Gene Kranz, to worry at the side effects of so much time exposed to electronic machinery. (This was in the late 1980s and early 1990s, when half a dozen of Fehrenkamp's associates, some of them as young as forty, all died of cancer or leukemia.)

Lately he had just grown bored with the process. He had taken part in telecons for over a hundred Shuttle missions. After the first sixty, he began to realize there were no new problems to be solved. None, that is, that required his particular expertise.

Of course, this may have been due to his loss of authority. People no longer listened to his words as if they were being handed down from Mount Sinai.

This telecon was the most interesting in five years, however. For one thing, Fehrenkamp was taking part from his bed in Titusville Community Hospital rather than a conference room in Building Two at the Johnson Space Center. For another, instead of a dozen NASA and contractor staff taking notes and offering advice around the table, he had only Curt Freitag, who still had a black eye and a bandage on his head from their accident.

The real reason for Fehrenkamp's excitement was the nature of the telecon. It wasn't just a routine flight readiness review—the subject was a genuine space crisis, the closest thing to Apollo 13 the American space program had faced in over thirty years! A chance to erase the failure to rescue *Columbia*!

If you weren't excited by that sort of challenge, and daunted by the obstacles, go home. Or, in Fehrenkamp's case, retire and become a "consultant."

"Okay, then, item two," Fehrenkamp said, consulting his written notes. (He had never made the transition to laptops.) "Orbiter status."

The KSC manager of launch operations spoke briefly on the repairs taking place in *Discovery*'s payload bay. "We've taken a good look at the delamination on the module with both ultrasound and thermography. We're ready to fly with it as is."

"You've looked at the load limits during ascent?" Fehrenkamp said. Even if the damage to Raffaello didn't appear to be a serious problem on the ground, the payload still had to survive the stress of launch and especially—given the potentially toxic nature of the "materials" to be returned—entry.

"Payload integration here," a female voice said. "We've run assessments that are beyond flight path limits, and the loads are still bearable." Representatives from JSC and Marshall concurred.

The telecon had moved with incredible speed and energy. Hell, Fehrenkamp thought, maybe we need *more* crises. Another dozen items were quickly covered, from early rendezvous options and propellant fuel loads to communications links, as well as the status of the three crew members aboard Alpha. "Tango's hanging in there," the rep from life sciences reported. "He's feverish and he's presenting the initial stages of X-Pox, but very slowly. Given what we know of X-Pox so far, which is very little, and what we know of its progression in microgravity, which is zero, it's impossible to predict when he'll reach, uh, the terminal phase. Our best guess is he still has two weeks from today."

"Until May eighth?" Fehrenkamp said. He needed to be able to visualize these dates on a calendar.

"May eighth, plus or minus two days."

"Which means he could be beyond hope as early as the sixth. Which, someone correct me here, is the first day we can *possibly* launch the rescue."

A pause. The energy seemed to have bled out of the group as they were confronted with the one thing that annoyed engineers as often as the weather: human biology and its unpredictability.

Fehrenkamp saw that he needed to change the subject. "What about the E-Thirteen guys?"

The JSC representative for the Alpha crew was outgoing chief astronaut Steve Goslin. "Morale is good, not great," Goslin said. "The water is up to their chins, but so far they aren't drowning."

"Let's hope they don't get hit with a wave," said an unknown voice, to general laughter.

"All right, then," he said, "orbiter and team are good to go NET May six. Thank you all—"

Through the speaker, Fehrenkamp could hear shuffling and clicking as participants disconnected. Not all of them, however. "Les, Steve McDowell, MOD. What about the Russian option?"

"Still on the table," Fehrenkamp said. He was unable to resist an automatic glance at Curt Freitag, who looked away, unable to watch his temporary boss lying. "We would all prefer to have the rescue accomplished by our crew using the prime package."

McDowell made no comment. Not wanting to invite further policy discussions from a group he could not see or control, Fehrenkamp said, "Your focus is on getting the orbiter on orbit, period. No matter what the Russians do, *we're* going to be flying. The other option is not your concern. Not today."

"Copy that," McDowell said, with the slightest hint of sarcasm. He logged off.

"I'm done here," Fehrenkamp said, feeling vaguely uneasy and not knowing why. The style and number of disconnects was off. "Are we still on-line?"

"Les, it's Terry Doolan. Gifford's with me." The associate administrator for spaceflight and the head of the Alpha program at HQ. Yes, they might very well have open issues to discuss with Fehrenkamp, especially since he had been laid up for several days.

"And Goslin."

It was unusual to include the chief astronaut in a discussion at this level, but Goslin was being groomed for a move up the NASA ladder—and he had recently returned from Russia.

"What's the order of the day?" Fehrenkamp said, trying to control the agenda, even if he didn't know what it was.

"Option C," Doolan said. "China."

"Well, I know there's been talk—" Fehrenkamp said.

"The Russians are not going to make it, Les." That was Goslin, clearly impatient.

"And we're not going to be ready until the sixth," Doolan said. "That's clear."

"It's not clear that we need to launch before then."

"Not to you, Les." That was Gifford. "But we're getting pounded by the White House, by the Hill, by the press. It's not just X-Pox hysteria; most people aren't worried that we're going to unleash the plague on Earth—"

"Good thing, given that it's already unleashed." Fehrenkamp could feel his face flush. He was getting angry.

Curt Freitag could see it, too. "Do I take notes?" the assistant mouthed, holding up his laptop. Fehrenkamp shook his head. Then Freitag started to rise. "Should I go?" Fehrenkamp pointed to the chair.

Doolan was talking. "Les, you've been a little out of the loop lately—"

"You mean because I'm in the hospital?"

"This isn't about you, Les," Goslin said, breaking in. "We need to get this guy off Alpha, now. The Chinese are willing to give it a try. They can guarantee a launch by the fourth."

"With hardware that's been flown, what, three times?"

"Three manned orbital tests, four unmanned," Goslin said.

"Compatible docking hardware?"

Now it was Gifford's turn. "The Shenzhou docking system is a licensed version of the universal Soyuz TM or Progress unit."

"Can they carry SAE-Two?"

Doolan: "Yes, and with room to spare. Their orbital module is thirteen percent larger than the one on Soyuz."

"Fine," Fehrenkamp said, knowing he had already lost the battle. "The basic hardware *might* work. But what about the tracking and communication system? What have they got, four ships and a couple of stations? What kind of coverage is that?"

"It's the same kind of coverage the Soviets used successfully for thirty years," Goslin said.

"Well, lack of coverage was one of the reasons half of the early Soviet docking missions failed."

"That was thirty years ago: Shenzhou's onboard computers can do the job alone."

"It's your station, Chris," Fehrenkamp said, addressing Gifford. "Do you really want some strange vehicle flopping around up there with thirty-year-old tracking?"

"No," Gifford said. "But I also don't want a millionaire with X-Pox dying on the station. And that is what's going to happen, if we don't pull the trigger here."

Fehrenkamp closed his eyes. His right arm—no, his whole right side—ached. Time for meds. Time to get off this stupid telecon. "What do you use to rescue Tango? Chinese haz-mat gear?"

"The SAE-Two payload is sitting at Sheremetyevo Airport in Moscow," Doolan said. "It hasn't been unloaded. We've got State on this, and we can fly it to China this afternoon."

"Okay, one last question," Fehrenkamp said, feeling it was one question too many. "Who flies this mission? A couple of Chinese astronauts?"

"One Chinese pilot, obviously. Plus one of our people. The third seat on the spacecraft is for Tango."

"It's going to be damn hard to physically get an astronaut to China, much less give him *minimal* training. I mean, opening the door or using the toilet, forget about using the SAE package. In what? Five days?"

"Agreed," Goslin said. "Which is why I sent Mark Koskinen to China two days ago."

Koskinen. Two days ago? "Why him?"

Doolan piled on. Obviously he had to have approved the assignment. "He knows Soyuz, which is the closest thing to the Chinese vehicle."

Then it was Gifford. "And he's *short,* which sounds like a joke, but the Chinese have stringent height requirements for their guys."

Goslin delivered the coup de grâce. "And, you know this as well as I do, Les—Mark Koskinen has proven himself in difficult situations."

Fehrenkamp was really in pain now. How many times was he going to be reminded of the STS-100 fiasco that had claimed the life of astronaut Cal Stipe? "Well, then, I can hardly object."

Another ten minutes of discussion followed. The trio of Doolan, Gifford, and Goslin knocked out decisions on half a dozen matters, any one of them worth a week's study and a stack of paper—at least as NASA operated here in the twenty-first century.

It reminded Fehrenkamp of the decisive way the agency had decided to fly Apollo 8 around the Moon. His admiration was tempered by one realization: in sponsoring Steve Goslin and saving his astronaut career, he had created a monster.

THE DIVINE VESSEL

"Five minutes, Mark."

"Shay shay," Mark said, using one of his four hard-earned Mandarin phrases: *xie xie*, meaning "thank you." He was strapped into the right-hand of three seats in the descent module of Shenzhou or "Divine Vessel" number eight, the one taken by what the Chinese called the "flight task expert."

Major Yu Guojun of the air forces of China's People's Liberation Army sat in the commander's couch to his left. The third seat, normally occupied by a "load expert," was empty. The savings in weight of a third crew member—even a typically compact Chinese crew member—allowed the Divine Vessel to carry three hundred kilograms of additional payload. Given the size and mass of the SAE-2 equipment crammed into the cylindrical orbital module atop the vehicle, every kilogram was needed.

And, four days from now, that seat would be filled by Tad Mikleszewski, known even to Major Yu as "Tango."

"Four minutes."

The last ten days had been the busiest of Mark's life. Even the frantic last-minute training he'd endured for the STS-100 flight six years back had not prepared him for the long hours, the amount of material to be learned, the sheer strangeness of the environment. It was as if he had really landed on another planet.

He had arrived in Beijing after a sixteen-hour flight that left him exhausted. He had not fully adjusted to the time shift in flying from Moscow to Iowa for his mother's funeral; in continuing around the world he seemed to have convinced his body that he had lost about

1.5 days. He was twelve hours out of phase, and a day behind at that.

He and the small NASA integration team had arrived at Beijing Capital Airport at night—by intention? Then they were piled into a bus and driven to the northwest side of the city.

The team numbered five. In addition to Mark, there were two engineers, one from JSC, one from NASA's Marshall Space Flight Center. The mission operations directorate had its own representative, a trainee flight controller named Burke whose primary qualification for the job was that he had studied Mandarin for two years in college.

There was also an astronaut support person—Wayne Shelton, also known to Mark as Kelly's ex.

"Anybody know where we're going?" a sleepy Shelton asked, as the bus crawled through streets crowded with pedestrians, bicyclists, and even horse-drawn wagons. Shelton and Mark had been selected in the same astronaut candidate group—the Worms—and had gotten along fine in training. But Mark made the earliest flight of any member of the group, and six years later, Shelton was one of the three Worms still waiting. In Shelton's place, Mark would have felt bitter, but the support astronaut gave no sign that he did. Perhaps he merely hid his emotions well.

Just as he hid any sign that he and Kelly were ever a couple.

"To the Haidian District," Mark said, having committed a great deal of data on the Chinese manned program to memory during his time at Star City. "We're probably going to a facility the Chinese call 'Aerospace City,' sort of a Silicon Valley of their rocket and satellite business. That's where they have a training center that is apparently known as the 'Red Chamber.' "

"Sounds ominous," Shelton said. The NASA team had been met at the airport by a group of Chinese officials—one for each foreigner. The greeting had been brisk and businesslike; Mark was sure the escorts had worked with Westerners in the past, on earlier satellite or launch vehicle programs.

Now the five escorts sat at the front of the bus. Shelton nodded at them. "I suppose we could always ask them."

"Gentlemen!" Mark yelled to Chinese escorts. He was loud enough that he startled the other sleepy members of the NASA team. "Are we going to the Red Chamber facility in Haidian District?"

A hurried exchange of Mandarin, then, in English: "Yes. You will live there. We'll arrive in twenty minutes."

Mark turned to Shelton. "There you have it."

The Red Chamber was actually rather bland, a collection of buildings that had the feel of a mid-sized software company—except for the occasional presence of a uniformed guard, which, after half a year at the Russians' Star City, Mark found unremarkable.

When the bus pulled through the gates of the Red Chamber, shortly after ten P.M. local time, another group was waiting to greet them—this time including Wang and Yu, the two *yuangyuan* Mark had met in Russia. Had Wang and Yu been Russian, Mark would have happily kissed them. Without thinking, he bowed. After a beat, the *yuangyuan* did the same.

As the group struggled with luggage, language, and directions, Shelton nudged Mark. "Hey, they're *Chinese,* not Japanese."

Mark laughed for the first time in a week.

There was a residence block at the Red Chamber, more of a dormitory than a hotel or apartment. Three rooms had been cleared for the NASA team. The two engineers were assigned to bunk together, as were Shelton and the guy from MOD.

Only Mark was given a room to himself. He protested, but Yu explained it: "You are the *yuangyuan.* You need quiet."

"I get the feeling we kicked some other *yuangyuan* out of their rooms." Mark knew that the members of the Chinese astronaut team lived in the Red Chamber during the week, returning to their families in apartments elsewhere in Beijing for the weekend.

"Yes. But they are happy to live elsewhere for such a short time. The launch could take place within two weeks."

"Do you know who will be commanding the mission?"

"There are two names under consideration," Yu said. "Captain Bao, and me."

"I hope it's you. I don't know Captain Bao."

"His name means 'good luck.' " It took Mark ten seconds to realize that Yu was joking and that there *was* no Captain Bao.

And now here they were, one hundred fifty feet above the Gobi Desert on a night in early May, something Mark would not have believed possible as recently as a week ago.

The Tango Midnight rescue had faced obstacles that ranged from the political to the physical. The political situation was being handled at a level higher than Mark's pay grade, for which he was grateful.

But during his ten days in Aerospace City he was never able to escape the physical challenges.

For example, the Chinese had put two *yuangyuan* on the very first Shenzhou flight in 2003. A year later, they had launched four men on a pair of vehicles. More relevant to the immediate mission, Shenzhou-6 and Shenzhou-7 had performed a rendezvous and docking.

Putting Shenzhou-8 on a trajectory that would ultimately reach the International Space Station was a question of timing: the launch from Jiuquan had to take place as the plane of Alpha's orbit was passing through the site. Alpha itself would be hundreds of miles ahead, and higher than Shenzhou-8's ultimate orbit, but over the course of forty-eight hours, Shenzhou would gradually catch up. (A lower orbit required a higher velocity.)

This rendezvous model provided the quickest arrival time with the least expenditure of propellant. Even the Shuttle orbiters, which carried substantially greater amounts of prop, used the two-day approach. (Which also had the benefit of allowing crew members to adapt to space before performing mission-critical tasks.)

The Chinese preferred to launch at night, to simplify visual tracking. Unfortunately, International Space Station Alpha didn't have a launch window that fell during hours of darkness. In fact, the only available launch time was in the early morning, shortly after sunrise.

There was no other option, so the Chinese embraced the inevitable.

Rendezvous also required a crew to perform critical maneuvers during the unfortunately named "terminal" phase of rendezvous, and here is where Mark thought the rescue mission would fall apart. The simulator at the Red Chamber was primitive—it was literally a wooden mock-up of a Shenzhou cabin containing only the instruments needed for rendezvous. Looking out the window, a *yuangyuan* saw only a circular target, nothing resembling another spacecraft. Certainly nothing resembling the massive silver bulk of a Harmony module on the side of the Alpha space station.

Yet, the pilot of Shenzhou-7 had managed to train himself sufficiently to nose his spacecraft into its twin adapter on Shenzhou-6.

"Three minutes."

Mark told himself that the Russians had trained for, and accomplished, rendezvous for thirty years now, most of them with rudimentary simulators. It would all work out.

Or it wouldn't.

Mark shifted in his pressure suit, to the extent he could move at all. He and his commander were strapped in so tightly that they had practically been molded to their seats. (Yu's seat was, in fact, molded to his body. There had been no time to make one for Mark, but his size and weight were a close match to one of the other *yuangyuan.*)

From his time at Star City, Mark knew there was a slight bit of wriggle room inside the suit. The Chinese model was a direct copy of the Russian Sokol suit, even down to the bizarre way you closed up the soft cloth undergarment: you backed into it, then gathered the loose fabric from chest and stomach into a knot, which you then twisted and sealed with a rubber band! It was a strong rubber band, but still! Mark would have dismissed the concept as ridiculous had he not seen a pressure test at Star City. The rubber band held just fine.

"Two minutes," Yu said. Then he listened to additional commentary before telling Mark, "They are holding the countdown."

"Why?"

"Loss of communication with one of the tracking ships."

Mark was actually relieved. First because things had been going *too* smoothly. The Long March–Divine Vessel combination had made seven successful launches over six years, but it was hardly a mature system. Even now, every Shuttle mission suffered one or more nagging glitches or holds.

Second, the scale of the problem suggested a fix wouldn't take long. Which was good: the launch window for a Shenzhou to Alpha was six minutes.

Mark realized that his commander was almost too tense to speak. He gave him an elbow, a move easily accomplished, since their suits were touching. "Relax," he said, with a confidence he didn't truly feel. "I've done this before."

"You should be the commander," Yu said.

"No way. That's a job for a pilot. Besides—" He pointed a rubbery hand at the control panel. The instruments were laid out just like those in a Soyuz, so Mark knew what they were. At least, theoretically. "—I don't read Mandarin."

"I could teach you what you need to know."

"Speaking of teaching, have you learned the astronaut's prayer?"

"No."

Mark told him. Yu was still laughing when the crew had to answer a call from the Beijing Aerospace Command and Control Center a thousand miles to the east. From the repetitive nature of the phrasing, Mark guessed it was a comm check.

Mark wondered if his father and sister were able to watch. Was the launch being broadcast live?

Where was Kelly? For that matter, what day was it? He had been cut off from communication with the world outside Aerospace City since his arrival. Yes, messages had come through the NASA team, but every one of them had been strictly operational. Even those had ceased upon his arrival here at Jiuquan, the Chinese launch center in Gansu Province.

What would Americans think of their first views of Jiuquan? A mixture of familiarity and mystery. For example, Jiuquan's vehicle assembly building looked like a smaller-scale model of the one at the Cape, down to the design of the giant doors that allowed the launch vehicle to be trucked to the pad vertically. Its design *had* to have been "borrowed."

Then there was the Shenzhou itself, roughly based on the Soyuz, even to the layout of instruments inside the cockpit. True, the Shenzhou had an orbital module that was cylindrical, not spherical, and equipped with a pair of solar panels. The vehicle was also slightly larger in its dimensions than the Soyuz. Nevertheless, it, too, would look as though it had been borrowed.

The difference was, the Chinese had actually licensed Soyuz designs from the Russians back in the 1990s. A good thing, too, or the docking equipment would have been completely incompatible with the modules on Alpha.

However, the launch vehicle itself—the Changzheng or Long March–2F, was an entirely homegrown product. It consisted of a first stage with a cluster of four YF-20 engines, surrounded by four smaller strap-on liquid-fueled rockets, each with a single YF-20. There was a second stage powered by a single YF-22 engine.

The whole vehicle, Shenzhou and Changzheng, massed a million pounds. The engines had a liftoff thrust of 1.3 million pounds—

Sudden chatter on the comm loops. Yu sighed. "We are resuming the countdown at two minutes."

"Shay shay."

The Long March–2F was said to be "highly" reliable. In truth, Mark was less concerned about this ascent than he had been about his launch on the Shuttle. With the Shuttle, if something failed while the twin solid rocket boosters were burning it was, in the words of one veteran astronaut, "curtains." There was no escape system, no hope for anything but death on impact with the surface of the Atlantic.

Like its Russian parent, the Soyuz, the Divine Vessel had a small escape rocket mounted on the nose of the fairing that enclosed the spacecraft proper. In case of a major malfunction during boost—or even on the pad—it would ignite, pulling the crew cabin to a safe distance.

Even knowing this, as the time to liftoff counted down, Mark began to feel apprehensive. Being less concerned didn't mean he didn't care. Was he entering the last five minutes of his lifetime? Four days from now, would his sister and Kelly be gathered at the same Lutheran cemetery in Marshalltown, Iowa?

Don't be stupid, he told himself. There won't be enough left to put in a casket—

"One minute, Mark," Yu said, forcing himself to smile, a gesture that was probably alien to Chinese air force pilots. "Good luck."

"Shay shay."

And what of Major Yu, his companion on this mission? In the forty-five years of manned flight, no two space travelers had ever been thrown together so abruptly for so complex a task. True, they had gone through twenty hours of simulations. But in human terms, they had barely shared a meal together, outside of one obligatory exploration of the food locker aboard Shenzhou. Yu was from a port city called Tianjin not far from Beijing; his father had been a ship's captain. The *yuangyuan* was younger than Mark—thirty-four to Mark's thirty-nine—and married. Did he and his wife have a child? Mark had never seen a picture or heard Yu mention one.

Mark wondered what Yu knew about his American passenger? Little more.

No matter, they would be linked forever, either as the two heroes who saved the X-Pox-infected millionaire in a daring space rescue, or the two screwups who failed.

Or the two unlucky bastards who died trying.

Mark felt, then heard, a rumbling and vibration through his back. Several indicators on the control panel changed color.

Up they went.

Tango Midnight, here we come.

Mark couldn't wait to see the look on the millionaire's face when he opened the hatch to Harmony.

ON THE BEACH

Kelly Gessner set her personal alarm for four P.M. the afternoon of May 4, and headed for the television in the living room of the beach house, feeling as confused as she had ever felt in her life.

It was the sleep-shifting, of course. Once a "firm" launch time had been established—10:15 P.M. on the evening of May 6—the crew of STS-124 had begun sleep-shifting. In a normal training flow, this required the crew to move to special quarters at the Johnson Space Center, where each night's bedtime would be an hour later. The crew would wake up an hour later, and the whole day's schedule would be adjusted accordingly. Windows would remain covered; extra bright lights would help fool the astronauts' biorhythms into acting as though daylight hours were shifting. (Their trainers and control center teams also had to sleep-shift, to some extent, without benefit of special quarters. Kelly tried to remember that when she caught someone yawning, or forgetting a piece of key information.)

Since the ULF-3 crew had had to move to the Cape early, sleep-shifting was taking place in the beach house two miles south of launch complex 39. The house had been used by generations of astronauts, all the way back to Mercury, for preflight parties and even some quiet nights. The crew quarters in the ops and checkout building would have been better, in some ways, but none of the hundreds of other staffers was used to the procedure. So mission commander Latham had suggested the beach house, and the decision proved to be a good one.

Except for Kelly, who had interrupted her shifting by taking the trip to Iowa; she had spent the rest of the week trying to catch up with Latham, Ames, and Herron, without much success. She was waking at the wrong times, feeling sleepy in the middle of what was, for the other astronauts, a workday.

Beyond that, she felt vaguely strange, as if she were coming down with a case of the flu. One troubling "night" she had awakened convinced she had X-Pox. She had even gone to the mirror to search her body for signs of the rash. Fortunately, there was nothing.

But she still felt off.

This "morning," however, she dragged herself out of bed earlier than the others in order to watch the launch of Shenzhou-8. When the CNN cameras shifted to a live shot of Jiuquan, she felt her pulse quicken. Everything looked so strange! Here was a vehicle assembly building that looked a lot like the one a few miles north of her. But the landscape seemed wrong—who wanted to launch over hills?

The gantry was fine, but the rocket was unfamiliar. It looked a little like a late-model Delta III with those first-stage strap-ons. But the vehicle at the top was clearly a Soyuz.

She forgot about her objections when the screen showed a view from inside the cabin: a Chinese astronaut in the center seat, and to his right, a Caucasian who might possibly be Mark Koskinen.

The count reached zero . . . the engines of the Long March first stage lit up.

"Am I missing it?" Diana Herron flew into the living room, bare feet slapping on the wood floor. She landed on the battered couch, cross-legged in shorts and T-shirt, like a sorority girl hoping to catch sight of the latest bad boy rap star.

"Right on time," Kelly said. The Long March with its Shenzhou was rising into the predawn sky of China.

"God, can you imagine? Flying with the fucking Chinese!"

"Two weeks ago I would have laughed at the idea." Kelly hated to agree with Herron, but she had no desire to get in an argument this early in their "morning."

They watched in silence as the strap-ons burned out, fell away, then through shutdown and ignition of the second stage. By now

Shenzhou-8 was sixty miles high and headed across northern China toward the Pacific.

"You think they're going to do it?" Herron asked.

"Do what?"

"Can they get that man out of Harmony without screwing up the whole station? Forget bringing him back alive; I don't think anyone's expecting that."

Kelly had asked herself the same question since learning of Option C for China: could you depend on a program with two years of manned operational experience to execute a rescue mission?

At a comparable point in their manned program, the Soviets launched one Vostok with a male cosmonaut followed two days later by another Vostok and the first female space traveler. No rendezvous, of course; the Soviets were five years away from that.

NASA was flying Gordo Cooper on an eighteen-hour Mercury mission. But America was already committed to landing a human on the Moon—

Oh, hell, the Chinese were ready! And looking objectively at Mark's skills, he was a good choice. He had dogged persistence, a trick memory and that ability to pull a Koskinen—to come up with some wild idea, a Grand Gesture out of left field, and make it work. "Yeah, they can do it," Kelly said.

"If they do, where does that leave us?"

"We're flying to Alpha." Kelly smiled. "One of us is going to have to fill out that expedition crew."

Herron stared at the television for several moments.

Shenzhou was now in orbit; animation showed the Shenzhou separating from the second stage, solar panels deploying from its propulsion module and orbital module like wings. "I'm sorry I keep pissing you off," Herron said abruptly.

Kelly was so startled by this conversational first strike that she could only say, "What are you talking about?"

"Sleeping with your boyfriend."

"Oh, that." Kelly was surprised at how humiliated and angry she felt. It was not that she had somehow "lost" Wayne Shelton. He was bright and good-looking and, fidelity aside, a decent human being. He would probably make some woman an acceptable husband someday.

But not Kelly. That had been clear for some months, since Mark Koskinen had shown up at her front door. Wayne must have sensed this—not that Kelly was at all ready to take responsibility for his treachery in not only cheating on her, but cheating on her with a colleague! In their one and only postdiscovery conversation, she had bitterly suggested that if Wayne wanted to cheat on her, there were hundreds of strippers, cocktail waitresses, secretaries, and horny, lonely housewives up and down the Gold Coast. Picking a fellow astronaut—a fellow crew member, for God's sake—was as mean as it was stupid.

"I've got to be honest, Diana. That did cost you some points with me."

"I don't expect this to make much difference, but I am in love with him."

Now, *this* was a surprise. Diana Herron, the one female astronaut who seemed determined to sleep with every suitable man she could find, and some that were completely unsuitable, trothing her love for Wayne Shelton? "I don't believe that."

"He asked me to marry him," she said, then quickly added, "*after* you two, uh, broke up."

Marry Diana Herron? Wayne? Kelly had felt nauseous all morning—now she literally wanted to vomit. But she took a breath and said, "Well, then, all I can do is wish you both the best."

"Thank you. And I'm sorry I've been such a screwup in training. I'm really not like this. I don't know what's been wrong with me."

"Love does strange things to people, Diana." Kelly couldn't hide the sarcasm.

"I'm good, you know. In school, in the air force, I was always at the top of whatever class I took. I got selected, how bad could I be?" This was a common argument put forward by the small percentage of astronauts who simply couldn't hack mission training. Diana Herron was hardly the first, and nowhere near the worst.

Maybe it was the queasiness, or the weird hour, or the sight of Mark blasting into space on a Chinese rocket, but Kelly felt the bare stirrings of sympathy for Herron. "It's probably because in school and even in the air force, you were never totally terrified."

"What?"

"It's *fear,* Diana. The one thing none of us ever talk about. When you get assigned to a mission after all those years of training, one part of you is feeling smug and arrogant and happy. But there's another part of your brain that's saying, 'Hey, stupid, don't forget . . . you could get killed here.' You know, 'Why are you doing this to us?' "

"I don't feel afraid. I'm aware of the risks—"

"I know. I felt the same way before my first flight. I was calmly aware that I had a one-in-a-hundred chance of dying in a horrible manner. The whole *Challenger* nightmare—the vehicle has broken up, I'm sitting there in the dark, strapped in, suffocating as the cabin falls toward the ocean.

"I was able to tell myself that, hell, everyone dies, if it's my day, it's my day. At least I'm doing something I wanted to do.

"This whole strategy worked fine up to about three minutes before ignition. Then I literally started shaking. If someone had swung the white room back to the orbiter and said, 'Anybody change her mind?,' I'd have been out of there like a shot."

"But you went back and flew two more times. This will be your fourth!"

"Yeah. On my next mission I felt that same clutching terror all through training. Not constantly, but it was the last thing I thought of every night and the first thing I felt every morning. And that was *before Columbia.*" The reentry disaster that had killed another crew of seven, seventeen years almost to the day after *Challenger,* had destroyed her sleep for the next year. She had sat in the flight engineer's seat, right behind two Shuttle pilots, on an entry. She refused to imagine the confusion she would have felt on seeing temperature warning lights for left-side tires. She would have assumed a sensor problem.

But then, to see the whole display light up with red warnings . . . not just temperature, but unusual firings of the reaction control jets, an unplanned opening of the speed brake, severe elevon deflections. Then the whole vehicle yawing left, then right—

Then what? An explosion as the orbiter broke up? A plunge into darkness and terror as she realized that she had seconds to live?

Herron stared at her as if Kelly were speaking a foreign language. "Why do you keep doing it?"

"I guess it's because I think that living in space—which is the reason we're here at all—is worth the pain and the risk. Living on Alpha is more dangerous than living in Houston. The Moon and Mars would be worse yet." Kelly had never articulated these thoughts. Maybe the waves of nausea were washing away some internal emotional barriers.

Herron looked doubtful. But then she threw her arms around Kelly. "I'm really looking forward to flying with you."

The hug was mercifully brief. Then Herron went back to her room.

Kelly rushed to the bathroom, where she threw up.

Moments later she had scrambled an egg—not remotely her usual breakfast—and eaten it, and was feeling better than she had in days.

Since Iowa. Since, specifically, the morning after her night with Mark Koskinen.

The night she had *not* used birth control.

Now she felt fear—and not the fear of death in space. The fear of a gigantic change in her life.

The fear of trying to explain to Steve Goslin and the rest of

NASA why she might not be the best candidate for an immediate tour on International Space Station Alpha.

Brad Latham walked into the kitchen, hair tousled, yawning. " 'Morning," he said. "Did the Chinese get off okay?"

"Sure did," Kelly said.

"But we won't know squat until they dock in a couple of days."

"Nope."

"Oh, well. Hose and I have to shoot landings this morning or this evening or whatever the hell time it is." He looked around the kitchen. "Hey, scrambled eggs. What a good idea!"

On the morning of Friday, May 5, Viktor Kondratko slept past seven for the first time. He was still in his coffinlike cabin at 7:45 when he was awakened by a *thump!* Nate Bristol was moving a piece of equipment through Zvezda, and hit the hatchway hard enough to make a sound that carried over the general drone of Alpha's equipment. Misjudging momentum and distance was also an easy mistake to make, even after two months on orbit. "Sorry," he said.

Viktor quickly saw that the equipment Bristol was moving was an Elektron air generator. There were two aboard Alpha, one online and one spare that was stored in Progress. The Elektron was the most troublesome piece of machinery on any spacecraft, often breaking down. The Expedition 12 crew had performed a changeout just prior to Viktor's arrival on Alpha. Now, apparently, it was the 13 crew's turn.

"So the Elektron is down."

"Since about four A.M."

"And we're on candles?"

"Yes."

The lithium-perchlorate "candles" were cartridges that could be ignited to produce oxygen. They had originally been developed for use on Soviet submarines. Later they were adapted to space station use. Viktor hated them, since they required regular replacement while serving as a constant reminder that your life depended on a very fragile backup system.

They also gave the station's atmosphere an odor that was noticeably different from that of the Elektron. Chemical analysts claimed they did no such thing, but as far as Viktor knew, none of these analysts had actually been aboard a station.

Viktor was eager to rage at Bristol, but the astronaut disarmed him, saying, "I was already awake when the alarm squeaked, so I got it very quickly. You were sleeping so soundly I couldn't wake you." He made one of those wry American faces Viktor had learned to recognize, if not appreciate. "You're the *commander,* Viktor. Talk about candles—you've been burning them at both ends. I thought you could use an extra hour's sleep. Only one of us can work the screwdriver at a time, anyway."

Rather than start an argument that would inevitably lead to delays in the work schedule, Viktor chose to embrace the inevitable. Besides, his training at Star City, from psychologists and other specialists who had thirty years of Russian space station experience to study, had prepared him for the change in personal dynamics once the crew was reduced to two. With three or more cosmonauts, one could exercise authority.

A crew of two *had* to be a partnership. "Why don't I take a look at the BMP?" This was a unit that scrubbed organic contaminants out of the station's atmosphere.

"I just did that," Bristol said. "It's fine, for now."

"Let me know if you need help. I'm going to check on Tango."

Mikleszewski had given Viktor a scare by falling unconscious four days ago. The only action Viktor could take then—short of opening the hatch to Harmony—was to trigger a caution and warning alarm. The jangling bells had roused the sick millionaire just enough to inject himself with a stimulant from the medical kit.

Relaying directions from the medical support staff at Houston, Viktor had kept Tango stabilized. The man had X-Pox, however; there was no doubt about it. The only mystery was how long it would take the mutated strain developed in Harmony to kill him.

And whether help would arrive in time.

As he floated into Unity, Viktor grabbed the daily summary off the printer. The Chinese vehicle was operating normally; it would arrive within twenty-four hours, bringing his comrade Mark Koskinen. They had had a brief comm link last night, little more than a "Hello, Viktor," "Hello, Mark" exchange. Viktor hoped they could speak again prior to docking.

"Good morning, Tango!" Viktor said, forcing himself to sound cheerful.

"What's the word?" Tango sounded like a man in pain.

"Shenzhou will be here tomorrow morning."

"That's good news." Now he wheezed.

"One more day." Viktor tried not to be astonished—or even offended—at the amount of effort being made to rescue this one man. He remembered his country's nuclear submarine *Kursk,* which had sunk in three hundred feet of water in 2000. Three hundred feet was nothing! The ship itself was twice that length! If you'd stood it on end, half of it would have been dry!

Yet over a hundred sailors from the Northern Fleet had drowned in the icy darkness, doomed by a combination of secrecy, inertia, and sheer incompetence.

The same sort of secrecy—this time for corporate reasons—and technical incompetence had locked Tango inside Harmony.

Well, so far he had survived longer than the poor sailors on *Kursk*.

"I suppose we should go over the—" Tango coughed. "The procedures."

"Absolutely. We'll have a training session this afternoon," Viktor said. "Why don't you get yourself some food?" Viktor wouldn't have objected to a little breakfast himself.

"Not hungry."

"Drink something, then. Water."

"Shit!" Bristol's voice carried into Unity from Zarya next door. Viktor was startled, not because the astronaut didn't normally use profanity; he was a sailor, after all. But because his voice sounded so resigned.

Then Viktor smelled the smoke. "Wait one," he told Tango.

He hauled himself out of Unity into Zarya, which was already smoky, to find Bristol trying to peer into the BMP. "Is it on fire?" Viktor asked, ready to grab for the nearest extinguisher. Aside from a violent collision with another spacecraft, a fire was the last thing you wanted in a space station. It not only used vital oxygen, it filled the modules with smoke and carbon dioxide.

"I don't think so."

Viktor didn't see flame, which propagated either as a jet or as a sphere. "What happened?"

"I was venting the contaminants." This was a routine procedure that cleared the BMP's cartridge. It was like emptying Alpha's toilet reservoir, but much less work. "The goddamn cartridge must have been hot. When I closed the valve, it started smoking."

Viktor shoved his hand into the unit, as far as he dared. He felt a panel that was hot, though not painfully so; the rest of the unit was fine. "All we can do is let it cool down." He waved at the smoke. It was not getting any worse. The other scrubbers would suck it out of the atmosphere within a few hours.

"What do we tell Houston?" Bristol asked.

"We don't need to tell them anything. They'll know." Viktor slapped Bristol on the shoulder. "Don't worry. I'm not going to become the stoic Russian commander. Their monitors will show them that we had a problem with the BMP. They will also show that the temperature is falling, and that the air is clearing.

"I'll tell them we're fine, but really, Nate, I want them concentrating on *that* situation." He pointed toward Unity in the general direction of the Harmony module.

"I wish we could cut that son of a bitch loose. Not Tango," Bristol said, correcting himself. "Harmony. We're never going to be able to clean it up. Not so anyone with brains will want to use it."

"We *can't* just cut it loose," Viktor said. "The great minds who designed the station ordered us to disable the pyros, remember? The module has no independent propulsion. If we close the hatches and disconnect, it will simply float away, and probably take away part of a truss or another module as it goes."

Bristol started coughing. "Christ, now I sound like Tango."

"Let's get out of here. We have a very busy day ahead of us."

They moved into Zvezda as Viktor Kondratko did something he had never done before.

He actually prayed: *Hurry, Mark!*

TERMINAL PHASE

"I see it."

Mark Koskinen saw the silvery shape of Alpha from the right-side window of the Shenzhou-8 orbital module. The station was presenting its starboard side, making it look like a train composed of silvery cars of different sizes. Behind it was the black of space, a reassuring sight. Shenzhou-8 was approaching the station from below; had Mark seen the blue and white of a sunlit Earth behind Alpha, he would have been worried. A Shuttle, with an experienced pair of pilots, the vast experience of mission control, and a load of propellant, *might* make a successful docking from almost anywhere in the proximity of a target.

Mark wasn't so sure about Shenzhou-8. An approach to the station from a little too high and far away risked the feared "whifferdill," an orbital Bermuda Triangle in which diminishing fuel and diverging rates would ensure that Shenzhou-8 and Alpha would never link up. Shenzhou-8 would have to break off the docking.

And Tango would almost certainly die.

"I see it, too," Yu said from Mark's left. He had his eye up to a periscope-like display overlaid with figures showing distance-to-target, rate of closure, and a dozen other parameters. "We are station-keeping," Yu said, first in English, then in Mandarin to BAACC.

At the moment the rendezvous and terminal phase maneuvers were being performed automatically by Shenzhou-8's guidance system as commanded from BAACC. The calls between Yu and BAACC were confirmations of thruster firings and their timings, ensuring that the readouts aboard the spacecraft matched those on the ground.

Mark was glad BAACC had taken the lead, since the *yuangyuan* commander of Shenzhou-8 had been ill for almost two days. Space adaptation syndrome, still the scourge of four out of ten astronauts and cosmonauts over the last forty years, hit Yu two hours after launch, when the crew began the grueling process of removing their pressure suits.

Mark and Yu were in the orbital module, bracing each other so zippers could be undone, and somehow got upside down in relation to the local vertical. The difference between what the brain felt ("I'm floating rightside up!") and the eyes saw ("I must be standing on my head!") was the usual trigger for nausea, at least during the first day or two in microgravity.

Based on his experience aboard STS-100, Mark sensed the impending unpleasantness, and closed his eyes while slowly aligning himself with the internal up-and-down of the module. He was also able to use a series of autogenic feedback techniques he had studied years back—a NASA version of a mantra that actually seemed to minimize discomfort.

Yu was not so lucky, expelling a cloud of milky vomit. The smell almost made Mark do the same, but he held his breath as he fished a barf bag out of the pocket of his launch suit.

"I flew aerobatics in jets!" Yu had protested. "I never got sick like this!"

Mark reassured the commander that prior immunity to motion sickness had no bearing on susceptibility to SAS. "One of our guys who got sickest in space had flown with the Thunderbirds," Mark said. "Then you have older, chubbier people who never feel a thing."

"Chubby astronauts?" Yu was gamely trying to carry on, a real challenge, given that he was literally green in the face.

"Well, chubby cosmonauts." In spite of the rigorous physical training schedule at Star City, the Russians still managed to launch an amazing number of space travelers who were overweight or cigarette smokers.

Yu grew more comfortable once he was out of the suit, and moved carefully during the rest of the first day. In fact, he strapped himself back into the command pilot couch and talked to BAACC, which fed images of the latest heroic *yuangyuan* to a billion or so television watchers.

Mark concentrated on checking out the haz-mat suits and medicines in the SAE-2 package. If the crew expected to don them in a timely manner after reaching Alpha, at least one prior rehearsal in microgravity was necessary. He also reviewed data on the layout of the Harmony, and continued his study of Shenzhou. While the descent module seemed fairly familiar, given its resemblance to its Russian parent, the orbital module was almost entirely original. There were still cabinets whose contents—hidden behind the boxes and bags of the SAE-2 material—Mark simply didn't know.

Yu's recovery suffered a major setback after the crew's first meal in space. Mark wanted to blame the food—who the hell ate curried shellfish *anywhere,* much less on orbit? But he realized his reaction was unjustified. Shenzhou's menu was Yu's. There had been no time to select, prepare, and load a dozen "Western" meals for Mark. While Chinese food as defined by the managers of the Shenzhou program bore little resemblance to the "Chinese food" Mark knew from living in the United States, he found he could eat most of it.

By the second morning, Mark's only lingering problem with the diet was the lack of coffee. He had to settle for a bag of hot tea. Well, hot colored water.

Yu's condition progressed from the miserable to the occasionally queasy. He was able to run through a haz-mat-donning test.

Mark, meanwhile, had half a dozen brief downlinks of his own, four with Wayne Shelton at BAACC, and another couple directly with the ISS support team in Houston. And shortly before the start of maneuvers on the second day of the mission, Mark was able to speak directly to Tango. "I hear you're riding to my rescue," Tango said, his voice sounding horribly weak. Mark blamed the poor reception on the fact that the signal had to be routed through Korolev, then Houston, then BAACC, and back.

Or so he hoped. "They told me you ordered takeout. Will this be cash or charge?"

Tango wheezed. "Get here in thirty minutes and there'll be a hell of a tip."

"Insurance regulations keep us from speeding, sir. Just be patient," Mark said, wondering why he felt compelled to banter with the dying millionaire. Maybe it was the knowledge that hundreds of millions of people could be listening. It was not as though he was a stranger to death—or dying men.

Mercifully, the comm session ended, as the crew of Shenzhou-8 turned to the all-consuming business of orienting the spacecraft for a series of burns that ranged in duration from two minutes to seven seconds.

Once Shenzhou was on station with Alpha, within a few hundred meters, close enough that the two vehicles were, essentially, traveling in the same orbit, the terminal phase began.

Alpha's current orientation was called LVLH, local-vertical, local-horizontal, with its nose or plus-X flying forward and its floor or nadir toward the surface of the Earth. The Harmony module was docked to Unity, jutting out to starboard.

On the comm loop, Mark heard a three-way conversation between Yu and Shelton at BAACC, with Viktor Kondratko included. Viktor reported the beginning of Alpha's final predocking maneuver, rolling the station to starboard so that the Harmony module pointed directly toward the Earth, on what was known as the R-bar.

Shenzhou slowly climbed up the R-bar, its onboard computer firing the vehicle's small reaction-control thrusters once, twice, three times. To Mark's eyes, there was no immediate effect, which was reassuring. Why hurry? The slower the approach, the less chance for a major mistake. And a major mistake this close to Alpha might involve a collision that could damage the two-hundred-ton station, utterly destroying Shenzhou.

During the terminal phase, Mark's job was simply to watch Alpha and tell Yu if the station moved the wrong direction. He would have liked to do more, but there had been no time to train him as a Shenzhou flight engineer.

His system was crude, but effective: as soon as Yu told him they were station-keeping, Mark used a red crayon to draw a grid right on the window glass. Alpha should grow within that grid—but it shouldn't *drift.*

Mark saw now that Alpha was closer, but still in the same part of his window. So far, so good. At least fifty vehicles—manned and unmanned—had docked with the International Space Station since its first elements were launched in late 1998. Not one of those dockings had failed, though there had been some that required a second try.

None of the dockings, of course, had involved relatively untested Chinese technology.

Closer now. Another thruster tweak, another confirmation from Yu to BAACC.

Alpha was drifting out of the window, moving left. "We're diverging!" Mark called. "Drifting left!" Mark turned just in time to see his commander staring at the instruments, as if he could not trust them.

Yu uttered a sharp phrase in Mandarin and literally raised a hand, as if to protect his face. An annunciator was beeping.

Mark slid into the seat next to Yu, and even with his limited knowledge of Shenzhou flight procedures and instrumentation, could see that guidance had *failed.*

"Reboot it," he said.

Yu was already punching the buttons. Waiting. If he had spent most of the mission looking green, he was now quite pale.

Shenzhou *lurched.*

Yu swore again. "Manual," he said in English, and grabbed the controller.

Mark desperately wanted to remind Yu of his training—for example, on orbit, thrusting in the direction of travel would put your spacecraft into a higher orbit—with a slower velocity. But Yu was already calmly reading numbers to BAACC. His training seemed to have taken over.

Mark pushed himself back to the window. Alpha was much closer now, almost filling the window.

Whump! Whump! Yu commanded thruster firings.

"Too much!" Mark shouted, unable to keep silent. *He could hear the grinding screech of a collision, feel the deadly pop in his ears as air blew out of the spacecraft—No,* he told himself. *We're not screwed yet.*

Whump! Another firing.

The circular docking adaptor slid into the center of Mark's window. Then, as expected, it moved backward. Fine: Mark's view was biased to the right. The adaptor and its twin on the nose of Shenzhou should be lined up.

They were ten meters away.

There was nothing else for Mark to do. He floated back to his couch and lightly tugged on his straps. "Go for it," he said, quietly.

Seven meters, four meters, zero. Shenzhou shuddered and even swayed, then settled.

The docking light on the console came on.

Now Yu proudly informed BAACC that the docking had been accomplished. Mark keyed his own microphone. "And, Houston, from Shenzhou—we have capture with Alpha."

He clasped hands with Yu. Both of them realized their hands were shaking.

It seemed crazy to Mark to break for a meal while Tango lingered inside the Harmony module. But then, Armstrong and Aldrin had stopped to have dinner between landing on the Moon and venturing out to the lunar surface. Work in space was strenuous; Mark and Yu hadn't eaten in five hours.

So they worked their way through a selection of what the Chinese called food "bricks" as they donned their plastic haz-mat suits and opened the medical kit. Mark couldn't help glancing at the docking hatch. Tango was on the other side, probably no more than two meters away.

The only immediate glitch was communications. Shenzhou should have been able to talk directly to Alpha by now, but either the Chinese antenna had failed, or the one on Alpha was blocked. Mark had received a hello and congratulations from Viktor and Nate Bristol, who told him that Tango was "packed and ready to go." But the conversation had been relayed through the three control centers, and sounded as forced and phony as Mark's earlier exchange with the millionaire.

What was he going to find on the other side of that hatch? Mark would be first through; it would be his job to use the sniffer that would give him a reading on the level of contamination inside the module. Then—

Well, it depended on conditions in Harmony. The night before the launch of Shenzhou-8, Mark had been given a set of "mission rules" by Steve Goslin during a phone call. "You have three goals: Save Tango. Save Alpha. Save the planet from X-Pox."

Mark respected Steve Goslin. The Marine was a steady if unspectacular pilot, honest, straightforward to a fault. His sense of humor ranged from nonexistent to goofy, and that's what Mark assumed, responding in kind: "No problem. Any particular priority? I mean, I figure saving the Earth from X-Pox ought to be near the top of the list."

"Whatever it takes. Nobody down here has enough data to make informed judgments about the situation. You're going to be on-site. The clock will be running. Comm might be an issue. It's not as though we're going to be looking over your shoulder."

Mark realized that Goslin was *serious.* Ignoring forty years of NASA precedents, where crew actions were scripted down to the level of "open tube, squeeze toothpaste," where major decisions were made by flight directors, the chief astronaut was offering Mark nothing more than *guidance.* "Wow. Okay."

"Things happen for a reason, Mark." There was the religious side of Steve Goslin.

"You may be right about that." Given the events of the past six months, Mark was no longer eager to discount the possibility of divine intervention—or interference—in human affairs. "What would you do?"

"I'm not there."

"I mean, knowing what you know so far—which of those three goals would be number one?"

The line was silent for several seconds, long enough for Mark to wonder who might be listening in. (The idea that the conversation was private struck Mark as extremely unlikely.)

Finally Goslin spoke. "Save the station, Mark."

Since then, Mark had agreed with Goslin's choice, rejected it in favor of saving Tango, rejected *that* in favor of recovering whatever vaccine Tango might have developed, then circled back to saving the station.

With every evaluation, he was reminded again that he didn't have sufficient data to make the decision.

"Pressures are equal," Yu reported, his voice strangely muffled in Mark's headset. He was sealed in the descent module. NASA and the Chinese had been willing to risk contaminating the Shenzhou orbital module, since it would be discarded in space, but not the entire spacecraft. "Open the hatch."

Mark immediately began cranking the handle that disengaged the seals. None of the hatches on Alpha or visiting spacecraft was locked, in the sense that they had keys or combinations. But they were most definitely secured against sudden changes in pressure or an accidental bump.

The SAE-2 package held a box of basic tools: hammer, crescent wrench, two types of screwdriver, knife, and power drill. Mark could have disassembled Harmony's hatch from his side, if Tango were complete disabled. Fortunately he was not.

Not so far, anyway.

"Shenzhou hatch open," Mark reported. Through the circular passage, he could see the matching exterior surface of Harmony's aft hatch cover. Would it open? He reached in with his yellow-gloved hand and knocked.

The hatch began to open, away from him, then got stuck half-way. Mark edged forward, braced himself against the side of the passage, and pushed on the hatch, which swung away.

He blinked in the bright lights of the Harmony interior. There, floating sideways, head to Mark's left and looking haggard and pink, was Tad Mikleszewski, aka Tango Midnight. "Did you order the pepperoni pizza?" Mark said, unable to stop himself.

Tango's arms fluttered, as if he couldn't decide whether to extend a hand to shake, or to simply grab his visitor. "Yeah," he croaked. "That was me."

Without thinking about the potential for contagion, Mark took Tango's hand and pulled him upright. Even through the protective plastic of the suit, Mark could feel that Tango's temperature was high. The man was sick.

"Thank God," Tango said. "Thank God you got here."

Mark reported contact to Yu, then took Tango's headset. Without removing his haz-mat hood, he yelled to Viktor Kondratko that he was safely in Harmony.

"*Khorosho!*" Viktor yelled in answer. "Good!"

"I'm going to have a look around. Give me ten minutes." He was speaking not only to Viktor, but to Major Yu and the various control teams in Beijing, Moscow, and Houston.

He turned to Tango, his first priority. Not only was the man suffering from the papular rash, he was also showing lesions on his neck and arms. Mark suspected that if he took off Tango's grubby shirt, he would find that the patient's torso was covered.

"Do you have any pain?" Mark asked, feeling like a physician making a house call.

"Oh, yeah." Without being asked, Tango lifted his shirt. Mark had to will himself not to look away. The last thing Tango needed right now was to be treated like he had the Black Death. X-Pox was spread via inhaled air droplets or aerosols; Mark was still safe and secure inside his suit.

"I'm febrile—feverish," Tango said. "I am definitely showing signs of an X-Pox infection in the last fourteen days, though not a classic case."

"How so?" Mark said, grateful that his patient was capable of making the diagnosis.

"Some symptoms are more advanced. These pustules," he said, indicating his chest. "The fever is intermittent. I have moments of great clarity. I've also been . . . crazy at times."

"Crazy."

"Irrational. Angry. I may have broken things."

Mark glanced at the mismatched collection of processed samples scattered around Harmony. "Have you taken anything?"

Tango smiled, and for an instant looked just like the arrogant millionaire he had come to know at Star City. The words, however, were those of a sick man. "I just don't remember." Tango seemed faint. "You got here just in time." He began to wheeze, each spasm wrenching his body into a flailing twitch. In microgravity, these twitches turned the man sideways and upside down.

It must have taken Tango's last stores of strength to open the hatch and greet Mark. "Let me get you some juice," Mark told him, tugging on a trailing cord attached to medical and sensor kits and a set of fresh cartridges for the BMP air filter on Harmony.

"What I really need," Tango said, obviously in pain, "is a bucket of ice."

Mark held up a pair of cold packs from the kit. He wrapped one in Tango's discarded shirt, then helped the patient place it against his neck.

Moments later, Tango had consumed a dozen fluid ounces of juice and was wearing a fresh shirt. He floated in the wide part of Harmony, talking to Viktor and the control centers while Mark took inventory.

The sniffer showed that the atmosphere inside the module was indeed contaminated. Not only were there traces of X-Pox—even a trace was enough to cause the air to be considered poisoned—but carbon dioxide levels were high, and so were an odd collection of other substances.

Mark could feel the heat and see the bright light. Had Tango tried to cook the virus out of the module? Or were the high temperatures just a side effect of continuing research? It was obvious that the Eridan glovebox and other processing equipment had been in use, possibly as late as this morning. The displays were lit, the surfaces were warm.

More intriguing, there were literally dozens of samples—bags and tubes—taped to walls and cabinet surfaces in the lab area. Glancing at the labels, Mark saw that they were all dated after April 17. The other markings were mysterious and might as well have been in Mandarin.

The rest of the module's internal volume was cluttered with tools, including marking pens, as well as unopened bags and boxes that Mark recognized as ISS cargo. There was also an astonishing amount of litter from parcels that had been opened, as well as bags filled with other substances. Mark remembered that Harmony didn't have a toilet. He gave those bags a lot of room as he continued to the other end, near the hatch that led into the Unity module and Alpha.

The sniffer was still showing high levels of contamination. Mark was resigned to the idea that the whole interior would have to be vented. Russian documentation on the module claimed that its electronics were hardened against vacuum; Mark hoped they were telling the truth.

But as he moved back to the module's control panel, he realized that venting Harmony was not an option.

Whether deliberately, or bumping around in his delirium, Tango had smashed the controls.

Four hours later, Mark had dragged Tango into the Shenzhou orbital module and zipped him into a sleeping bag. Tango was still running a fever, but Mark had given him an anti-inflammatory. Tango was still conscious, but groggy, either from the X-Pox or sheer fatigue.

Mark had been busy on the closed Shenzhou link, getting Yu's approval before bringing Tango aboard. "The module's already exposed, isn't it?" the *yuangyuan* said.

"Correct."

"Then it doesn't make any difference where he is. Put him where you think he needs to be."

Yu also agreed to stay put in the descent module. For one thing, it kept the *yuangyuan* from being exposed to X-Pox. For another, it allowed him to work through the tedious business of rebooting Shenzhou's guidance system, which had failed during the terminal phase. It was needed for the "contingency maneuver" the crew had simulated prior to launch.

Now Mark faced a decision. According to the timeline, he should have been able to vent Harmony by now, and reenter the module minus his haz-mat suit.

But venting was now impossible. And he had replaced the filters on the haz-mat suit twice. He only had two more in stock.

He was finding it difficult to work in the suit. Not only was he sweating and fogging up the tiny faceplate, he couldn't reach, couldn't see, couldn't hear. (He had to wear the comm headset over the plastic hood of the suit.)

He wasn't able to do what he needed to do. So, fully aware that he was exposing himself to X-Pox, he opened the suit.

He took a breath. Felt much the same.

He didn't expect to get sick immediately, or possibly at all. While Tango was hardly in a biological-isolation garment, he *was* zipped into a sleeping bag and not actively breathing or sweating in Mark's face. The new air filters had had some time to start purging the atmosphere inside Harmony.

Mark needed to be able to speak with Viktor Kondratko in Alpha using the intracrew system. Five hours after docking, with the night shift working at BAACC and Korolev, he was finally able to ask his Russian colleague, "How long will it take you to get a collision avoidance maneuver scheduled?"

Alpha routinely used the engines of a Progress supply craft or a docked Shuttle to raise its orbit by several miles. (Day by day, thanks to the cumulative effects of atmospheric drag on the massive structure, Alpha fell several hundred meters closer to earth.) Once or twice a year, the whole station might require a lesser maneuver to avoid colliding with space debris. In neither case could the crew just flip a switch and make it happen.

"Two hours minimum," Viktor said. "But why do we need it?" Mark told him. "You are out of your mind, my friend."

"What else are we going to do? This thing is a toxic hulk. They will *never* let you open that hatch."

Viktor fumed silently at the obvious truth. "What reason do I give Houston? A collision-avoidance originates with *them*."

"You make the request like this: 'Houston, a message from Shenzhou: Koskinen requests a medical conference.' A small group of flight dynamics folks will know what it means. Anyone else who happens to be listening in will think it's about the contamination aboard Harmony."

"All right," Viktor said, though the unhappiness was plain in his voice. "Then what do you do?"

"I really don't know, Viktor."

"Are you *sure* this is the right choice?"

"Yes," Mark said. "Just be standing by for disconnect."

Five hours and thirty minutes after docking, Yu reported that Shenzhou's guidance was back on-line.

At docking-plus-seven hours, twenty-three minutes, with Alpha passing over southern Africa, well within range of the Chinese tracking station in Namibia, station commander Viktor Kondratko fired the latches that disconnected Harmony from the Unity module.

In the descent module of Shenzhou-8, Major Yu Guojun briefly fired his small forward-facing reaction control thrusters, causing the sixty-foot-long combined Shenzhou-Harmony vehicle to back away from Alpha at approximately two feet per second.

As Alpha flight engineer Nate Bristol observed from the Destiny lab module, and Shenzhou flight task expert Mark Koskinen watched from the orbital module, the vehicles made a clean, if agonizingly slow, separation.

Once Shenzhou-Harmony was clear of Alpha's solar arrays, which stretched a hundred feet to either side of the core structure, Yu fired the thrusters again, dropping his vehicle into an orbit that was slightly lower than Alpha's.

Ten minutes later, with Shenzhou-Harmony no more than a twinned pair of bright objects below, Alpha performed a "collision avoidance" maneuver, raising its orbit by several feet per second.

Save the station first, Steve Goslin had suggested. Mark had done that.

As for saving Tango Midnight, much less the people of Earth—well, so far he was batting one out of three.

Too bad he wasn't playing baseball.

"He did *what?*" Kelly said, still blinking sleep from her eyes, and feeling the first stirrings of what she now believed to be morning sickness.

"Mark had Shenzhou undock from the station," Diana Herron told her. "*With* Harmony!"

"Where did they go?"

"Apparently they're just station-keeping. They moved off a couple of hundred yards, then Alpha maneuvered. They can probably still see each other!"

Kelly glanced at the clock: three P.M. To her body it might as well have been A.M. She had planned to get up "early"—4:30 or so—just to see how the Shenzhou docking had gone. She had assumed she would awake to find Mark and his Chinese partner busy tending to Tango, then venting and sanitizing the module.

Not *this*.

"Did they have some kind of problem?" Spacecraft didn't go to the trouble of docking just to pull apart after four or five hours. Similar incidents had only happened twice in the history of spaceflight, once on a Soviet space station mission in 1971, when the crew had not been able to open a hatch, and even earlier, on Neil Armstrong's infamous first flight, Gemini 8. Armstrong and his pilot, Dave Scott, had docked Gemini to an Agena upper stage for several hours, only to perform an emergency separation when a thruster on the Gemini started firing uncontrollably.

"Nobody knows. The comm from the Chinese dealie hasn't been good, and the guys on Alpha aren't saying much, either. One minute

Mark was reporting that Tango was sick, but alive—a couple of hours later they were saying they had undocked."

Five minutes later, Kelly joined Herron, Latham, and Ames in the living room. The television was playing. To Kelly's quiet astonishment, there was no commercial coverage of the situation in space. The set was tuned to NASA Select TV, the official channel of the space agency. There was no commentary at the moment, and no air-to-ground conversation between Houston and either Kondratko or Bristol. The screen merely showed the position of Alpha, somewhere over the Pacific, and another spacecraft on the same path, a little ahead and, according to the figures displayed in the corner of the screen, a bit below.

Diana Herron was more outspoken, having grabbed the remote and quickly clicked through half a dozen news outlets, finding several live reports about the death of a popular singer, and nothing on Alpha except a news crawl. "Look at this shit! Doesn't anybody *care*?"

"Ask yourself this," Latham said. "Does anybody really understand the problem?"

"Do we?" Kelly said.

Ames barked a laugh. "Since when has ignorance ever stopped us?"

"Stopped us from what?"

"Goslin's on his way over," the pilot said. "Apparently we're going to be launching tomorrow instead of Thursday."

"It's not just that they backed Harmony off Alpha," Goslin said. "That's a good thing."

He had arrived in a Ford hybrid with KSC markings, to Latham's open disgust. "No self-respecting pilot should be driving something like that." Kelly was too busy scrambling eggs to comment.

Goslin bounced into the beach house carrying a briefcase, taking over the kitchen table. "The problem is with Shenzhou. They had a critical guidance failure during docking, got it patched, lost it again, and got it back. *For now.*"

Goslin glanced at Kelly, which embarrassed her. "Shelton's there in Beijing, and he says they are looking at a manual reentry."

"It's been done," Latham said.

"We figure they can do it," Goslin said. "The question is where or when." He looked around the kitchen. "I don't suppose there's an atlas anywhere . . ."

"Try the TV," Kelly said.

They all moved into the living room, where NASA Select was showing almost an entire Earth hemisphere, with the South Pacific disappearing on the left, and the west coast of the United States crawling in from the right. "This'll have to do," Goslin said.

"Okay, Shenzhou usually operates in an orbit inclined to forty-four degrees. In nominal ops, they have two primary landing zones within China, meaning that in the best of circumstances, they have two shots at a landing every day.

"But this mission launched at fifty-two degrees to reach Alpha, which really takes the secondary zone out of play. If they miss the primary zone, when they come around again they're too far east."

Latham interrupted. "They still have a good shot at landing once a day. What's the problem? Shenzhou's consumables are good for a week, even with a crew of three, aren't they?"

"They probably don't have a week," Kelly said, quietly.

Goslin pointed at her with his pen: correct. "That's what's got us nervous. We don't think Tango's going to last a week. He might not last three days, and they've already blown the landing option for today."

The United States now took up a third of the screen. Ames tapped his finger on California and Arizona. "Why can't Shenzhou land here? We can perform recovery as well as the Chinese."

Latham looked at his pilot. "Come on, Hose, people are freaked out about having Harmony reenter over the *Pacific*. What are they going to say to a Chinese spacecraft full of X-Pox thumping down near *Vegas?*"

"We *are* making plans for an emergency landing in CONUS," Goslin said. "But there are other factors driving this: we want what Tango cooked up."

"What, a nastier kind of X-Pox?" Herron said.

Goslin shook his head. "The people at Korolev managed to download processing data from Harmony over the past week. A lot of it was cached, and a lot of that needed to get to specialists.

"Anyway, they think he was on the right path. That is, working in micro-G might have given him some kind of substance that could be more effective, either as a vaccine or a treatment.

"The point is, we don't want to throw it away—"

"—And getting hold of it once it's in China is going to be as expensive as it is difficult," said Latham, who was not a fan of either the Russians or the Chinese.

"So here's the deal," the chief astronaut said, leading the team back to the kitchen. "The flow teams put the pedal to the metal and will have the bird ready for launch tomorrow. The traj people dug up direct ascent profiles they had done years ago, and crew systems had some early-orbit ops procedures, including RMS captures, in the same files." Goslin opened his briefcase and started distributing workbooks.

"It was probably old DOD stuff," Ames said. For ten years NASA flew occasional missions for the Department of Defense, most of them deploying satellites. Even Kelly knew that there had been more exotic plans in the works, including missions that would rendezvous with and snatch enemy satellites.

"Some of this is going to be familiar," Goslin said, indicating the briefing books. "Some of it will be new. To go with the new procedures, we'll be adding some special EVA equipment to the package. Anybody remember the PRE?"

Latham had started shaking his head halfway through Goslin's statement. Kelly had been waiting for him to explode, and now he did. "No way! If we go tomorrow, there's no time to sim! Come on, Steve! We're moving up the launch; don't fuck us up even more."

Ames jumped in with his own objections, and so did Herron.

To Kelly's surprise, Goslin remained composed, almost serene, as they vented. The chief astronaut's face usually flushed red in response to challenges like this; not today. He was as calm as if he were telling a five-year-old that she needed to eat her broccoli. "Guys, I understand your objections. Five years ago, I'd have said the same thing.

"Here's the deal. Between the four of you you've got, what, thirty years of spaceflight training. Half a dozen missions between you. You know everything there is to know about the orbiter, the RMS, and the EVA gear. If not, we have all failed.

"You're going to have the whole team working with you. They're out there now, about ten thousand of them. Don't tell them you can't be ready."

Ames wasn't ready to give up. "Well, there may be ten thousand people on the team, but if it goes wrong, they're just unhappy: we're the four casualties."

His commander was less heated, but just as pointed. "Worse than that, we're the four casualties who took the whole program down with them. You think it was bad after *Columbia*. What does a lost orbiter do to Alpha?"

Goslin's voice was calm. He didn't even look at Latham and Ames. "I'm *sick* of operating with the attitude that we can't afford to screw up. Life doesn't work that way. We're so concerned about safety that we're paralyzed. It's time we started taking some goddamned chances!"

The idea of Goslin taking the Lord's name in vain was as shocking to the astronauts as the core of his statement.

"Now," he said, his face truly red, "I'm looking for a crew that says, 'Yes, sir, we're going to take the hill!' And if you can't tell me that, *I'll* fly the mission. And I can pick up the phone and have three other people in here in an hour."

It was so silent in the beach house that Kelly could hear the waves brushing the beach. Latham was staring at a spot on the wood floor about two-thirds of the way between his feet and Goslin's.

Then he raised his head, his face breaking into the biggest smile Kelly had ever seen. "Okay, Skipper," he told Goslin. "We'll take your goddamned hill."

The five of them spent another half-hour reviewing the accelerated schedule and changes to the flight plan. The orbiter would be launched tomorrow on a direct ascent trajectory that would bring it into proximity with Shenzhou and Harmony ninety minutes later.

"We're planning to grab Harmony with the RMS," Goslin was telling Ames, who would serve as lead operator for the orbiter's remote-manipulator arm.

"Not to bring it aboard, though," Latham said.

"No. Just to hold it and Shenzhou long enough to get those guys and their cargo off. Everything goes into Raffaello, and the Chinese command the whole stack into a fiery reentry."

Latham looked at each of his crew members, forcing a smile. "It's a big hill, but we can take it, right, gang?"

Goslin closed up his briefcase. "I imagine you want to shoot some landings. Then we'll have a little sit-down at the crew quarters afterward.

"Miss Gessner, would you walk out with me?"

Goslin tossed the briefcase into the front of the Ford before speaking. "I know we talked about having you join Viktor and Nate to finish out E-Thirteen, but no one thinks there's going to be time to do a capture on Harmony, then another rendezvous with Alpha, followed by even a minimal off-loading of supplies."

"I'd be amazed if we had the prop, much less the time."

"Only if Barracuda flies that rendezvous without wasting a

pound. Yeah. So it's not going to happen. I'm sorry. It's got to be wrenching going from a six-week mission to one that will probably be twenty-four hours."

"Don't apologize. It's actually a relief." For the past two days, she had been holding a lively internal debate on the question of her physical condition: what to say? And when?

According to the astronaut code, of course, there was no physical problem that justified blowing a flight assignment. You only backed out if you suffered an injury that kept you from doing your job.

But Kelly saw that Goslin was offering and demanding greater openness and honesty. "Steve," she said, "I may be pregnant."

For the first time in days, she saw utter surprise on Goslin's face. His mouth literally opened, then closed. Then it opened long enough for him to say, "Uh, how far along?"

"Not very far," she said. "Let's just say, less than a month."

"Have you done a test?"

She shook her head. "Not yet. I will if you want me to. I'll pull out of the mission. Burnside's got EVA experience." She laughed. "And he's got exactly the same amount of training for this EVA as I do, which happens to be zero."

"What about morning sickness? If you're throwing up in a suit, it's a bad day for everyone."

Kelly had been obsessing over that very issue, presupposing, of course, that the discomfort of the past few days was morning sickness. Well, whatever it was, it had vanished when she ate protein. "I can treat it. Just make sure we get some powdered eggs added to my menu."

Goslin nodded. "So you want to go."

What did she want? One more flight in space, so she could put four on her résumé rather than three? Even if everything went smoothly—not likely, given the improvisational planning—she faced one or two days that were so busy she wouldn't be able to look out the window. It wouldn't be fun.

On the other hand, she would have a chance to save the life of the father of her child. Putting it like that—"Yeah. I'm the best man for the job," she said.

Gender-blending statements like that tended to fluster Goslin—the old Steve Goslin, that is. He simply nodded and said, "Policy says I should ground you. But, what the heck, one of my great-grandmothers rode a wagon train while she was expecting. That *had* to be more dangerous than this."

"Even with radiation exposure, one or two days in space is not a health threat."

"Well, then, as Gus Grissom used to say, 'Do good work.' " He seemed paralyzed for a moment, as if he didn't know whether to shake her hand or kiss her. "Did you want to ask me something?"

"Yes," Kelly said. "What have you done with the real Steve Goslin?"

Goslin stared for a beat, not getting the joke. Then he flushed red and laughed. "He's gone. The old Steve Goslin died when Les Fehrenkamp wrecked up his car."

TANGO MIDNIGHT

Tango drifted in and out of fever dreams, vivid, colorful adventures at Star City that were much more real than the dull world he found when he awoke, swollen and itchy, in the flat gray interior of the Shenzhou's orbital module.

He *believed* it had been ten hours since Mark Koskinen had knocked on the hatch of Harmony, four since the Chinese spacecraft had backed away from the station.

Or was it twenty hours and fourteen? He wasn't sure. Had he eaten? He wasn't sure. Mark had forced him to drink water, juice, but had he also given him medicine? He wasn't sure.

If it was medicine, it wasn't working. Tango could feel himself tiring, fading, burning into ash.

He was dying, and not only did he not have the strength to fight it—he didn't want to. For his many sins, he deserved to die!

What was the alternative? Survive so he could return to Earth, to business? How much more money could he make? For the past several years, "wealth" had just been numbers on a screen. He had visited every exotic place he had wanted to visit, bought (then sold off) cars, airplanes, boats. He had slept his way through a notable collection of women, from secretaries to actresses. Sex, even with next year's version of Rachel Dunne, didn't have much of the old lure at the moment.

Find a cure for X-Pox? He'd screwed that up.

What else went on the negative side of the ledger? Oh, yes, the failure of the X-39 program. The development of a cheap, reusable, easily maintained, single-stage-to-orbit spacecraft was *always* a dream, but one he could have chased a little while longer. Losing another ten million dollars would not have impoverished him; it was only a third of the amount he had spent for the flight on Harmony.

Certainly the people at Spacelifter who lost jobs would have appreciated a more heartfelt commitment.

Then there was the small matter of endangering the existence of the $40 billion International Space Station, the human race's one, and for the near-future, *only* outpost in space.

Of course, Tango had had help in endangering the station, from the unknown, unknowable, overworked, underpaid, drunken, or just plain sullen technicians at the Institute for Biological Machine-Building who had assembled the Eridan glovebox that, years later, wound up inside the Harmony module.

Correction: how could he blame them? These workers certainly had not expected their handiwork to be launched into space. More likely they were using the best materials they had to build devices that would work tolerably well on Earth. Yes, they might have suffered leaks, but leaks were an acceptable risk.

(The glovebox might have been originally designed for use with benign substances, too. But, then, *anything* short of a handful of plutonium or pure VX nerve gas was less dangerous than X-Pox.)

A small amount of blame could be shared by Tango's various commercial partners, including the Eternal Frontier Society, Rosaviakosmos, Krunichev, Star City, and Tango's associates in Pyrite itself. All of them had been willing—eager—to take his money to help their own causes. None of them wanted to look too closely at Tango's methods . . . fearing that the mission would vaporize along with the cash.

"What about the cash?" A voice was speaking to him. Koskinen, most likely. Tango could no longer be certain. His hearing was as blurry as his vision—as his thoughts.

"Nothing," he croaked. Had another hour passed? Two? What difference did it make?

But Koskinen's presence reminded Tango of another reason he

should be condemned: he was very likely taking two other human beings to their deaths, Koskinen and the mysterious Chinese astronaut who had yet to show his face.

Tango wasn't so far gone that he didn't see a smidgeon of irony in Koskinen's fate. The astronaut had haunted him for years, from Spacelifter to Star City, and now in orbit! Well, Koskinen knew the risks. How he had managed to get himself to *this* place at *this* moment was a mystery Tango would have loved to explore, back when he cared whether he lived or not. The astronaut wanted to share Tango's life and work—how did he like it now?

Stop. That was the old Tango talking—Tad Mikleszewski. He had spent ten days locked up in a contaminated space station module. He had, for the first time in thirty years, ample time to reflect on his life, on the many mistakes he had made.

To remember the people who hated him.

God, what a list. How far back did he want to go? To Eli Lilly? To the lab workers whose work he had stolen? To the corporate rivals he had sabotaged? What were their names again? It was terrible to think that he had made so many enemies for so many years that he had *forgotten* them. Stupid. They certainly hadn't forgotten him. Some were probably sitting around their shitty little tract homes in Indianapolis eagerly awaiting Tango's slow, public death.

Stick to the more recent enemies. Everyone at Spacelifter. Dozens at NASA and Star City. Quite a few in various offices of his businesses, especially those in Los Angeles who saw him in person.

Rachel Dunne.

Here was an interesting question: did Rachel Dunne go on the list of to-be-forgiven? It was Rachel Dunne who had, with the classic instinct of actresses everywhere, decided to sleep with the most powerful man on her movie set. At Star City, for the misguided *Recoil* project, the most powerful man happened to be Tango.

Tango had been through the same sort of sexual hit-and-run before, and knew from the first kiss just how long the relationship would last. He had been the one to break it off, a month after it began, a month before the launch. Rachel had taken the news with suspicious ease. To be fair, the actress had never said anything about being in love with Tango. Hell, looking back, he wondered if she even *liked* him.

So it was no surprise that a month later, she was involved with Viktor Kondratko. Being angry about that was like blaming a puppy for pissing on the floor.

The real source of his burning anger toward Rachel Dunne was what she had done to Leslie. *Leslie* had fallen in love with the actress; she had never admitted it to Tango, but, hey, a father knows these things.

Even a father who never knew his daughter was gay until she came out to him at the age of twenty-six.

Leslie had been in the United States when Tango and Rachel began seeing each other. When she returned to Star City, three weeks into the affair, she obviously connected the dots. Tango certainly made no effort to hide the affair from Leslie. While he had grown to accept his daughter's lesbianism, he had not evolved far enough to realize that she would be attracted to a woman he might know—especially a semifamous actress.

Tango was certainly not evolved enough to think that Rachel Dunne—who could have successfully seduced any human male south of the pope—might respond sexually or emotionally to his gay daughter. But she had. They had.

Or so it seemed. It was so goddamn hard to tell.

To his immense relief, Leslie had never directly confronted him, never even mentioned Rachel to him. Upon learning of the affair, she had simply fallen silent, a typical response for Leslie in any setting, much less Star City, where she felt isolated and unhappy. Seeing that Tango had broken up with Rachel, she had resumed speaking. Tango's only real clue that Leslie and Rachel were together was catching a glimpse of them talking—not touching, merely talking—one spring day in the woods outside the Orbita.

Tango had felt happy for his daughter, who seemed to have no one special in her life. And worried, because Rachel Dunne was not a lover to depend on.

As she proved during her first hours on the International Space Station.

Tango wanted to blame Kondratko, but failed, partly due to male solidarity, but mostly because he was sure the Russian didn't know about the relationship between the two women. (He was conveniently out of the way aboard Alpha from early March. Tango was pretty sure reports on Rachel Dunne's romantic activities were not part of the routine air-to-ground traffic.)

No, it was entirely Rachel's fault. The morning of the accident, after a week of hearing giggles and moans floating through Alpha's atmosphere at odd hours, following several encounters with an obviously hastily re-dressed Kondratko or Rachel, Tango had finally told the actress, "Do you have any idea what this will do to Leslie?"

"Since when do you care what happens to your daughter?"

The response could have come from Rachel herself—Tango had begun to recognize a formidable, if inconsistent intelligence in her—or from some exchange in a well-learned script.

Either way, it had shut him down, left him fuming.

Left him prone to making mistakes in his work.

He woke again, damp with sweat that collected on his face and in his eyes. The orbital module was empty, the lights turned down low. The only sound Tango could hear through the constant roaring in his ears—the sound of his body burning itself up—was that of a single whirring fan.

More hours had passed. Where was Koskinen?

Tango's throat was dry. He clawed at the zipper of the sleeping bag and tried to escape. The effort caused him to sweat even more.

Eventually he had the bag open, and began searching the lockers for something to drink.

Fortunately, Koskinen or the Invisible Chinese had left a drink bag taped to the wall. Tango greedily sucked down the contents, which turned out to be tepid green tea. No matter; he was able to swallow.

And think clearly. For the last time?

There was a small window in the orbit module. He pulled himself to it and looked out. Shenzhou was flying southeast across the western United States just as night fell in the Rockies. There was a storm over western Colorado, with giant clouds piled halfway to orbit, or so it seemed. Their shadows stretched all the way to Nebraska.

Then night fell below, leaving puddles of city lights scattered against the blackness—

Behind him the Harmony hatch opened. Koskinen, blinking sleepily. "How do you feel?"

"How do I look?" Tango said, appalled at the croaking rasp his voice had become.

"Like shit."

He didn't like Koskinen. Didn't want to talk to him. "Go away!" he said.

"Wish I could, man." Koskinen started collecting sample bags that were taped to the front of lockers.

Turning back to the window, Tango forgot his anger. The spacecraft was over the Atlantic now . . . a circle of moonlight sailed across the smooth black surface below. "So here we are. Can you get the Chinese guy to turn this thing around? I'd like to see the Moon."

"The poor guy needs his rest. He's got a busy couple of days ahead of him."

Tango accepted this. He had no interest in the next couple of days. The future was the next five minutes. "Funny," he croaked.

"What?" Koskinen was somewhere behind him, opening and closing lockers.

"Got this great view—we're in a goddamn spaceship—just left

the goddamn space station. All I can think about is a girl problem. And my daughter."

Koskinen took him by the shoulder and turned him away from the window. "What should you be thinking about, Tango? The mass fraction? The future return from asteroid mining? If people are really going to live in space, they're going to be obsessing about their children and relationships, not that visionary shit."

"You don't sound much like an astronaut, Koskinen."

"I have it on pretty good authority that I'm a poor excuse for an astronaut." Koskinen held up a pair of samples, one in a bag, one in a tube. "Now, you need to tell me what this stuff is."

Tango only wanted Koskinen to go away. But he put his face so close to Tango's that even through his fever, the sick man could smell sweat mixed with some kind of Chinese spice.

"Let me go back to sleep."

"You mean, let you die? No. Not until you finish what you started. Some of this is X-Pox, but some of this is attempts at a vaccine. Primary cultures, diploid cells, continuous cell whatever. This is not my field. I need to know which is which."

Tango opened his mouth to croak a reply, then closed it. He wanted nothing more to do with Koskinen, or X-Pox, or anything. The sleeping bag beckoned. He tried to reach it.

But Koskinen blocked his way. "Do you have any idea of the shit we're in here, Tango? Our pilot is locked up in the descent module. I don't dare let him open this door. We've got a guidance computer that keeps dropping out.

"We've got two reentry opportunities before we start to have consumable problems." He rapped on the hatch that led to the Harmony module. "And, oh, by the way, we're still hooked up to your fucking plague ship. No one wants us to land until it gets sterilized.

"And *I'm* sick."

"What?"

"I've got X-Pox, Tango. And I think it's the nasty version you were playing with, because it sure seems to be working fast. Look at this rash."

It was hard for Tango to see anything in the half-light, especially through the sweat collecting in his eyes. He needed his glasses for close work. Where were they? "I can't see!" he said.

"Then feel my head, goddamn it!" Mark took his hand and put it on his forehead. It was hot. "Now," he said. "Are you going to save my life or not?"

THE GRAND GESTURE

For the next hour Mark walked Tango—painfully and slowly—through every sample, both the virus itself and the different types of vaccines, he had rescued from Harmony. Mark had studied the collection enough to track the progress of Tango's X-Pox dementia. The first set of samples was labeled numerically, and even dated.

As things progressed, however, the numbering and dating grew irregular, then disappeared. One set of materials was not labeled at all.

Making the process more difficult was the variety of sizes and shapes, and Mark's own clumsiness with the materials. Most astronauts became competent lab techs, if only in self-defense. Operating scientific equipment was one of the requirements of the job, especially for space station missions.

But Mark had missed that training; STS-100 carried no scientific gear to speak of. And in the intervening years there had been no need for him to acquire those skills.

He was also feeling light-headed and generally unsure of himself.

Mark and Yu had not separated Harmony from Alpha entirely on impulse. The radical procedure wasn't even their idea, at least not entirely. It was one of the options that had been under consideration prior to the Shenzhou launch—a rather desperate one. *If* Tango was seriously ill. *If* Harmony was not totally contaminated. *If* the module could not be vented.

The postseparation goal was then to deorbit Harmony over an unpopulated part of the planet, and return with Tango aboard Shenzhou-8.

With a perfect onboard guidance system, that might have

worked. It might still work, but when? Who was working the problem? And where? In Houston, Beijing?

Shenzhou-8 had been out of contact for hours now. Acquisition of signal was still ninety minutes off when Tango finally identified his most promising sample vaccine. It was in an unmarked bag that Mark realized, to his horror, he had almost discarded.

Mark took a pen and wrote "The Real Deal" on it.

Just in time. Tango was completely covered in rash and pustules. Even allowing for the puffiness associated with being in space, the millionaire didn't look like himself anymore. In the unlikely event that he survived, he was going to have a tough time facing a mirror.

Worst of all, the man was now slipping into unconsciousness. Mark had to shake him to get a response. "Did you use it on yourself?"

"Huh?"

"The Real Deal? Did you inject it?" It was an important question; if Tango had tested it, it sure wasn't working.

"No."

"Why not?"

"Can't," Tango said, then struggled for words. "Use needle."

Can't use needle? Because he was afraid? Or too sick to handle one?

Well, no time like the present. Mark found a syringe from the collection of materials brought over from Harmony. He dipped it into the Real Deal soup, then jabbed Tango's upper arm, just as he had seen in training, years in the past.

The man was so far gone that he didn't flinch.

Mark wondered if he had done the right thing. One look at Tango's eyes convinced him: Tango Midnight was going to die soon. The injection might postpone that; it was unlikely to kill him more quickly.

Whether Mark would be around to judge the wisdom of his actions was another matter. Before shutting down for the night, Yu and

Mark had discussed their options. If the guidance system stabilized, if air and power held out, if weather in the prime landing zone remained within limits, they had one good chance at reentry each day for at least two, and possibly as many as four days.

Given Tango's condition, it would be better to return as soon as possible.

If a nominal reentry proved to be impossible, Mark and Yu agreed they were going to try it anyway. They preferred drowning in the ocean or slamming into the side of a mountain to slow suffocation in orbit.

They would maneuver Harmony into a return trajectory first, one that would cause it to burn up over the ocean. It would help if they could figure out a way to safely vent the contaminated module first. That was a problem Mark would be working through the day.

Shortly before six A.M., Shenzhou time, Yu called Mark on the intercom. "We will be in contact with the control center soon."

Mark had hoped so. He updated his commander on his actions with Tango. Yu supported Mark, but what else would he say?

The commander admitted feeling cramped after twenty-four hours in the descent module. "But I spent a week in this couch during training," he said. "At least here I can float a little."

The air supplies aboard Shenzhou-8 wouldn't last a week, not with both descent module and orbital module drawing the supply down separately. The spacecraft was using 50 percent more air than it should.

Mark and Yu were eating a cold breakfast when Shenzhou-8 flew within radio coverage of one of the Chinese tracking ships, and everything changed.

"Shenzhou, BAACC," Wayne Shelton said on the comm link, pronouncing the Beijing center as "back." "Wayne for Mark through Long View Two."

"Good morning," Mark said, trying to add enthusiasm and energy he certainly didn't feel.

"I've got some big news for you. STS-One-twenty-four, Space

Shuttle *Discovery,* launched safely at twelve twenty-two A.M. Central Daylight Time this morning."

Mark's head was stuffy—whether from space adaptation syndrome or something worse made no difference at this point—and so his hearing was impaired. Or maybe he simply couldn't believe Shelton's message. "Say again, please."

"*Discovery* and a crew of four were launched this morning. Barracuda and Hoser along with Diana Herron and Kelly Gessner."

"What's the mission?" Mark was baffled. Was this an Alpha resupply flight? What would *Discovery* be doing?

"They're *coming* for you, dude, and they'll be there before you know it. But it might be tricky. Are you ready to copy procedures? We don't have constant comm."

"Start talking!"

The message that *Discovery* was on its way—and expected within six hours!—was great news. Mark had calculated his chances of surviving the mission with an emergency Shenzhou landing at less than 50 percent.

But there were still major problems. According to the nominal plans uplinked by Shelton, *Discovery* was to take the crew off Shenzhou. The question was, how? "I know this will be the next thing on your list of open items," Mark said, "but it's number one on mine: the orbiter can't dock with Harmony. No mating assembly."

"Correct. The idea is to do a capture with the RMS," Shelton said, referring to the orbiter's robot arm. "BAACC will put Shenzhou-Harmony in a minus-Z orientation."

"Barracuda will want our thrusters inhibited."

"On the list."

"We might want to be able to turn those suckers back on. Just in case the grapple gets hairy."

"These procedures assume nominal ops," Shelton said patiently. "Uh, we're working a number of scenarios."

"Okay. I'll shut up until you're through."

It was a good thing he had. Reading up just the "nominal ops" took the entire pass through the Long View 2 tracking ship, then a second pass through Long View 4.

Discovery's proposed capture of Shenzhou and Harmony was nowhere near the most radical idea on the table. Shuttle orbiters had grappled a number of unmanned spacecraft over twenty-four years, from errant comsats to a wayward spy satellite. Having a crew aboard the target would make the process a bit easier.

But flight managers also proposed to have the RMS draw Harmony-Shenzhou close enough to the orbiter that its nose docking mechanism—the one formerly used to connect with Alpha—would butt up against the receptacle on the orbiter.

The two units would not latch; there would be no seal that would allow crew members to move freely through a connecting tunnel. But the "soft capture" would free the RMS to move the EVA astronauts up to the hatch on Shenzhou's orbital module. (Harmony didn't have one.) Mark was appalled at the number of operational compromises in the plan.

Yet, getting the crew *off* was an even greater challenge.

Yu would remain where he was—inside the descent module—while Mark and Tango would retreat to Harmony. The orbital module would be sealed off, and vented, so that *Discovery* spacewalkers Gessner and Herron could enter.

Another problem: Shenzhou did not carry pressure suits that were rated for EVA. The lightweight Sokol-style ascent suits were designed to protect a crew against an emergency depressurization. They did not have independent oxygen packs, which would be the first requirement for EVA. "We've rigged a pair of tanks and hoses that will be compatible," Shelton had said.

Okay. What about the fact that there were only two pressure suits on Shenzhou, but three crew members? Shelton and the ground team had planned for that, too. Mark and Yu would wear the suits with these new tanks, while Tango would be stuffed into a man-sized pressurized bag called the Personal Rescue Enclosure that had been developed for spacecraft rescue thirty years ago.

There was a flaw in that plan, too. Mark *knew* it, but he was too overwhelmed to see it—

The problem with spaceflight, Mark concluded, was that it required a massive group of human beings and huge amounts of expensive, unique equipment to do even the simplest goddamn thing—like take a walk.

Mark checked on Tango, who was even more hideous-looking and just as feverish. He ran through the updates with Yu, then turned to the one task he could accomplish: storing the precious vaccine samples so they would be protected against vacuum.

And trying to figure out a way to safe the Harmony module.

"Shenzhou, *Discovery*. Shenzhou, *Discovery*."

Mark was startled at the sound of Kelly's familiar voice in his earphones. "Mark, did you hear that?" Yu was on the same loop.

"Yeah," Mark said. "*Discovery,* Shenzhou. Hey, Kel. You're talking to me and to Major Yu Guojun. Say hello."

"*Ni hao,*" Kelly said, in passable Mandarin.

"We look forward to your arrival," Yu told her. "Mark, I have some work to do." Yu clicked off, so that Mark and Kelly could have a moment's privacy. During their maneuvers toward Alpha, Mark had mentioned his resumed relationship with Kelly. Of course, there was no real privacy on the link.

"We have direct comm, in case you hadn't noticed."

"Thank God."

"How are you doing?" she said.

"Good enough, now that the cavalry is here." This was the truth. While he was hardly at his best physically, he did have energy. More important, he was eager to face the next set of challenges.

"And Tango?"

"He needs to go home, Kelly."

"We'll be there on our next pass," she said. "Look for us in eighty minutes."

He sighed with a sense of relief that surprised him. "I missed you," he said, no longer caring that their personal exchanges could be heard by millions of strangers.

"I missed you, too. We've got to stop meeting like this." An old joke, but a strangely appropriate one, given their history.

"How are you doing?" Mark asked, picturing Kelly on the flight deck of the orbiter, looking out the aft windows at the SpaceHab module in the brightly lit payload bay.

"Pretty good, considering that I'm upside down in the airlock with Diana." Of course! If Kelly and Diana were going to do an EVA today, they had to prebreathe to purge nitrogen from their systems. They were probably both in their water-cooled underwear and about to don the massive EVA suits. "In fact, I've got to get off the line and put my mask back on."

She and Mark turned the comm over to Kevin Ames and Major Yu.

The rendezvous took place as the spacecraft flew over the Mediterranean. Even while engaged in the business of storing Tango's samples inside a series of bags, as well as stuffing everything that could float inside the lockers of the orbital module, Mark managed to steal a few seconds to glance out the window.

But Yu had already maneuvered the stack to the Harmony-down orientation. The window on the orbital module not only looked perpendicular to the axis of *Discovery*'s arrival, it pointed backward along their trajectory. Mark was more likely to see the big bright light that was Alpha. (How were Viktor and Nate Bristol managing on the station? Mark had not communicated with them since undocking. He had barely *thought* about them.)

Less than six hours after the report of its launch, *Discovery* was there, a hundred meters below Harmony, its backdrop the blue of the Med and the browns of the Arabian Peninsula. Mark realized that Yu and Brad Latham were talking on the loop, quick exchanges of numbers punctuated by frequent use of the word "okay."

Tango was still in his sleeping bag. In the last hour, his condition had changed: instead of feeling hot to the touch, he was now cool, clammy. For a moment Mark thought he had died. But a touch to the neck showed that Tango's heart was still beating.

Goddamn good thing. Mark was not up to CPR.

He hauled Tango through the tunnel into Harmony, and secured him next to his samples.

"Mark, they're moving in for capture now," Yu reported.

Mark pushed himself to the Harmony window, gaining his first view of the tail of the orbiter *Discovery*. No sign of the robot arm, which was undoubtedly positioned several degrees around Harmony, near the grapple fixture.

It had to be a tense time on *Discovery*. Two astronauts buttoned up in suits inside the airlock, ready for egress. Latham and Ames at the aft position on the flight deck, one controlling the orbiter, the other maneuvering the arm, each extremely aware that thirty tons of mass was floating a few meters away. If *Discovery* and the Shenzhou-Harmony combination collided, even gently, it would be a bad day for all aboard.

"Fuck," Ames said on the open loop. "It's not firing." He meant the end effector on the arm, an open cylinder crossed by a series of wires. When the "capture" command was entered, the wires would fasten on the grapple fixture.

"Try it again," Latham said, his voice calm, like a golfer advising a partner to sink a two-foot putt.

"No joy."

"We got a soft latch, at least?" Latham said. Was the end effector around the Harmony grapple? Tiny cameras mounted on the RMS would tell Ames yes or no.

"Looks like it."

"Good enough for government work," Latham said. "Any

rates?" Had the touch of the RMS caused Harmony to rotate?

"Negative."

"Okay," Latham said. "Kelly and Diana, go for depress, egress, and the rock climb."

Rock climb? With the RMS needed to "hold" Harmony in place, Kelly and Diana would have to climb the arm up to the hatch on the orbital module, a distance of at least fifty feet. The idea of looking up from the payload bay and seeing a five-story silver structure looming above you—Mark felt queasy. He hoped Kelly and Diana had taken their antinausea drugs.

They also had to be gentle. The robot arm was actually rather fragile: a flight article could not be tested on Earth, since it would collapse of its own weight.

Still, from the traffic on the comm, Kelly and Diana were going ahead.

The process of depressurizing the airlock, configuring the rescue ball, and other items would take the spacewalkers the better part of an hour.

According to the timeline, Mark was to use that period to don his pressure suit and retreat to Harmony, sealing its hatch as Yu vented the orbital module.

Only now did Mark spot the flaw in the plan:

Both pressure suits were inside the descent module with Yu. The sealed descent module. There was plenty of time to open the hatch and get the suit. Sufficient time for Mark to don it and check it.

But not without exposing Yu and the descent module to X-Pox.

Yu saw the problem at the same time. "Mark, how are we going to do this?"

"Without contaminating your module, you mean?"

"Yes. I'm willing to open the hatch, of course—"

Mark couldn't let him do that. *Think! If Yu stays in the descent module, what does it mean?* How would Mark and Tango get to *Discovery*—

He heard a scrape on the wall of the module. Someone's EVA

boot. A moment later, Kelly said, "We're almost there, guys."

And Mark said, "Yu! I'm closing the hatch. Go ahead and vent the orbital module."

The Chinese commander had been incredibly patient, until now. "What the hell are you talking about?"

Mark told him. Kelly and Diana and the astronauts on *Discovery* heard it, too. "Jesus Christ," Latham said. "We've had enough improv for one day, Mark!"

"Brad, we all slipped up. The suits are with Yu. And I'm not going to contaminate that module." While Mark listened to a heated exchange between Latham, who quickly saw Mark's point, and Houston, Mark sealed the hatch. Yu confirmed that venting was in process. (Slowly, Mark hoped; the outrushing air might act like an attitude control jet, pushing Shenzhou and Harmony around. Nobody wanted that.)

While the air-to-ground discussion was still going on, Yu reported venting complete. Kelly called, "Okay, I've got the hatch open. I'm in."

Five minutes later, Diana was in, too, followed by their bulky rescue gear. "Closing the hatch now. Tethers hooked outside." Kelly and Diana were connected to *Discovery* by safety tethers, but they had to disconnect them in order to close the hatch on Shenzhou.

"Do you have any room in there?" Mark asked.

"Well, more than we had in the airlock," Diana said, speaking directly to Mark for the first time. That wasn't much; the Shuttle's airlock was so small that two EVA-suited astronauts could not fit unless one turned upside down.

"You have pressure," Yu said. Air had been pumped back into the orbital module. "You can open the hatch."

Mark was already busy undoing the latches. Then he swung the circular covering back, and almost butted heads with Kelly Gessner.

It would have been painful, at least on Mark's end: Kelly was wearing her bulky white EVA suit, complete with red stripes (so flight controllers could differentiate between Kelly and Diana) and helmet. They managed the clumsiest hug in the history of human relations.

Then Kelly examined Tango. "How does he feel?" Kelly couldn't take off her gloves and helmet.

"Cool to the touch."

"That's bad." Mark wasn't actually hearing Kelly; her voice was traveling through the comm link with a fraction of a second's delay. It added to Mark's growing sense of disorientation.

"Yeah, that's what I was afraid of."

"We better get him to the orbiter."

Diana Herron was already pushing the rescue ball through the hatch. It was still in its yellow transfer bag. Mark and Kelly quickly pulled it out and deployed it. "It looks like a big, thick-skinned balloon," Mark said, dreading the looming struggle to insert the unconscious Tango into the ball.

"It *is* a big, thick-skinned balloon."

"Good point." Kelly's ability to maneuver was limited, but she was able to steady Tango as Mark extracted him from the sleeping bag. "What next?" she said. "Mask first, then into the ball? Or the other way around?"

The rescue ball would hold pressure—hence its thick, multilayered skin made of the same material as Kelly's suit. But it possessed no life support equipment: the rescuee had to wear a mask and oxygen tank much like a scuba diver. "Mask first," Mark said.

He got the mask on Tango's face, and the oxygen pack strapped to his chest. "Is it working?" Kelly said.

Mark leaned close. "Yes. He's fogging the mask." *For now,* he added silently.

Forcing Tango into a crouch, and zipping him into the ball, took twenty minutes. Mark was panting and sweaty by the time they were ready to seal it. "What about the samples?" Kelly asked. "Do you want to put them with Tango?"

Mark looked at the precious cargo. "Too big, I think." He retrieved the yellow bag that had formerly contained the rescue ball.

"Let's use this. One of you can attach it to your suit, right?"

"We've got all kinds of tethers. Sure."

Mark hauled the bag with the samples into the orbital module, where he helped Diana Herron hook it to her suit. Then it was back to Harmony, where Kelly had Tango safely zipped up. With internal pressure, the rescue ball looked like a soccer ball three feet in diamater.

"Oh, shit!" For one horrifying moment, Mark thought the inflated ball was too big for the Harmony hatch.

"Don't worry," Kelly said. "This was one thing we thought about. It'll squeeze through."

It did, but now there was absolutely no extra room inside the orbital module. Mark would have to brace himself to get the hatch closed. "It's going to take us an hour to get him to *Discovery*, then come back," Kelly said.

"Don't worry. I'm not going anywhere."

The orbital module was vented again. Diana and Kelly opened the hatch and exited, taking the rescue ball and Tango, and the sample bag, with them. Mark did not envy them the climb down to the orbiter.

"Do you want me to re-press the module?" Yu asked.

"No, don't waste the air," Mark said. He was fine in Harmony.

After the hour of intense activity, Harmony seemed strangely quiet, like a ghost ship. Well, in a sense it was, or would soon be.

"They're in the lock," Latham reported. "Diana and Tango and the luggage."

"Copy that," Mark said. All right, the necessary work was done. Tango was aboard the orbiter. Kelly would remain in the payload bay while Diana transferred the X-Pox victim and the potential vaccines to the Raffaello module. Once she had Tango squared away, she would return to the airlock with the rescue ball.

The process was scheduled to take an hour. It took more like two. Kelly parked herself in a corner of the payload bay and took a nap, or so she claimed.

Mark took a last look around Harmony. In a day, at most two, it would be diving into the Earth's atmosphere, where the extreme heat of friction would cause it to break into smaller pieces, which would burn up. Fragments would reach the surface, nothing more.

Oh, yes, some X-Pox particles would undoubtedly escape, fed by the heat. But the atmosphere inside the module had been cycled through filters for the better part of a day. It wasn't as contaminated as it had been.

Still, it would be best to vent it. But how?

Something would occur to him. Or it wouldn't.

"How's guidance looking?" Mark asked Yu.

"It has been operating perfectly all day."

"Good news. You're going to need it." Once Mark and Yu agreed to keep him isolated in the descent module, the *yuangyuan* commander was committed to flying a reentry by himself. "At least you won't have me along to screw things up."

"You're being unfair," Yu said. "You have left me in a difficult position. If something goes wrong, *I* get blamed. If you were along, I could always point to you."

Mark laughed. Major Yu had made a joke. He was now an official space traveler.

Mark was sealed inside Harmony when he heard a thump on the hatch. The orbital module was repressurized. Kelly had returned, tugging the rescue ball. "Where's Diana?" Mark said, seeing that Kelly was alone.

"Waiting in the payload bay," she said. "It got a little tight in here last time. We were afraid we'd tear something."

"Let's get this thing open." Mark wriggled his legs into it, and realized that it smelled like ancient gym socks mixed with something worse. He made a face so pronounced that Kelly saw it through the limited vision of her helmet.

"That bad?"

"I'll be breathing through a mask."

"Mark, it's probably filled with X-Pox."

"What alternative do I have? I'm not going to open the hatch to the DM." Kelly still seemed uncertain. "What is it?"

Kelly had the mask and oxygen kit out of the transfer bag. "We took twice as long with Tango as we should have," she said. "I don't know if there's enough oxygen in this pack to get you to *Discovery.*"

There it was. All the wild maneuvers of the past six months, beginning with Kelly's phone call on the Day of the Dead, through his return to Houston, transfer to Russia, encounters with Tango, Leslie, Rachel Dunne, Viktor, the Chinese—here he was, looking at a death sentence.

And his unwilling executioner would be the woman he loved.

"What was it rated for?" he said, afraid that he knew the answer.

"Ninety minutes." Yes, that was the answer he remembered.

"No spares."

"We were lucky to find one set of equipment. Nobody was expecting . . ." She trailed off.

He could open the hatch to the DM. He could risk Yu's life, too. Why die alone? Both of them could try to make it to *Discovery* using the ascent/entry suits—

"Wait, wait. You had oxygen kits for our suits, didn't you?"

"Yes, but—"

"Where are they?"

"In the orbital module."

He took both of them. They were completely different from the emergency pack originally designed for use with the rescue ball and its unique mask.

But they contained oxygen, enough for an hour or more. They had tubes and valves that would feed air. The tube and mask just needed to fit.

Mark got a knife from the SAE kit in the orbital module, and sliced the ends off one of the spare packs. Then he cut the hose on the rescue ball's kit. "Hand me that tape."

He had used most of a roll of duct tape during his hours inside Harmony, fastening sample bags to the wall so they wouldn't be floating around.

Now he used it to marry the suit pack to the rescue mask.

He slipped it onto his face and started to wriggle into the rescue ball.

"I was waiting for this. The Grand Gesture."

"You haven't been watching, Miss Gessner. We've had a couple of Grand Gestures today."

"Oh, God, Mark, how do you know that's going to work?"

"If I turn blue in the next five minutes, we'll both know. Now, if you love me, you'll zip this bag and get me aboard *Discovery.*"

Kelly stared at him through the glass of her faceplate. "I guess I better. Since I do love you."

The bag was floating, sealed, in the middle of the orbital module, when Kelly said, "Harmony hatch—open or closed?"

Mark was about to say "closed" when that long-awaited "something" finally occurred to him. "Open!" he said. "But close the Shenzhou side and dog it."

It took Kelly several minutes—she had never worked with this hardware—while Mark breathed in, breathed out, breathed in again, all the while wondering if his patched system was working, or if he was living on residual air inside the ball.

He wished he could see better. There was only a tiny piece of clear plastic a foot in front of his face. It showed him nothing.

Then, with a final good-bye to Yu, Mark felt himself towed into open space.

His breathing was fine, steady, for several minutes. The ball twisted at the end of its tether, and during one revolution he saw the looming silver and white payload bay, including the flat top of the Raffaello module.

Another revolution. Kelly laboriously working her way down the RMS.

Sleepy. He was floating now, in the warm darkness. After *Discovery* departed, Yu would separate the descent module from the orbital module. Once he was clear, BAACC could command the orbital module (which had its own small maneuvering engines) to push Harmony into a steep return trajectory that would burn it thoroughly.

And as it separated from the orbital module, the open hatch would vent the X-Pox-contaminated atmosphere into the purifying vacuum of space.

"Mark!" His mother's voice. "Come inside now, honey. It's getting late."

THE REAL DEAL

"I think he's awake."

Mark Koskinen blinked at the ceiling. White, with bright lights. A room somewhere.

Somewhere on Earth, not in a spacecraft.

Kelly Gessner's face moved into view, brushing back the hair from her face. Her eyes looked swollen, as if she had been crying. Her hair was damp, too. Mark saw that she was wearing blue NASA flight coveralls, the kind Shuttle crews donned upon landing after shedding the heavy orange launch-and-entry suits.

She was the most beautiful woman he had ever seen.

"You can talk to him," a voice—obviously a doctor's—said from elsewhere in the room. "I'll be outside."

A door opened, then closed.

"Hey," he said to Kelly.

"It's all right," she whispered. "You can say, 'Where am I?' Or even 'What happened?' "

He found a hand, squeezed it. "Okay. In any order you want."

"You passed out during the transfer. You were getting oxygen, but the carbon dioxide buildup in the rescue ball got too high. The mask's filter was saturated."

"Have to work on that."

"Yeeesss." She smiled indulgently. "We slapped a new mask on you; you started breathing normally. And we went right into reentry prep. We landed two hours ago, and you're at the Cape medical office."

"Wow." Mark pushed himself up to a sitting position. "What about—?"

"Tango? He's in an iso tent in the next room." Kelly sat on the bed next to him. The feel of her thigh against his was soothing.

"Can I see him?"

"No one's going to stop you." Kelly stood. "He's conscious. They *think* he's going to live."

"Good." Mark pushed back the sheet. He was still wearing the polo shirt and shorts he had worn in Shenzhou . . . when? A hundred years ago. Bare feet. The tile of the hospital room floor was smooth and cool.

He stood, swayed. Kelly steaded him. "Mark, Tango said you got X-Pox."

"He did?" Mark smiled. "Then where's your mask?" He took one step, then another. Yeah, he could master this walking business with a little practice.

Kelly took his arm as they moved out the door and down the hall. Just as they reached Tango's room, which was guarded by a member of the KSC security staff, Kelly said, "By the way, Yu made it. Landed in Mongolia about fifteen minutes ago. He's not out of the spacecraft yet, but they're talking to him and he seems fine." No, they wouldn't have let Yu out of the descent module yet. They were probably tenting the site before washing it down with decontaminant.

"I'm glad," Mark said, as quietly as he could. "That poor guy risked everything for a bunch of people he didn't even know, and probably wouldn't have liked." He raised his voice in greeting. "Hey, Tango!"

Tango Midnight—Tad Mikleszewski again, according to the name tag and chart—blinked at Mark, and forced a smile to parched, swollen lips. "Koskinen. When will you stop haunting me?"

"Now. From this moment on, our lives officially diverge for all time to come."

"In that case, thank you for your efforts." He coughed. "There'll be a little something extra in your paycheck this week."

"I'm just a civil servant, Dr. Mikleszewski. I can't accept gratuities."

Tango grunted. "The doctors say you don't have X-Pox."

"I guess they should know what they're talking about."

"You lied."

"I figured it was the only way to get you to concentrate long enough to give me some information. If you believed I was infected."

"Why would I care what happened to you? As you may have suspected over the past six months, if not the past six years, I'm notoriously selfish."

"True," Mark said, and he wasn't kidding. "But you were sick." He smiled. "You weren't yourself."

"Fine, fine. But why would you trust me to synthesize a working vaccine in the first place? You said I was a bad lab tech. Too arrogant."

"Yeah. I believe the exact phrase was 'arrogant son of a bitch,' " Mark said. "But I never, ever said you were *stupid.*"

Mrs. Mary Gessner
Requests your presence at the wedding of her daughter
Kelly Kathleen Gessner
to
Mark Richard Koskinen
Son of Mr. Glenn Koskinen

3 P.M., Friday, August 18, 2006
At Grace Community Lutheran Church
1980 Chestnut Drive
Marshalltown, Iowa

EPILOGUE: GRACE COMMUNITY

"How do you feel?"

Mark Koskinen realized he had asked Kelly Gessner this question at least three times in the past ten minutes. But, then, these were unusual circumstances for the two of them.

They were standing at the altar in Grace Community Lutheran Church in Marshalltown, Iowa, as Reverend Conrad Eckerle prepared to join them in holy matrimony.

"I'm fine, fine," Kelly said, her voice quavering and her hands shaking like a Shuttle flying on solid-rockets.

Scheduling a wedding for August, in Iowa, was a risk. The weather was likely to be hot, with high humidity, almost as bad as that of Houston. The bugs, it was said, might eat you alive.

But Mark and Kelly had found luck. An early cold snap had blown through central Iowa the night before, bringing a thunderstorm. This particular Friday in August had dawned sunny and unseasonably cool.

Perfect weather for an afternoon wedding. Especially with a pregnant bride still prone to morning sickness.

"Ladies and gentlemen," Reverend Eckerle said, "we are all gathered here—"

And so they were. Standing with Mark were Viktor Kondratko and Jay Pollack. With Kelly, Diana Herron and Mark's sister, Johanna.

In the church, almost within reach, were Mark's brother-in-law, Lewis, and the girls, Cayley and Madison. Glenn Koskinen, of course, more frail than he'd been in April, but still alert, and determined to live long enough to hold his next grandchild. Kelly's mom and, of course, her brother, Gerard.

Lanny Consoldane. Steve and Debbie Goslin. Les Fehrenkamp, recently retired from NASA and about to become professor of space policy at Texas A&M.

Yu Guojun and his wife, flown from Beijing courtesy of Pyrite Industries. And the pockmarked but very much alive Dr. Tad Mikleszewski, formerly Tango Midnight.

And his daughter, Leslie, accompanied by Miss Rachel Dunne. The actress had somehow managed to shed the paparazzi that had hounded her since her return from Alpha.

Mark held on to Kelly's hand, nodding at the reverend's words without truly hearing them. He thought about what he had done, and all that he still needed to do. He was about to become a husband. Then, soon enough, a father. Both roles were far more intimidating than flying in space.

Eventually, Mark knew, he would begin to think again about his astronaut career. Not necessarily about going to orbit himself, but helping others make the journey more economically, usefully, safely.

Pyrite was back in the game. Tango had already contracted with the Chinese to fly a medical-processing system on Shenzhou, one that would be totally dedicated to the production of the Real Deal vaccine in microgravity. (The Real Deal had passed its first clinical trials, but was proving difficult to mass-produce in Earth's gravity.) Sale of the vaccine would not only be beneficial to thousands of sufferers, it would be incredibly lucrative.

So lucrative that in a few years, Tango would be able to afford a flight to the Moon. At least, that was the conversation Mark had overheard last night, when Tango and Yu greeted each other.

And if that worked, it was on to Mars—cold, dry, airless, forbidding—and still the most useful real estate in the solar system beyond Earth itself.

Human beings would live there some day. And not just steely-eyed professional astronauts, but mothers and fathers and people from China, and millionaires and actresses, too.

And if not Mark Koskinen and Kelly Gessner, then their children.